EASY
MEAT

EASY
MEAT

JOHN HARVEY

A MARIAN WOOD / OWL BOOK

Henry Holt and Company ◆ New York

Henry Holt and Company, Inc.
Publishers since 1866
115 West 18th Street
New York, New York 10011

Henry Holt® is a registered trademark
of Henry Holt and company, Inc.

Published in Canada by Fitzhenry & Whiteside Ltd.,
195 Allstate Parkway, Markham, Ontario L3R 4T8.

The lines from "Tami Jane Tells Him What Has Been
on Her Mind for a Long Time" by Albert Baker
reprinted here in chapter 16 are taken from
The Sounds of Wings (Slow Dancer Press: London, 1995).

Library of Congress Cataloging-in-Publication Data
Harvey, John
Easy meat / John Harvey.
I. Title.
PR6058.A6989E27 1996   96-7307
823'.914—dc20   CIP

ISBN 0-8050-5495-2

Henry Holt books are available for special promotions and
premiums. For details contact: Director, Special Markets.

First published in hardcover in 1996 by
Henry Holt and Company, Inc.

First Owl Book Edition—1997

A Marian Wood / Owl Book

Designed by Michelle McMillian

Printed in the United States of America
All first editions are printed on acid-free paper.∞

1 3 5 7 9 10 8 6 4 2

Although this novel is set in a real city, it is a work of fiction and its events and principal characters exist only in its pages and in the author's imagination.

EASY
MEAT

1

The last words Norma Snape said to her youngest that Thursday: "You let me get my hands on you, you little tripeshanks, and I'll wring your miserable neck!" Like so much of Norma's life, their memory would haunt her, words like angry fingers down her throat, again and again until she all but choked. And Nicky—it's doubtful whether, between the slam of the door and the ring of his own high-pitched laughter, Nicky heard a thing.

It had started the way it so often did, the four of them tumbling over one another inside the small, flat-fronted terraced house: Nicky's sister, Sheena, out of the bathroom at last and slamming from room to room in search of a clean blouse, her green factory overalls, a right shoe; Nicky, barely fifteen, down the stairs three at a time, chanting along to the Walkman that hung from the belt of his jeans. "Mum, you seen my blouse?" Sheena called. "Mum, where's all the toast?"

"Mum, I thought you were going to iron these?" Only the eldest, Shane, fair hair and slate gray eyes, eight days short of his eighteenth birthday, was still; flush in the center of the worn settee, eating toast and drinking his third mug of tea while he watched *The Big Breakfast* on TV.

"Mum . . ."

Norma, hair not combed out, still not properly dressed, opened the back door to let out the gray cat, and the dog, which had been scratching at the outside of the door unheeded, scuttled to its empty bowl and began to bark.

"For Christ's sake," Norma said. "Don't you start."

On the enamel drainer alongside the sink, used tea bags bled orange onto spilt milk; a half-eaten bowl of soggy Cocoa Pops sat speckled with coffee granules. Shane's best shirt hung drying from the back of a chair; cotton knickers made a patchwork quilt along the radiator top. Norma pulled a can of dog food from the back of the fridge and began to search for the opener.

"Nicky, get out of my bloody way!" Sheena's voice.

"Get out of the way yourself!"

From the other room, Norma heard a punch and a slap and then, above the sound of the TV, Shane's warning shout. Norma stubbed out the smoldering end of the cigarette she had lit earlier and forgotten, and fished another from the packet. Unable to find her lighter, she bent her head and lit the cigarette from the stove.

"Mum, I thought you were going to iron this blouse?" Sheena stood in the doorway, cream blouse in one hand, outline of her ribs visible between her off-white bra and the top of her short black skirt; she still didn't seem to have found her other shoe.

"Will you cover yourself up, for Christ's sake," Norma said.

"Yeah," said Nicky, pushing past her into the kitchen, "nobody wants to see your feeble tits anyway."

2

"No? Then how come you're always hanging round out-side the bathroom every morning?"

" 'Cause I'm nearly shitting myself, that's why, waiting for you to plaster your spots with Poly-Fila."

Sheena swung out at him with her blouse, flicking it at the kidney-shaped burn mark discoloring the left side of his face. Dancing out of the way, laughing, Nicky collided with the table and then, as he stumbled off balance, kicked the dog's food all across the floor.

Jesus, Norma thought, when's he ever going to grow up? "Right!" she shouted. "That's enough. Nicky, you get down there and clean up that mess. And Sheena, get shifting out of here or you'll miss your bus. A few more times late and you'll be for the sack."

"Again," laughed Nicky.

"Shut it!" Norma said.

"I don't suppose," said Shane, stirring himself during a commercial break, "there's any more tea in the pot?"

"That's right," said Norma, "there's not."

As Nicky went to move the dog's bowl, the animal nipped at his hand and Nicky hit it smack on the nose with the bowl's edge. Straightening its front legs, the dog showed its teeth and growled but then, thinking better of it, backed off into the corner and whined instead.

"Pick on someone your own size," said Shane, fetching his brother a kick in the shin.

"Nicky"—Norma pointed from the doorway—"I want that cleared up by the time I'm back down here. And you can sort out the crap by the sink as well."

"Why bloody me?"

"Because I told you to, that's why."

Shane chuckled and went back to watch the TV.

When Norma came back down ten minutes later, wearing an old jumper and sagging stretch pants to do her morning stint of cleaning in the pub, she found Nicky with his hand inside her bag, purse open, the last ten pounds she had about to make their way into his pocket.

"You scuttering little bastard! What d'you think you're doing?"

They both knew the answer to that.

Fear for a moment brightening his eyes, Nicky squeezed around the back of the table and made a dash for the back door. For a big woman, Norma moved fast, faster than Nicky might have thought. He had the door six inches open when with the flat of one hand she slammed it shut and with the other she slapped the side of his face, where the skin wrinkled liverish up from his neck.

"You thieving geck!"

"Here." Nicky held the two five-pound notes toward her, high above his head.

As Norma reached for them, he swiveled fast and left her catching air, the door yanked open wide enough and then pushed shut.

"You let me get my hands on you, you little tripeshanks, and I'll wring your miserable neck!"

She followed his laughter out into the yard, the bins and the empty rabbit hutch, the rusting shopping cart that had somehow found its way from Qwik Save and never made its way back. Stepping through the gate into the narrow alley that ran between the rows of houses, she stared after her son as he ran, not hurrying now, a lazy jinking step between the dog shit and the broken glass. At the alley's end he stopped and waved the stolen money once in triumph, before disappearing from sight into the street.

Norma shivered and turned back toward the house.

"Locking up, that's what he wants." Sheena was standing with her overall buttoned, ready to leave.

"Here," Shane said, offering his mother his packet of Silk Cut. "How much did he get this time?"

Lighting the cigarette, Norma drew in the smoke and slowly exhaled. "Only all I had." And then, as she lowered herself onto a chair, "You'd think somewhere along the line he'd learn his bloody lesson, wouldn't you?" But even the petrol bomb, thrown by an angry neighbor whose house Nicky had burgled twice within the same week, hadn't done that. Oh, yes, when he'd been laid up in the hospital, sure enough, Nicky had confessed the error of his ways; and those evenings when Norma had patiently tended to the burn marks on his arms and legs, blistering across his chest up to his neck and face, then Nicky had promised her, time and again, that he would change.

From his trouser pocket, Shane took a small fold of tens and twenties and pressed one of the twenties into her hand. Norma looked into the gray of his eyes. Don't ask, a voice told her, if you don't want to know. "Thanks," she said. "Thanks, love. Thanks."

Norma had grown up in Rotherham, the daughter of a steel-worker and a mother who, in the lengthening intervals between six children, had worked behind the counter in the local shop. Norma had been the last born, the one who broke her mother's spirit and finally her heart.

By the time she was three years old, her father had thrown in his lot with a walleyed girl of seventeen who had come to the house one evening selling lucky heather; Norma knew him only as a memory, an envelope of curling photographs, an edge of bitterness, sharp on the blade of her mother's tongue.

So Norma had spent her early days in a carry cot beside the jars of sweets and newspapers on the counter, alternately fussed over or ignored. Whenever she cried, she was passed from one customer to another, the recipient of much chin-chucking and baby talk, a great deal of cupboard love and all of it transitory; her mother was ever the last to pick her up, the first to put her down.

"It was you, drove your father away." The accusation, for years unspoken, had been present only in her mother's eyes until the day, slipping back from the shop unsuspected, she had caught Norma and the ten-year-old Gary Prout exploring each other behind the living-room settee, Norma's gray skirt inelegantly hiked over her face. "You, you little slut, it was you!"

Norma was nine and she thought her mother was probably right; after all, two of her brothers had been feeling her up for years.

When Norma was thirteen, the family upped and moved to Huddersfield, a house in Longwood with dark corners and the persistent smell of damp. The two eldest had left home long since, one pregnant and married and miserable, the brother off in the army, drunk in the pubs of Aldershot or Salisbury more nights than not. Norma was filling out fast, almost full grown; with a little makeup and heels she could pass for sixteen, eighteen even, in pubs and she did. Men nudged one another in the street and stared. Hands going nineteen to the dozen, older lads bumped into her in the corridor at school. One of Norma's biggest thrills, the one she remembered because it involved neither hurt nor harm, was waiting until the lights went up in the interval at the pictures, and then, in the tightest of sweaters, walking slowly, left to right, across in front of the screen. Like a movie star, Norma could feel eyes following her every move.

Of course, as her mother never tired of warning her, there was only one way for it to end. Norma hid the pregnancy successfully for almost seven months, wore her clothes loose, a fat girl getting fatter, nothing more.

When the baby came, three weeks early, it seemed to slip from the folds of her body like a fish, bloodied and wriggling, sliding between the midwife's hands. They let Norma hold it for a minute, wet against her neck and cheek. Too long for what they meant to do.

"Baby's small," the midwife said. "Tiny. We'll have to pop him into an incubator, just for now."

Her mother and the hospital arranged for the adoption: there was no need for Norma, underage, to sign the forms.

"Forget it, lovey," her married sister told her. "Plenty more where that came from, you'll see."

There were but she did not.

Michael. In that brief time that she held him, she had known his name. Spoken it to him, soft and wondering beneath his cries. Michael. She never saw him again, or knew where he was. And although now, she supposed, there were ways she could take and means, she had never tried to track him down. Norma liked to think of him happy somewhere, content: a grown man he would be, maybe with a family of his own.

When her mother's man friend, the reason they had moved to Huddersfield, backed Norma up against the cellar wall one night and tried to squeeze her breasts, Norma hit him with the coal scuttle hard below the knees and told him if ever he touched her again, she'd cut off his dick and feed it to the ducks. After that, he could never walk in the local park without his eyes beginning to water. And Norma learned there were things in her life she could control if she tried.

So when she became pregnant again, so stone in love with Patrick Connelly she could no more think of life without him than the air that she breathed, it was a fully thought-out, premeditated act. On Norma's part, at least.

Patrick was part-Irish, part-Scottish, part-wild, at twenty-nine, almost ten years older than Norma herself; he had drifted from Cork to Edinburgh to Glastonbury, a gentle hippie with the most violent of tempers, a musician with a raw and rudimentary guitar technique and the voice of one of Satan's angels—or the lead singer with the Stylistics, at least. Weekends, Patrick would take the train to Manchester or Leeds and busk; midweek, he sang with an uneven eight-piece soul band in the local pubs. One night, eyes closed, when he was singing Al Green's "Tired of Being Alone," Norma, emboldened by the drink, walked up to the stage and stroked the inside of his thigh.

They lived in two furnished rooms above a shop near the station. Sometimes, Patrick hit her and she hit him back; a big girl—a big woman—growing bigger, Norma was learning to punch her weight. When, one night, blissed out on the aftereffects of some good grass, Patrick said that what he wanted most in the world were children, a family, Norma took him at his word.

During her pregnancy, he left her four times, staying away the Lord knows where for weeks, before moving his few things back in again. He tried to talk her into an abortion and when it was too late for that, pushed her down the stairs of a double-decker bus, traveling between Paddock and Longwood.

Norma took out an injunction against him, but once Shane was born, he began deluging her with flowers stolen from nearby gardens, sang to her from the corridor outside the ward. Five months after they had moved back in together, Patrick shook Shane so hard to stop him from crying that he cracked three of the baby's ribs.

Norma had a friend in Nottingham, Rosa, who had two kids of her own, but was otherwise living alone. It took Norma no time at all to pack her belongings and the baby onto the bus and travel south. They shared expenses, shared the chores, complained about the social—miserable, conniving bastards, how're we supposed to live on this?—sang in the pub on Friday nights, played bingo, watched TV. This was it, Norma decided: men were shit.

She met Peter at Rosa's sister's wedding; after the reception they went back to the house together, Norma and Peter, Rosa and some bloke none of them had set eyes on before or since. Rosa found a bottle of Drambuie and they drank it from chipped mugs; the man nobody knew passed round a few splifs. When they paired off, Norma went with Peter. What harm was there in that? A quick shag between friends.

The harm was she fell in love.

Small and gentle was Peter, with delicate fingers that could read her body as if it were braille, soft dark eyes and lashes, long and curving like a girl's. Whenever Norma rolled on top of him in the night, she was frightened she might crush the breath from out of him.

He played with Shane and rocked him on his knee, even though Shane was slow to laugh and quick to cry. Norma read the look in his eye. Sheena was born when Shane was two and Nicky no more than eleven months later.

It was you, drove your father away.

Nicky screamed whenever Peter touched him, kicked out if ever he picked him up. It got so that he would start to cry whenever Peter walked into the room. The only one who could quieten Nicky was Norma herself; his eyes would follow her from place to place; as soon as he could crawl, he would only crawl to her; the only way she could get him to sleep was to take him into her bed.

Peter spent nights on a borrowed mattress laid on the floor, nights on the couch, nights away from home. "I can't take this," he told Norma. "I can't take this anymore."

"It's all right, love," Norma said. "Nicky'll come round, you see. You're his dad, after all."

But Peter stopped coming round himself before the boy had the chance. When Norma arrived back from the shops one afternoon, all of his things had been cleared out of the cupboards; the suit he had worn for best, so strangely like the one her own father wore in one of those old photographs, no longer hung in its place inside the wardrobe.

There was no note. Twice a year, Christmas and birthday, he would send a card to Sheena, always with a different postmark, never with a return address.

Norma told everyone she didn't care: hadn't she and Rosa always said men were shit. But when Shane suddenly went off the rails a few years later, she was forced to admit she couldn't cope, not with them all, and Shane went off for the first of his two spells in care. Just to give your mum a break, love, the social worker had explained. He's a good lad, she'd said to Norma, I'm sure he understands. If he did or not, Shane never said. Especially after being released back home the second time, Shane never said much at all.

"You not going into work this morning," Shane asked, "or what?"

Norma was sitting at the kitchen table, smoke drifting from her cigarette. "Yes," she said. "Yeah, soon."

Shane shrugged. "Suit yourself. I'm off out, right?"

Norma nodded: one more cup of tea, one more cigarette, one more something, she'd pick herself up and get on her way.

2

"I don't want anyone to get too carried away about this," the Head of Geography said, wriggling out of his anorak as he came into the staff room, "but there was a rumored sighting of a lesser spotted Snape earlier this morning."

"In the general vicinity, is that?" asked one of the Maths staff, glancing up from the crossword. "Or actually, you know . . ."

"On the premises, apparently. Somewhere in the vicinity of the toilets. Natural habitat."

"We ought to put a sign on the notice board, perhaps? Must be quite a few members of staff who've never had the chance to see one at close quarters. After all, I don't suppose he'll be here long."

"Difficult to predict," the Head of Geography said, "the migratory habits of the Snape."

From her seat across the room, where she was vainly trying to get another set of English folders marked before the bell,

Hannah Campbell didn't think it was so funny. The last time Nicky Snape had showed up in her class, a perfectly decent lesson on haiku had been fatally disrupted in less time than it took to count to seventeen. Then again, she knew that if Nicky weren't in school, the chances were he was out getting himself into even more trouble, adding to a list of offenses and misdemeanors that, even in this catchment area, was truly impressive. She knew all of that, but even so . . . Hannah sighed as the bell sounded, assigned a mark to the open folder, capped her red Uni-Ball micro deluxe, and climbed to her feet. Another day.

Nicky was letting a couple of the younger kids examine the label of his black cotton Hugo Boss shirt—not the right size for his skinny frame, but it was difficult to be particular when you picked up clothes the way Nicky did most of his. Today he wore it loose, so that was fine, unbuttoned over a black T-shirt that had been yanked high to hide as much as it could of the burns that spread up from his chest. His black denim jeans were turned over at the waist. On his feet were Reebok trainers, scuffed and coming away at one heel; they would have to be replaced.

"Snape, what the fuck are you doing here?" one of the other youths asked, straggling into the building.

"They begged me," Nicky said. "All of 'em, down on their hands and knees."

"Yeah, but you're here anyway."

"So what about Macbeth and the witches?" Hannah Campbell asked. "Do you think he believes them or what?"

"Yes, course he does," said a girl near the front.

"Okay, why?"

" 'Cause he does."

"Yes, but why? I mean, would you?"

"Would I what?"

"If you were on your way home across the Forest . . ."

"Miss, I don't go home across the Forest."

"If you were walking across the Forest and just past the Park and Ride you saw these three weird old women—"

"Tarts," shouted somebody.

"Scrubbers."

"Prostitutes."

One of the lads at the back jumped up and stood beside his desk, hand extravagantly on hip. "Hey, Macbeth, duck, lookin' for business?"

"All right, all right." Hannah smiled and allowed the laughter to subside. "Let's get back to the question. If you were stopped by three people you didn't know and who looked pretty strange into the bargain, and they told you that something was going to happen in the future, would you believe them?"

"Depend what they said, Miss."

"All right, Wayne, and why's that?"

"If they said what you wanted to hear, Miss, you'd believe 'em."

"Yeah, like winning the lottery."

"Seven million."

"That bloke, right, shot himself 'cause he never bought the winning number."

"He couldn't know the winning number, stupid."

"Yes, he could, 'cause it was the one he picked every week, only this week he never did it."

"Daft sod."

"Okay," said Hannah, "calm down a minute and let's think. Isn't what happens with the witches and Macbeth a bit like what you've just been talking about?"

"There's no lottery in *Macbeth*, Miss."

"No, but it is about getting what you want most in the world, isn't it? Becoming king. All that glory, all that power. All your dreams come true."

"Never happens, Miss, does it?" A girl off to the side this time, flicking her hair away from her face with a Biro. "Dreams comin' true an' that."

"Do you mean in the play or ever? In real life, say?"

"Ever."

"That bloke," someone said from near the door, "the one as worked in the factory. Won all that money and couldn't cope with it, went back to Pakistan."

"Should've took all his mates."

"Family."

"Fazal along with 'em," Nicky said. It was the first time he had spoken during the lesson, happy fiddling with the Casio digital diary he'd pocketed on his last visit to Dixon's.

"I can't go back, clever," Fazal called back, "'cause I've never bloody been."

"Right," Hannah said firmly. "We'll have no more of that." And then, taking a few steps toward Nicky, "What do you think, Nicky? D'you think that's one of the things Shakespeare's trying to get us to think about, what happens when we get what we want most?"

Nicky pushed a few buttons on the keyboard of the diary and the day of the week came up in French. Why didn't she leave him alone and ask somebody else?

"Nicky, do you think he's saying something about ambition in this play?"

"Fuck knows."

"I'm sorry?"

"I said I don't know."

"Why don't you know?"

Nicky pushed the pocket computer across the desk. "If he wanted anyone to understand what he was on about, he should've written in normal English, shouldn't he?"

"But he did, the normal English of his day."

"Yeah, but that's not our day, is it? It's not now. If you

expect us to read it, why doesn't someone put it into proper English so's we can all understand?"

"Yeah, Miss," someone called out. "Or give it subtitles."

"Then stick it on Channel Four."

"How many of you think that Nicky's right?" Hannah asked. "Shakespeare would be better translated into contemporary language?"

A chorus of shouts suggested that many did.

"All right, but if we did that, what would we lose?"

"Nothing."

"All that lousy spelling."

"Words you can't understand."

"Yes," Hannah said, "you'd lose the words, you'd lose the language. In fact, it wouldn't really be Shakespeare at all."

Loud cheers, then: "Story'd be the same, Miss."

"I know, Wayne, but don't you think the reason we still bother with Shakespeare after all this time is not so much the stories but the language he told them in? After all, his actual stories weren't so different from anybody else's. In fact, he borrowed most of them from other people anyway."

"When I did that, Miss, you wouldn't even give me a mark."

"I don't think, John, Shakespeare copied it out word for word, right down to the spelling mistakes."

Laughs and jeers.

Hannah glanced at her watch. "How many of you have seen *Pulp Fiction*?" About half the class, but almost everyone had seen some clips on TV. "And *Natural Born Killers*?" Two thirds.

"Right. Two films with quite a lot of violence—"

"Not enough, Miss."

"Bloodshed, violence, criminals and murderers as central characters—quite a lot like *Macbeth*, in fact. But tell me, apart from the basic stories, Quentin Tarantino's *Pulp Fiction* and Oliver Stone's *Natural Born Killers*, what's one of the most obvious differences between them?"

"John Travolta."

"*Pulp Fiction*'s longer."

"*Natural Born Killers* is crap."

Hannah raised a hand for quiet. "Isn't one of the most important differences in the dialogue, the use of language? Isn't the Oliver Stone film all quick-editing and MTV effects, whereas *Pulp Fiction* is full of scenes with people just talking?"

"Like the bit where they're in the car, going on and on about when you're in France, what d'you call a Big Mac?"

"In *Reservoir Dogs*, Miss, when they're all sitting round that table—"

"Yeah, talking 'bout Madonna . . ."

"Right," Hannah said, "that's it. Talking. Language. Isn't that what Tarantino loves? If you took all that dialogue out of *Pulp Fiction*, that would change it so much it wouldn't any longer be his film. It certainly wouldn't be as good. And if you took the language out of *Macbeth*—"

"It'd be over quicker."

"—it wouldn't be as good either. It certainly wouldn't be Shakespeare."

Before Hannah could say anything else, the bell sounded for the end of the lesson and everything was lost to a scraping of chairs, the clamor of private chatter, and the movement of thirty-one pairs of feet.

"Nicky," Hannah tried, "can I just have a word?"

But Nicky, like the witches, had vanished without trace. As had Hannah's purse, which had been pushed down to the bottom of her bag, between her work diary and a Snickers bar she'd been saving for break.

3

Nicky had a grin that left room for him to eat his pizza slice and speak at the same time. "Roland, you're lucky I bumped into you, right? Just the thing you've been looking for. Exact."

Roland tipped sugar into his coffee, two sachets and then a third; the last occasion he had bought something from Nicky, a pair of Marantz speakers for thirty quid, he ended up paying twice that amount to get them repaired after only ten days.

"Here," Nicky said, sliding what looked at first glance like a glasses case across the table.

"What the fuck's that, man? Polaroids or shit?"

"Look at it, here. Look."

Roland shook his head. "You got to be joking, man, wha'do I want with that?"

Nicky couldn't believe it. How could Roland be so thick? "Business appointments, that's what this is for. Business.

You're the one, always telling me how you've got to be this place or that place, meeting someone here, somebody there, doing some deal or other. And sometimes you forget, right? You've told me. Sat there and told me. Well, now if you had this . . ." Experimentally, Nicky fingered a few of the tiny buttons. "See, this is perfect, right? Neat. What d'you call it? Compact. Slips into your top pocket, inside pocket, anywhere. But everything you want to know, Roland, okay—phone numbers, addresses, appointments—you can store it right in here, yeah? SF-8350. Do anything you want except send a fax or E-mail, and there's probably some way you can adapt it to do that. And look, look here, look—how about this?—it can only translate stuff into nine languages. Nine. You believe that? Bet you didn't know there were nine fucking languages."

Roland picked up the digital organizer and stared at the word *mercredi*, blinking faintly back at him from the top of the oblong screen. "Fuck, man. Why you fussin' me with this shit?"

"Gonna do you a deal, aren't I?"

Roland laughed and bit into his cherry pie, coming close to burning his tongue. "Shit! Why's the stuff in these things always so bleedin' hot?"

"Thirty quid," Nicky said, easing the last piece of mushroom away from his pizza and scraping it onto the side of his paper plate. Never could stand mushrooms, they made him sick. "Come on, Roland, yeah? Thirty quid."

Roland pressed a button and the screen went blank. "Nothing, man. Not interested, okay?"

"Twenty-five."

Roland shook his head.

"Okay, twenty."

"Nicky, how many times I got to tell you? Now get this piece of junk out of my face."

Shit! Nicky dropped the pizza crust onto the table,

18

screwed up the paper plate, snapped the organizer shut, and pushed it down into the back pocket of his jeans as he got to his feet. "See you, Roland."

"Yeah."

Fifteen meters short of the door, Nicky spun round on the heels of his Reeboks and hastened back. "Here." Leaning over Roland from behind. "Fifteen. You can sell it for twice that."

"Ten."

Nicky balanced the machine across Roland's cup. "Done."

Roland laughed and laid the note in the palm of Nicky's hand.

Ten, Nicky was thinking as he headed back for the street, ten and the fifty that was in old Campbell's purse, I can get myself something decent for my feet instead of this old crap I'm wearing now.

If Mark Divine noticed the few daffodils that remained unpicked or untrampled on the wedge of green beside the school entrance, he gave no sign. Four hours' sleep was the most he'd caught last night. How many pints of bitter? Six or eight, and then the woman he'd been stalking round from bar to bar only laughed in his face as she climbed into a cab. Two o'clock it must have been before he'd stumbled into bed. No, nearer three. And this morning there'd been Graham Millington, lip curling up beneath his mustache as he delivered a bollocking over some petty bit of paperwork Divine had somehow neglected to get done. "What are you now?" Millington had asked. "Twenty-seven, is it? Twenty-eight? Ask yourself, maybe, why it is you're still stuck at DC when there's others, give you three years or four, shooting past like you're standing still?"

It had been on the tip of Divine's tongue to say, "What about you, Graham? Sergeant since before I bloody joined and about as like to move on as one of them statues stuck round the edge of Slab Square." But he'd said nothing, had he? Bit his tongue and sulked around the CID room till this call came through, some teacher who'd got her purse nicked from her bag in class. Serve her right, most like, Divine had thought, for taking it in with her in the first place. But it gave him a reason for getting out and about, at least. Hannah Campbell, he could picture her now. Short frizzy hair and flat-chested, blinking at him from behind a pair of those bifocals. Hannah, anyway, what sort of a name was that? Somewhere on the back shelf of his memory, Divine remembered an Aunt Hannah, the kind with whiskers on her chin.

"Can I help you?" The woman in the office looked up from her typewriter and regarded Divine with suspicion.

"DC Divine," he said, showing her his card. "CID. It's about the incident this morning. Hannah, er, Campbell. You'll know about it, I reckon."

"Please take a seat."

Why was it, Divine wondered, he only had to set foot inside a school, any school, to feel the cold compress of failure shriveling his balls, packing itself around his heart?

She was waiting for him in a small room on the first floor, the only light coming from a long, high window through which he could see bricks and sky. Two of the walls were lined with shelves, sets of tatty books with fraying covers, some of which didn't seem to have been moved in a long time. Wasn't there supposed to be a shortage of books? Divine wondered. Hadn't he heard that somewhere? So what was wrong with all these?

"Miss Campbell?"

"Hannah."

Divine showed her his identification as he introduced

himself and sat down across from her, a narrow table in between.

He could see right off he'd got it wrong. She was younger than he'd imagined, for a start. Middle thirties, maybe; possibly even younger. Scrub the glasses, too. Her hair was longer than he'd pictured, bushing out a little at the sides and back. Light brown. Under a tan jacket she was wearing a lilac top, three buttons to the neck. Lilac or purple, he could never be certain which was which. A black skirt, calf length, and comfortable shoes on her feet.

"I spoke with two officers already," Hannah said. "Explained to them what happened, as best as I know."

"Uniform, yes. Routine."

"And you're a detective, isn't that right? CID, that's what it means?"

Divine nodded, resisting the idea that, ever so slightly, she might be sending him up.

"And you'd like me to tell you what happened?"

"Yeah, that's right."

She looked at him, the natural cockiness of his face offset by the tiredness round his eyes.

"Aren't you going to take notes?" Hannah asked.

Only when Divine had taken out his notebook and pencil did she begin.

"So do you think you'll catch him?"

"Nicky Snape?"

"That's who we've been talking about, isn't it?" They were walking along the bottom corridor, Hannah escorting him off the premises, out of school.

"You seem pretty certain it was him," Divine said.

Hannah shrugged. "My purse disappeared, Nicky disappeared, both at the same time. Added to which, he does seem to have a penchant for this sort of thing."

"A what?" Divine wondered again if she was sending him up.

"Stealing. He's been in trouble before."

The laugh lines crinkled around Divine's mouth. "Just once or twice."

"And you didn't catch him then?"

"We caught him right enough, courts bounced him off out again. Can't hold 'em, you see. Not that young. Twelve when he started, thirteen." Divine looked around them, windows and doors. "You must know what it's like, mixing with them every day."

Hannah didn't say anything, carried on walking until they had passed beyond the office and were standing on the shallow steps outside. The building was sending shadows long across the tarmac and there was a bite still in the spring air. Hannah was conscious of Divine looking at her, her neck and breasts.

"You make it all sound pretty much a waste of time," she said.

"Catch him with any of your property still on him, credit cards, say, someone might actually have the nous to stick him away."

"And is that likely? Catching him like that, I mean?"

Divine pushed out his chest a little, stood an extra inch taller. "Best detection figures in the country this year past, you know, Notts."

"Really?"

"Clear-up rate per officer of fourteen cases a year."

"That doesn't seem," Hannah said, "an awful lot."

"Better'n anybody else, though, isn't it?"

"Statistics." Hannah smiled. "To get a real sense of it, you'd need to set that figure against the one for the amount of crime that took place. You know, to see it in the right perspective."

"Yes, well," Divine said, gazing away, "I can't bring to

22

mind what that was, not exactly." It was 148 crimes per 1,000 of the population, the second highest after Humberside, he knew it by heart. He said, "I'd better be going, then."

"All right." She hesitated a moment longer before turning back into the school.

"Look, I don't suppose . . ." Divine began, a slight flush on his cheeks.

"No," Hannah said. "I'm sorry, not a chance."

4

"You'd think," Skelton said, "when you get something right, the last thing anyone would want to do is mess about with it and run the risk of losing everything you'd gained."

From the chair opposite the superintendent's desk, Resnick grunted something that might be taken for agreement.

"You know and I know, Charlie," Skelton went on, "most forces in the country would give their eyeteeth for figures like these."

Nodding, Resnick shifted his weight from left buttock onto right. The idea of a Serious Crimes Unit in the county had been mooted before, but now, with changes in the Police Authority, it looked as though it might actually be going to happen.

Skelton was toying with a pencil, daring to disturb the symmetry of his desk. "You know what it'll mean, don't you? Two-tier policing, that's what it'll mean. All the high-fliers and bright boys stuck in together where they can polish one another's Ph.D's and the rest of us left penny-anteing about with stolen mountain bikes and traffic offenses."

Resnick wondered if in a way that wasn't happening already. Helen Siddons, for instance, the bright young DI who had paused at the station long enough to set a seismograph beneath the crumbling structure of Skelton's marriage. She had been made up to inspector at an age when Resnick was still shy of sergeant; now here he was in his mid-forties, inspector still, and where was she? Holding down a chief inspector's post in Somerset. As Reg Cossall had put it a few nights back in the pub, "If that self-seeking cow'd had the luck to be black as well as female, she'd've been superintendent by now, never mind fucking chief inspector!"

"No, Reg," Graham Millington had laughed, "it were better'n inspector she was fucking, it was our Jolly Jack."

Looking across at Jack Skelton now, Resnick wondered if that had been true. Oh, Skelton had fancied her, Siddons, clearly enough, and she had turned that to her advantage. But whether it had gone beyond the lingering glances and the barely covert looks, Resnick didn't know. And besides, it hardly mattered: what mattered was what Alice Skelton thought had happened. Adultery in the mind as hard to shake as love stains on the sheets. The last time Resnick had been round to the Skelton house, it was like watching bear baiting between barely consenting adults.

"Still, with any luck, Charlie," Skelton said, "we'll both be up and gone, the pair of us, before it happens. Put out to grass with a pension and whatever they give you nowadays in place of a gold watch."

Resnick didn't think so. Skelton, maybe, but as far as he himself was concerned, retirement was something lurking in the last gray hours before morning; one of those beasts like cancer of the prostate that stalked you in your sleep.

"Lynn Kellogg, Charlie." He had waited until Resnick was almost at the door. "Okay, is she?"

Resnick was slow to answer, wondering if there was something he should have noticed, something he'd missed. "Fine. Why d'you ask?"

"Oh, no reason." Skelton looked at Resnick across the broad arch of his fingers. "She's started seeing that therapist again, that's all."

No reason then, Resnick thought as he headed back along the corridor toward his own office, was not exactly true. As he well knew, there were reasons enough.

Fifteen or so months ago, Lynn had been kidnapped by a man Resnick and his team were tracking down. The man had killed twice before, women whom he had tantalized with the prospect of freedom, before brutally ending their lives; it was a game that he played, and he had played it with Lynn, alternately being kind to her and then threatening her, keeping her cold and in chains. By day he was capable of speaking to her in the soft tones of romance, and at night, in the cramped blankness of the caravan, he would masturbate over her as she feigned sleep.

After a lengthy trial, at which all of this was painfully dragged out for everyone to read about in their newspapers and see replayed each night on their TV, the man's pleas of diminished responsibility had been disregarded and he had been sentenced to imprisonment for life. A minimum of twenty-five years.

By the time she herself was little more than fifty—younger than her own mother was now—Lynn knew he could be walking the same streets, breathing the same air. At the turn of any corner she might meet him, hear him again, clear across the clamor of a crowded bar, asking could he buy her a drink; his fingers tapping at the window the next time her car broke down, face peering in, drizzled out of focus by the rain, the lilt of his voice, that smile . . .

And there were other things that had been stirred into consciousness by the experience, things that Lynn was struggling to forget.

She was at her desk when Resnick entered the CID office, back toward him, a slight hunch of her shoulders as she made notes on her pad while talking on the phone. Kevin Naylor, like Lynn a detective constable in his twenties, was accessing the computer, checking through incidents of arson in connection with a recent fire in which an Asian boy of four had died. Graham Millington, Resnick's sergeant, sat with an elderly black woman, coaxing her through the circumstances of a robbery she had witnessed in a local bookmaker's, three thousand pounds stolen and the manager recovering from serious head injuries in the Queen's Medical Centre. The other desks were empty, officers out and about in the city, asking questions, knocking on doors.

Inside Resnick's office, a partitioned corner of the narrow room, the telephone started to ring. By the time he had entered and closed the door behind him, it stopped. One glance at the jumble of papers on his desk, and he reached into one of the drawers for a half-empty pack of Lavazza caffé espresso and filled the coffee machine his friend Marian Witczak had given him as a present. "For you, Charles, to treat yourself well. I know how much you like good coffee."

The last drops, black and strong, had not finished percolating through before Resnick, unable to distract himself any longer, pushed open the office door and called Lynn Kellogg's name.

"Coffee?"
"No, thanks."

She kept her hair cut short now, defiantly, brushed forward at the front just like a boy's; the only slight curl, as if to spite her, curved in front of her ears and the plain gold studs that she wore. She had never won back the fullness or the color of her face. She wore black cotton trousers, a black, round-necked top. No rings.

"Jack Skelton was asking me how you were."

She hadn't forgotten how to smile, at least with her eyes. "And you told him?"

"As far as I knew, you were fine."

"That's okay, then."

Resnick brought the cup toward his mouth, but didn't drink. "Except, apparently, you're not."

Lynn looked at him and saw a sad man with sad eyes. When he had been the first to arrive at the caravan where she was being held captive, she clung to him and thought that she would never let him go. Now that was proving all too true: through therapy and jagged dreams, the memory of him persisted, the bulk of him hard against her, the tears in his eyes.

"The hospital," Resnick said.

"Dr. Carey."

"You've started seeing her again."

Lynn sat forward, hands pressed between her thighs. "So much for confidentiality, then."

Resnick set the cup back down. "As far as what's said, whatever passes between you, of course that's true."

"But if I've gone back into therapy . . ."

"We have to be concerned."

"That I might be cracking up?"

"Concerned for you."

She laughed. "Because I might not be able to do the job?"

"Yes." He looked away and Lynn laughed again.

"What?" Resnick said. "What?"

"Nothing, it's just . . . No, it's okay, I know you're only doing your job, too."

Resnick shifted again, uncomfortably, in his chair. "It's the nightmares, then? They've started up again. Is that the problem?"

"Yes," Lynn said. "Yes, that's right. Same old thing."

The lie hung between them, tangible as smoke.

"You feel okay, though," Resnick asked. "About the job? Carrying on?"

"Yes. Really I'm fine."

"You'll let me know if there's anything I can do?"

"Of course." She was on her feet by the door, avoiding his eyes.

"Your caseload," Resnick asked. For whatever reason, he didn't want her to go. "What's most pressing?"

"That lad, I suppose. The one who absconded from the Secure Unit . . ."

"Hodgson?"

"Martin, yes. He could be anywhere, of course. Manchester, London. But I had a call earlier from Vice, thought they might've spotted him, touting for business out on Forest Road."

Resnick sighed, all too familiar. "Who are you liaising with?"

"Sharon, Sharon Garnett."

"Give her my best."

"Right, yes, I will."

Just a moment longer Lynn hesitated before going back through the door. Already her phone was ringing again and Graham Millington, having finished with his witness, was waiting to ask her about overtime. Divine was back at his desk with a copy of the *Post* and a brace of Jamaica patties from the baker's on Hartley Road.

In his office, Resnick scanned the response from the Police Authority chairman to claims that the recent Audit Commission survey comparing police forces' efficiency was scarcely worth the paper it had been printed on. He opened an envelope addressed to him in Marian Witczak's precise hand. *Is it true you are never at home anymore, Charles, and, if so, who is feeding all of your beautiful cats?* She had enclosed an invitation to a dance at the Polish Club for this coming weekend. Underneath the line *Dress Informal*, she had added, *But please bring dancing shoes!*

Resnick pushed it out of sight beneath a pile of crime reports, dancing the last of several things occupying his mind. For no clear reason he could discern, unless it was the coffee in the cup that he was holding, the words to an old Bessie Smith blues came filtering to the surface, something about waking up cold in hand.

5

Nicky Snape had been a busy boy. At the back of a pub edging onto the wholesale fruit and veg market he had sold one of Hannah Campbell's two credit cards for twenty pounds; less than thirty minutes later, in the pleasant surroundings of St. Mary's Rest Garden, her checkbook and check guarantee card had exchanged hands for double that. Cutting through the Victoria Centre toward the Mansfield Road, he had chanced to bump into Sally Purdy, who was just leaving the Magistrates' Court, having a few minutes previously been released on her own recognizance on charges of fraud. Purdy sent Nicky back inside to Tesco's to buy a six-pack of Tennents, two of which she shared with him on one of the benches opposite Peachey Street; she then bought the remaining credit card from him for three five-pound notes and an unopened can. "You give my love to Shane now, will you do that for me? Tell him I was asking after him, make sure that you do." Nicky could see how that would go down well with his brother, and with a belch and a quick wave of the hand, consigned the idea to oblivion.

He treated himself to a Whopper and fries from Burger King and was finishing them off, window-shopping on Cheapside, when his eyes fell on a pair of purple and red Sanmarco walking boots, Gore-Tex lined. No way he could boost them out of there, the boots cost Nicky pretty much all he'd made in the past hour, but what else was money for?

He left his old Reeboks in the shop and was wearing his new boots when he met his mate, Martin Hodgson, in the bowling alley by the Ice Stadium. Martin was not so many months younger than Nicky, but more slightly built; his over-sized check shirt hung loose and open over a beige Sweater Shop jumper, black jeans rolled up over high-top trainers. At first glance, it was tempting to dismiss him as soft, but that would have been a mistake.

"Fuck!" Nicky exclaimed. "Thought you was fucking locked away."

"Nah. Only that kids' place, weren't it? Not a real fuckin' prison at all." Martin pushed the fall of dark hair from where it shielded his dark eyes and grinned.

Martin was about the only person Nicky had ever gone on jobs with, breaking and entering in and about the Meadows, which was where Martin lived. Most times, Nicky preferred to stay on his own, a low-profit, low-risk sort of business. Martin, though, was a laugh, which was why Nicky went with him; the only thing was, Martin didn't seem to know what risk meant.

"So what you doing, hanging about here?" Nicky asked.

Martin nodded in the direction of the nearest lane. "Seeing how many spares I can get in a single game."

They bowled for the best part of an hour and then, when Martin went to buy more cigarettes, Nicky noticed he was holding what had to be close to a hundred pounds.

"Up on the Forest last night," Martin explained, offering

Nicky a king size. "Would've scored more'n this, but the coppers came sniffin' round. Bastards! Had to clear out."

Nicky stared at him in fascination. "What d'you have to do?" he asked.

"Easy." Martin laughed. "Hang around, just down toward the trees, like, till some punter comes along . . ."

"But how d'you know?"

"You always know. Sometimes they want you to go in their car—I always charge extra for that, mostly you just do it there. Cemetery's a good place."

"Yeah," Nicky said, "but what d'you have to *do*?"

"Jesus! What d'you think? Wank 'em off, that's the easiest. That's a tenner. Sometimes they want to suck you off, that's twenty. Nothin' to it."

"But you don't let 'em . . ."

"Stick it up me arse? What d'you think I am? Fuckin' mental? Think I want to get AIDS or something?"

"No. No, course not."

"This bloke once, though, dead rich, Mercedes, nearly new. Offered me a hundred if I'd go with him, back to his hotel." Disgust and dismay mingled on Nicky's face. "He had a condom," Martin said, "so it was okay. Give me these poppers, you know, amyl nitrate. After a bit it never hurt much at all."

Nicky thought he was going to throw up. He nipped out his cigarette and started to walk quickly away.

"Hold up!" Martin called. "Where you off to now?"

"Home," Nicky said. "Supposed to have been in school, haven't I."

"Nah," Martin said, catching him up. "You don't want to do that. I'm meeting Aasim later. You want to stick around, chill out, we'll have some fun."

Sharon Garnett was wearing a short red skirt over ribbed tights, a dark cotton jacket buttoned over a cream shirt;

as if she weren't tall enough already, she was wearing boots.

"Blending in with the scenery?" Lynn asked, the hint of a smile in her eyes.

"Something like that."

"I got you half of bitter, that all right?"

"'S'fine."

They had agreed to meet in the Lincolnshire Poacher, a pub that promised good beer, good food, and a courtyard out back, which was where they now sat. It was early evening and there was a decided nip in the air, the temperature down below fifty.

"You working?" Lynn asked.

"Yes, later. You?"

Lynn shrugged. "Depends."

"Martin Hodgson?"

"Yes."

Lynn had first arrested the youth when he was thirteen, on the run from a children's home and caught by an alert store detective in Woolworth's with several hundred pounds' worth of computer games stashed inside the Head sports bag he'd stolen just an hour before. Since then, he'd been arrested and charged more than thirty times, running a succession of social workers, short-term foster parents, and police officers ragged. Unable to find sufficiently secure local authority accommodation within the county, Martin had finally been sent to a custom-built facility in Northumberland on a temporary basis. When a place became available at the Amberdale Secure Unit, reasonably close to the city, he was brought back and placed there. Eight days later he escaped and had been living rough ever since.

"Fifteen, isn't he?" Sharon asked.

Lynn shook her head. "Fourteen."

"Some future ahead of him."

Lynn nodded and drank her beer.

◆◆◆

By that time, Nicky Snape and Martin Hodgson had met with Martin's friend, Aasim, and they had decided to go off to Derby, where one of Aasim's cousins worked as an attendant at the multiplex cinema and could get them in free. The first car Martin broke into they couldn't get started, but the second, a two-year-old Honda Civic that had been parked on Lenton Road in the shadow of the Castle, that was fine. Aasim had stolen his older brother's license, so Aasim drove.

"You still applying for CID?" Lynn asked Sharon. They were walking up the Mansfield Road, heading round the block to where Lynn had parked her car.

"Not really," Sharon said. "Not since the last time."

"What did they say?"

Sharon laughed. "Asked me if I was interested in a place in the Domestic Violence Unit."

Sharon had begun her police work in London, for her a second career after a spell in community theater, and domestic violence was where she had quickly become sidelined. Not that it wasn't important, even interesting, but Sharon bridled at the obviousness of the thinking—woman, black woman, area with high ratio of Afro-Caribbean and Asian families, let her deal with them, she speaks the language. But she didn't want to be the token friendly face and she didn't want to be a social worker—she had done her share for her sisters, up and down the motorways of the country, putting on agitprop plays about incest and wife battering. What she wanted was to be out on the street, solving crime, serious crime, something that would further quicken her wits, sharpen her already sharp reflexes; something to make the adrenaline flow.

And now? Well, most nights, one way or another, she was on the streets at least.

"How d'you feel about Vice?" Lynn asked.

"You mean, am I for it or against it?"

It was Lynn's turn to laugh. "I meant working it."

They paused at the corner. Ahead of them, the Victorian headstones of the cemetery on Forest Road East were beginning to stand out, white against the gathering dark. Lower down the hill, the floodlights of the five-a-side soccer pitch were sharpening into focus. The broad expanse of the recreation ground eased away to the left, trees shielding the open tarmaced car park for the daily Park and Ride and, beyond that, the Goose Fair site. It was early yet for many of the prostitutes who worked the area to be on the street, and most of the cars that passed Lynn and Sharon seemed to be heading for other destinations rather than seeking out business. Give it another hour and the curb-crawling would have begun in earnest.

"The girls," Sharon said. "I even like them, sort of. The regulars, anyway. Not the little scrubbers who train over on an Away Day, then scuttle back home on their high heels like Cinderella. They're the ones who'll do it without a rubber, some of them, take risks, the stupid tarts."

"And the boys?" Lynn asked. They were turning the corner into North Sherwood Street, Lynn pleasantly surprised to see her car still there where she'd left it.

Sharon stopped. "No, it's . . . I don't know, but somehow it's not the same. I can't, I suppose I can't understand—I mean I can *understand*—but I just can't relate to what's going on. And some of them—God, it turns you over—they seem so bloody young."

"Fourteen."

"Younger."

They were walking again, Lynn fishing in her bag for her keys. "The lad you contacted me about, you think it was him, Hodgson?"

"What I saw, from the picture, it could be, yes."

36

"I'll meet you, then. Later. If that's okay? Ten o'clock?"

"Better half past."

They made the final arrangements and Sharon stepped back to watch Lynn make a U-turn and drive away. A nice woman, she thought, straightforward—a little too straight, maybe, uptight even—but no side. Sharon liked that about her. If only she'd take a bit more trouble with herself, she could be nice-looking, too.

6

Laden with Pepsi and cartons of popcorn—sweet for Nicky, salted for Aasim, Martin had mixed—they watched *Dumb and Dumber* and then went into one of the other screens to see *Poetic Justice*, which Aasim insisted on seeing because one of his mates had told him there were shots of Janet Jackson naked from the waist up. "What's new about that?" Nicky had wanted to know, but they went anyway. Fifteen minutes into the movie, when they realized what they were hearing on the soundtrack was meant to be poetry, they kicked back their seats and left. "I don't care what her tits are like," Martin said on their way through the foyer, "I'm not listening to no fucking poetry."

It was a wonder that Miss Campbell hadn't been there, Nicky thought, sitting up the back taking notes.

They left the Honda in the Showcase car park and took an Escort in its place.

"Wait up," called Martin as they were turning past the Assembly Rooms and in sight of the bus station. "This is as good a place as any."

"What for?" Nicky wanted to know.

"You stay put," Martin told him. "Make sure no bastard nicks the fucking car."

So Nicky popped a Polo in his mouth and lit a cigarette, while Martin and Aasim made their way between the bus stands toward the toilets. Aasim, two years older than Martin, was almost a foot taller, a mustache already thick upon his lip. Martin had met him first in the children's home, Aasim sitting on the top bunk looking at the pictures in *Penthouse* and *Hot Asian Babes* and listening to his Bangra tapes, over and over again.

Twenty minutes and three cigarettes later they were back: Martin had sixty pounds in twenties, fifty in tens, and three tatty fives; Aasim had blood drying from a cut alongside his mouth and a graze across his fist.

"Better'n a bank," Martin said with a grin. "Now let's get the fuck out of here. This place gives me the runs."

"Where we going?" Nicky asked.

"What do you care?" Martin said. "Just wait and see."

But Nicky was already thinking that wherever it was, it probably wasn't the place he most wanted to be. Sitting around kicking his heels while others were off doing stuff wasn't his idea of a good time.

"I'll tell you what," Aasim said, "when we've finished this, let's go to a club."

This was Chinese take-away, sweet and sour, chicken and cashew, chicken chow mein; Nicky had ordered two portions of toffee banana as well and now Martin was only reckoning they were for everyone, reaching over into the back of the Vauxhall with his plastic fork.

Oh, yes, another car. As soon as they had reached the ring road, Martin insisted on taking over the wheel and within less than a mile had wrapped the near side of the Escort around a bollard, after which Aasim had made a detour across the grass to the Social Sciences car park of the university and liberated a Fiesta XR2.

"Fuckin' students, man, got too much money. What's some fucker on a grant doin' with a car like this?"

"Maybe it belongs to some teacher," Nicky suggested. "Lecturer, whatever they're called."

"Don't make me piss myself, man. Whatever sort of teacher drives a fuckin' XR2?"

Nicky finally got tired of fending off Martin's fork and let him have it all, tipping the contents of the container forward across the seat and into Martin's lap.

"Fuck it, Nicky! Just fuckin' watch it, right?"

But Nicky was rapidly getting to the point where he didn't give a shit.

"Syrup all down my tossin' jeans!"

"Be cool," Aasim said. "Make you taste sweet."

Martin laughed and, in disgust, Nicky lowered the window and threw all that remained of the food out onto the street.

"Right," Aasim said, setting the car in gear. "We wasted enough time already, right?"

"Where we going?" Martin asked, still brushing away at his clothes.

"Clubbin', I told you."

"Not me," Nicky said.

"Come on, you got to. I know this guy, right, works the door at the Black Orchid, yeah? Won't cost us nothin'."

It was beginning to grate on Nicky more than a little, the way Aasim knew someone who worked *everywhere*, some cousin, uncle, aunt, or brother. He'd bet anything you liked, mention somebody doing the most far-out job you could ever think of, personal bodyguard to Madonna, something stupid like that, and Aasim would swear on whatever it was they swore on that he knew the bloke's Siamese twin.

When the XR2 pulled up outside the club, both Nicky and Martin got out but neither of them moved toward the door. "Suit yourselves," Aasim said. After he'd parked the car and talked his way inside, the two of them jumped into a cab that had just dropped off four girls with skirts up around their tits and headed into town.

Sitting in the back, Martin did his best to persuade Nicky to work the Forest with him. Martin, he'd get some punter back into the trees and then Nicky could jump him; the two of them would beat the shit out of him and take him for whatever he had. "They'll never do nothing about it," Martin assured him. "Not the coppers nor nothin'. Married, most of 'em, that's why."

But Nicky wouldn't budge. He left Martin cadging a light from a tart on the corner of Waterloo Road and took off down Southey Street, heading for home.

"Smoke?" Sharon asked.

Lynn shook her head.

"I know, I keep trying to give it up." Sharon lowered the window on her side of the car a crack before she lit up.

The streets were busier now, small knots of girls in different shapes and sizes, gossiping at corners, blowing into their hands. Others, most often in pairs, walked slow along the pavement's edge, a quick dip of the head toward any car that drew near.

"No lads," Lynn said.

"Not yet."

The drill was, park for a while where you have, as far as possible, an unimpeded view of one stretch of the territory; next, drive around the circuit at a steady pace, eyes peeled, letting the ones who knew you know you were about, casting a careful eye over anyone new on the patch. Look out for trouble, warn persistent punters away. Every now and again, there would be a lot of conspicuous action, rounding the girls up and taking them in. Fines in the coffers, a small knee jerk in the direction of the moral majority. Keeping the trade under wraps.

"You seeing anyone?" Sharon asked, stubbing out her cigarette and resisting the temptation to light another.

"Sorry?"

"A bloke, you know."

"Oh. No." In the close proximity of the car, Lynn felt herself beginning to blush and blushed all the more. "How about you?" she asked.

Sharon smiled, almost a laugh. "Depends what you mean. Not in the regular sense, no. Friday nights at the pictures, Saturdays a take-away and a couple of videos from Blockbuster, nothing like that."

"But?"

To hell with it! Sharon lit up anyway, lowered the window a further half inch. "There's this one guy, I don't see him often, just, you know, when we can fix it. When he can."

"Married, then?"

She did laugh this time. "Of course he's married."

Lynn stared out through the window; what she thought were shapes moving was probably nothing more than the wind in the trees. "He won't leave her. You know that."

"He'd better not!"

"You know you're just saying that."

"Like hell I am. Leave her and what'll he expect? Me to dump his washing in the machine last thing at night, collect

42

his suit from the cleaners, cook, be nice to his kids. I've had a belly full of that once on my own account; I'm not about to fall for it again."

"What is it, then? Why do you keep seeing him?"

Sharon drew in smoke and exhaled slowly through her nose. "Sex, why d'you think?"

It was quiet inside the car, each woman aware of the other's breathing, the heat of her skin.

"I don't know if I could," Lynn said. "Not unless . . ."

Sharon barked out a laugh. "Unless you loved him?"

"Unless I thought it was leading somewhere."

In the semidarkness, Sharon was looking at her. "You're young, you'll learn."

"I hope not."

Sharon lowered the window a little more and tapped ash out into the air. "Look, me and him, we spend the night together, most of it, once every two or three weeks. He's a nice bloke, a good lover. Treats me with respect. He's never aggressive or overdemanding unless I want him to be; he's got great hands and a lovely cock. And he makes me laugh. You think I should be holding out for what? A co-signee for the mortgage and someone to help me push the trolley round at Safeway?"

For a while Lynn didn't answer. "Maybe not," she finally said. "Only . . ."

"Only what?"

"After you've . . . after you've been to bed and . . ."

"And done the deed," Sharon laughed.

"Yes, if you like. And he's gone back home to his wife, well, how do you feel?"

Sharon put her hand on Lynn's arm. "Somewhere between having had a Turkish and a long massage, and being seen to by the Dynarod man."

The laughter of the two women filled the car and when it faded, Lynn said, "Look, what's that? Over there."

"Where?"

"Over there."

Nicky had walked past the house three times now, a two-story end-terrace with lace curtains at the window, even those above street level. The kind of house, the kind of street where people put milk bottles out last thing at night, but no one had done that here. Okay, he thought, it was getting late but not that late; most of the other houses had lights showing in their bedroom windows at least. Not here. He turned along the side of the house to where a narrow ginnel ran into the darkness, giving access to the backs.

For as much as five minutes he stood in the center of the rear yard, letting the darkness gather round him. A few doors along someone was playing their television too loud, someone else was singing, one of those pathetic songs his mum would sing when she was in the kitchen and thought no one else was listening, or when she came back from the pub after last orders and didn't care. There was a gap at the top of the window at least an inch wide and his guess was that whoever lived there had forgotten to close it tight. So simple, Nicky thought, so why was he still standing there when by now he could have been in and out? Another ten minutes and he'd be home. Nicky took a pace toward the window then another; as far as he was concerned, most of the evening had been a washout and here was his chance to finish it on an up.

Face close against the glass, he saw, beyond his own reflection, the contours of the neat back room, everything ordered and in its place the way old jossers' homes were. Some of them, anyway. The ones that didn't babble on at you in the street, half-drown in their own dribble, sit in their own piss. Yes, he bet whoever lived here dusted it every morning, moving every sodding ornament on the shelf. Nicky had done places like this before, money hid away in the most stupid places, obvious, inside vases, between the pages of Bibles, biscuit tins. Three hundred he'd found once, three hundred almost, pushed up the arse of this donkey, a present from Skegness.

Easing himself silently up onto the tiled sill, Nicky slipped his fingers over the top of the window and began to slide it down.

7

Nicky stood still long enough to let his eyes grow accustomed to the light. Table, chest of drawers, sideboard, mantelpiece, chairs—gradually, the details sharpened into place. Family photographs. He had already turned the key to unlock the back door and slipped back the bolts; he could be out of there in seconds if he had to. But he wasn't going to have to. Wherever they were, the people who lived here—off on one of them geriatric coach trips or boring the balls off their relations—they weren't here. Quiet as the sodding grave.

He would do this room first and then the front. No rush for a change, Nicky, take your time.

Brian Noble had followed the boy down into the trees.

He had driven past him twice, the boy standing in shadow at the edge of the streetlight's fall, holding his cigarette down by his side, cupped inside his hand. Noble had parked the car on the nearest of the side streets, careful to push anything that might be stolen beneath the seats. One of the women had called out to him, asked him if he wanted a good time, but that wasn't the kind of good time that interested him. He could get that at home.

The first time he walked on past, just slowing enough to judge the boy's age—fourteen or fifteen, soft flesh still around those hard eyes. On the way back he spoke, stopped and asked him for a light.

"You don't want a light," the boy said.

"Don't I?"

"Fifteen quid," the boy said, not looking at the man directly, glancing back and forth along the street.

"What for?"

The boy showed him with an almost elegant gesture of the hand.

"Doesn't that seem rather a lot?" Brian Noble asked.

"Suit yourself."

Noble was gazing at the boy's face, the dark hair that hung loosely across his forehead, the first beginnings of a mustache darkening along his upper lip. He imagined the pubic hair around the boy's cock and felt himself grow hard.

"Suppose there are things I want to do to you?" Brian Noble asked.

"Cost you."

"Of course."

The boy stared at him now. "Well?"

Across the street a car, an Astra, dark blue, slowed almost to a halt and a woman jumped out of the backseat before the car had come to a proper stop. "Wanker!" She stepped off the pavement, middle finger thrust high into the air as the car accelerated away.

"I have a car," Noble said.

"Fancy that."

"We could go to it now, it wouldn't take a minute."

"No." He didn't know why, but he didn't fancy it. "No," the boy said. "Back here."

Noble looked at the headlights from Gregory Boulevard, strung in perpetual motion through the trees. "It doesn't look so very comfortable," he said.

"Suit yourself."

The boy ground the nub end of his cigarette beneath his shoe and started to move away. Noble detained him with a hand, restraining yet gentle on the boy's arm. "All right. Have it your way."

"The money first."

"What, here? Where everyone can see?"

"The money."

Noble fingered fifteen pounds away from the fifty he had pushed down into his trouser pocket before leaving the car; his wallet he had locked for safety inside the glove compartment.

"I thought you wanted something more," the boy said, looking at the money now in his hand.

"Let's just see, shall we? See how we go. I think that's enough to be going on with."

Without another word, the boy turned and Brian Noble, not without the exhilaration of fear, followed him down toward the trees.

Nicky had upturned every jar and ornament, opened every box and drawer, and all he'd come up with was a few pounds' worth of five-p pieces inside a half-size whiskey bottle and a postal order for one pound, forty-two. It went without saying they had neither a stereo nor a VCR, just a poxy plastic radio that wasn't worth taking and a postage-stamp TV that was more state of the arc than art.

He would have to try upstairs. See what, aside from the old man's best trousers, they kept under the mattress.

Under the worn tread of the carpet, the stairs squeaked a little and groaned, however lightly Nicky placed his feet.

"Slowly," Brian Noble said, his voice a hissed whisper. "Go more slowly. That's it, that's it. There."

He was leaning back against the rough-hewn stonework of the cemetery wall, its unevenness poking hard against his shoulders, the back of his head, base of his spine.

"That's it, that's lovely. Go on, go on."

The boy stood close alongside him, always looking away, his elbow pressing into Noble's arm. Noble wanted to dip his head and kiss the V of hair, dark at the back of the boy's neck, but knew that if he did the boy would pull away. Instead, he set his right hand softly against the boy's waist, and when there was no resistance, slid it down over his hip and round until his finger ends were resting on the boy's buttocks. He felt the boy's muscles tense and prepared to pull his hand away, but it was all right, there was no need.

Faint, he could see the headlights along Gregory Boulevard, strung like a moving lantern between the trees.

"Christ!" the boy complained. "How much longer you gonna be?"

"It's okay, okay. Just . . . here, here, touch me here as well." And he caught hold of the boy's other hand and thrust it inside his open trousers, tightening it around his balls.

"Oh, God! Oh, good! Oh, God, oh, holy Christ! That's it, that's it!"

Hips thrust forward, back arched, Noble's head smacked back against the cemetery wall, once, twice, three times as he came between the fingers of the boy's hand. "Oh, God! Yes!" Eyes closed, he bit down into the flesh of his lower lip and groaned his pleasure and release, even as the boy was squatting low to wipe away the semen from his hand on the rough grass.

When Brian Noble reopened his eyes, the figures were standing silent between the nearest trees.

"We are police officers. . . ." one of them said and the boy was away, leaping for the cemetery wall, both arms hooked over and pulling his legs after, one foot on top and the other swinging round as Lynn caught hold of his ankle tight and dragged him back, the boy kicking now, kicking and swearing, punching out at her with his fists until the other one joined in, the pair of them hauling him back across the grass and twisting him round, arms tight behind his back and close enough to snap the handcuffs shut about his wrists.

"Hello, Martin," Lynn said, rolling him round onto his side. "Nice to see you again."

Martin jerked back his head, but she was ready for him and the mouthful of phlegm sailed harmlessly past.

Brian Noble had sunk down to his knees in front of Sharon Garnett, shaking, tears in his eyes.

"You do not have to say anything," Sharon was saying. "But it may harm your defense if you do not mention when questioned something that you later rely on in court. Anything you do say may be given in evidence."

Through his tears, Noble looked up at her.

"Do you understand that?" Sharon asked.

Noble nodded.

"Well, if I were you, I'd zip myself up. Nippy, these squirrels can be, this time of year."

Eric Netherfield had gone to bed each night for the past dozen years with a length of railing on the floor within reach. He had picked it up one day from a skipful of rubbish where a house was being cleared. "What on earth've you dragged that back for?" his wife, Doris, had said, and Eric had given his usual little shrug. "Come in handy someday, just you see." Since the burglaries had started in earnest, up and down the

50

street, the last thing Eric did each night, after dropping his teeth into the glass beside the bed and wishing Doris God bless and good night, was trail his fingers down toward that piece of iron, as if touching it for good luck.

Up until now, it had done the trick.

Standing back behind the bedroom door and struggling to control the wheezing from his chest, Eric listened as the pressure on the last stair caused it to squeak.

All Nicky saw, a faint bundle off to one side of the high bed, was Doris, one hand clutching at the turn of the sheet. He waited a moment longer, to be certain that she was asleep, then stepped inside the room.

Eric brought the railing down with all the strength he could muster, aiming for the head but striking the top of the shoulder with such force that the weapon was nearly jarred from his hands.

Nicky cried out at the sudden, searing pain and stumbled back across the room, the old man coming at him now, swinging that damned bar toward his face. Why the hell wouldn't he just let him run? The third time the man swung at him, Nicky was in the doorway; he ducked inside the man's arm and came up fast, head-butting him in the face. The iron bar fell past him and bounced haphazardly down the stairs.

Across the room, clothes pulled toward her skinny chest, the old woman was sobbing. Blood trickled from her husband's nose.

Stupid fuckers! Deserve whatever they fucking get! "Where's your fucking money?" Nicky yelled, driving him back into the room.

Eric made a fist at him and Nicky punched him in the neck, then barged him against the wardrobe hard. Wheezing heavily, Eric sank down to his knees.

"Where's . . . the . . . fucking . . . money?" Nicky shouted

51

in the man's ear, punching him in the head to emphasize each word.

Slowly Eric raised his head. "Sod off, you little toerag!" he said, spittle on his lips.

Nicky stood back and kicked him in the chest.

"Don't! My dear God, don't! You'll kill him!" Doris cried, and scrambled on all fours across the bed toward them.

Eric had collapsed against the foot of the wardrobe and no longer moved.

"Eric! Oh, Eric!"

Nicky pushed Doris back across the bed and raced down the stairs as fast as he could. At the turn, his foot hooked under the length of iron and he tripped and fell headlong.

"Jesus! You bastard! You fucking bastard!"

Winded, aching, Nicky leaned forward, hands on knees. The piece of railing had rolled close to his feet and now he picked it up and with a shout swung it at arm's length, sending every ornament and picture from the mantelpiece flying. His wrist and shoulder where the man had hit him, he thought they might be broken. In the mirror, he caught a glimpse of his reflection, white and scared. Stupid cunt! What'd he have to have a go at him for? Why didn't he let him just run? The mirror was hanging from a chain; he smashed it and smashed it again. It wasn't enough.

Back upstairs, Doris Netherfield was leaning over Eric, massaging his chest. When Nicky burst back into the room, she cradled herself across her husband to protect him, clinging to him as Nicky raised the bar above his head, then brought it down, time and again until his arms had begun to ache and he had had enough.

Seeing the blood for the first time, Nicky ran.

8

Resnick's house was a substantial detached property in Mapperley Park, a short distance to the northeast of the city center. Situated on the curve of a narrow crescent, it was separated from the road by a white stone wall and a small area of lawn. There was a passage at the side, wide enough to park the car that Resnick seldom used, and beyond that a ragged garden of grass and shrubs, a cherry tree that needed pruning, and a shed in sore need of creosote and nails. The cherry tree was already shedding blossoms.

Almost immediately past the hedge at the garden's foot, the land fell steeply away over the allotments of Hungerhill Gardens, and the heart of the city was exposed. Between the railway station and Sneinton windmill, the floodlights of the two soccer grounds showed up clearly, perched on either side of the Trent. Terraced houses that had stood in stubby rows since the turn of the century shared the land with curves and courts of new development that was already starting to look careworn and old. Along the canal, warehouses with peeling fronts, home to flocks of graying pigeons if little else, stood beside architect-designed office buildings and the new marina, and a shopping park of superstores encouraging need and envy, good ambition and bad debts. From where he might stand, at an upstairs window or the garden's edge, Resnick could not see the night shelters, the needles discarded below the old railway arch, the benches and shop doorways where the homeless slept, but he knew they were there.

The interior of the house was dark, the furniture heavy and largely in need of replacement. On the ground floor, at the front, was the living room, comfortable and large, in which Resnick would sometimes sit up late, listening to music, occasionally finding something that interested him on the TV. Past the middle room—a dumping ground for boxes and old magazines, whatever Resnick could not bear to throw away—was the kitchen, large enough to house a scrubbed dining table, a miscellany of pots and pans, an antiquated stove, a refrigerator stuffed with packages from the deli, cat food, and bottled beer.

The stairs, broad, with carved wooden banisters, curved up from the center of the house toward Resnick's bedroom, the bathroom, other rooms he rarely entered. At the top of the house one room had been reduced to bare boards, layers of wallpaper stripped from the walls and not replaced. A man Resnick had been pursuing, a murderer, William Doria, had killed himself there, in front of Rachel Chaplin, a woman whom Resnick had thought, however briefly, he might have loved. Resnick had labored to remove the stains of blood from his sight, but that was all and not enough; they hung still in that room on the air, floated like feathers, pink-tinged and soft, that brushed his face and stirred his memory, would not let it rest.

Resnick rarely went there, climbed those stairs. He had

tried moving once, thought of it many times, but somehow he had stayed. A family house, though he had no immediate family, unless you included the cats and he did not. Cats were cats and people people and Resnick knew the difference, he was clear on that. To all intents and purposes, he lived in just three rooms and let the rest succumb to dust.

When he arrived home that evening on foot, after buying Millington and the CID team a quick round in the pub, the black cat, Dizzy, was waiting for him, as usual, atop the length of wall. Automatically, Resnick reached out a hand to stroke the animal's glossy fur, but Dizzy turned away from his touch and, tail raised, presented Resnick with a fine view of his backside as he ran along the wall and then sprang down toward the door, anxious to be fed. A neat encapsulation, Resnick thought, of man's relationship with cats.

Inside, two of the others, Miles and Pepper, threaded themselves between his legs as he walked toward the kitchen, sifting through the mail he had picked up from the floor. Bud, the fourth and last, eternally young and stupid, lay wedged, for no apparent reason, midway through the cat door, mewing pathetically. Dropping straight into the bin the usual conglomeration of circulars and catalogs, advertisements for a double CD or cassette collection of *Songs That Won the War*, and invitations from his bank to come in and discuss his financial affairs, Resnick bent down and prized open the cat flap and Bud came sprawling through.

Fifteen minutes later, he had fed them, ground coffee and set the kettle on to boil, improvised a sandwich from scraps of Stilton, a few fading leaves of rocket, a rasher of cold, cooked bacon, and the last of a jar of mayonnaise. The *Post* had arrived, offering free tickets to Butlins, free flights to Spain, six hundred pounds' worth of holiday vouchers *and* free beer. Pretty soon, Resnick thought, the entire population of the city would be off sunning itself and singing "Viva España!" and the crime figures would take care of themselves.

In the front room, he dropped into an easy chair and closed his eyes. When he opened them again, the night was gathering close around the windows, the coffee was cold but still drinkable, and the sandwich—the sandwich tasted just fine. As he ate it he stared across the room at his recent acquisition, a brand-new CD player to complement his stereo; his nightly project, working through the tracks of the ten-disc Billie Holiday set he had bought himself the Christmas before last.

What would it be this evening?

"Some Other Spring"?

"Sometimes I'm Happy"?

"I Got It Bad (And That Ain't Good)"?

When the call came through, he was listening to "Body and Soul," the '57 version with Harry Edison taking the bridge. Resnick recognized the slight catch in Kevin Naylor's voice as the younger officer struggled to keep his emotions in check.

"Alive?" Resnick asked, frowning.

"Yes, sir. Last I heard. The old woman, though, got to be touch and go."

"Anyone gone to the hospital?"

"Mark, sir."

"Not Lynn?"

"Already out. Something to do with this kid as absconded."

"Right. Call Graham, tell him to meet me at the house. And you, stay there till I arrive. And for Christ's sake, don't let any bugger trample over everything."

Without waiting to hear Naylor's reply, Resnick set down the receiver and headed for the door. Near enough eleven-thirty and it was going to be a long night. He found his car keys on the table in the hall and grabbed a topcoat from the hooks beside the door. Long and likely cold.

Unaware, though she was never really that, Billie Holiday sang on in the empty room.

Graham Millington, burly, hands in pocket, was pacing the pavement inside the area that had been cordoned off, firing an occasional scowl in the direction of those bystanders who were still lingering in the wake of the sirens' call. Naylor stood in the doorway, face paler than usual in the fall of the streetlight, one of those faces that were forever young until the day that suddenly they were old.

Resnick parked at the opposite side of the street and strode across.

"Break-in, looks like," Millington said, falling into step.

"Entry?"

"Round back. Shimmied in through the window."

"How many?"

"Hard to say as yet. By sight of what's in there, happen half a hundred of 'em."

Resnick blinked. Something was pulsing away behind his left temple, some premonition of pain.

"I've this minute had a call from Mark," Naylor said. "Woman's in the operating theater, crushed skull. Brain damage, sounds like. Serious."

"And the husband?"

"Be okay, I think. Cuts and bruises. Shock."

Resnick turned toward the street, faces indistinct between curtains pulled back. "Witnesses? Anyone seen running away?"

Naylor fidgeted uneasily on the step. "None come forward, sir, as yet."

"Chances are this wasn't the only house broken into. Get yourself about, find out what you can. We'll organize a proper house-to-house first thing."

"Yes, sir."

"Think he'll ever break the habit?" Millington asked, watching Naylor in sports jacket and khaki trousers walking toward the next-door house.

"Which habit's that?"

"Calling you sir."

Resnick didn't bother to reply. He was looking at the turmoil in the small back room, like one of those newspaper photographs showing the spread of damage some distance from the epicenter of an earthquake. A small world turned upside down.

"Something got him in a rare snit," Millington said.

"Him?"

"Them. Maybe."

Resnick surveyed the shattered ornaments, broken picture frames, the shards of mirrored glass. In his mind's eye it was the work of one man, one pair of hands, a sudden unleashing of bewildered rage. Which was not to say that others had not been present, looking on.

"It happened up here," Millington said, close by the foot of the stairs.

Resnick nodded, cast his eyes around one last time before going up. Shielded by the seat of a fallen chair, something caught his eye, shiny and plastic, a library card, computerized. Gloves already on, he bent down and picked it up carefully between forefinger and thumb.

The moment Resnick entered the bedroom it was like stepping back in time. The way the blood seemed to have spun, spiraling around the walls, across the bedspread and the wardrobe face. And the smell of it. The smell he could never clear from his mind.

"Looks like they got trapped somehow," Millington said, "between here and the end of the bed."

"Yes."

Behind Resnick's temple the same nerve triggered again, a pulse of memory. If he closed his eyes, he knew he would hear, along with the cries of those who had been attacked where he now stood, the screams of Rachel Chaplin, jagged and sharp, echoing from the upper bedroom of his own house. Would see the dead man's savagely self-mutilated body lodged between floor and wall.

"Think he was trying to knock it out of 'em, where they were hiding whatever he were after?"

"I don't know, Graham." Stretching his leg across the perimeter of blood, Resnick moved to the far side of the bed. "I don't know if whoever did that was being that rational."

"Makes you wonder, doesn't it? How come she came off so much the worse for wear?"

Resnick was staring at the space, the floor. "Whatever damage was done, it was done there. She must have been leaning over him, protecting him in some way. Whatever way she could."

Naylor called up from below and a few moments later appeared at the door. "People two doors down, sir, friends of the Netherfields ..." Netherfield, Resnick thought, up to that moment he had not known their name. "... seems the husband, Eric, always kept this piece of iron railing beside the bed. In case of burglars, that's what he always said."

"Right," said Resnick. "Find that and I wouldn't mind betting we've found the weapon that did this."

Sounds from below informed him that the Scene of Crime team had arrived, and while they photographed and dusted,

Resnick and Millington could make themselves scarce, make themselves useful elsewhere.

"You'll be wanting to get out to Queen's, I reckon," Millington said by the front door. "I'll just hang on and give Kevin a hand here. Get a start on the morning."

Crossing the street toward his car, Resnick checked his watch: morning had already started.

9

"Why did you run away from the home, Martin?" Lynn asked.

From under the fall of dark hair, Martin Hodgson squinted back at her in disbelief.

"Why, Martin?"

"Why d'you think?"

"I don't know, I'm asking you."

"If you don't know, you must be thick."

"And if I were you, I'd watch my mouth."

Leaning back in his chair, Martin contorted his face and peered downward. "All I can see is me top lip."

She controlled the urge to slap him hard across the face, kick the chair out from under him, cocky little sod, and see him sprawling on the floor. For a moment she wondered whether if someone had done that to him sooner, and hard enough, he would still have turned out the way he had; or was he like he was because that had happened too many times?

"When we brought you in," Lynn said, "you had over a hundred pounds in your pockets."

"So?"

"So where did it come from?"

Martin shook his head; the same expression was back on his face again, sullen and hard. "Where d'you think?"

"Tell me."

"You shouldn't be doin' this, interrogating me on me own. You know how old I am, you know the rules."

Despite herself, Lynn smiled. "Interrogation? Is that what this is?"

"Yeah. What else'd you call it?"

"It's just a chat."

"You mean, I could get up and go?"

"No."

"Then I should have someone here, right?"

"Social Services've been informed."

"Bollocks to that. I want a brief."

"As soon as one can be found."

"Then I'm not sayin' another thing till he comes."

"Just tell me about the money."

"What about it?"

"Where it came from?"

Martin squinted up his eyes. "You know where you found me, right?"

"You got it on the Forest?"

"Yeah, grows on trees."

Caught her! Lynn sat on her hands, staring at the ceiling. Grinning, Martin let his chair rock forward and then slowly folded his arms across the table and lowered his head. Fourteen, Lynn thought, fourteen and he must have been in this situation half a hundred times. She tried to think of the worst thing she might have done, growing up on her parents' poultry farm in Norfolk, by the time she was fourteen. The front of Martin's hair had fallen forward across his wrist and she could see the back of his neck, narrow and exposed. She wondered whereabouts along the line the caring had stopped, the real caring; how long it had been since anyone, any adult, had held him, touched him in anything other than anger or sexual need? From the shift in his breathing she thought he might be asleep.

It was less than ten minutes later that he stirred and opened his eyes. "Ambergate, you're goin' to send me back there, right?"

Lynn nodded. "Right."

Resnick had spoken briefly to the senior registrar in neurosurgery; Doris Netherfield was still in the operating theater and it was impossible to determine with any certainty which way it would go. Up to the present, Doris was just about holding her own, that was the best she could say. They had contacted her immediate family, who were on their way.

Resnick thanked the registrar and went down to the ward.

Sitting beside Eric Netherfield's bed, Divine was browsing through the pages of yesterday's *Today.*

"Spark out, boss," Divine said, on his feet and gesturing down.

"Did he say anything?"

"Kept asking about his missus, that were all."

"Okay, get along home. I'll want you in first thing."

"You're sure, 'cause I don't mind. . . ."

"No, hop it. I'll just hang on here a minute, have a word with the doctor, whoever's on duty."

Divine didn't need telling a third time.

It was the staff nurse who was in charge, a bright-eyed woman in a blue uniform, to Resnick's eyes improbably young. "We gave him something for the pain," she said, "poor old boy. I'm hoping he'll sleep as long as he can."

"I'll not disturb him," Resnick said.

There was a bandage round Eric Netherfield's head, light patches around it where the hair had been shaved away. The arm that poked from the end of hospital pajamas was shiny and gray. Resnick was thinking about the last time he had seen his own father alive.

"Did you want a cup of tea?" the staff nurse said from behind him.

Resnick took it and sat beside the bed, listening to the old man's halting, stubborn breath. He had sat, virtually alone, in a side ward with his father, thirty-six hours, watching the occasional movement of the older man's mouth, each gasp of air into his damaged lungs like rust scraping against rust. "Go home," the sister had said. "Get some rest. We'll call you if there's any change." When the phone rang somewhere between four and five, the change had been that his father was dead. It was the hour those calls had come ever since.

Resnick was finishing the tea, about to leave, when Netherfield spoke. "Doris," he said, his voice barely audible, little more than a croak.

"She's all right," Resnick said. "She's being looked after. She'll be fine."

"She did it for me," Eric said. "She were protecting me."

"I know."

The man stretched out the fingers of his hand and Resnick placed his own between them, leaning close over him, smelling his old man's smell.

"The person who did this . . ." Resnick began.

"A lad, nothing but a lad."

Resnick was about to ask more, but Netherfield's head had slipped a little to one side and his eyes were closed. His fingers, long and bony, were tight around Resnick's hand. As the sound of the old man's breathing steadied down, Resnick continued to sit, arm at an awkward angle, unable to move.

After several minutes the staff nurse came along and freed

64

Resnick's hand, slipping the old man's fingers beneath the edge of the sheet.

"You can go now." She smiled.

Resnick hesitated, waiting for her to add, We'll call you if there's any change.

The litter of half-smoked cigarettes in the ashtray at Brian Noble's side had grown to the edge of overflowing, though, in truth, he didn't smoke. Rarely, at least. Occasionally, after a meal. He looked at his watch and, again, counted the patches on the opposite wall where the paint had begun to flake away. Shifted awkwardly on the hard seat. Got up, sat down.

"Surely you aren't intending to charge me?" he asked, and Sharon stared back at him, eyebrow raised.

"But whatever with?"

"That's just it," she said. "It's difficult. So many possibilities, you know what I mean?" She shrugged. "Gross indecency, that's the usual, isn't it? That'd be a start."

"Look, my wife . . ."

"Oh, yes." Sharon grinned. "There's usually one of those."

He demanded to make a phone call and dialed his own number, hanging up at the first ring.

"No one else you want to try?"

"No. Thank you."

And then they kept him sitting there, looking in from time to time, uniformed officers mainly, once to offer him a hot drink, once a sandwich that was stale, occasionally a head would poke round the door and stare and disappear.

When Sharon came back it was with a lamb kebab inside pita bread. "Sorry to have kept you waiting. It's been a busy night."

Noble said nothing.

Sharon held out the kebab toward him but Noble shook his head.

"Not hungry?"

"I'm a vegetarian."

She looked at him quizzically. "You don't like meat?"

"That's right."

She was still looking at him, a smile at the corners of her mouth. "You surprise me." Sharon picked up a cube of lamb with her fingers and lifted it to her mouth.

"Please," Noble said, "tell me . . . ?"

"What?"

"What you're . . . what you're going to do?"

"With you?"

Noble looked up at her and then away; he couldn't stand the mixture of contempt and mockery in her eyes.

"Did you read," Sharon asked, "about that boy? They found him in a wood down near Bristol, a week or so ago? What was left of him. It was on the news, remember? Nine, wasn't he? Nine years old."

"Look," Noble said, alarmed, "I don't know why you're telling me this. That's nothing to do with me. Nothing at all. There's no . . ."

"Comparison?"

"No."

Sharon sat on the corner of the table and crossed her legs, one high above the other. "You're not a pedophile, is that what you're saying?"

"Of course I'm not!"

"No," Sharon said. "You just like sex with young boys."

Resnick had driven back to the station by way of the Netherfield house. So far, there was no indication that any of the adjacent properties had been broken into. It had been a one-off.

Back in his office, coffee brewing, he was placing a call to the hospital when Lynn Kellogg knocked on his door.

"Not quite ready yet," Resnick said, indicating the coffee machine.

Lynn smiled, a tired smile, there for a moment and then gone.

"The Hodgson youth," Resnick said, "you've got him back in custody."

She nodded.

"Well done."

"Earlier this evening, he was hanging out with Aasim Patel and Nicky Snape."

Resnick's interest quickened. He knew the Snape family well. Shane, the eldest, he'd arrested on a charge of aggravated burglary; the last time he talked to Norma it had been about Nicky, just a day or two before the lad was firebombed in a vigilante attack.

"Nicky wasn't with him, then, up on the Forest?"

"Apparently not. There was some kind of argument by the sound of it. Last he saw of Nicky, he was setting off for home."

Resnick didn't even need to look at the map. If you drew a straight line from the Forest Recreation Ground to Radford, it would pass right through where the Netherfields lived.

First light was filtering up above the rooftops when Millington and Naylor arrived, Graham Millington, with a broad grin, holding aloft a narrow object secured inside two plastic bags.

"Kevin here found it. Dustbin, two streets off."

It was the length of iron railing from beside Eric Netherfield's bed.

10

Resnick caught a couple of hours' sleep in his office, chair pushed back, legs forcing a space for themselves among the reports and memos that littered his desk. When he woke it was to the sound of Graham Millington clattering the kettle and treating the otherwise empty CID room to a muted rendition of "Oh, What a Beautiful Morning."

Resnick had his first mug of tea in his hand before realizing that the phone had failed to ring: Doris Netherfield had survived the night.

"What's all this I hear about Serious Crimes?" Millington asked, lighting only his second Lambert and Butler of the day. The expression of unallayed martyrdom that Madeleine assumed if ever he dared to smoke at home was no longer anything he could bear to watch.

"Going on around us, Graham, all the time."

Millington narrowed his eyes through the spiraling cigarette smoke: what the hell was the boss doing, cracking jokes at this hour of the morning? He presumed it had been meant as a joke.

"You know what I'm on about," Millington said, "this new Serious Crimes Unit."

Resnick sighed. "Yes, and the answer is, I don't know a whole lot more than you."

"But if you were to guess?"

"I'd reckon it'll get as far as Finance, someone will throw a fit about resourcing new office space, extra personnel, and it'll get lost on its way back to the drawing board."

Even as the words were being spoken, Resnick wasn't certain how far he believed them, but neither did he want to face the ramifications the establishing of the squad might have for his career. And not solely his own, Millington's as well.

Divine and Naylor arrived within moments of each other, Divine chirpier than the bags beneath his eyes suggested he would be. "Tea mashed, then, Serge?" he said, reaching for his favorite mug, decorated with a fading cartoon of rugby players and odd-shaped balls.

As usual, Naylor was quiet, easy even among four people to forget that he was there. It was a characteristic that, in the right circumstances, made him the good detective he could be.

Millington caught Resnick's glance toward his watch. "Uniform backup?" he asked.

Resnick shook his head. "Let's not start World War Three, Graham. It's only one youth, after all."

A sardonic smile played round the edges of Millington's mouth. "Well, that's okay, then, in't it? Piece of piss."

In his panic to get away from the Netherfields' house, Nicky hadn't even realized the iron railing was still in his hand. Quickly, he had dumped it in the nearest bin and continued to run. Only when he was within sight of his own home did he stop, chest tight, tears stinging his eyes. Only then did he consider the blood that was splashed across his clothes and staining his face and hands. No way he could go in like that, no way. Backtracking, he climbed into a garden and took two towels from the line, leaned against a wall deep in shadow, and rubbed at his skin, his shirt and jeans. It was still likely that if he went home now someone would be up: Sheena, listening to Blur and looking at some stupid magazine; Shane slumped down in front of a video, Jean Claude Van Damme or Bruce Lee; his mum, sewing buttons back on Shane's shirts or lost in a world of her own, reading one of her trashy romances, Mills and sodding Bloom.

Keeping clear of main roads, quick to cross away from any passersby, Nicky walked and walked, trying not to think about what might happen, what had happened, what he would do if the man or the old woman died.

When he finally turned his key in the front door, legs aching, it was gone two. All of the lights in the house were out. Quick to slip off his boots, Nicky was on his way to the stairs when he heard a muffled groan from the front room: slowly undulating shapes stretched along the settee; his brother was shagging Sara Johnson yet again.

On another occasion, Nicky would have stayed there and watched, but now there were more pressing things. In the bathroom he locked the door before switching on the light.

Jesus Christ!

He might have thought that black wouldn't have shown the stains so clearly, but there was no denying them, thick patches that seemed to have been thrown across his shirt and T-shirt as if he had ridden a mountain bike fast through mud. More across the top of his jeans. And the blood was not only smeared across his skin, it was sticking to his hair. Nicky stripped to his underpants and socks; took off the socks. He thought about rinsing the shirt out in the sink, letting the jeans, perhaps, soak in the bath, but realized there was too little time and anyway, it would never work. He fetched a bin liner from the kitchen and bundled the clothes inside. First thing in the morning, he would get them good and lost. Burn them, that was the thing.

Oh, shit! Footsteps on the stairs. The door handle turned but didn't give.

"Hang on a minute," Nicky said.

"Nicky?" Shane's voice. "That you?"

"Yeah, I shan't be long."

"What the fuck you doin' in there?"

"What d'you think?"

Nicky waited until his brother had walked away before returning to the sink. At least the water was still hot. He found an old scrubbing brush beside the bath and lathered it with soap. He would have to wash his face, clean between his fingers, beneath his nails, shampoo his hair. As he looked into the reddening water, he saw the woman's gray head breaking below him, felt the impact of the blows reverberating back along his arms. Who'd have thought the old girl had as much blood in her as this?

Why didn't he run? Take whatever money was in the house, what he had himself, and run. A bus to Manchester, Glasgow, London, anywhere. He could lose himself in London, knew kids who had. Kids who came back with stories of money and crack, of picking up punters on Victoria Station or at Funland in Leicester Square. Doing the kind of stuff Martin Hodgson would have been out doing last night. At the back of his throat, Nicky felt himself beginning to retch. The sensible thing was to stay here. Bugger off and they'll take that as telling them, fair and square, sticking two and two in their hands and saying, Right, what's that? No, the thing to do was stay cool, get rid of the clothes, go to school.

Just as his mum was getting up, Nicky fell fast off, sucking at his thumb.

Norma was down in the kitchen when the cars arrived, two of them, Naylor and Divine, hurrying round to the back to cut off any possible escape. If she heard them, taking the carton of milk from the fridge, she gave no sign. Sitting down here with a cigarette, quiet, a fag and a cup of tea was the best part of the day.

First up the path, Resnick stood aside, allowing Millington to ring the bell and knock. The sergeant paused, then rang the bell again.

"Bloody hell! Who's this?" But Norma, padding to the front door in her slippers, knew whoever it was, the news would not be good. Seeing the two men standing there, Resnick whom she recognized, Norma felt a sudden pain fire, sharp, across her chest.

"Your Nicky," Millington said. "Is he in?"

"Of course he's bloody in." But she was not looking at Millington, but at Resnick, trying to read the expression in his eyes.

"You can see where it's heading, Norma. Clear as I can myself." Resnick's words, the last time he had been to her house.

"What d'you want him for?" Norma asked.

"One or two questions," Millington told her, "about what he was up to last night."

"Last night he was here," Norma said, "along of me, all evening." It was a response as automatic as drawing breath.

"I think we'd best ask him that," Millington said.

Norma stood her ground, not knowing what to do.

Resnick shifted half a pace toward the doorway. "Norma, I think maybe you should let us in, don't you?"

Millington wandered off into the front room and then the kitchen, while Resnick stood with Norma near the foot of the stairs.

"He's still in bed, then?"

"Course he bloody is."

Resnick set his hand upon the banister and she took hold of his wrist. "You call him, then, Norma. Fetch him down."

At the edge of his eye line, Millington had reappeared, slowly shaking his head.

"Norma," Resnick prompted.

Heavy, she turned and called Nicky's name; set her foot upon the stairs and called again.

In his room, Nicky was instantly awake and throwing back the clothes.

"Nicky, it's the police."

He grabbed a pair of old jeans and was still pulling them on as he threw up the window and scrambled out onto the sloping roof above what had once been the outside lavatory.

"Nicky!"

First Resnick, and then Millington, elbowed past Norma and took the stairs at a run.

Nicky slithered down the steeply angled roof, dislodging tiles as he went. One of his hands caught at the old iron guttering and it broke. Twisting as best he could, Nicky half-jumped, half-fell, and then he was away, jumping the old rabbit hutch and vaulting the gate, straight into Divine's arms where the detective waited behind the wall.

From the upstairs window, Resnick watched as Nicky swore at Divine and struggled, until Naylor had his arms behind him and between them they'd put on the cuffs.

"Kick me again, you little bastard," Divine said, "and I'll have your balls for breakfast."

Resnick, closing the window, didn't hear. Shane was out on the landing, pulling a pair of cords up over his boxer shorts. "What the fuck's going on?"

"It's okay, nothing to bother you."

"Well, s'pose I want it to bother me?"

"I'd remind you what the magistrate said, last time you were up in court."

"Fuck the bastard magistrate!"

"I daresay," Resnick sighed. "Now, why don't you go downstairs, look to your mum? Make her a cup of tea if nothing else."

Shane pushed past him and slammed the bathroom door shut behind him.

Norma was in the kitchen, head in her hands.

"I'll take a look round," Millington said, and Resnick nodded and went to put the kettle on himself. Within five minutes, Millington had found the bin liner full of bloodied clothes stuffed under Nicky's bed.

"Take them in," Resnick said. "Let Forensic have them, first thing." He glanced at Norma. "I'll be along directly." He fished out the used tea bags, tipped the lukewarm tea down the sink, and set to making some fresh.

11

Resnick watched her walk across the playground, hair moving lightly in the freshness of the wind. Despite all the forecasts, the temperature had dipped a further five degrees and, in the CID room that day, Millington had been mithering on about having to take his geraniums in again, safe out of the frost.

"Hannah Campbell," the school secretary had said. "She's taking a drama group in the main hall. Should be through anytime in the next half hour."

In no hurry to return to the station, Resnick had elected to wait.

Nicky Snape's interrogation had been careful and slow. For the best part of the first hour, his mother sitting alongside him, a solicitor just behind, Nicky had said nothing; then, after continued questioning, Resnick and Millington alternating, he admitted to spending the first part of the evening with Martin Hodgson and another friend. Where?

Cinema. What did you see? Nicky told them. Had he been near the Netherfield house? No, he had not been near the Netherfield house. Didn't know what they were on about? Didn't know where it was.

"Nicky," Resnick had said, "listen to me. We're doing tests now. They're going on while we're talking here. The blood on the clothes we found underneath your bed, blood around the sink in your bathroom at home, blood on a length of iron railing we found near the house—whose blood, Nicky, do you think that is? Do you think it belongs to that woman lying up at Queen's in intensive care, just about hanging on to her life? Do you think that's what we're going to find?"

Nicky had stared at the table, his hands clenched together. Beside him, with very little noise, Norma had started to cry.

"Whatever you know about this, Nicky," Resnick had said. "Anything at all, I think you should tell us now. Let's talk about it now, you and me, while we're here. While we can."

Norma had turned away, unwilling to look at her son, afraid to, and Resnick had leaned, almost imperceptibly, forward. "Nicky, this house we're talking about, where all of this happened, were you there?"

Nicky's reply was so quiet it was almost as if he hadn't spoken at all.

"Sorry, Nicky, what did you say? Could you just say that again for us please?"

"I said yes. Yes."

Norma hid her face in her hands and began to sob.

"But all I did was break in, right? I never touched nobody, never hit no one. I never even saw nobody, none of that stuff you said. All I did was get in downstairs at the back. I never even went upstairs."

"All right, Nicky, one thing at a time. We'll get to that later." And when the solicitor requested a break for his client, Resnick was happy to accede. He had wanted to get out of the station, clear his head, find something else, unde-manding, to do. He had come here.

Hannah was wearing a cotton jumper beneath her jacket, pale blue, and she had white and blue trainers on her feet. He liked the way she walked, purposefully but not hurrying, a leather bag slung over one shoulder, another, an old brief-case, packed and battered, tight against her side. She slowed to speak to two boys who were engaged in one of those argu-ments young boys are forever into, a push here, an angry word there, and only when they had shuffled grudgingly away did she carry on toward where her car was parked, a Volkswagen Beetle, painted red.

Resnick got out of his own car and moved to intercept her. "Hannah Campbell?"

With a slight jump, she turned.

"Sorry, I didn't mean to startle you."

"That's all right." She was trying to place him—one of the parents, another teacher she had met somewhere at a confer-ence and forgotten?

"Charlie Resnick. Detective Inspector, CID." He held up his identification for her to see.

"My," she said, eyes widening. "I *am* going up in the world. Last time it was only a—what do you call them?"

"Detective Constable. DC."

"An odd sort of a name . . ."

"Divine."

Hannah smiled. "He should have gone to ecclesiastical college, become a priest."

Resnick grinned at the thought and she saw something in his eyes that had not been there before.

He watched her place the briefcase on top of the car and turn back to face him. With the light as it was, he thought he could see traces of red, faint in the brown of her hair.

"Don't tell me you've recovered my purse?"

"Not exactly."

"Just the money and the credit cards."

"I wish I could say we had."

Hannah smiled. It had been a long day and the extra session she'd just had should have left her exhausted but instead it had picked her up, renewed her energy. And here was this shaggy man, hair askew, fawn trousers too baggy, brown jacket unbuttoned or it would have been too tight. She couldn't decide if the top button of his shirt was missing, or if, shielded by the knot of his tie, it was simply undone.

"So what is it?" Hannah asked. She liked the way his eyes stayed focused on her instead of wandering off as so many people's did. It gave the impression that he was honest, and she wondered if that was true.

Resnick took her library card from his wallet.

"Where did you find that?" she asked.

He told her, light on the details of the injuries the Netherfields had suffered, but making sure she understood the seriousness of what had happened. The skin prickled at the back of her neck when he mentioned Nicky Snape. When he had finished, she stood awhile saying nothing, fiddling with a tissue, blowing her nose.

"When you spoke to DC Divine," Resnick said, "you said you thought it was Nicky Snape who stole your purse."

"Yes, that's right." Somehow, absurdly, Hannah wished that she had not.

"When we brought Nicky in, he had some money on him, though not a lot. As yet it's unclear where he got it from. No sign of your credit cards, I'm afraid."

"That's okay. It's not exactly important, is it? I mean, not after what's happened." She looked at him. "I don't see why you're bothering with this at all."

"The card, if he did take it from you, if it was in your purse that morning, well, it places him there, in the house."

"I see."

"And it would have been in your purse?"

Hannah nodded yes.

"As it turns out, it likely isn't crucial. There's other evidence enough."

Hannah looked away from Resnick toward the Boulevard and saw men walking their dogs on the sparse green of the Forest, the slow blur of cars. "Of course, I knew he was always bunking off school, getting into trouble, but this . . ." She turned back to face him. "It's difficult to believe."

Resnick gave a slow shake of the head. "I know. It's not the kind of thing I'd've reckoned him for at all."

"You don't think it could have been somebody else? I mean, with him?"

"That's not what he's saying."

"I see."

Below them, homecoming traffic was slowing to a crawl. "I should be going," Hannah said.

"Me, too."

Neither one moved.

"What will happen to him?" Hannah asked. "Now, I mean?"

"Oh, most likely he'll be taken into local authority care. Secure accommodation somewhere. Until the trial."

"And then?"

Resnick shook his head and stepped away.

Hannah's keys were in her hand. "Be seeing you." It was one of those things you said; it didn't mean anything.

"Yes," Resnick said.

From the window of her car she watched him, shoulders more hunched than they should be, head a little bowed. She sat a moment longer, wondering without reason if he might turn back, find something more to say. When he didn't, she turned the key in the ignition, backed the car round, and headed down to join the traffic. She had one final glimpse of

Resnick as he drove off in the opposite direction. That young detective, she thought, so full of himself, the one who had almost asked her out—why was it never the ones to whom you might have said yes?

The investigation went pretty much as Resnick had anticipated; Hannah read the reports in the newspaper the next day, though for legal reasons Nicky's name was omitted. Nicky was remanded into the care of the local authority awaiting trial. Hannah got on with her teaching, poems and book reports, *Break Point*, *What About It, Sharon?* and *Macbeth*. For Resnick, other things came pressing in, the way things do. A suspected arson attack on a café specializing in Caribbean food; a youth of thirteen who stole a delivery van and drove it into a bus queue, leaving one person dead and four more seriously injured; one doctor who was accused of illegally prescribing drugs, another of procuring an illegal abortion; a gang of teenage girls rampaging through the underpasses around the city center, mugging two women and a twenty-seven-year-old man. A little shy of six in the morning, a Sunday, Resnick had a call from the Social Services emergency duty team: Nicky Snape had been found hanging from the shower in the children's home where he was being held.

12

The building was separated from the road by a parade of tightly packed firs. Its brick and concrete fascia and high barred windows told of decades of institutional use: children's home, assessment center, now secure accommodation that was less than secure. There were plans to sell it into private hands; a certain amount of modification and a coat or two of paint and it would make a perfect old people's home. Resnick recognized the police surgeon's car at the curb; the ambulance was parked on the curve of the drive, tight to the front door. He rang the bell. Six-thirty: out of the east the sky leaked a stubborn light.

The door was opened by a man in his early thirties, slightly built with thinning hair. He glanced at Resnick's identification and stepped back. "Paul Matthews, I . . . Mr. Jardine's busy with the Director of Social Services, on the phone, er . . . He asked me to show you where . . . where it happened, and then he would like to talk to you later. Before you go."

Resnick stepped onto the worn parquet flooring of the hall. The death of a minor in custody: he thought it would be a long time before he—he and those officers who came after him—would be taking their leave.

"It's the bathroom on the second floor."

Resnick nodded and followed him toward the stairs. Voices echoed faintly back and forth along cold corridors; the interior smelt of disinfectant and waste. Several yards short of the bathroom, Matthews stopped and stared at the floor.

In the moment before he went inside, Resnick had an image, clear and defined, of what he would see. For neither the first time nor the last. He turned the rounded handle and went in.

Nicky Snape lay on a sheet of thick polythene, which had been doubled beneath him on the bathroom floor. He was naked to the waist and his soiled pajamas had been lowered below his buttocks to midway down his thighs. Across the cage of his ribs and taut between his hips, his skin stretched opaque and milky white. The bruising at his neck and underneath his chin had already darkened to a color that was neither black nor purple. Old burn marks stood out kidney red in the bright overhead light. In death his face was that of a child.

"Charlie."

Resnick heard the police surgeon's voice, but continued to stare. So small and broken there.

"Asphyxiation, Charlie. Dead, what? Couple of hours, hour and a half." Parkinson offered Resnick a mint and when the inspector refused, popped one into his own mouth. "You see the way the lips have turned that shade of blue? And there, the nail beds of the hand."

Bending, Resnick saw the skin around the fingers chewed raw, nails bitten down to the quick.

"There was a towel by the body, wet and twisted tight. What he used, Charlie, most like."

Resnick could see it, coiled against the edge of the shower stall, white with a faint blue stripe.

"Your boys'll find fibers aplenty, like as not." The mint cracked between the surgeon's teeth.

"You didn't take him down?" Resnick asked.

Parkinson shook his head. "He was propped up against the wall there, back against the tiles. Staff, I suppose."

Resnick squatted close to the body, wondering if, when he was discovered, Nicky's eyes had already been closed. An illusion he allowed himself for a moment, if he stayed there close the boy would wake.

"What was he, Charlie?" Parkinson asked, fidgeting things back into his case. "Sixteen?"

"Not that."

Not ever, Resnick thought. He rose to his feet. Millington would be here soon, roused from his blissful bed, and then Scene of Crime, bemoaning the disruption of their Sunday, even as they counted the overtime. Others, too. Senior social workers in once-good suits engaged on damage limitation, eager to off-load the blame.

"Nasty burn marks," Parkinson observed. "Not above a year old. Caught in a fire or some such, I suppose."

"Firebomb," Resnick said. "A little surprise as he was walking home. Local vigilantes out to teach him a lesson."

"Tearaway, then, was he?"

"Fond of what wasn't properly his own."

"Well," Parkinson said, snapping the case shut, "not so different from the rest of us there. But now, if you'll excuse me, no excuse for not getting on the green bright and early this morning, at least."

"No, I suppose not."

"You don't play, do you, Charlie?" The surgeon voiced it as a matter of regret.

Resnick shook his head.

"Ah, well. I'll give Jack Skelton your regards."

Paul Matthews was waiting in the corridor. "Mr. Jardine—if you're ready, I'll show you the way to his office." Resnick looked at him carefully; understood that it was more than tiredness lining his eyes.

"You were the one who found him," Resnick said.

Matthews flinched and looked away.

"What time was that?"

"Five, it would've been . . . Not long after five."

"You were the member of staff on duty?"

"Yes."

"Just you?"

"No, my colleague, Elizabeth, she . . . It was routine, you see, I was just checking the bathroom. Routine." His words were beginning to collide again, haphazard; at his sides, his hands were never still. "As soon as I went in there, I could see—Nicky, I mean—I could see what had happened, what he'd done. The towel, he'd fastened it around the pipe to the shower. Behind the . . . behind the showerhead . . . he . . . ."

"It's all right, take your time."

"I could see the way his neck was twisted off to one side . . ."

"Yes."

". . . and he'd, you know, messed himself. I mean, I could tell that he was dead, Nicky, dead already. It was too late. There was nothing I could do."

"You took him down?"

"Not right away. I . . ."

"But you checked for vital signs?"

Matthews's eyes were birds trapped in the space of Resnick's gaze. "I didn't know what to do. Whether I should touch him or not, I wasn't sure. Elizabeth, she was . . . like I said, she was on duty with me. I ran for help."

Resnick struggled to keep his temper, keep the incredulity out of his voice. "You left him hanging? Without establishing that he was dead?"

Matthews scratched hard at the side of his face. "Yes, I mean, no, not for long. Just till . . ." He looked at Resnick imploringly. "He was already dead. He was."

"You phoned the emergency services?"

"Yes."

"You and not your colleague, Elizabeth."

"I'm not . . . I'm not . . . It might have been Elizabeth, I'm not sure."

Resnick steadied him with a hand on his arm. "All right. We'll talk some other time. You can make a statement to one of my officers later. Now let's not keep your Mr. Jardine waiting any longer."

Hand on the banister, Matthews pulled in air gratefully, gathering himself together before leading the way.

The name had been written in black copperplate on a white card—DEREK JARDINE—and slipped into the brass frame attached to the oak-finish door, more letters after it than in the name itself. The sound was hollow when Resnick knocked.

"Inspector." Jardine raised himself from his chair to shake Resnick's hand. "Please, take a seat."

Beneath the curtained window and along one wall, shelves stood thick with books on social work and young offenders, bound copies of professional journals and reports. A write-on, wipe-off calendar bearing staff names and duties was fixed to the other side wall; beside it, without apparent pattern, an array of photographs—the youngsters, Resnick assumed, who had passed through Jardine's hands. On top of the gray filing cabinet close by the director's desk, framed by a browning ivy and a spider plant that had known better days, was a photograph of Jardine himself in cap and gown, receiving an academic scroll.

Thirty years on, the face was more fleshy, thin lines had appeared, crisscrossing the nose and cheeks, blue like Roquefort cheese. Dark hair, graying at the temples, was receding; small flakes of dandruff decorated the shoulders of his dark blue suit.

"Of course, this is terrible," Jardine was saying and Resnick nodded, waiting for the second "terrible" to follow, which it predictably did.

"A young boy."

"Yes."

"A tragedy."

He could be, Resnick thought, rehearsing the vicar's empty speech. "Last night, this morning, when the incident occurred—you weren't on the premises?" He hadn't intended it to sound hostile, but from Jardine's expression he could see that it had.

"I can't be here all of the time, Inspector."

"No, of course. I didn't mean . . ."

"I left, in fact, quite late. Nine-thirty or ten. My staff contacted me at home this morning when the . . . when Nicky's body was discovered."

"And that was Paul . . . ?"

"Paul Matthews, yes." Jardine's eyes narrowed and he leaned forward, chest pressing the edge of the desk. "Inspector, you do appreciate we shall be carrying out a full internal inquiry. I've discussed this already with the Director of Social Services. In the meantime, I must ask you not to question any of my staff unless either myself or a solicitor is present." He settled back into the curve of his chair. "I have no doubt whatsoever the inquiry will establish that, as far as we are concerned, correct procedures were followed."

If the correct procedures had been followed, Resnick thought, then maybe a boy wouldn't be lying out there dead. He said nothing, but Jardine read the accusation, unmistakable in Resnick's eyes.

"Nicky's mother," Resnick said. "She has been informed?"

When Resnick left the building less than ten minutes later, it was with a sense of relief. Graham Millington had arrived moments earlier and met Resnick outside, a few crumbs of toast still caught in his mustache. Easy to imagine Madeleine sitting her husband down at the kitchen table: "Graham, you're not going off at this hour without something inside you. You know how your stomach plays up when you do."

"Straightforward enough, then?" Millington said, apprised of the details.

"Who knows, Graham? The lad's dead, no two ways about that, but how and why . . . ?"

"Topped himself, though, didn't he? I mean, it was suicide?"

Resnick sighed. "That seems the most likely—at present."

Millington looked back at him quizzically, eyebrow raised. "You've no reason to suppose . . ."

"No reason, Graham, to suppose a thing. But there's a social worker in there, Matthews, ready to come apart at the seams. And the director, Jardine, getting the hatches battened down like he was in a time of siege."

"Or cholera," Millington said quietly.

"Sorry, Graham?"

"It's a book the wife was reading. . . ."

"I daresay, Graham. Anyway, stick around, keep Scene of Crime on their toes. Soon as they're through, you can release the lad's body to the hospital. Oh, and Graham, so you know, Jardine gave me the benefit of a lecture, no talking to the staff without his say-so."

"And without a Social Services solicitor to hold their hand."

"Most likely."

"Ah, well." Millington grinned ruefully. "Do what we can, eh?"

"By the book, Graham. If there is anything amiss here, we'll not want to let it slip away."

Millington nodded and walked toward the entrance. The morning air was cold and the sky was an almost unbroken gray. Whatever had happened to spring? Resnick thought. At the end of the drive, he looked back toward the tall windows and saw the faces staring down.

13

It was still early on Sunday morning. Kevin and Debbie Naylor lay beneath the duvet, Kevin on his back, Debbie curled over on her side; softly, from the adjacent bedroom, the sounds of their daughter holding a long and complicated conversation with one or other of her stuffed animals.

"Kevin?"

"Hmm?"

"What you thinking?"

"Nothing."

But just by reaching out a hand and touching him, Debbie could tell that he was lying.

"Kevin?"

"What?"

Debbie laughed and slid one leg across his, the laugh stifling against his chest.

"Deb."

"Mmm?"

"She might come in at any minute."

"Not if we close the door." She moved her head again and her mouth found his nipple.

"Ow!"

"Shhh."

"Is it, you know, all right?"

"Of course it's all right."

Some months ago Debbie had had a miscarriage; she didn't want to wait too long before giving their only child a little sister or brother.

"Kevin?"

But Kevin was smiling as he rolled off his back toward her, the whole thing easy between them now, easier than it had ever been. Just for a second she tensed when he touched her but then quickly relaxed. His mouth at her neck, her breast, and then her hand around him, guiding him in.

Deftly, Lynn Kellogg fashioned for her mother the story of her Saturday-night date; at seven on the dot, her young man, an accountant with a local firm of solicitors, had picked her up at the housing association flat where she lived. They had gone to see the new Alan Bennett play at the Playhouse. Well, not new actually, an old one revived, but with that actor her mum had always liked in *The Likely Lads*. No, not him. The other one. Yes, very good. Funny. And then they'd gone for something to eat at Mama Mia. Yes, tagliatelle. Italian, that's right. Very tasty. And, yes, of course she'd be seeing him again. No, she didn't know exactly when.

She could almost hear her mother, sitting in the kitchen of their Norfolk poultry farm, making calculations, crossing fingers, counting chickens, hatching dreams.

What Lynn had actually done the previous night was read two chapters of a Tom Clancy, walk around the corner for a take-away chicken korma from the Maharani, pop open a can of Carlsberg, and watch Andy Garcia and Meg Ryan drinking their way through *When a Man Loves a Woman* on a rented video.

All those things her mother wanted for her—marriage, babies—Lynn thought she was happy to forgo them all, if that meant she didn't have to go through all of the crap that seemed necessary to get within even spitting distance of them.

"How's Dad?" she asked, breaking across her mother's words.

"Oh, Lynnie, he's fine. Right as rain. Out there with his blessed birds since the Lord knows when. He'll be in soon for his bit of breakfast, you see."

Almost two years ago, Lynne's father had been diagnosed as having colorectal cancer, cancer of the bowel. He had an operation, treatment, regained weight, resumed work, almost as if nothing more could happen. It was like sitting on a time bomb, Lynn thought, waiting for the news, imagining what was slowly growing inside him.

"Lynnie, your dad's fine. Honest."

Her mother who believed in dreams.

For Norma Snape the best Sundays were not present but past. She could remember when she was still with Patrick, waking late in that bed in Huddersfield, sunlight patching across the room and Patrick sitting propped on pillows beside her, building his first joint of the day. Then lying there, getting more and more stoned until finally the munchies overcame them and they raided the refrigerator for leftover pizza and chocolate-chip ice cream. Al Green on the record player all the while: "Let's Stay Together," "Here I Am (Come and Take Me)," "Call Me (Come Back Home)."

Or later, Sundays with Peter, his hands fluttering at her back like wings, barely touching, never still. Sheena, nine months old, fast asleep close alongside her, thumb in her mouth, hair fair across her eyes. The rise and fall of the child's tiny chest no more than the delicate pressure of Peter's fingers at the base of her spine. The tension within her as she bit into the soft underside of her lip, waiting for his hands to move lower.

Norma stirred and reached for the mug of tea she had fetched earlier and which had long since grown cold. Faint from downstairs she could hear the sound of the television, though she'd swear that she'd heard Shane go out the best part of an hour since. She fidgeted the sheet around her and reached for a magazine. She could hear Sheena now, running herself a bath. But not her Nicky, he wasn't there for certain. Shut up in that place, poor little bastard, shut up in that bastard home. This afternoon she'd get herself up nice, go out and see him, take him some chocolate, cigarettes, something special, something for a treat. No matter what he'd done, when it came down to it, he was her son; there was no getting away from that, no getting away from it at all. She'd just stay there ten minutes longer, get up for good then, mash some fresh tea. She lit a cigarette and flicked toward the problem page—anyone else's but her own, they were a cinch.

She was still lying there, half an hour later, when the doorbell rang.

When it became clear that, whoever it was, they weren't going to go away, Norma pulled on her dressing gown and shuffled to the upstairs window, overlooking the street.

"What the hell . . . ?"

She saw Resnick looking up at her and what she saw in his eyes drove into her stomach like a fist.

Downstairs, she could see him silhouetted through the mottled glass panels at the top of the door. Impatient with the bolts, her fingers finally fumbled back the door.

"Norma . . ."

It was still there in his eyes and in the way he stood.

"It's Nicky, isn't it?"

"Yes."

"Something's happened to Nicky."

"I'm afraid so, yes."

Norma's hands were at her sides, clenched; for a moment she closed her eyes.

"Norma, I think we'd best talk inside."

"Tell me."

"Norma . . ."

She caught hold of him, the lapel of his coat. "Fucking tell me!"

Resnick's breath snagged in his throat. "He was found earlier this morning. Norma, he . . ."

"He's dead."

Resnick's voice was quiet, each word screaming in her head. "Yes. Yes, Norma, I'm afraid he's dead."

She flung back her arm and her hand smashed through the glass of the door. What came from her mouth was more of a hiss than a scream. Resnick caught her and held her close, her breath against his face. Blood ran from her palm and wrist, down past her finger ends onto the floor.

"Norma, come on. Come on now, let's get inside."

He led her, half-dragging her, along the short hall. Sheena was standing, white-faced, a towel wrapped round her, at the foot of the stairs.

"Help me get your mum into the front room."

Sheena didn't move.

Over and over again, Norma was saying Nicky's name. Resnick maneuvered her onto the settee and raised her arm so that her hand was level with her head. Cartoon dinosaurs were doing battle on the TV.

Resnick looked round at Sheena, silent in the doorway. "Get a clean towel, tea towel, anything as long as it's clean. All right? Now."

There were slivers of glass visible in the fleshy part of

Norma's hand, below the thumb. "What . . . happened?" she gasped. "Nicky, what happened?"

"Let's get this mess sorted first. . . ."

"No! No. Tell me, I want to know."

Careful, Resnick eased the longest of the glass shards away; he was holding Norma's arm upright with his hand. Sheena came back carrying a hand towel. She had pulled on a T-shirt and jeans. "It's all I could find."

"That's fine. Now phone for an ambulance. . . ."

"No." Norma was sobbing, shaking her head.

"An ambulance, this wants seeing to properly. And get the kettle on, let's have some tea, all right? Sweet tea."

Gingerly, Resnick fingered out another piece of glass and set it carefully with the first, on the floor by the settee.

"Mr. Resnick, please . . ."

He held her other hand as well. "He was found in one of the bathrooms with a towel around his neck. He was hanging. It looks as if he took his own life."

She pulled away from him so hard that he was unable to hold her; punched and slapped against him as the cries tore from her throat and didn't stop until he had caught her wrists and pinned them back and by then the front of his shirt and the side of his face were smeared with blood.

"It's okay, Norma," Resnick said. "It's okay, it's going to be all right."

But Norma could only remember Nicky's face as she chased him away, holding her ten pounds aloft and laughing. *You let me get my hands on you, you little tripeshanks, and I'll wring your miserable neck.*

14

When Resnick first worked with him, Jack Skelton had begun his days in track suit and running shoes, jogging a couple of miles down the Derby Road toward the university, one lap round the lake and then back up the hill, forehead glistening with sweat and good intentions. Now he lit his third or fourth Bensons of the day between the car park and the rear door of the station, and his breath was audible by the time he reached the second flight of stairs.

Time was, too, when Resnick would have had his work cut out to be at his desk before the superintendent of a morning, but this Monday he had almost finished briefing Millington and the rest of the team before Skelton arrived.

It had been a weekend like many another. Half a dozen break-ins either side of the Alfreton Road and the same number in the narrow streets at the back of Lenton Boulevard. In one of these, the burglars had made themselves jam and peanut butter sandwiches, opened the mail, then sat around long enough to watch the recording of that Saturday's *Match of the Day*, which had been left in the VCR. All of this while three lads slept upstairs, out to the world.

A van had been stolen from round the back of a bakery in Radford and driven into the canal behind the Raleigh cycle works. Two men had got into a fight in the early hours, which resulted in one biting off the first finger of the other at the tip; the victim had walked into accident and emergency at the Queen's with the finger safe inside a condom he had been keeping providentially in his wallet. And at a little before seven that morning, three girls wearing face masks, one of them in what looked like a school uniform, had tried to hold up the petrol station by Abbey Bridge with what proved to be a cucumber inside a plastic bag.

"Another week, eh, Charlie?" Millington had said, stubbing out his cigarette.

"Least we don't have Nicky Snape to fret about," Divine said, getting to his feet.

Resnick shot him a look that would keep his head down for the rest of the day.

"The Hodgson youth," Resnick said to Lynn as she walked by, "safely back at Ambergate?"

Lynn nodded. "Till the next time."

"Good work there."

"Thanks."

"The man they picked up with him . . ."

"Brian Noble."

"Vice decide to charge him or what?"

Lynn shook her head. "More trouble than it was worth in the end. Gave him a warning and kicked him free." She smiled. "What's the betting he was in church yesterday with his wife and kids, giving thanks."

Across the room, Kevin Naylor turned his head from the telephone. "The hospital, sir, Doris Netherfield . . ." The skin tightened apprehensively around Resnick's eyes. "No change, apparently. Still holding her own."

"Good," Resnick said, releasing his breath. "Thank God for that as well."

Skelton was waiting in his office and listened with barely concealed impatience while Resnick made his report. There were more pressing things on his mind.

"Don't know how you managed it yesterday morning, Charlie, out where that kid was found, but you got a hair stuck up the director's arse of sizable proportions. I had the ACC on the phone to me last evening, Assistant Director of Social Services had been onto him, asking whatever investigation we carry out, you wouldn't be the officer in charge."

Resnick grunted in response.

"According to Jardine, you questioned staff without his authority."

"I talked to one, the man who let me in. What was I supposed to do, maintain strict silence?"

"And then, apparently, you all but accused Jardine of culpability in Snape's death."

"That's nonsense. I accused nobody."

"All right, then, implied."

Resnick looked past Skelton's head toward the window; with what seemed unnatural slowness, a plane from East Midlands Airport was making a diagonal pass across a blue-gray sky. "I'd be tempted to wonder, all this defensiveness, if he hasn't got something to hide."

"The suicide? You think there's something not kosher?"

Resnick shrugged. "Not necessarily. But if that is what happened, I'd like to know the reasons why."

"The way he attacked that old man, kid or not, he might've been facing some heavy time. Maybe it was the thought of being shut away."

Resnick shook his head. "I think it would've taken more than that."

"Bullying, then, some of the other youths, is that what you think?"

"I don't know. Could be a lot of things."

"Or nothing at all."

Resnick shifted heavily in his chair. "Dead fifteen-year-old, that's what there is."

Hands clenched behind his head, Skelton leaned his chair back onto its rear legs. "There will be a police inquiry, of course. Routine. The ACC mentioned Bill Aston. What do you think?"

"I thought he'd been put out to pasture long since."

"Not exactly. They found him an office the size of a shoe box up at headquarters and gave him bits of paper to push around the desk."

"You make it sound like occupational therapy."

Skelton unclasped his hands and set his chair level. "Kinder than kicking him free a few years short of his pension."

"And you think he's right for this?"

"Like I say, it's a suggestion."

Resnick remembered Aston, a tall figure with iron gray hair and steel-rimmed glasses, ramrod straight. As a uniformed inspector, he would run his morning parades with a fine-tooth comb. Buttons smeared with Brasso, creased jackets, dirty shoes—all enough to earn a reprimand at least. Cleanliness and Godliness and the chief constable sitting up there at the Lord's right hand. Resnick had worked with him after Aston moved across to CID and found him thorough, painstaking, devoid of imagination. Policing changed and Aston had not. Turning forty, he saw advancement pass him by. Chief inspectors' posts came and went and he devoted more and more time to his work as a lay preacher and governor of the local primary school; he had been shuffled aside.

"He'll do a careful job," Skelton said. "By the numbers, you know that."

"He'll be polite."

"You'll have a word with him, make sure he's primed? You know the family pretty well."

"Yes, I'll tell him what I can."

"Good." Skelton was on his feet. "Jardine's objections aside, you'd not really have fancied this yourself."

"Probably not."

"Oh, and Charlie . . ." This when Resnick was almost at the door. "Had a call from your mate, Reg Cossall. Setting up an operation in Radford, undercover. Fraud, theft, dealing. Drugs Squad have got their oar in, too. Wants to know if we can spare a body? Three nights or four. Somehow he's scared up some overtime."

Uncertain, Resnick shook his head. "We're shorthanded as it is, you know that."

"Charlie, it's only a couple of nights. Divine's kind of thing, this, isn't it?"

Resnick shrugged. "If it's going to be anyone, better Naylor. Then at least the money might go to good use. Divine'll drink it away and scarce notice the difference."

"As you say, Charlie, up to you." Before Resnick had left the office, Skelton was reaching for the phone.

It was ten to one and Resnick was about to take a bite out of his turkey breast and cranberry sandwich when the officer on duty called up from the front desk. There were two visitors to see him, Norma Snape and her son, Shane.

Naturally a big woman, Norma seemed to have suddenly shrunken on her frame. The black dress she wore hung from her shoulders like poorly fitted curtains; her face, previously full, had become gaunt. Darkness around her eyes suggested many tears and little sleep.

Alongside her, Shane was taller than Resnick remembered

him, fitter; aside from frequent trips to the betting shop and pool hall, clearly he had been working out. He wore loose-fitting blue jeans and a gray sweatshirt and his fair hair had been zealously trimmed. Standing alongside his mother at the entrance to the CID room, Shane fixed his eyes on Resnick and dismissed him as so much piss and wind.

"Let's go into my office." Resnick held open the door and ushered Norma toward a chair. Shane preferred to stand.

"Can I get you anything? Tea, coffee?"

No reply.

Resnick walked around his desk and sat down, Shane's eyes following him all the way. "Norma, how've you been?"

"How d'you think?" Shane snapped back before his mother could speak.

"And your hand, Norma? How's your hand?"

"Never mind her bloody hand. That's not why we're here." He stared at Resnick. "My brother was in your charge and he died—that's why we're here."

Resnick eased back his chair and sighed. "Not directly in my charge. The local authority—"

"Bollocks to the local authority! You arrested him." Shane's finger jabbing toward Resnick's face. "You. You're the one as dragged him out the house, banged him up in here, got him up in court. And what happened to him, what happened to him, right, that's down to you, too. Your fucking fault!"

His fist was now little more than inches from Resnick's face. His voice more than filled the room. Millington knocked on the door and entered without waiting to be asked. "Everything okay, boss?"

"Thanks, Graham. Everything's fine." Resnick didn't look at his sergeant, didn't take his eyes off Shane Snape.

"Right, then. If you're sure." Millington slowly withdrew, leaving the door ajar.

Shane and Resnick were staring at each other and neither would look away.

"Shane . . ." Norma reached up with her bandaged hand and touched her eldest's arm. "Please."

With a flex of his muscles, Shane lowered his fist and stepped away. Resnick watched him for ten, fifteen seconds more and then, apparently, dismissed him from his thoughts. "What is there I can tell you, Norma?"

"My Nicky," Norma said, leaning closer, "never mind what happened to him in the past, no matter how bad he got hurt, he'd always bounce back. Always. Even that time those bastards threw that petrol bomb at him. Nicky, he was laughing and joking about it while he was still in the hospital. That's why I don't think he would ever have done a thing like that, Mr. Resnick, took his own life. It's not the way he . . . not the way he was. Not unless there was good reason, something we don't know about. Something that happened to him while he was there."

"Norma, there'll be an inquiry. . . ." Behind his mother, Shane laughed a short, bitter laugh. "Two. One carried out by Social Services, and another that we'll conduct ourselves."

"Bloody whitewash," said Shane. "That's what that'll sodding be."

"You, Mr. Resnick," Norma said, "you'll be looking into it yourself?"

Resnick shook his head. "A senior officer will lead the team. Very experienced. You couldn't ask for anyone to be more thorough. . . ."

"But you knew Nicky, really knew him. This bloke, whoever he is . . ."

"He's a good man, Norma, I can assure you of that. And I shall be giving him all the help I can."

A smile showed fleetingly on her face and slipped away. "Nicky's body, the funeral . . ."

"We'll release it as soon as we can. I'll do my best to find out today and let you know. Okay?"

For a moment, Norma let her head drop forward, eyes closed. Shane started to say something, but Resnick's quick look told him he had already said enough. Resnick got to his feet and started around the desk to help Norma from her chair, but Shane placed himself in his way.

"Come on, Mum, let's get out of here."

Millington stood alongside Resnick, watching them go. "Aggravated burglary, wasn't it? What he was up for last?"

Resnick nodded. "I believe so."

"Next time, praise God, someone'll send him down for a nice long time."

Resnick turned aside, went back into his office, and closed the door. Untouched, his sandwich waited for him on his desk, but after all the empty words he had offered Norma Snape, his appetite had deserted him. He took hold of the sandwich and dumped it in the bin.

15

Resnick had a call from Bill Aston late that afternoon. For some minutes they exchanged pleasantries, gossiped about the Job. "Changed a lot since our day, Charlie. Used to be, all you did was put on that uniform, walk into a pub, anywhere in the city, people looked at you with respect. Now they'll as like spit in your face as ask the time of day." Resnick waited for him to get to the point, smarting a little under the implication: as far as he was concerned, this was his day still.

"Thought we might have a jar, Charlie? Once I've got my feet under the table. One or two little things, this Snape youth, background, you could fill me in on."

"I had the mother here today," Resnick said. "Doesn't see Nicky as the suicidal type; not without there was a powerful reason."

"Only to be expected, given the circumstances. Upset, bound to be. Distraught. Probably shouldn't give her too much credence in the circumstances."

"She's the lad's mother, Bill, nonetheless. As a family, I think they were pretty close."

"If there's anything nasty in the woodshed, Charlie, I'll poke it out."

"I told her you'd do a good job."

"Thanks, Charlie. Thanks for that. And our little drink some evening?"

"Ring me, Bill. Anytime."

"I will, Charlie. Thanks again."

As Resnick rode the escalator upstairs in the Victoria Centre, he was thinking about what Aston had said. They were near enough of an age for him to recognize what the older man had described, the shifts and slippages of the last twenty years. And what lay ahead? Promotion into the new Serious Crimes Unit, always supposing that memorandum became reality, or a little room of his own at HQ, a rubber stamp with which he could mark out the end of his days?

He stepped off the escalator and walked toward the market, nodding in the direction of the dozen or so elderly Poles who stood in their gray raincoats and shiny shoes, reminiscing about the good old days fifty years or more before. Resnick's father, had he lived, would have been among them, stooped by now and shrunken, an exile from the country of his childhood, the country of his youth.

Resnick entered the market past the corner music stall where the *Tremeloes' Greatest Hits* was permanently on offer at a special marked-down price. Ahead of him, shoppers hesitated before slabs of local cheddar and blue Stilton, mushrooms and courgettes, potatoes—reds, whites, and the first Jersey Royals—Granny Smiths from France and New Zealand, strawberries from Israel and Spain, thick-stalked cabbages in lustrous green grown no more than a mile or two up the road. Deeper into the market, incongruously, bottles of perfume could be bought, machine-made Nottingham lace, electrical gizmos, and Hoover bags by the dozen, kids' shirts and jeans for which Council clothing vouchers were gratefully accepted.

Resnick was heading for the Polish deli, where the cheese-cake stared back at him like a government health warning, threatening to push him that extra ten pounds over on the scales. The approximate ideal weight for a male with your body frame is . . . Resnick didn't want to know. He made his purchases—several of the salamis sliced thin, a loaf of crusty rye bread with caraway, sour cream—and carried them over to the Italian coffee stall. Someone had left a *Post* on the counter and he skimmed through it while waiting for his espresso. Sea-fishing gear had been stolen from a shed, thirty-two prizewinning budgies from a garage; a masked burglar had sat comfortably on a seventy-nine-year-old woman's bed and chatted with her for thirty minutes before making off with her jewelry. He had asked her if she wanted a cup of coffee and when she declined, said he would make her tea instead. It was almost enough to make crime seem cozy, the stuff of Ealing comedies and Dixon of Dock Green. Except that Resnick knew what had happened when Nicky Snape broke into the Netherfield home, and it wasn't a friendly bedside chat, a pot of tea. Doris Netherfield might be stable and responding to treatment, but her condition was still serious; her husband was nursing his injuries at home, and Nicky Snape had been found hanging from a bathroom shower. That was in the paper, too, front page. ALLEGED AGGRESSOR FOUND DEAD. Resnick's own name was in paragraph three.

Setting down the espresso, the assistant tapped the paper. "Good riddance, no?"

"No. Not at all."

The assistant shrugged, uncomprehending, took Resnick's money and turned away to serve an attractive young mother, well-built, bright-eyed, kids fidgeting on stools at either side of her, taking the occasional kick at one another behind her back. "Cut it out, you two. I'll not tell you again." Automatically, Resnick's eyes went to her left hand, third finger. No dad at home, presumably, whom she could offer as a threat. A good thing or bad? He wasn't sure.

"Another, Inspector?"

Resnick pushed the empty cup away. "No thanks, not today."

He was almost out of the market when he saw her, in the center row near the exit, buying flowers.

Hannah Campbell had left her VW in the underground car park and taken the lift to Tesco's, where she had compromised her usual healthy purchases with a Sara Lee ready-baked Pecan Nut Danish Pastry, an impulse for which she had felt more than a twinge of guilt at the checkout. The two bags of groceries she had locked into the boot of her car, before going up to the market for vegetables, salad stuff, and cheese. It was the sign announcing wreaths and floral tributes that stopped her in her tracks.

Of course, what had happened to Nicky—rumors, innuendo, the story imperfectly patched together piece by piece—had been all over the school the entire day. Shock and genuine sympathy in the staff room had been shot through with a malicious righteousness that had made Hannah heave. Smug elegies of the I-told-you-so variety. At least one overheard remark about Nicky's positive contribution to classroom overcrowding.

Floral tributes and wreaths: Hannah asked the aproned woman in charge of the stall about the price of a bouquet. Lilies, those nice carnations, daffs, they're lovely this time of the year. Resnick stood at the end of the aisle, watching her, hair falling across her face as she bent forward toward the flowers; if he went to speak to her, what would he say? Far easier to walk away.

He was downstairs, hesitating outside HMV and considering a quick foray through their meager jazz section, when Hannah spotted him.

"Inspector Resnick?"

Seeing her reflection in the shop window, he smiled.

"It sounds silly," Hannah said when he was facing her, "calling you inspector like that. Like something out of a play. J. B. Priestley. You know, *The Inspector Calls.*"

Vaguely, Resnick thought that he might. "Charlie, then," he said.

"That's your name? Charlie?"

He nodded—"Yes"—and shifted the bag he was carrying from hand to hand.

"Somehow I never think of policemen doing their own shopping."

"Someone has to."

"I suppose so." She smiled. "I know."

He looked at the flowers she was carrying; didn't know what more to say. "Well . . ." A lurch to the left, not really a step away.

"I nearly phoned you," Hannah said, "earlier today."

"How come?"

"What happened to Nicky. I just . . ." She pushed a hand up through her hair and stepped back, almost into a pushchair that was being steered past. "I don't know, I wanted to talk about it, I suppose."

"To say what exactly?"

She smiled again, just the eyes this time. "That's it, I don't really know. That's why in the end I didn't phone."

"There probably isn't a great deal I could tell you. . . ."

"No, of course not. I understand."

"But if . . ."

"Yes?"

For the first time he smiled, his whole face relaxing into it, opening wide.

"You haven't got a few minutes now?" Hannah asked.

Resnick shrugged, glanced toward his watch without registering a thing. "Why not?"

She led him to the food court, where they bought cappuccinos in waxed paper cups and carried them toward the raised section of seating at the center. He found it strange to be in the company of this woman he scarcely knew, a good-looking woman, casually but nicely dressed, a large bouquet of flowers in her hand. For no discernible reason, a phrase from "Roseland Shuffle" sprang into Resnick's head, Lester Young soloing against Basie's sprightly piano.

"Is this okay?" Hannah asked, looking round.

"Fine."

She set the flowers down carefully on the seat alongside. "I was going to take them to Nicky's mother," she said. "Now I'm not so sure."

"I didn't realize you knew him that well."

"I didn't. Not really. To be honest, I don't think anyone at the school did, not in the last couple of years anyway. He was scarcely there." She sipped at her coffee and cradled it in her hands. "It's awful to say it, but I'd go into my English class, the one Nicky was supposed to be in, and if I saw he wasn't at his desk, I'd be relieved. It's not that he was disruptive exactly. Not all the time anyway. Mostly, he'd just sit there and let it wash over him. Never say a word. But occasionally he'd latch on to something, some idea of his own, at a complete tangent from what the rest of the class was doing, and keep on and on about it, question after question, till it was all I could do to get the lesson back on track."

Hannah stopped and drank a little coffee, looked across into Resnick's patient face, the skin that wrinkled past the corners of his eyes. "Perhaps I shouldn't have let that matter. The plan for my precious lesson, I mean. Aim, method, conclusion. Perhaps there were more important things."

"My guess, by the time he got to you, there'd not have been a great deal you could do."

Hannah gave a wry smile. "Give me a child until he's seven—isn't that what the Jesuits say? Or is it nine? Either way, they're probably right, don't you think? Or in your book, are criminals born and not made? Nature or nurture, Charlie, which are you?" Even as she said it, she was surprised at the ease with which she used his name.

He had noticed a green fleck in her right eye, close to the iris, and was trying not to stare. "Some people," he said, "they'll engage in criminal behavior no matter what. Maybe it's psychological, something in their genes, deep in their childhood, who's to say? But average, run-of-the-mill crime, you just have to look at the figures. Unemployment, housing . . ." Resnick gestured with the palm of one hand. "Worse those problems are, higher the rate of crime."

"Tell that to the government," Hannah said sharply.

Resnick tasted his coffee; despite the paper cup, it was better than he'd thought. "This last election," he said, "local. How many? Sixteen Conservatives kicked out. For Labour almost a clean sweep. Fifty seats on the council now to one Tory, couple of the other lot. I'll be interested to see, by the year's end, how much difference it's made."

"You don't think that's a little too cynical."

"How about realistic?"

"And kids like Nicky, you don't think there's anything that can be done? Not with things as they stand?"

He sighed. "If it can, I'm buggered if I know what it is."

"Locking them up, though? Prison. Short, sharp shocks. Boot camps—isn't that what they're called? Do you really think that's the answer?"

"I doubt it puts them on the straight and narrow; figures disprove that."

"But still you carry on, shutting them away."

Resnick shifted a little awkwardly on his seat. "No. The courts lock them up. Or they don't, whatever. What we do, what I do, if I can, is arrest those who've broken the law. Not my laws, not my punishment either."

"But you must agree with them, the courts, what they do, or you wouldn't carry on doing it."

Resnick pushed back his chair, crossed his legs. "Are we having a row?"

Hannah smiled. "No, it's a discussion."

"That's all right, then."

"But is this your way," she asked, "of avoiding the question?"

Resnick grinned and shook his head. "Youths Nicky's age and younger, persistent offenders, they might get arrested— what?—thirty or forty times in a year. More in some cases. They're too young to be put in prison. Bail, supervision orders, none of that does a scrap of good."

"You think they should be shut away."

"I think society needs protecting, yes. . . ."

"And Nicky?"

"Look." Resnick was conscious of his voice being louder than it should, louder than the space allowed. "I saw that old woman after she'd been beaten about the head, the old man. I'm not saying what happened to Nicky, whatever the reasons, is right, of course I'm not. But he was accused of a serious crime, he had to be kept in custody. Surely you don't think he should have been let back on the streets?"

"If it were a choice between that and him ending up dead, yes, I do. Don't you?"

Resnick glanced around at people at other tables, just about pretending not to listen to their conversation. The coffee was beginning to grow cold.

"I'm sorry," Hannah said. "I'm not trying to make you feel guilty."

"You're not." Resnick shook his head. "I'm sad about

what happened. Sad for Nicky's mother. Nicky himself. But what I don't feel is guilt."

"I do," Hannah said quietly. "I do."

"I don't suppose I can give you a lift anywhere?" she asked. They were standing in front of the telephones, near the glass doors that opened out onto the Mansfield Road.

"Thanks, no. I'm fine."

"Okay, bye then." She started to walk away.

"The flowers," Resnick said. "Shall you be taking them or not?"

"Yes, I think so."

"Good. I think Norma'll be pleased." He stood his ground as she walked off in the direction of the lift, plastic bag of shopping swinging lightly from his fist.

When Hannah turned around moments later, before the lift doors closed in front of her, he had gone.

16

A social worker from the Youth Justice Team had called twice and on each occasion the door had been slammed in her face. A reporter from the local BBC radio station had her DAT Walkman hurled back into the street and the crew from Central TV had buckets of water emptied down on them and a spade taken to one side of their van. Shane threw a punch at a stringer for several national tabloids when he came across the man quizzing neighbors in the local pub. "We'd not said a thing to him, had we, duck?" Hard-eyed, Shane had stared them in the face, smashed an empty bottle against the bar, and slammed out: all that rage and nowhere, so far, to bleed it out.

Norma's friend Rosa arrived midafternoon with a bottle of white port and a dozen roses, convinced Norma to go into the bathroom and wash her face, put on some makeup, and change her clothes. With the afternoon racing from Market

Rasen as whispered commentary, the two of them sat on the settee while Rosa plied her friend with glass on glass of port, seizing Norma's wrists in her sudden, flailing fits of anger, holding her tight whenever she gave way to tears, Norma's body shaking inside Rosa's stubborn arms. "The stupid, stupid geck! Why ever did he want to go and do a thing like that?"

Sheena hovered at the edges of the room, watching the two women, riven by the force of her mother's tears, which she could not hope to replicate. She went into the kitchen and made tea she never drank, smeared slices of bread with jam she never ate. In her room, she turned her radio up high to drown the sounds of mourning: Lisa l'Anson in the afternoon. Blur. Oasis. Nirvana. Pulp. Take That.

As the racing gave way to *Terrytoons* and *All-American Girl*, Norma slept in Rosa's arms, twitching suddenly with the vividness of her dreams. "Michael. Oh, Michael," she moaned.

"Shh, now." Rosa gently stroked her head. And then, as Norma opened her eyes, "Who's Michael? You kept saying Michael."

"The baby I lost."

Rosa squeezed her hand. "That was Nicky, sweetheart. You're confused, that's all."

But Norma knew what she had meant. "No, it was Michael. My little Michael." And felt again the final thrust and tear, saw him small and bloodied in the mid-wife's hands.

When Hannah arrived outside the Snape house, there were twenty bunches of flowers lining the pavement, others leaning beside the front door. She hesitated, thinking it through, uncertain what she might actually say; she was bending to place her bouquet with the others, turn away, when Sheena

113

came out into the street. Hannah knew her, had taught her in her last year at school, the same school where she had taught Nicky.

"Hello, Sheena, I'm Miss Campbell. I don't know if you remember me."

She had been a feckless girl, easily led. Left to her own devices, she would fidget with her Biro, pull at her lank hair, decorate the name of whichever boyfriend she aspired to along the edges of her desk, across the front of her notebook, the back of her arm.

"Sheena, I'm sorry about your brother. I really am." From her reaction, Hannah couldn't tell if the girl remembered her or not, though she supposed she did. "I brought these flowers for your mum," Hannah said.

Without speaking, Sheena pushed open the front door and waited for Hannah to step inside.

"Mrs. Snape?"

Hannah found them in the kitchen, Norma and Rosa, hunched over the small table, cigarettes and tea.

"Sheena let me in. I'm . . . I was Nicky's teacher, one of Nicky's teachers." Neither woman looking at her, she stumbled on. "I wanted to say I was sorry. And to bring you these." For a few moments longer she held on to the flowers, before laying them down on the table.

"These from the school, then?" Rosa asked.

"Yes. I mean, no, not exactly. I brought them myself."

"So there's nothing from the school?"

"I'm sorry."

"Bastards, not a sodding word."

"Look," Hannah said, "I think I'd better go. I didn't mean to intrude."

"Yes," Rosa said, "I think you better had."

She was at the door when she heard Norma's voice. "You his special teacher, then? Class teacher, whatever it is?"

"No." Hannah turned back into the kitchen. Norma's eyes

114

were raw and finding it difficult to focus. "Not really. I was his English teacher, that's all." Norma blinked and blinked again. "He was a nice lad, cheerful. I liked him."

The room expanded to accept the lie, lifted it to the ceiling wreathed in smoke.

"I will go now," Hannah said.

As she shut the front door behind her, Hannah leaned back against it and closed her eyes. The backs of her legs were shaking, her arms burned cold. *All my pretty ones?* All she could think of were Macduff's words when Malcolm told him that his children had been killed. And what, Hannah, she asked herself, what bloody good is that?

The rain that would saturate the flowers outside Norma's house, mashing the decorated florists' paper against the twisted stems, caught Resnick half a mile from home, no raincoat, plummeting down from a darkening spring sky. Like stair rods, his mother-in-law might have said, back when he had a mother-in-law. By the time he had slipped his key into the front-door lock, his hair was plastered flat against his head, water dripping from his nose and squirreling past his collar, down his back. As the door clicked open and swung back, Dizzy darted from the shelter of a neighbor's shrub, one touch upon the wall, then in.

Careful, Resnick emptied the contents of his bag, paper-wrapped packages nestling in puddles of water. He took off his coat and hung it over a chair, rubbed a towel briskly through his hair. The meeting with Hannah Campbell kept replaying, sporadically, in his mind.

"Are we having a row?"

"No, it's a discussion."

Automatically, he forked food into the cats' bowls. Is that what it had truly been, a discussion? Academic? Impersonal? Certainly that wasn't the way it had felt. But what did he know? Teachers, perhaps that was what they liked to do, take words and push them back and forth like dominoes, a game to exercise the mind.

He was building a sandwich, waiting for the kettle to boil. Four slices of fresh garlic salami overlapping across rye bread, a pickled cucumber sliced narrowly along its length, goat's cheese that he crumpled between his fingers, a single, thinly cut shallot; finally, the second slice of bread he drizzled with extra-virgin olive oil before setting it on top and pressing the sandwich closed, encouraging some of the oil to seep down before he sliced the whole thing in two.

Tinker, tailor, mother-in-law, wife. Slowly, he poured boiling water onto coffee grounds. He had not heard from his ex-wife, Elaine, since two Christmases ago, not seen her in twice as long. He knew that she had remarried, redivorced, seen the inside of more than one psychiatric ward. When he last saw her, it was like meeting a stranger, someone who had lived for a long time in another country and spoke a language he didn't understand.

"Are we having a row?"

"No, it's a discussion."

Rather than wait until the lift doors closed across her face, he had walked away.

When the phone rang, it made him jump.

"Charles, I am surprised to find you in." Marian Witczak's voice, tinged with the accent of a homeland in which she had not been born, which she had not visited until her teens. "I was wondering, Charles, about the dance. This weekend, you remember? I wonder if you have made up your mind?"

"Marian, I'm not sure."

He could feel her disappointment as eloquently as words.

"It's difficult, Marian, you know that. To promise. I never know what's going to crop up."

"All work and no play, Charles, you know what they say?"

116

"Look, I'll try, that's all I can do."

"You remember, Charles, that time we persuaded the accordion player to forsake his polkas for 'Blue Suede Shoes'? Well, it is the same band again."

"Marian, I'm sorry, I have to go. I'll be in touch, all right? I'll let you know."

He ate one half of the sandwich standing near the stove, the other sitting in the front room, listening to Frank Morgan play "Mood Indigo," the wind curling the rain against the tall panes.

Norma sat up suddenly and opened her eyes. Rosa had been home to sort out the youngest of her own kids and then returned. They had eaten Birds Eye lasagna and chips and drunk two cans of Kestrel, got through the Lord knew how many cigarettes. Norma had slept. "Nicky's dad!" she shouted, waking. "Peter. How'm I ever going to get in touch with Nicky's dad?"

Sheena had an address, written on a sheet of torn paper, in pencil that was beginning to smudge and fade.

"How long've you had this? How long?"

"On my birthday," Sheena said, "when I was fourteen. It was tucked inside the card."

Norma rubbed her eyes. Peterborough. "No saying he's still there now, he could be anywhere."

"You'll let him know, my dad?"

"Here." Norma pushed the paper back toward her. "You let him know. You're the one he give his address to."

Hannah sat in the chair near the upstairs window, a sweater round her shoulders to foil the drafts. With the curtains still open, she could see the rain silvering past the streetlights outside, before it was lost against the blackness of the small park facing where she lived. The mug that had held her peppermint tea lay cold in her lap. She was reading a collection of

117

new poems she'd picked up in Mushroom, the soundtrack for *The Piano* playing in the background.

> *As though a man is no more than fear and fire*
> *for a woman to feed and carry like a torch.*
> *As though a woman is no more than light at the*
> *end of a long and hard tunnel. As though my*
> *sweet life needs it. As though ache could be*
> *enough to smooth the edges of a desperate day.*

How different would her life be if she had married, had a child? The same issues, tugging at her beneath the tide of her life. She had her own house, a job—a good job, one most days she valued, and which she thought of as in some small way doing good. Her Visa bill was paid up at the end of each month, her mortgage was manageable, she went abroad three times a year, enjoyed the company of friends. If she saw a new book or CD she fancied, she could buy it without too much thought. Aside from those children she taught, the only person she was feeding and carrying was herself.

Her choice.

Why, then, did she feel as empty as the china mug she cradled in her lap, as pale and cold?

Shane walked up to Pete Turvey in the main bar of Turvey's local and head-butted him in the face. "You, you bastard! You fucking slime!" Blood was running down Turvey's forehead into his eyes, half-blinding him. "You're paying for what you fucking did." Shane brought his fist back level with his shoulder and punched Turvey in the face, breaking his nose. Shane's own shirt was ripe with blood and snot. "Here!" As Turvey sank to the floor, Shane brought his knee up hard and broke his nose a second time. It had been Pete Turvey and his brothers who hurled a firebomb from their car into Nicky Snape's path, though it was never proved. Shane caught hold of Turvey's shirt and hauled him off the ground.

"For pity's sake," called someone, "leave the poor bastard be. You'll kill him, sure is that what you want?"

Shane let Turvey go and the back of his victim's head collided with the bar; then he walked ten feet away, swiveled back, and kicked out at Turvey's chest, burying the toe of his boot in Turvey's gut.

"For Christ's sake," came the same voice, "call the law, why don't you?"

Shane slapped two pound coins on the table and ordered a pint of best.

He had it almost finished when the door spun open and Turvey's two brothers arrived. They had others with them: Gorman, who toured around with the fairs, taking on all-comers in the boxing tent; Frankie and Edgar Droy; and Carl Howard, who had served an extra eighteen months in Lincoln for assaulting one of the screws with a bucket, causing him to need twenty-one stitches in his head.

This was what Shane wanted, to be lost in this. They started on him there, inside the bar, beside Pete Turvey moaning over his twice-broken nose and broken ribs. They hauled him off into the urinal, Shane hardly even bothering to fight back now, almost unable to raise his hands. Finally, they dragged him out into the street and left his body slewed across the road, only the sound of police sirens saving Shane from more of a beating.

While a young uniformed officer talked to the landlord, who had seen nothing—maybe a little scuffle, nothing to write down in his little book—Shane was in an ambulance, heading for Queen's. More than an hour later he would be in the cubicle next to Pete Turvey, waiting for the same doctor to examine both their injuries.

◆◆◆

It was a bad sign, Resnick knew, when he played Monk last thing at night, the pianist's fractured attempts at melody obeying no logic but their own. He was a big man, as Resnick was big; Monk's fingers stabbed down at single notes, crushed chords into the beauty of an abstract painting, twisted scaffolding seen in a certain light.

Almost an hour ago, certain it would not be there, Resnick had checked through the phone book and found Hannah's number, written it, for want of somewhere else, in Biro on the back of his hand. Now he stared at it from moment to moment, sitting near the phone. One of the cats jumped onto his lap and he shooed him off as "Solitude" came to an end. He pointed the remote control and set it off again.

> *As though a woman is no more than light at the end of a long and hard tunnel. As though my sweet life needs it.*

Wetting his thumb, he rubbed the numbers from his skin.

Norma Snape lay in the dark of her room and when she slept she cried and then when she woke she cried some more.

17

Where had Bill Aston read that every pound you put on after age forty takes twice as much effort to get off? And eighteen months sitting behind that desk at Police Headquarters hadn't helped. Fortnightly game of golf aside, for too long the only exercise he had been getting was walking the pair of Jack Russells he and his wife, Margaret, had bought after their youngest son left home. Which was why, on the second of January that year, he had instituted his daily swim. There were two pools close to where they lived, Rushcliffe and Portland, and Aston alternated between them pretty much at will. Some days he would stop off on the way to work and put in ten lengths; other times he would call in at home and pick up the dogs, have his swim, and then walk them before returning for dinner.

"Should have got a real dog, Dad," his eldest had said on a brief visit home. "A Labrador or a retriever, something with some size. Chase those two sorry specimens the length of the garden and they're worn out. Expect you to carry them back."

But Aston was happy enough with his Jack Russells—they would sit in the back of the car if he went for a drive, the pair of them quite content—and as for Margaret . . . well, if Bill had thought these were going to be her new babies, he was wrong, but just as long as they didn't get under her feet . . .

He rustled his paper aside and peered in the direction of the kitchen clock: still time for one more cup of tea. He reached for the pot.

"Bill," Margaret said, coming back into the room, "are you sure you want to wear those shoes?"

Aston swung his leg round and glanced down. "What's wrong with them?"

"I mean with that suit."

Gray suede with dark blue, why not? "Yes, love," he said, "they're fine."

Margaret was dressed to go out herself, an early appointment at the hair salon on Trinity Square and then she was meeting her friend Barbara for coffee in Jessop's.

"No swim this morning?"

Aston shook his head. "Evenings all week, I should think. While this lot goes on, anyway."

Impulsively, she kissed him on the top of his head, behind the ear.

"What was that all about?" Aston asked. Unbidden displays of affection had not been Margaret's style for years, no more than they were his own.

Margaret smiled. "I'm pleased for you, that's all. Putting you in charge of this inquiry. Something important again. Well, it's no more than you deserve."

"Thanks, love," Aston said dryly, finding it difficult to respond. "Right now, though, I'd best be off."

"You will give me a lift in?"

"Yes, of course." He swallowed down most of his tea and tipped the remainder into the sink and started to run the tap.

"Leave that, Bill. Sally's here today, she'll do all of that."

He looked at her, a dumpy woman with spectacles, wearing a green plaid suit and court shoes, and was surprised by the strength of the conflicting emotions that he felt.

A few minutes later, Margaret beside him, Aston was backing the Volvo out from the drive of the thirties suburban house they'd lived in now for nineteen years. Around him, on either side, neighbors' gardens glowed green from the previous night's rain.

"You remember Charlie Resnick?" Aston said. "Seems he knew this Snape, the youth in the inquiry. I've got to meet up with him some night this week for a drink. Could well be back a bit late."

Margaret remembered Resnick well enough, around the same height as her husband but broader—broader still now, most likely. It was years since she'd seen him. But he was a nice enough man, she thought, not foul-mouthed like some of them.

"You ought to invite him round, Bill. Supper. He might appreciate that."

And he might not, Aston thought, but nodded anyway.

"We used to have people round for dinner all the time."

Aston grunted. "We used to do a lot of things."

Margaret rested her hand on his knee and tried not to notice when he flinched.

Khan was waiting for Aston in reception. Five years in the force, at twenty-seven he had benefited from the aftershock of a well-publicized case in which two Asian officers had taken the police authority to court for racially discriminating against them and blocking their advancement. Khan had successfully completed his probation, spent his time in a Panda car and out on the beat; now he was in Central Division CID and confidently expecting to be made up to sergeant. The inquiry into Nicky Snape's death would broaden his experience. His tasks were to take notes, facilitate the timetable, keep on top of the documentation, and stay alert to any nuances that his superior might miss—and to drive the car.

He greeted Aston with a sir, a handshake, and a smile. Five minutes later they were making their way toward the Derby Road, slowed a little by the residue of rush-hour traffic. When they arrived, Derek Jardine greeted both men with brisk enthusiasm and ushered them into his office for coffee and a drab selection of biscuits. There were still twenty minutes before the case conference was due to start.

Phyllis Parmenter, heading up the three-strong team from the Social Services Inspectorate, was already present, balancing cup and saucer on one hand and chatting to the local authority solicitor. Jardine introduced her to Aston and stepped away. Khan snagged the remaining stale bourbon biscuit and examined the photographs on the director's wall.

The conference room had been set out with pads of lined local authority paper, black Bics and sharpened pencils, water glasses, ashtrays, and copies of the agenda. The first item was to establish the methods by which the joint investigation should proceed. If we get that far by coffee time, Khan thought, glancing round the table, I shall be well surprised.

And he was: they would consider the pathologist's report and then begin interviewing the staff, starting with Paul Matthews and Elizabeth Peck, both of whom had been on duty the night Nicky died, and finishing with Jardine himself. The youth who had shared a room with Nicky would be brought in, along with another of the lads Nicky had apparently befriended. If either the police or Social Services teams found a need to re-interview separately, that was their prerogative. It was agreed that it was desirable, if possible, for a joint statement to be issued when the inquiry came to an end.

"One point I think I should like to make clear," Phyllis Parmenter said. "Our aim here is to ascertain all that we can about the circumstances of Nicky Snape's death. It may be, and I have no wish to prejudice the inquiry by saying this, that we discover there are certain procedures which would benefit from overhaul or change. If so, I'm sure we would all agree this can only be beneficial. But what we are not concerned with primarily here is blame; in these sad and unfortunate circumstances, we are not, I think and hope, looking for scapegoats."

Especially, Khan thought, if they're to be found among the local authority staff. He edged a sideways look at Aston, who was nodding in thoughtful agreement.

Resnick had tapped Millington on the shoulder as they passed the small café near the fire station and, with a grin, the sergeant had performed a circuit of the roundabout and parked. Resnick had had a lousy night: broken sleep and nightmarish dreams. Finally, at something short of four, he had barefooted downstairs; thirty minutes later he was sitting with rye toast and coffee, Bud and Pepper vying for the prime place in his lap, while he tried to concentrate on a biography of Lester Young. To complicate matters, he was listening, not to Prez, but to Monk. *Alone in San Francisco.* Between the notes, the sentences, he was wondering about Norma Snape, alone but not alone in Radford; about his ex-wife, Elaine, hoping that she was not alone anywhere. And Hannah: he was thinking about Hannah. The seriousness that turned down the corners of her eyes when she talked; the way that same seriousness would break suddenly into a smile.

"What's it to be?" Millington asked as Resnick slumped into a seat near the window.

His face brightened. "Oh, a bacon sandwich, don't you think, Graham?"

"Is that with the egg or without?"

"Without. But a sausage wouldn't go amiss."

"Tea?"

"Tea." The coffee here still had to catch up with the post-powder age.

They ate in near silence, Resnick enjoying the salt, slightly fishlike taste of the smoked bacon, not inquiring too deeply about the occasional gristly blob that the sausage vouchsafed. Later, as Millington relaxed with a Lambert and Butler, Resnick asked about Madeleine's latest forays into amateur dramatics and adult education and received a lecture about the perils of living with a wife who is simultaneously reading Karen Horney and Kate Millett for her course on "Feminism for Beginners" and rehearsing the part of a frustrated middle-aged wife in an Alan Ayckbourn farce.

"Bit difficult for her, that, Graham. The play, I mean. Well outside her experience, I should reckon."

Millington drew in smoke and examined Resnick keenly; if that was meant as some kind of joke, he couldn't see the humor. Of late, Millington had taken to eyeing the kitchen knives with suspicion.

Resnick, however, solid food inside him, was beginning to feel better. The day might be salvaged after all. "All right, Graham," he said, scraping back his chair. "Let's not waste any more time."

Once inside Queen's, they checked on Doris Netherfield, who was still making cautious progress and treated them to a pale smile. Her husband was making slow but significant progress at home. Shane Snape was propped irritably between hospital pillows, fiddling with the headset of his radio. One side of his face showed some deep bruising and a neat line of stitches butterflied its way from behind one ear onto his neck, but apart from those injuries he had got off surprisingly lightly. Nothing broken. Another day and he would be discharged.

"Morning, Shane," Millington said breezily. "Run into a spot of bother?"

He and Resnick took seats at either side of the bed.

"I've got nothing to say," said Shane.

"The people who did this," Resnick said, "you're not in a position to identify who they were?"

Shane shook his head.

"And the name Turvey," Millington offered, "that doesn't ring any bells?"

Shane shook his head again.

"Coincidence, then, Peter Turvey sustaining all those injuries the same time as yourself? Same place?"

"Must've been."

"There's no chance, then," Resnick said, "that you'll be making a complaint, pressing charges, anything like that?"

"None."

"Fine." Resnick started out of his seat. "All right, Graham, we might as well go."

Shane looked surprised that they were letting him off so lightly, had just begun to relax back against the pillows when Resnick swiveled on his heels faster than a man of his size might be expected to, something like a dancer. From nowhere he was leaning over the bed, his right hand gripping Shane's shoulder where it was bruised and swollen, finger ends not so far from where the line of stitches finished.

"Understand me, I don't give a toss how you spend your evenings, what flotsam you hang around with, but I do care about your mother. She's had a hard enough time as it is, bringing up the three of you, and now after what's happened to Nicky, you're the last thing she should have to worry about." Resnick increased the pressure with his hand, enough to force tears to the edges of Shane's eyes no matter how much he fought to deny them. "So stay out of trouble, right? Or I'll come down on you so fast you'll wish you'd paid attention." Resnick relinquished his grip and stood tall. "Okay, Shane. Think you can learn something here?"

Shane stared back at him, humiliated, angry, a single tear making a slow track down his face.

Whistling "Winchester Cathedral" while they waited for the lift, Millington was still surprised by the force of Resnick's anger.

Sheena had not clocked in at the factory since Nicky had died. The first day, the Monday, she had phoned in and explained; the second day she had said her mother still needed looking after. Her supervisor had been understanding, told her to take whatever sick leave she was entitled to and suggested that she make an appointment to see her GP on her own account, have him prescribe a tranquilizer, Valium, that new stuff even—what was it?—Prozac, that's the one.

This morning Sheena had said nothing to her mum, had left home with her uniform ironed and folded in a plastic bag from Tesco, wandered without direction until she ended up in the Old Market Square, watching the gang of youths that sprawled extravagantly on the worn grass near the public lavatories, drinking Strongbow cider and shouting at any passerby who wore a suit. They were the usual sprinkling of latter-day punks and Goths, lads with pink Mohicans or hair spiked out around their heads in blue-tipped stars, chains that hung from the pockets and lapels of torn leather jackets, ripped jeans, smaller chains dangling from their ears and the corners of their mouths. Tattoos. Girls younger than Sheena in tight T-shirts and skinny, black-legged jeans, rings through their ears and noses, mouths darkened into little black beaks. Sheena sat a safe distance away on the low stone wall, wrists trapped between her knees. No way she was about to go near them. The clock above the Council House sounded the quarter hour.

"Here."

She turned with a start, almost losing her balance. Janie Cornwall was close behind her, usual superior expression on her face, an open packet of Embassy in her hand.

"Go on, have one."

Sheena blinked up at Janie, her hard young face framed by frizzed-out hair. At the other side of the street, outside Debenham's, Janie's friends stood watching. Lesley Dawson, Irena, Tracey Daniels, Dee-Dee, Diane. Janie shook the packet again and with a breathed thank-you Sheena took one and angled back her head as Janie, leaning forward, lit it for her.

Sheena drew in smoke and held it down inside.

After a quick glance back toward her pals, Janie lit a cigarette for herself and sat down. "Your brother, we're cut up, like, about what happened."

"Thanks."

"You must be feeling like shit."

"Yeah. Yes, I am."

Janie had been in Sheena's year right through school, they all had, Lesley, Dee-Dee, and the rest. Girls whose breasts were obvious sooner, whose periods had started earlier, who were forever bringing scratty little notes to excuse them from games. They would smoke openly on the way to school and light up again the minute they set foot on the Boulevard. They were the ones who boasted they had done it at thirteen, gone all the way, and Sheena had believed them, jealous, frightened, in awe. When, after school, Janie and the rest had huddled among the cars parked on the Forest, laughing with boys who were as old as Shane and older, Sheena had loitered close enough for them to call her over but they never had. Now this. Nicky's death had given her notoriety at second hand, made her acceptable where she had not been before.

One of the girls called out to Janie, who turned her head and gestured for them to go on ahead. "We're going up Diane's," she said to Sheena. "Why'n't you come?"

At the far side of the square, Janie took Sheena's Tesco bag from her and dropped it, uniform and all, into a green council bin.

Diane and Dee-Dee were black. Except for those times when they had briefly fallen out, they told everyone they were sisters, even went out dressed in the same clothes, though it wasn't true. Their families never spoke to one another and would cross the street to avoid contact. Dee-Dee's father was a minister in the Pentecostal church and Diane's was doing fifteen years in Lincoln for shooting another drug dealer in the face at close range. When Dee-Dee fell pregnant just eighteen days short of her fifteenth birthday, her father prayed for her while her mother took her to the clinic to arrange for an abortion. As soon as Diane heard, she went out and got herself knocked up by a friend of her brother's and miscarried after eight weeks. The next time she was more fortunate. The baby was called Melvin and Diane's elder sister had looked after him until Diane finished school, at which point Diane and the baby's father were given temporary accommodation in a high-rise the council was planning to demolish. The father had left but the flats were still standing.

"Fucking lift!" Diane screamed, kicking at the graffitied doors. "Never fucking working!"

Diane's neighbor had been looking after Melvin, and Diane collected him to show him off to Sheena.

"Gorgeous, in't he? In't he fuckin' gorgeous?"

Tightly curled black hair, coffee skin, wide brown eyes— Sheena had to admit that he was.

The girls all bundled into Diane's living room to play with

Melvin and watch TV, pass round the bottle of vodka that Irena had lifted from the corner shop. Seated on the floor by the settee, Lesley carefully rolled a couple of spliffs. An hour or so later, when Janie tipped some pills into Sheena's hand, she didn't think twice, popped them into her mouth and swallowed what was almost the last of the vodka to wash them down.

Peter was waiting when Norma got home from visiting Shane at the hospital, sitting on the uneven paving stones where days before Nicky's flowers had huddled haphazardly against one another. He was leaning back against the wall when Norma saw him, a hand-rolled cigarette between his fingers, his feet bare, shoes neatly placed alongside him, socks rolled into a ball. Something lurched through Norma like a fist and she thought she was going to be sick.

Peter spotted her and stared, then pushed himself slowly to his feet. My God, Norma thought, how he's changed. Most of the hair had gone from his head and what remained was flat against his scalp and dark. His face had never been full, but now the skin seemed to be stretched too tight across his forehead and both cheeks had sunken in. Inside a striped shirt, his chest appeared to have collapsed inward, though a little potbelly strained awkwardly against the top of his trousers. How long was it since she had seen him? Twelve years? More? She had never imagined he could look so old. He could not have been more than forty-five.

Norma could no more stop the tears than she could stop time.

Peter tossed the nub end of the roll-up toward the curb and took her in his arms.

"Come away, you great geck! Let's get inside else we'll have neighbors goin' round with a hat."

In the kitchen she made him tea and toast while he told her how he had hitched three lifts from Peterborough to get there, the last a laundry van on its way in from the RAF base outside Grantham. He asked Norma how she'd been keeping, told her how good she looked in that blue and orange dress. Had she lost a bit of weight? Well, it suited her, there was no denying that. He asked her about Sheena and Norma told him she was at work; asked about Shane and looked concerned when she told him about the beating he had received. It was not till Norma had mashed a second pot that he asked about Nicky.

Without crying this time, clear eyed, Norma told him what she knew.

Peter was silent for a long time and then asked if the inquest had been opened and adjourned.

Norma nodded and Peter, one-handed, rolled another cigarette. "If you like," he said, not looking at her, looking at the pile of crockery heaped alongside the sink, "I could stay for a while. A few days at least. I'd not be in the way."

Norma didn't reply. She didn't know what Shane, when he got out of the hospital, might think. Nor Sheena either, for that matter—he was her father, she should be pleased, but after all this time who could tell?

"Just till the funeral, eh? That was what I thought."

"All right," Norma said. "All right."

He reached a hand to touch her but she pulled away.

At six-thirty that evening, Bill Aston plunged into the Portland pool and swam the first of twenty slow, deliberate lengths. After showering and drying himself down, he drove the short distance to the Victoria Embankment and walked the Jack Russells along the north bank of the Trent. All things considered, it had not been too bad a day.

Khan's girlfriend was seven years his senior. Light-skinned, lithe-limbed, and blond, Jill was a divorced woman with three kids who were spending the night at her sister's. She had trained as a dancer, worked as a model; now she was a part-time receptionist at Central Television and went to a dance class four afternoons a week. Khan liked to imagine he could still smell the sweat on her body.

"What was he like, then?" Jill asked. "This bloke Aston you're working with?"

"After he'd got over the color of my skin, d'you mean?"

She reached out to stroke his chest. "What's wrong with your skin? It's beautiful."

"Yes, well"—Khan grinned—"you'd not expect Bill Aston to feel the same way about it as you now, would you?"

"Oh, I don't know," Jill laughed.

"Not him. I doubt he's got the imagination."

Jill raised her legs and slid her bottom a little further down the bed. "What's he doing in charge of the inquiry into this kid's death, then?"

But by then Khan was in no position to answer.

18

"Old Fashioned Love." The opening growl from Vic Dickenson's trombone sounds like the fanfare from a fairground barker, but once piano and bass have settled into their gentle stride, he nudges the melody along respectfully enough, just the odd hint of jauntiness to keep sentimentality at bay; then, rolling out from the lower register with that tart huskiness that marks his playing, Edmund Hall takes the tune through a second chorus before the clipped notes of Ruby Braff's trumpet start to lengthen and unwind. Which is as far as Resnick gets, because now the phone is ringing and he reaches awkwardly toward it, fiddling the remote onto pause and then dropping it into his lap, where an aggrieved cat wakes with a start and jumps to the floor, one paw tipping the saucer that holds a half-finished cup of coffee growing cold.

"Hello?"

"Charlie. Thought you weren't there."

Friday night, Resnick thought, where else would I be?

"Wondered how you were placed for this drink we mentioned?"

Resnick angled his wrist around to look at his watch: twenty-five to nine. "You'll be wanting me to trek out there, I suppose?" He wondered why it had always been difficult to take them seriously, the suburbs south of the Trent.

"No need, I'm in the city. Just tidying up a bit of paper-work." Aston paused. "The Partridge, that's your watering hole, isn't it?"

"As good as any."

"Nine o'clock, then?"

"Best make it quarter past."

"All right, Charlie. See you there."

Resnick retrieved his cup and rose to his feet, releasing the pause into the beginning of Sir Charles Thompson's piano solo. Bud's head nudged repeatedly against the backs of his legs as he stood there listening, the cat urging him to sit down so that he could jump onto his lap. Only after the second trumpet solo and Dickenson's closing trombone coda, lazy but exact, did Resnick open the tray and drop the CD back in its case, switch off the stereo, carry cup and saucer into the kitchen to rinse, open the fridge on a well-honed impulse and lift out a slice of ham, wrap it around the last half-inch of Emmenthal cheese, something to nibble while he put on his coat and hesitated in the doorway, patting his pockets for his wallet, money, keys.

For whatever reason, the Partridge failed to attract the Friday-night gangs of youths who marauded through the city center, clad, whatever the weather, in shirtsleeves or the shortest of skirts, growing noisier and noisier as they moved from pub to pub, more and more obscene. Even so, it was crowded enough for Resnick and Bill Aston to take refuge in the deep V of the public bar, opposite the door to the gents.

135

"Sure that's all you want, Charlie? Not fancy a chaser?"

Resnick glanced at the bottle of Czech Budweiser and shook his head.

"Drop of scotch, no?"

"Thanks, Bill, I'm fine."

Aston himself was sitting with a half pint of mild, which Resnick knew from experience he would nurse through the coming half hour, or however long the conversation took.

Not wanting to shout it out for all and sundry, needing to be heard above the rise and fall of Friday-night conversations, Resnick hunched his shoulders forward and leaned in. Aston listened attentively, a nod here and there, while Resnick filled him in on the Snape family background. Resnick's relationship with the Snapes had begun when, as detective sergeant, he had questioned Shane about the provenance of two dozen videocassettes that had been in the youth's sports bag when a uniformed officer stopped him at past two in the morning, crossing Radford Boulevard. Nicky had first come to Resnick's official attention at the age of eleven, when he was caught climbing through the skylight of a neighbor's house. At Norma Snape's request, Resnick had given the boy a royal rollocking; enough to put the fear of God into him, that was how Norma had described it, though it could only be said to have worked in that, as far as anyone knew, Nicky had never since that day set foot inside a church. Other people's houses, that had been a different matter.

"Poor little bastard," Aston said feelingly. "Growing up like that, never stood a chance."

Resnick leaned back and lifted his glass. "She did her best."

Aston shook his head. "Never going to be good enough, though, is it, Charlie?" And Resnick drank his beer steadily, while Aston delivered his sermon on the breakdown of the social fabric and the lost virtues of the two-parent family.

When it was over, he excused himself and went first to the gents and then to the bar.

"The inquiry, Bill," Resnick said, emptying the second bottle into his glass. "How's it all going?"

"Oh, shouldn't take long to wrap it up, I'd say. Seems all pretty much aboveboard."

Resnick regarded him skeptically. "No funny business, you think? Nothing untoward?"

"No, Charlie, not so far as I can see. Oh, supervision might've been a mite lax the night he died. But if it's reasons you're looking for—ill treatment, bullying . . ." Aston gave a quick shake of the head. "Doesn't seem to have been the case."

"No clear reason, then? For him to do what he did."

"Not mind readers, Charlie. Not as if he left a note, nothing like that. The other lads, those that knew him, the youth in his room, all swear he never said a word about what he meant to do. Moaned on a bit, like; complained. But then that's just par for the course." Aston finally supped the last of his mild, froth sliding back down the glass. "Couldn't face up to being put away. If you ask me, that's what it was. He just couldn't face the thought of going to prison, poor little sod. Terrified. Just a kid, you see. Missed his mam."

Resnick waited until a sudden splurge of laughter from the table alongside had died down. "Social Services see it the same way?"

Aston nodded. "Pretty much. Right down the line."

I bet they do, Resnick thought, stains enough on their copybook already. He was on his feet, half his beer still untouched. "At least there's nothing to prevent the body from being released. His mother'll be pleased." He held out his hand. "Take care, Bill. And give Margaret my best."

Out on the street, Resnick crossed in the direction of what had once been Bobby Brown's Café and was now another boarded-up testament to free enterprise and the price you eventually had to pay. He thought about picking up a cab from outside the Victoria Stakis, but decided he would walk instead. If Aston had found nothing suspicious, then maybe there was nothing to find. Why, then, did Resnick find that so difficult to believe?

By the time he had reached the Sikh temple, he was starting to feel vaguely peckish and began inventorying the contents of his refrigerator; he thought there might be enough left for a decent sandwich before turning in. He could sit up a while longer and listen to those Vic Dickenson sides again: "Runnin' Wild," "Keeping Out of Mischief Now."

"Here, take another one of these prawns while they're still going."

"No, it's okay. . . ."

"Go on. I've had more than my share already."

"All right, then. Thanks."

Lynn made two attempts at lifting the king prawn from its chili sauce, before setting down her chopsticks and resorting to a fork.

"Good, aren't they?"

"Great." Actually, they were too spicy for Lynn's taste, but she wasn't about to say. It had been Sharon's idea, the pair of them having a night out together, and the choice of the restaurant had been Sharon's, too. They had met earlier and had a couple of glasses of white wine in one of the wine bars near Lynn's flat in the Lace Market, moving on when the place had begun to get really crowded and the offers of drinks from predatory males were more than they could shrug off or gracefully turn down.

In the end, Sharon had rounded on one of the more persistent—a good few years younger than herself and certainly no taller—caught hold of him by the lapels of his mid-blue, beautifully tailored Kenzo suit, and told him that if he wanted to get sorted in front of his mates by a woman who taught a class in self-defense and close combat, he should just carry on as he was. She could tell from his wilting body language which option he was going to choose. Sharon straightened him out, brushed him down, and gave him a quick peck on the cheek; the man blushed deep red and retreated into the huddle of his friends.

"Don't you hate all that?" Lynn asked, once Sharon had perched back on her stool.

"Want to know the truth?" Sharon grinned. "Actually, I enjoy it."

Now they were at a window table in Ocean City, looking out at four lanes of traffic heading north up Derby Road. They were still attracting more than their fair share of sidelong looks—two youngish women eating alone, one black, one white—and Sharon in a long, loose denim skirt, a denim shirt over a soft gray fitted top, was the focus of most of them. If in some respects that left Lynn relieved, in others it didn't help at all. Just about the last thing you needed, self-image at the low ebb, was playing second fiddle to someone who was not only sure of herself, but looked great into the bargain. And was nice with it.

Lynn could imagine their laughing conversation back in the wine bar, those blokes who'd fancied themselves in with a chance. "Mine's okay, pal, but I wouldn't go near yours on a dark night with a stick."

"Here," Sharon said, tipping the bottle of Australian Chardonnay over Lynn's glass. "You might as well finish this off, too."

Lynn laughed. "I shall be pissed."

"Not working tomorrow, are you?"

"No, thank God. Nor Sunday, neither. Not unless anything major crops up."

Sharon raised her glass. "Lucky you. We're top-handed tomorrow night. Boss wants a bit of a crackdown. Scare the balls off the curb crawlers, promise to print their names in the paper, send letters home to their wives. Haul in the girls and keep them overnight, pack them off bright and early with a two-hundred-quid fine. All that does, send them back on the streets to earn some more." With a flourish, she finished her wine. "Sometimes I think the magistrates do more to keep the trade going than the pimps."

Lynn nodded and popped the last piece of oyster mushroom into her mouth.

"Right," Sharon said, looking round for a waiter. "A couple of banana fritters, coffee, and they can phone a cab for us. Drop you off on the way to mine." She winked. "All tucked up before midnight, eh, safe and sound."

Curtains drawn, only a table lamp at the far side of the room burned its subdued light. Through the speakers, the sound of Steve Jordan's guitar chording evenly above the rhythmic swish of Jo Jones's brushes, while in the easy chair, the smallest of the cats nestling his head beneath his chin, Resnick slept, his breathing a soft counterpoint to the sounds of Sir Charles Thompson, gentling his piano through the tune of "Russian Lullaby."

19

While Resnick had slept, a house across the city had been torched and now stood gutted, the third instance of serious arson on the Bestwood Estate that month. The incident had taken place at two in the morning, four kids under the age of fourteen asleep upstairs, the youngest of them only escaping serious burns when his mother dropped him from the bedroom window into the arms of neighbors below. Certain in their own minds who had caused the fire, other members of the family had been intercepted on their way across the estate by hastily summoned police. A sawn-off shotgun and a pistol were found beneath the rear seat of the car they were driving.

As an excited local radio reporter informed Resnick that morning, an emergency meeting had been called at which the city housing chief and other officials would discuss with police additional ways of constraining an estate that was seemingly in the grip of mob rule. Resnick sighed as he buttered toast. He knew that extra officers had already been

141

drafted in and that during the past few weeks alone there had been around fifty arrests; he also knew that most of those arrested would by now have been released on bail.

Interviewed by the reporter, the city council leader said they were preparing to take legal action against the eight families who were at the heart of the trouble. "We have no qualms about evicting," he said. "The trouble is that we need witnesses—and witnesses can be intimidated."

Resnick remembered his team going round Radford, door to door, trying to uncover information about the incident in which Nicky Snape had been petrol-bombed. After days of intensive questioning, it had proved impossible to persuade anyone who knew anything to make a statement. If Nicky could be put into the hospital, so could they.

The result was a stubborn silence: distrust of the police, fear of reprisals.

Resnick opted for raspberry jam. While the other cats weren't looking, he forked the last of the Whiskas into Bud's bowl before throwing the can away. There was a note from Marian Witczak with the mail, reminding him in her ornate, slightly Gothic hand, of the Polish Club dance that evening. Before his second cup of coffee, Resnick phoned the station and got a jubilant-sounding Kevin Naylor, the third of whose nights on observation with Reg Cossall had resulted in five arrests for drug offenses and three additional charges of passing counterfeit money and attempting to defraud the post office. Resnick could imagine Cossall's obscene expressions of delight.

"Well done," he said to Naylor. "Good work. Now get off home and get some sleep. I'll not want you propping your eyes open when you're back on duty."

Resnick had only that second put the phone down when it rang again. Instantly he recognized Millington's somewhat nasal, bemused tone. In the background he could hear somebody practicing scales; after her triumph in the title role of

The Merry Widow, Madeleine was preparing herself for the amateur operatic season once again.

"Morning, Graham. What can I do for you?"

"I was just wondering," Millington said. "You've not heard anything about upping staffing levels? Ours, I mean."

Resnick hadn't heard a thing.

"Just I caught a whisper things were lightening up; few new bodies transferring in. Thought Jack Skelton might've mentioned something. Only, if it's a case of staking a claim, well, that team of ours has been overstretched for more time'n I care to remember."

What his sergeant was preferring not to recall was the murder of DC Dipak Patel several years before, stabbed in the street when he intervened in a street brawl, his attacker never identified, never apprehended.

"This whisper, Graham, you wouldn't like to be more specific as to the source, I suppose?"

"Rather not, boss."

Just so, thought Resnick, nobody likes to get caught talking out of turn. "Okay, Graham, thanks for the tip. I'll give Skelton a ring now, see if there's anything can be done."

"Right," said Millington, and then, barely disguising the smirk, "Off to the match this afternoon, I daresay? Another bit of history in the making."

Resnick lowered the receiver onto Millington's laugh. After a season in which the club had hired and fired almost as many managers as their strikers had managed goals, today's game was County's last mathematical chance of avoiding relegation. Resnick didn't like to think about it.

He dialed the superintendent's number and was greeted by Alice Skelton's shrewish voice, each syllable like lemon rind squeezed through a grater. "Jack at home on Saturday morning, Charlie? Be reasonable. Why remain in the bosom of his family when there are stupid little golf balls to be hit about? Or in Jack's case, more like skewed into a bunker."

"Thank you, Alice," Resnick said pleasantly. "Perhaps you'll tell him I called."

He poured his second cup of coffee and drank it black while reading the Review section of the previous day's *Guardian*; not a natural choice of newspaper for Resnick—hardly the police officer's friend—but recently they'd started a jazz CD review that was halfway decent. Dizzy Gillespie leading a big band that included Clark Terry—now, that did sound interesting.

After telling himself he wasn't going to go near the County ground, Resnick turned up with five minutes to spare and found a seat on the same side he had stood in previous seasons, Saturday after alternate Saturday, surrounded by the same loose group of moaners and celebrants with whom he had shared the dubious delights of being a Notts supporter. But now government edicts had been followed and the old place was transformed into a smart all-seater stadium, the price of admission had just about doubled, most of Resnick's friends had drifted away, and after finding all that money for improvements, the club had failed to find a similar amount to improve the team.

On this particular Saturday there seemed to be at least two players in home-team shirts—minimum-wage recruits from a youth-training scheme, most likely—who Resnick was at odds to recognize and, from the way they began playing, the rest of the side were none the wiser.

Trying to defend their goal, two County players collided with each other, jumping for the same ball. For Resnick it was the last straw. Fifteen minutes before the end, head bowed, he turned and made for the exit, shoulder to shoulder with all those other supporters who had opted to do the same.

After that he knew a night in his own company was not a good idea: he considered phoning Hannah on the off chance that she had no plans for the evening and might consider going out with him. But by the time he reached the main road, he had dismissed the idea from his head. Against all of his previous inclinations, he would go to the Polish Club instead.

He had bought the light gray suit six years ago or more and insofar as he had a favorite, this was it; there was only one small stain that he could find, a dark patch near the lapel, which mostly came away when he scraped at it with a fingernail. He ironed a pale blue shirt and knotted his dark blue tie with more than usual care.

The bar in the Polish Club divided the large room into two unequal halves, and in the larger of these, the one with a small stage for the band, he found Marian seated at the bar.

"Charles! You are here! Come, come, come over and join us. Oh, you don't know how good it is to see you." As Marian squeezed his hand and enthusiastically kissed both of his cheeks, Resnick thought he was beginning to get the idea.

Wearing a black dress with a discreet white bow, a single strand of pearls at her neck, she was surrounded by several of those married men in late middle age whose fortnightly frisson came from flirting with her out of earshot of their wives. Her hair had been pushed up high on her head and was held in place with a silver barrette; silver earrings accentuated the slenderness of her neck. She was an elegant woman, some would say beautiful; some of those standing by her, Resnick assumed, frequently did. They had stepped back reluctantly to let him through and now continued to stand there, grudgingly, while Marian plied Resnick with questions, offered to buy him the vodka of his choice, smiled into his eyes. Ten minutes more and they had slunk away, back to their wives.

"You're looking happy, Marian."

"Not beautiful?"

"Of course."

"Desirable?" She was laughing at him with her eyes.

Why was it, Resnick wondered, and not for the first time, that in all the years he had known her—since, almost, they had been children—he had never entertained about her one sexual thought? Was it that, along with her beauty, she wore her Polishness so obviously on her sleeve? That to think of her as a partner—any kind of serious partner—would be to step back into a life he had all but rejected. His parents' life, a life in exile. Strangers in a strange land.

He looked around the room at the women in their flared dresses, the men, some of them, in bow ties, the children who skittered between the tables got up like miniature editions of their elders; out on the dance floor, two couples essaying a waltz to the accordion-led band; photographs of fallen generals on the walls.

"Charles, what are you thinking?"

Resnick smiled. "Oh, nothing important."

"Some dreadful crime?"

He shook his head. "Marian, I promise you it wasn't that."

For a moment she rested her hand on his arm. "You know, Charles, one of the things that would make me most happy? If one evening, like this evening, you would walk in here with a beautiful woman on your arm, someone with whom you are in love."

Despite himself, Resnick laughed. "Marian, you're just a dreamer."

"Oh"—she brought her face close—"and you are not?"

"I think," Resnick said, finishing his vodka and turning toward the band, "it might almost be time for us to have that dance."

Waltz over, the elderly couples moved slowly back toward their seats, the accordionist tested his fingers with an exploratory flourish and announced the first polka of the evening. Marian slipped out of her high heels into a pair of flat shoes she had brought expressly for the purpose and took Resnick's arm as they stepped onto the floor.

Forty minutes later, with only two brief intervals, they were still there, perspiring lightly, Resnick's tie loose at his neck, top button of his shirt unfastened.

"You see," Marian laughed, colliding with his chest as the number came to an unruly end. "You see what fun you are having? And why you should come here more often?"

Resnick dabbed at his temples and looked longingly toward the bar. "I think I need a drink."

She caught at his hands. "In a little while." Mischief danced in her eyes. "I had a talk with my friend the band-leader earlier. I think I know what they are going to play now."

When Carl Perkins wrote it, it's doubtful he ever imagined it sounding exactly this way, but Polish rock 'n' roll was what it was, "Blue Suede Shoes" what it is. One of the things Resnick had learned from his uncle, the tailor who had been to America and returned with a love of jazz and the jitterbug, was how to jive; who Marian had learned it from, Resnick had never known. But together, Resnick's unbuttoned jacket performing a dance of its own, while not sensational, they were pretty good.

"Roll Over Beethoven."

"Tutti Frutti."

"Little Queenie."

Resnick missed his footing, failed to catch Marian's out-stretched hand, and came close to trampling a small child underfoot. It was enough. And this time he would brook no argument.

They walked around into the second bar and found two seats; while Marian went to refresh herself in the ladies, Resnick chatted with the waistcoated barman and came away with two cold beers. I wonder, he thought, whether Hannah can dance like that? Oh, Charles, and you are not a dreamer? He should never have let her into his mind. When Marian returned, he excused himself and went outside to the phone. He had no real expectation that she would be in, but she picked up on the third ring.

"Hello?"

"Hannah?"

"Yes."

A slight pause, and then, "I didn't think you'd be there."

"Who is this?"

When he told her, there was a small silence before she said, "And was that why you phoned, because you thought I wouldn't be here?"

"No."

He could hear music, faint and distant, something she was listening to, guitars. "Is it too late," he asked, "for you to meet me for a drink?"

20

Hannah had gone to the smaller of the two Broadway cine-
mas that afternoon and seen a Tunisian film, *The Silence of
the Palace*; herself and perhaps half a dozen others watching
a woman returning from exile to a newly independent country and slowly coming to terms with the demands of present
and past. The woman, a singer, among other women for
whom silence was the only option. Hannah had sat at the end
of the row, close against the wall, trying not to fight against
the deliberately slow passing of time, fighting her prejudice
against the harsh sounds of Arabic. Gradually, the film had
won her over, so that, by the end, she was immersed in its
rhythm, and when she left, the voices and the movement in
the CaféBar next door seemed relentless and loud. She
resented the traffic and the crowds out on the streets. Crossing the end of Clumber Street toward the Old Market
Square, she thought she spotted Sheena Snape among a

group of half a dozen or so girls, noisily blocking the pavement outside the bank.

There were young men in the square wearing football shirts with black and white stripes, threatening to push one another into the fountain. Hannah maneuvered around them and walked up St. James Street and past the Tales of Robin Hood, heading uphill toward Lenton and where she lived in a terraced Victorian house overlooking a swath of grass and a children's playground, a church and a crown bowling green.

The light was blinking twice on her answerphone.

There were people, she supposed, who could take off their coat, change their shoes, put on the kettle, empty the rubbish, do any number of other things before pressing the button marked play. She was not one of them.

The first voice was her father's, calling from the French village to which he had moved three years before. Now his time was taken up in restoring a crumbling barn with the woman for whom he had left Hannah's mother, an architectural student and would-be writer almost ten years younger than Hannah herself.

"She'll leave you, Dad," Hannah had said, out there to visit last year, the pair of them sitting in the shade while Alexa busied herself inside. "You know that, don't you?"

He had taken both of Hannah's hands in his and kissed the bridge of her nose. "Of course she will. In time." He winked. "Just so long as we get this place finished first, eh? Then at least she'll leave me with a roof over my head to be miserable under."

On the tape, his voice was robust, happy; happier than she could ever remember him seeming in that commuter town in Kent, in every day on the seven twenty-three, home on the six fifty-four.

Hannah thought the second caller might be her mother, the family symmetry perfect, but it was Joanne, a colleague from work; she had a court booked at the tennis center at ten tomorrow morning and someone had dropped out of their doubles match, did Hannah want to take their place? Hannah thought that she might; she dialed Joanne's number, but the line was engaged.

She would try later. Now she made the tea and drank it with a slice of coffee-and-almond cake and that day's *Independent*. There was a frozen lasagna she could pop into the microwave, the makings of a salad, two piles of folders on the table waiting to be marked. She had treated herself to the new Marge Piercy and it sat, fat and white, on the arm of her chair in the window, asking to be read. *The Longings of Women.* Ah, yes, Hannah thought, we all know about those.

She was just pouring herself a glass of wine when the phone called her into the other room; certain it would be Joanne, checking about the tennis, she was ill-prepared for her mother's brittle cheeriness, wanting Hannah's advice about the holidays—walking in Crete or painting watercolors at Flatford Mill? Hannah understood it was her mother's way of saying, See how well I'm surviving, being positive, still turning your father's desertion into an oasis of opportunity. Go to Crete, Hannah wanted to say, you're more likely to meet a man. Some swarthy shepherd who will adore your trim, well-articulated body and white skin. As if that was all she—her mother—any of them—needed. *The Longings of Women* indeed!

Fifteen minutes later, not unkindly, Hannah told her mother there was marking she had to finish, replaced the receiver, and took wine and book upstairs to the bay-windowed room that she used as her study and looked out over the park. She had arranged a wicker armchair stuffed with cushions close against the window and, curtains open, she liked to sit there in the evenings, reading, glancing out at intervals to watch the light fading through the tops of the trees.

Her father had met Alexa in the same year that she started living with Jim, her second attempt at a stable relationship and, she had been certain, the one that would succeed. Jim's predecessor, Andrew, was a volatile Irishman she met when he was on a sabbatical from Queen's College, Belfast: a robust, round-faced scholar who wrote long, earnest—and now, Hannah realized, extremely bad—poems about the blackness of peat and the saving grace of the pudendum. Andrew, who on a good day could put an entire bottle of Jameson's away without blinking, and whose idea of good sex was to push her up against any convenient table and hoist her skirt up around her neck. On the first couple of occasions, though she thought it was politically incorrect to admit it, Hannah had found this distinctly exciting; after that, it had been a case of diminishing returns until all she associated Andrew's lovemaking with were sore thighs and bruised hips.

Jim was different: a peripatetic music teacher whom she first encountered schooling a nervous thirteen-year-old in national health glasses through the first movement of the Mozart clarinet concerto. Jim had taken Hannah's musical education in hand, too, had got her to realize there was more to Benjamin Britten than his love affair with Peter Pears and that it was possible to see a day of concerts featuring all six Bartók string quartets as more than an endurance test. They had lain in her bed and listened to Schubert, talking about where they would live when they were married, making up names for their children—Béla and Tasmin were Jim's favorites—and laughing about which reed instruments they would learn to play. A little less than two years later, Hannah still found signs of him around the house—a clarinet reed stuffed down behind the cushions of the sofa, the score of *Billy Budd* among the dusty folders in which she kept her old college lecture notes. Peripatetic had proved to be the right word.

At the end of another chapter, Hannah closed the book and stood for a while at the window, gazing out. Lights blinked like fireflies from across the park. Downstairs, she called Joanne and said yes to tennis, picked up a folder of work and put it back down, told herself she shouldn't really have another glass of wine and then, after she had poured it, crossed the room to the stereo and rummaged through the piles of CDs, which, since Jim's departure, had resumed their previous disorder. Mary Chapin Carpenter, Nanci Griffith, Rosanne Cash? She thought "Blue Moon with Heartache" might be a little difficult to take. "Shut Up and Kiss Me!" though, that was positive, nothing wrong with that. Maybe she should buy an extra copy and send one to her mum, something to put in her bag for Crete, along with sunblock and a Greek phrase book. Hannah had just set Mary Chapin Carpenter to play when the phone rang again. She nearly decided to ignore it.

"Hello?"

"Hannah?"

"Yes." She had no idea who it was.

"I didn't think you'd be there."

Then why on earth did you call, she thought, still trawling through the file of possibilities. Someone on the staff? A friend of Joanne's? Her partner for tomorrow? "Who is this?"

"Charlie Resnick, you remember we . . ."

Of course she remembered. She did now, now she recognized the voice. She could even picture him standing there, bulky, telephone to his ear, his mouth. "And was that why you phoned?" she said, smiling a little. "Because you thought I wouldn't be here?" She was surprised at how pleased she was that he had.

"No," he said, and then, "Is it too late for you to meet me for a drink?"

It was only when she put down the phone that Hannah realized she didn't know exactly where the Polish Club was; she hoped the taxi driver would.

She had changed outfits three times waiting for the cab to arrive, reverting finally to what she had been wearing when Resnick phoned, a soft gray cotton round-neck top over recently washed blue jeans, black shoes, flat and comfortable, on her feet. Front door open, she lifted a stone-colored linen jacket from the coatrack in the hall.

Resnick was waiting for her when she arrived, moving from the shadows at the top of the steps as her taxi drew away.

"You found it okay?"

"The driver did."

"You've been here before?"

Hannah shook her head.

The elderly man with white hair brushed back and a blue blazer, buttons shining, looked up at Resnick as he signed Hannah in, Resnick avoiding the questions in his watery blue eyes.

"Look," Resnick said; he had stopped her in the hallway beyond the desk, hand barely touching her arm. She was vaguely aware of deep red wallpaper, framed photographs, music from another room. "There are people here I know, I can either introduce you or—"

"Or we can hide in a corner."

He smiled. "Something like that."

Hannah smiled back. "I'm not the hiding type."

Marian Witczak took Hannah's hand as a doctor might receive a slide on which a rare and potentially dangerous specimen had been prepared. She made the smallest of small talk while Resnick was at the bar and, when he returned, excused herself onto the dance floor. So much for her wanting to see me on the arm of a beautiful woman, Resnick thought.

Hannah accepted the glass of lager and relaxed against the worn leather seat. "When did that finish?" she asked, looking off in the direction Marian had taken.

"What exactly?"

"Your whatever-you'd-call-it. Relationship. Affair."

"With Marian?"

"Uh-huh."

Resnick shook his head. "It never started."

Setting down her glass, Hannah smiled. "Well, that explains the welcome, at least."

They sat and talked for maybe half an hour, respective jobs, contrasting afternoons, Notts County seemingly as foreign to Hannah as Tunisia was to Resnick.

"You never go to the cinema?"

"Not really."

"I go to Broadway most weeks, I suppose. They show all kinds of stuff. You know, things you're not likely to see elsewhere, except on Channel Four."

"Like films from Tunisia." Resnick smiled.

Hannah nodded. He looked years younger when he did that, the broadening of the mouth, brightening of the eyes.

"You should go," she said. "They have some good films. They're not all Tunisian. And besides"—smiling—"they serve good food."

What had it been, she was thinking, the sauce that he had dripped onto his suit and failed to wipe away? Bolognese? Matriciana?

The call for last orders came from behind the bar. They were on their feet when the accordion swayed into the last waltz.

"Should we?" Resnick said, head angled, fingers reaching again for her arm.

"I don't think so," Hannah said.

But once outside she slipped her arm through his and suggested they walk a little. He asked her where she lived and she him. At the junction of Sherwood Rise and Gregory Boulevard, a black-and-white cab came toward them with its FOR HIRE light shining and Resnick stepped out into the road, arm raised.

"Oh, God," said Hannah as he held open the door. "Your place or mine?"

The cab dropped them off at the end of the Promenade. During the short journey they had said little, Resnick aware of Hannah's proximity, the sleeve of her jacket almost resting on his thigh, the sounds, faint, of her breathing, the way her hands rested in a loose cradle above her lap, fingers barely touching.

"This is it," she said, her voice, for that moment, unnaturally loud.

Resnick nodded: he had reasons for knowing this street. The houses, tall, to the left as they began to walk along the unmade road, little more than a path; to the right, iron railings and an uneven line of bushes and small trees that separated them from the park.

"I'm at the far end," Hannah said. "The terrace."

These houses they were going past, lights muted by curtains or filtered through lace, were semidetached; small gardens at the front, squares of grass bordered by shrubs or flowering plants. Indistinct, the sounds of voices, laughter, television, dinner parties winding down. Resnick exchanged automatic greetings with a man out walking his dog. As they passed the house where Mary Sheppard had lived, something in the pit of his stomach knotted and turned.

When Hannah paused to ease back the gate that led to the few terraced houses at the end, she saw Resnick's face, pale in the fall of the overhead light.

"What's the matter? You look as if you've seen a ghost."

It had been a cold night, far colder than this, and Mary Sheppard had been naked to the waist, next to naked below; Resnick remembered her legs partly raised, arms at extreme angles to the body. The officers who had arrived there before Resnick—Lynn Kellogg and Kevin Naylor had been the first—had covered her with a plastic sheet and then covered that with coats taken from inside the house. Resnick had lifted these back, looked at her with a borrowed torch. Her eyes had been open, gazing up, unseeing, at the moon.

He followed Hannah up the short path toward her front door. When she turned, key in her hand, it was almost into his arms.

"You are coming in? Coffee? A drink?"

For a moment he hesitated. "Maybe better some other time." Regretful, the slow shake of the head.

"You're sure?" She laid her hand on his, the cold hardness of the key, the sudden warmth of her skin. Resnick didn't move. Hannah was trying to see his face, read the expression in his eyes. After a moment, she turned and slipped the key into the lock, pushed back the door; there was a light burning, warm orange, in the hall. She looked back, then stepped aside as Resnick followed her in.

There was an old fireplace in the living room, decorated tiles at each side, a vase of dried flowers standing before the matt-black grate. Postcards stood on the mantelpiece, a small family photograph in a gray-green frame. A two-seater settee pushed up against one wall, two brightly covered armchairs, cushions on the floor. Not knowing where to sit, Resnick stood.

From upstairs he heard the flushing of the toilet, Hannah's feet upon the stairs.

"What's it to be?" She had taken off her jacket; he noticed, for the first time, two rings, silver with a glint of color, on the outside fingers of her right hand.

"Coffee, tea? There's a bottle of wine already open. It's not too bad. Actually, it's pretty good." She was smiling with her eyes.

"Wine sounds fine."

"Okay." She flapped a hand in the direction of the settee. "Why don't you sit down? Put on some music if you'd like. I'll just be a minute."

Resnick bent over a small pile of CDs beside the stereo in the corner of the room bearing names, mostly female, that he didn't know. He looked at the cover of the case that was standing empty, presumably what Hannah had been playing when he'd called. *Stones in the Road.* Resnick thought he knew some of those.

In the square kitchen, pouring wine, Hannah was amazed at the unsteadiness of her hand. Hannah, what the hell's the matter with you? she asked. And what on earth do you think you're doing?

"Here."

He was still standing there, too big for the middle of the room. When he took the glass, his fingers burned for an instant against the edge of her hand.

"Why don't you let me take your coat?"

"It's okay." But he put down his glass, shrugged off his suit jacket, and Hannah hung it in the hall, beside her own.

"Please, sit down."

Hesitating, Resnick took the settee. Not quite able to bring herself to sit beside him, Hannah sat in the easy chair nearest to the stereo.

"You didn't see anything you fancied?" she said, indicating the CDs.

"I didn't know."

"Not your kind of music, then?"

At last, Resnick smiled. "I'm a jazzman myself, I'm afraid."

"Well," Hannah said, reaching round for the controls, "nothing ventured . . ."

The sounds of a piano, tentative at first, rolled out across the room. Then a woman's voice, slightly husky, unaccompanied, warm but bare. Why walk, she was singing, when you can fly?

When the other instruments came in behind the vocal, Resnick thought, for the second time that evening, he could hear an accordion. He leaned forward and lifted his glass from the mantelpiece and, without drinking, placed it on the floor beside his feet. Hannah watching him, her lips moving, just faintly, to the words. The space between them seemed a million miles wide, uncrossable. Resnick moved his foot and the glass overturned, spilling wine.

"Oh, shit!"

"It's okay." Hannah was on her feet, heading for the door. "Don't worry. Don't worry." Returning with a tea towel in her hand.

"I'm sorry." Resnick was still sitting there, legs apart, all-but-empty glass in his hand.

"It doesn't matter," Hannah assured him, pressing the cloth hard against the carpet where the wine had spread. "That's why I bought this color. Nothing shows."

"It's my fault for being so clumsy."

"No, there. See? Nothing. Well"—laughing—"nothing much." Straightening, she placed her hand on his leg; as she reached her other hand toward his neck, the darkened towel fell away. His mouth was closed against hers and then it was not. Wine on his tongue. Somewhere inside Hannah's brain she was thinking, I should have waited for "Shut Up and Kiss Me!" but track six was too far on. Resnick's knees were tight against her side, his hand in her hair.

"Charlie," she said, some fifteen minutes later. He had swung one of his legs round onto the settee, and she was half-lying across him, trying not to get cramped or notice that

159

her hip was rubbing rather painfully against the settee's sharp edge.

"Mmm?" he mumbled, close against her face. His tie had disappeared and his shirt was mostly undone.

"Come up to bed."

At the door he stopped her, catching at her hand. "Look, Hannah, are you sure?"

He was startled by the ferocity of her laugh.

"What is it?"

"Sure?" she said. "I don't know if I can afford to wait that long."

The bedroom stretched across the top of the house between two sloping roofs. The floorboards had been sanded and polished; two chests of drawers and the wardrobe were in stripped pine. There were two rugs, one at either side of the bed, one white, the other blood red. Plants hung in baskets from the ceiling, fronds pushing up toward the light, which, even now, showed through the uncovered skylights, one at each side of the room. In the city it was never quite dark. Hannah would lay there some nights, staring up, vainly searching for stars.

Now she lifted herself up onto one arm and was surprised to find that she was still shaking a little; she had not made love to anyone since Jim and that already seemed longer ago than it was. So strange, the first time with anyone new; after the first blind excitement of caressing and undressing, the clumsiness of finding that fit, the almost stubborn awkwardness of it. She remembered in a film once she had seen— Robert De Niro, was it, and Uma Thurman?—charging at it headlong, a melee of arms and legs and sheets that ended up with the pair of them, startled and breathless, on the floor. And, of course, in movies there was never that embarrassing nonconversation about the condoms. Which of you, if either, has them and are they within reach? The answer had been on the upper shelf of the bathroom cabinet, behind the mouth ulcer gel and the spare dental floss, down on the second floor.

She noticed Resnick's breathing change and thought he might be asleep again, until, fleetingly at first, he opened his eyes.

"What time is it?"

Hannah narrowed her eyes toward the digital clock on the floor. "A quarter to four."

Resnick eased himself up onto his elbow and lay facing her, this woman he scarcely knew who had invited him into her bed. He felt honored and would have liked to have told her so, but couldn't quite find the words. He kissed a corner of her mouth instead.

"Do you have to go?"

"I ought to, soon."

"An early start?"

"Responsibilities." He smiled. "Cats. And I have to change out of this suit. That suit." The trousers were somewhere between the bed and the stairs.

"And if you stay the night," Hannah said, "it might mean something more."

He looked at her; in this light her eyes were gray-green, stone polished by water. "Might it?"

With a swift movement, she was out from beneath the duvet and on her feet. "We'll see."

Resnick watched her walk, barefooted, across the floor, the dark ends of pubic hair visible between her legs before she disappeared behind the door.

In the kitchen they sat and drank tea while the light slowly changed behind the window, Resnick dressed in everything save his suit jacket, Hannah in a T-shirt and chenille dressing gown, dunking stale dark chocolate biscuits, all she had been able to find. How, Hannah thought, had she ever kept chocolate biscuits long enough to go stale? Her self-control must be better than she'd imagined. Until tonight.

Resnick sat listening for the sound of a car engine; the cab company had told him twenty minutes to half an hour. When he heard it on the road near the rear of the house, he quickly swallowed down the last of his tea.

Slippers on her feet, Hannah walked with him along the narrow alley to where the driver was waiting.

"I'm not much good at one-night stands," she said.

"Neither am I." He didn't know if that was true.

She held two of his fingers tight inside her hand. "Then I'll see you again?"

"Yes. Yes, of course. If that's what you want."

On the pavement, he kissed her softly on the mouth and she kissed him back; she watched as the car drew away, out onto the Boulevard, indicator blinking orange light. Well, Hannah, she thought as she turned back toward the house, so the earth didn't move, what did you expect? At the gate, she laughed lightly. "You didn't even see stars."

The phone was ringing when Resnick entered the house.

"Charlie, where the fuck have you been?"

Taken aback by the ferocity in Skelton's voice, he didn't know how to respond.

"Where the hell was your bleep?"

There on the hall table; he had forgotten to transfer it into the pocket of his suit.

"What's happened?" Resnick finally asked.

"Bill Aston," Skelton said, his voice like sour milk. "He's dead. Some bastard's killed him."

21

You could see the lights of the emergency vehicles once you passed the corner of Meadow Lane and approached the bridge; patches of muted color bleeding out into the day. Mist hung in low gray rags over the surface of the river. Rain teased the air. A temporary covering had been set up on the flat spread of grass of the embankment, a tent of ill-fitting orange plastic around which lighting had been quickly rigged. Figures wearing dark blue overalls were already examining the surrounding ground on hands and knees. At the perimeter of the scene others were gathered in knots of conversation, heads bowed. It was Skelton who turned away from one of these and moved toward the road to meet Resnick, more than tiredness darkening his eyes.

"Jesus Christ, Charlie! Where were you?"

"When was he found?" Resnick asked, scarcely breaking his stride.

"An hour since."

"What was he doing here?"

"Walking his dogs. They're back there in one of the cars."

Millington was there, Divine, Reg Cossall, gray haired, hands deep in the topcoat he seemed to wear whatever the weather; other officers, in uniform and without. Resnick pushed one of the flaps of plastic aside with an arm and ducked inside. The police surgeon turned his head toward Resnick and then away. Whatever had been used to batter Bill Aston's head and face had been heavy and hard and wielded with frequency and great force. Beneath a coagulation of blood and hair and bone, it seemed as if the top of his skull had been stoved completely in. Lower down, more bone, sharp-edged, splintered through the skin. The globe of one eye, iris and retina, lay, barely attached, among the bloodied pulp of what had been Bill Aston's cheek.

Resnick had to will himself to stay there, bent over, as long as it took. There were mud and grass stains thick on the dead man's clothes, sports jacket and gray trousers, striped shirt. A smear of earth thick on the fleshy palm of his right hand. One of the nails, the finger end, deeply split. One of his shoes was missing, something the vibrant yellow of dog shit sticking to the heel of his woolen navy sock.

"Time of death?" Resnick asked.

Parkinson removed his spectacles, pinched the bridge of his nose. "Between four to six hours ago. Around one o'clock."

Resnick nodded and swung out of the tent to where Skelton stood smoking a cigarette. "All right," Resnick said, "what do we know?"

The superintendent waited until they were up on the road, the houses opposite—mock-Tudor, mock-Gothic, mock-something—at the end of their deep gardens, mostly dark. Skelton lit a fresh cigarette from the nub end of the last.

"This youth found the body around three A.M. He'd been sleeping rough, down by that bandstand, other side of the

164

Memorial Gardens. Woke up, started to wander, keeping out the cold. That was when he heard the dogs, barking and whining. Followed the sound to the body, so he says."

"Called it in?"

A shake of Skelton's head. "Not straightaway. Panicked. Ran off. While later—says he's not sure how long, half an hour, maybe more—he went back. Took another look. That was when he phoned." For a moment, Skelton turned his head, down toward the river, the splash of birds disturbing the water. "The two lads who arrived first, uniform patrol, they had no idea who he was. It was only after the ambulance had arrived, one of the paramedics found his wallet, kicked it up from the grass. About the only thing left in it, his warrant card. That was when all hell broke loose."

"The youth who found him . . ."

"At the station now. Being questioned. First reports, seems straight enough."

"And Aston's wife?"

Again, Skelton shook his head. "Would you want her to see him first like this?"

Cold air slithered down into Resnick's lungs like a wave; he could already see Margaret Aston's slow-collapsing face, the lance of pain stripping across her eyes.

"She's not reported him missing? Made inquiries, anything?"

For a second, Skelton's eyes were closed. "Not as far as we know." And then, "You know her, Charlie, don't you? Socially, I mean."

"Not well. Not for a long time."

Skelton nodded; not well was better than not at all. "There'll be an incident room set up at the station, Charlie. Whoever it was, we'll get him."

"Yes." It was almost fully light now to the east. Resnick sighed and began to walk back in the direction of the bridge.

"Charlie?"

165

"Yes?"

"You talked with him, didn't you? Aston. About the inquiry? That kid Snape's death."

Resnick nodded. "Friday night."

"There wasn't anything he said . . . nothing he said about it that might lead you to believe, well, that it had anything to do with this?"

"No. Nothing. But . . ."

"But?"

Resnick recalled the almost glib ease with which Aston had seemed to be accepting the Social Services version of Nicky Snape's death; had there been anything murky going on, Aston didn't seem to have been aware of it—unless something had come to light between his conversation with him in the pub and the attack. "No," Resnick said. "Not as far as I know."

Skelton released a slow breath of relief. "Mugging, then. Out on his own, late at night, someone saw their chance."

"Yes," Resnick said. "Likely that's how it was. We'll see."

Resnick stood with his back half toward the front door as the next-door neighbor eased his BMW out of the drive and onto the road. Birds were making a racket in the trees. The lock clicked open, and as the door swung inward, Resnick turned.

"Bill, I swear you'd forget your head if it wasn't screwed on, never mind your keys. . . ." Seeing Resnick, only half-recognizing him, she faltered into silence.

"Hello, Margaret." He made a move, unthreatening, toward her.

"Bill, I thought he'd gone out early. With the dogs. To . . . to . . ." But she had been a policeman's wife long enough to know this moment, to have rehearsed it often enough in the long flat hours before dawn.

"Margaret, why don't you let me come inside?"

Stubby, short, pink dressing gown tied round her, curlers

in her hair, she stood her ground, challenging him for the truth.

"Margaret, I'm sorry . . ."

She opened her mouth to scream, drowning out his words.

". . . he's dead."

Resnick caught hold of her and held her close, muffling her screams against his chest. Three minutes, more. When he was able to, he shuffled her far enough into the hallway to push the door shut at his back. It smelled of lavender in there, strong, like soap on his fingers, the palms of his hands. His shirt was damp with Margaret Aston's tears.

"Tell . . . tell me what happened."

"Why don't we go and make . . . ?"

Her voice was shrill and angry. "I don't want . . . ! I want to know."

Resnick took her arm, his hand steady beneath her elbow. "All right, but let's at least sit down."

The living room was at the rear of the house, fussy with tasteful ornaments and family photographs; the curtains, had they been fully open, would have revealed French windows and beyond those some eighty feet of flower beds and tidy shrubs, well-groomed lawn. As it was, they sat in facing chairs in the shadowy half-light, Margaret's face angled toward the other armchair, empty by the span of fireside, the one in which, Resnick guessed, her husband would more usually have sat.

He told her such details as were known, restricting the description of Aston's injuries to a minimum. She listened, straining toward him, head angled slightly to one side, her hands in her lap never still.

"Bill," she said when Resnick had finished. "Poor Bill. What has he ever done to deserve this?"

"Nothing, Margaret. Nothing."

She was on her feet. "I want to see him."

"Later, Margaret. Why not let it wait?" Gently, he led her

167

back to the chair. On his feet, he went to the windows and let light into the room.

"When you came to the door," Resnick said, "just now. You thought it was Bill, back from walking the dogs?"

"Yes."

"But when this happened, as far as we can tell, it was near the middle of the night. One or two."

He waited while she assimilated this.

"Yes, he . . . Sometimes he couldn't sleep. Not right away. So he'd go out again, a walk, anything rather than lie there. He hated that; there was nothing he disliked more. And this past couple of years it had got worse, much worse. That was why we moved, he moved across the hall—separate rooms, you see. That way, if Bill was troubled with his insomnia, he wouldn't feel guilty about waking me." She plucked at the hem of her dressing gown, some end of cotton she alone could see. "Not that I ever minded. Not . . ." And she was lost to tears again, flapping Resnick away when he came near.

He went to find the kitchen and left her there, unembarrassed in her own grief. If Bill Aston had gone out last night after midnight, taking the dogs with him, she would not have thought it unusual; and if she had slept through till morning, possibly gone to look for him in his room and found him not there, she could have imagined him up early, taking a stroll, nothing sinister or alarming there.

The tea was ready in the pot when Margaret, red-eyed, came into the room. "I do want to see him, now. You must take me to see him."

On his feet, Resnick tried the beginnings of a smile. "Let's have a cup of this, why don't we? I'll call the hospital, then drive you over. All right? Margaret, is that okay?"

She stood, staring at him, lost between table and door. How long till it was ever okay again?

22

Eleven forty-four: cigarette smoke hung like a gray-blue cloud from the center of the windowless room. Enlarged photographs of Aston's body had been tacked to the wall. Color. Black and white. High, to the right, a picture that had been taken eighteen months before, Bill Aston at the retirement party for a colleague, champagne glass held aloft, dinner jacket and tie, smiling and alive.

At right angles to these, a blown-up map showed the precise spot on the embankment where the body had been found; a second map, larger scale, delineated the parameters of the area—the deep southerly curve of the river, forming an almost perfect U between Trent Bridge and the old Wilford viaduct, the Memorial Gardens and the flat, open recreation ground, which led up to the predominantly council-owned Meadows residential area in the north; south, the civic blandness of County Hall and then more open ground, playing fields, and schools. Further along, a fully detailed map of the city and its surroundings had been marked with Aston's home, the office where he had been based, the local authority accommodation where the Snape inquiry had been carried out. On the far side of the photographs, also attached to the wall, were the two white boards on which the principal lines of inquiry would be followed and marked. A pair of linked video monitors had been set up at the rear; two computers, one of them on-line with the national Home Office computer, stood ready to access and disseminate information.

Copies of the pathologist's initial report had been handed out to those present: multiple fractures of the cranial cavity, severe damage to the upper and lower jaw, the mandible and orbit walls, rupturing of the blood vessels to the brain and consequent internal hemorrhaging. Damage to Aston's hands and bruising to the forearms suggested that he had put up a considerable struggle and made a determined, finally desperate effort to defend himself.

Skelton stood near the front of the room in close conversation with Resnick and the DCI in charge of uniforms. A little to one side, Reg Cossall, thick gray hair brushed back, inevitable cigarette burning from the curve of his hand, spoke in slow undertones to the inspector from the Support Department, emphasizing every sentence with a jab of a finger toward the man's chest. Skelton, more alive than Resnick had observed him for months, wearing a double-breasted suit that Resnick had never seen, glanced quickly down at his neatly written notes before slipping them from sight; as soon as this was over, he would go directly to the media briefing below. A last word to Resnick and he turned away; two steps forward and the heavy hum and burr of voices around him rose, then died.

Briefly, he introduced Harry Payne, the inspector from the Support Department, fifteen of whose officers would be responsible for the initial close search, and Jane Prescott, the sergeant who would be liaising between the investigation and

Force Intelligence. He introduced DC Khan as Bill Aston's assistant on the Snape inquiry, and finally the two civilian computer operators. Everyone else knew everyone else, pretty much.

Skelton cleared his throat. "I don't need to tell you a fellow officer has been killed. One of us." Nods of agreement, murmurs of assent and anger from all around. Skelton waited before going on. "Many of you knew Bill Aston; some of you, like myself, worked with him. He was a good officer. The old school. Decent. Fair. Scrupulous in everything that he did. After all of his years of service, Bill was due to retire at the end of this year. And now this."

Once again, the litany of voices as though in church, Skelton orchestrating them, call and response.

"We all know what happened in the early hours of this morning. You've all seen the photographs, read the report, some of you were present at the scene where Bill Aston's body was found. This was a callous, brutal attack and I know that you all feel as shocked as I do. And I know that what you all want is to get whoever did this, person or persons, banged up behind bars as soon as possible. We want a result and we want it fast. We want it for Bill Aston's widow . . . and before whoever was responsible for this can act again."

Skelton waited for the volley of sound, fierce and emphatic, to subside. He wanted every face turned toward him, everyone's attention exclusively on what he had to say.

"Before we set to work, I want us to be clear—there are dangers here. The last thing we can afford to do is rush headlong into this and let feelings, however strong, get the better of judgment. Nobody, none of you is going off at half-cock on this. It's too important." Skelton's voice clear now, no longer loud, no longer needing to be: silence around him in the room. "What we can't afford is to bring in the right person, the right people, and then not be able to make it stick. So we're thorough, exact, we work through channels, we check and then we double-check. And then when we've caught the bastard, he stays caught."

Acclamation. Skelton waited a moment longer before stepping aside. "Charlie?"

As Resnick began speaking, he moved across until he was positioned in front of the maps of the Trent. "The most likely scenario so far is that this was a random, unpremeditated attack, carried out for gain. Whatever he had on him at the time. They could have seen Bill as an affluent-enough-looking bloke, not so young, out on his own with a couple of little dogs. No threat there." Resnick pointed up at one of the maps. "Bill parked his car here, opposite the Memorial Gardens, and walked, as far as we can tell, in this direction here, along the embankment toward the bridge. When he couldn't sleep, this was something he did quite a bit, nothing unusual about it at all. We're presuming that whoever it was that attacked him saw him wandering alone, presumably nobody else around, and marked him down as an easy target. He was set upon here, close by these trees, and his wallet was found here, not far from the body, cash and credit cards gone." Resnick paused and looked around the room. "Margaret Aston says the most he would have been likely to have had with him was thirty or forty pounds."

"Bastards!" somebody said, loud and pronounced.

"Thanks, Charlie." It was Skelton's turn again. "Right. To specifics. Reg, anything and everything that happened on the embankment between one and four, anyone who set foot, anything that breathed, that's your bailiwick." Cossall shuffled a foot and gave the floor a half-smile. "So, supervision of house-to-house, that's down to you. All those places along Victoria Embankment, they can't all have been tucked up with their Ovaltine; anyone who heard anything, saw anyone, we have to know. And we'll be appealing for anyone who drove along that way after midnight, any late-night fishermen, joggers, whatever, to come forward. Anyone using the pub on his side of the bridge, especially around last orders, or walking back into the city from the TBI. We'll be using local radio, television news, the *Post*. Whatever information we get, once it's been processed, Reg, you and your team, get it prioritized, followed through.

"Charlie, your team, I want you to go in close. Forensics, anything found at the immediate scene—give us as exact a picture as you can of what actually happened. And the twenty-four hours leading up to the attack, we want to know where Bill went, who he spoke to, what he did. Cover ourselves, just in case. If we have to look further afield, that's where we'll start."

Skelton cleared his throat and wished for a glass of water; he was conscious of speaking for a long time. The troops were getting restless for action and it was time for the last push. "All right, one of the things we have to be wary of is tunnel vision. The most obvious suspect is not always the one that ends up in the frame, which is why, even though I don't think there's any connection, I'm going to be talking to Khan here about the inquiry Bill was heading into the apparent suicide of Nicky Snape. There may be no connection, but it has to be checked and eliminated. And there'll be other avenues. Cases Bill worked when he was operational, people he was responsible for getting sent down who've recently been released. Anyone else who might have held a grudge, the Job or personal. Anything out of sync. I don't see Bill as having been a man who made enemies easily, but we'll talk to Margaret, see what she says. Finally, any of you, any ideas you might have, different angles, things that seem to be in danger of being overlooked. Come forward. Talk to me. I want to know."

Skelton took a step back and inclined his head right, then left. "Charlie, Reg, anything you want to add?"

Neither did.

"All right, let's be moving. And good luck."

◆◆◆

Less than half an hour later, Resnick was back in his own
CID room. Kevin Naylor had just finished mashing tea.
Resnick sat on the edge of one of the desks, finishing off a
smoked chicken and cranberry sandwich that had been sent
across from the deli on the Circus.

"Okay," he said, taking a mug from Kevin and holding it
in both hands, "let's talk this through."

Millington was sitting close to Resnick's right, chair angled
back onto its rear legs; Divine was down toward the end of
the narrow room, chair reversed, legs spread wide; Lynn Kellogg sat with her head resting back against the left-hand wall;
Naylor, having handed out the tea, took up a position behind
one of the dark green filing cabinets and leaned forward on
both elbows.

"First things first. We already have somebody helping us
with our inquiries, this homeless youth who found the body,
phoned it in. Graham, I want you and Mark to question him
again, push him some more. Let's check out what he knows,
make sure he's telling us everything."

"You think he might've been involved, boss?" Divine
asked. "The attack?" Push him a little, he'd liked the sound
of that.

"Wouldn't be the first time, would it?" Millington said.
"Throwing off suspicion, reporting your own crime."

Resnick nodded and moved on. "Kevin, Scene of Crime
will have details of footprints, boot marks, in the area the
body was found—photographs, casts, whatever. Make what
sense of them you can. Other things aside, it should help us
to pin down how many people were actually involved."

"We are pretty definite, are we," Naylor asked, "we're
dealing with more than one person?"

Resnick swallowed a mouthful of tea. "That's my gut feeling, yes. Two at least, maybe more. Bill had kept himself rea-

sonably fit, he wouldn't have looked such an easy mark to one man on his own. And unless whoever struck the first blow managed to take him completely by surprise, I doubt that a single attacker would have been able to cause as much damage as this."

He shifted his focus across the room. "Lynn, we have to build up a detailed picture of Bill Aston's last twenty-four hours—everything he did, everywhere he went, anyone and everyone he spoke to. I'd like you to take care of that. I'll go with you to see Margaret Aston first off, introduce you. Then you're on your own."

"Right," Lynn said. "Thanks."

"Meantime, I'm going to go over the material from the Nicky Snape inquiry with Khan." Resnick set both hands on the desk and pushed himself to his feet. "Before you go off duty tonight, check back with me, let me know what you've got."

The last drops of water spurted noisily down into the jug of Skelton's coffee machine and, standing close by the side window, looking down, Resnick was aware of his stomach rumbling in sympathy. Past noon and, chicken sandwich aside, the last food that had passed his lips had been at Hannah's house hours before, a couple of chocolate digestives that had seen better days. For a moment he was thinking of her, Hannah, the skin around her hip, along her thigh, smooth and taut against his hand.

"Charlie?"

"Huh?"

"Milk or without?"

"As it comes."

Skelton took a seat and Resnick did the same. "Difficult not to think," Skelton said, "how close he was to retiring, poor bugger."

"Yes." And Margaret, Resnick thought, what kind of a life

for her? After all that time, that life, how could you hope to adjust? The kids, he supposed, there were always the kids, but then he wondered what kind of an answer that was.

"Press conference at one," Skelton was saying. "You're okay about that, fully briefed?"

"I can only say what we know, and up to now that's not too much."

"Good opportunity, though, ask for information, help."

Resnick nodded: they would be flooded with calls, extra staff on hand to log them in. Much of the information would prove inconclusive and conflicting; and then there would be the cranks, psychics, and backyard psychiatrists, two or three at least wanting to confess. He set his cup down in its saucer, placed them both on the floor. State-of-the-art coffee maker or not, Skelton's coffee always tasted like instant, and weak instant at that. He got to his feet, thinking that was all, but there was more.

"There's a young DC," Skelton said, "looking to transfer up from Leicestershire. Chance he might come here."

Resnick waited at the back of his chair. "Is this definite, or just rumor?"

"Definite as these things go."

"I thought there was a freeze on all recruitment?"

Skelton spread his hands, fingers wide. "In theory there is, but you know Finance, Charlie. Bloody unfathomable."

"This transfer, does he have a name? You said 'he.'"

"Vincent. Carl Vincent."

"And he's CID?"

Skelton nodded. "Five years."

"Still a DC?"

Nodded again.

There were all kinds of reasons, Resnick knew, why officers applied to transfer. Personality clashes, mostly; sometimes a case goes sour and they're looking for a fresh start.

Family reasons for needing to relocate, but this—nothing more than an hour's drive.

"Might be he'll be here in the next couple of days," Skelton said. "No bad thing, Charlie. This inquiry, you'll be needing all the bodies you can get. Have him plug a few holes, feel him out. You can afford to give it a while either way, see how it goes. If it turns out he's half the copper young Patel would have been, you'll not be sorry."

Resnick could still remember the first time he had met Dipak Patel, bright as tomorrow and eager to please. The first from his family to go to university, get a degree. The police force, Patel's father had said, why that? Such waste. Resnick remembered blood drying on the paving stones, the purplish hue around the wound, one single slashing blow that had found the artery by design or chance. A killer never caught. He remembered the father's face, the way it had twisted in; his uncomprehending grief.

Margaret Aston.

Norma Snape.

It went on, without end.

23

Norma had tried not to notice the smell on Sheena's breath when her daughter came in; not quite tobacco, not quite gin, it was grass, she knew, remembered it distantly but well.

"And where d'you think you got this?" she asked, angling back her head, the better to see the black leather jacket, studs around both pockets, zips unfastened along both sleeves.

"I don't *think*," Sheena said, doing her best to swerve past. "I know."

Norma grabbed the back of the jacket with one hand and swung her round. "So tell me."

Sheena gazed, not quite steady, not as steady as she would have liked to be, into her mother's accusing eyes. "Dee-Dee," she said. "That's where. My friend Dee-Dee, she lent it to me. Right?"

But before Norma could say anything more, Peter was in the doorway, three cans of Kestrel balanced one above the other on the palm of one hand. "Let's sit down, eh? Have a drink." Winking at Norma as he pushed one of the cans into her grudging hands; aiming a kiss at Sheena's cheek, which she only partly managed to evade. "Nice evening, eh, sweetheart? Good time?"

"I don't think," Sheena said, articulating overcarefully, "you should call me sweetheart."

"Oh, and why's that, then?"

Sheena thought about it and after some consideration decided that she didn't know. She sat on the arm of the settee and wobbled just a little.

"For Christ's sake," Norma said from the armchair beside the TV, "take that coat off indoors."

Sheena tried, but got her arm caught up in the sleeve and inexplicably couldn't get it free. Peter, finally, got up and helped her, Sheena starting again to laugh. Not laughing, really, giggling more like. "You're not to call . . . you're not to call . . ." Losing her balance, she began to topple backward, legs kicking high in the air, arms flailing, till all she could do was collapse backward against her father, Peter not strong enough to hold her, the pair of them sprawling on the carpet, sprawling and rolling until they ended up against the side wall, laughing and crying in each other's arms.

"For the Lord's sake, give over, you pair of great nazzle-heads!" Norma shouted, but soon she was laughing, too, despite herself, wiping her sleeve across her eyes before trying to take too much of the lager down at one time, coughing then so bad she couldn't see for the tears and Sheena had to hold her hands while Peter patted her back and whispered in her ear for her to get a grip.

When it was over Sheena wandered off into the kitchen just in case there was any of the ice cream from Tesco left in the freezer, mint and chocolate.

Peter switched on the TV and switched it back off, springing onto the settee with arms flung wide. "Let me call you sweetheart!" he sang at the top of his reedy voice. "You belong to me!"

"Sit down, you great gillifer," Norma called, "before you fall down."

Which he did, clean over the back of the settee onto his head. And came up singing. Norma and Sheena hauled him to his feet and pushed him down into a chair, Norma plumping herself in his lap, while Sheena sat across the room and spooned with exaggerated care around the tub of ice cream.

"Sweetheart," Peter whispered into Norma's bosom and she clipped him none too seriously around the ear and told him to behave and anyway, if that was what he was after, he had another think coming.

Which he did. And when Sheena finally got tired of sitting there, watching the pair of them pretending not to paw at each other, she sashayed out past them, her parting gesture to switch out the light.

"Peter, not here. . . ." Norma whispered.

"In that case," Peter said, "let's away up to bed."

Oh, God, Norma thought, how long's it been?

She lay awake, Peter beside her sleeping like a baby, his mouth slightly open close to her breast. Tears that Norma would cry later she had held back for fear of waking him, having to explain what she herself could not understand.

Whatever the deft magic of Peter's hands, he had not lost it all this time away. He would tell her little or nothing about the years between, how he had come to look so downtrodden, so ill, so very thin. There was a curving scar, low on his chest, crisscross markings, faint, where the stitches had been removed. A bruise, old and yellow, which clung deep to his left thigh.

Soft against her, Peter stirred and she stroked his head, what little remained of his hair; soft it was, like a baby's hair.

Don't let me think of Nicky, Norma prayed, don't let me think of him. Or of Michael, my lovely baby son.

Don't let me think of that.

Not any of that.

She turned, careful, onto her side and ran her other hand along Peter's flank, his skinny buttock, the knobs of spine cresting his curving back. She rested her head toward his and closed her eyes, seeking sleep.

24

The youth eyed the contents of the plate with suspicion. A sausage cob, more than a little mauled in transit, brown sauce sticking it to the skimpy paper napkin in which it had been wrapped.

"What?" Divine said, no more yet than a hint of aggression. Push it, Resnick had said, push him a little.

"What?" the youth said back. He could have been any age between seventeen and twenty-five and already he had admitted to both twenty-one and nineteen. His face was framed by a scrubby haze of beard, a few reddening pustules below his right cheekbone, whiteheads massing above his nose and across his brow. There was a small gold ring through the upper part of his left ear. He was wearing a combat-type jacket, gray cotton trousers, several T-shirts, one over the other, the uppermost bearing the exhortation NUKE THE WHALES!

Alongside Divine, jacket unbuttoned, top button of his

shirt unfastened above the knot of his woolen tie, Millington kept his counsel and said nothing.

"That's what you asked for, isn't it?" Divine asked. "Sausage cob."

"Not like that."

"You don't like the sauce or what? Don't like the sauce, scrape it off."

"It's nothing to do with the sauce, the sauce is fine."

"What, then?"

"Onions."

"What onions?"

"Exactly."

Leaning forward, carefully using middle finger and thumb, Divine eased back the top half of the roll. "No onions."

"That's what I mean."

"Do you think," Millington said, stirred to action, tapping the end of a Lambert and Butler on the surface of the table, "when all this culinary discussion is through, we could make a start?"

"You going to eat that?" Divine, pointing at the cob. "Or not?"

The youth shook his head.

Sliding the plate toward him, Divine reopened the roll, picked up the folded sausage, dabbled it around in the wash of brown sauce, and, a defiant glint in his eyes, brought it to his mouth. "Last chance?" Too late, the sausage disappeared into his mouth, two, three bites and it was gone, all save for a nodule of gristle that he delicately extracted from between his teeth and deposited back inside the cob, the whole of which, napkin included, he tipped from the plate into the metal bin beside his chair, where it landed with a soft but satisfying thump.

"This interview," Millington said, having just switched on the tapes, "timed at two twenty-three. Present are Detective

Sergeant Millington, Detective Constable Divine, and Mr. St. John."

Out of politeness, Divine stifled a belch.

Millington leaned in a fraction more toward the youth. "State your full name."

"You know my name."

Oh God, Divine thought, he's going to be one of those. Like the onions, all the way through.

"Full name," Millington said again.

"John Anthony Lawrence St. John."

Divine choked back a snort.

"Address?"

"I have none."

"Address?"

Just for a moment, light shone in the youth's eyes. "Wherever I lay my hat is home."

Smart-arsed bastard, Divine thought.

"Tell us," Millington said encouragingly, "about where you laid your hat on Saturday night."

Reg Cossall and his team were diligently knocking on doors. So far they had been mistaken for Jehovah's Witnesses, Seventh-Day Adventists, a succession of distant aunts and uncles, and supervisors from the cable-laying company who'd called to announce one of the workmen had put his spade through the electric again and the power would be off for the best part of an hour. Once problems of identification were sorted out, they generally received surprise, sympathy, a great deal of attention, but no definite leads.

"There *was* a noise, wasn't there, Geoff? An awful kerfuffle. I remember we switched off the TV, came out to have a look." A big woman in her fifties, this, Cossall himself the caller, along with a young DC; their house, on the embankment, backed onto the path near which Aston's body had been found. "Geoff?" She seemed agitated, her hands in and out of the patch pockets of her red and green apron, her mind, maybe, half on whatever she had left simmering on the stove. "When was that, Geoff? Getting on for eleven o'clock, is that when it was? About eleven o'clock?"

Geoff appeared in the hallway, *Telegraph* splaying over his hand, part of it, glasses tipped to the end of his nose.

"Yobs, that's all they are. Plain and simple. It's the same here every Saturday night now; come tipping out the pub, hooting and hollering and carrying on. And the kind of language they use, it beggars belief. But just yobs, nothing more. The sort your lot let have the run of the streets so the rest of us have to stay inside and lock our doors."

What, instead of boogying off down the disco, Cossall thought, swiveling the old lady's hips around the floor? Couple of cherry brandies and whip her back home for a little of the old adagio on the living-room carpet. He doubted if their carpet had seen more than lemon-scented shampoo and a good hoovering since it had first been laid.

"And the time, sir," Cossall said. "Can you be a bit more precise?"

"Like the wife said, in the region of eleven o'clock. Eleven-thirty. You can check your *Radio Times* or whatever, *Match of the Day*, that's what was on. That Scottish fellow, Hanson, too much of a know-all for my liking. And you can't understand half of what he says."

It was the same story all along: there had been a rowdy element fooling about on the embankment between eleven and eleven-thirty, but after that they had gone, made off across the playing fields toward the Meadows, several reports suggested. And good riddance. Two households mentioned a sports car revving its engine loudly at around midnight; one other seemed to recall hearing a motorbike with a faulty silencer. It could have been the same thing.

What this first trawl failed to deliver was anything that tied in with the attack on Bill Aston; but this was only the beginning, Cossall knew that. Once the pubs had been leafleted, the local media had done their work, it would be different, he was certain. A man brutally attacked only a hundred yards from houses, little more than that from a busy main road, someone must have seen or heard something, it stood to reason.

Suddenly it was warm. In Resnick's office, at least. A large blue fly, lazy and fat, had woken from its long sleep and now buzzed the corners of the room, bumped with soft, persistent spats against the glass that looked out over nothing much.

"This is everything? There's nothing more?" Resnick dropped the last stapled sheaf of papers down among the rest.

Khan responded to the implicit criticism by tugging at the cuffs of his shirt, sitting straighter in his chair. "The preliminary interviews, yes. Transcribed from tape."

"Preliminary? You were planning to interview some of these again?"

"It was a contingency, sir, yes. If necessary."

"And?"

Khan smoothed the palms of both hands along the tops of his legs; warm in there and he was starting to sweat. Soon, he thought, he would be able to smell it; how he hated that.

"I'm sorry, sir, I don't fully understand what it is you're asking."

"What I'm asking"—Resnick trying not to sound irritable, but doing so all the same—"is were there any definite plans, did Inspector Aston intend to speak again, officially, to any of these people?"

Khan took his time; the fly, which had lain silent for a while, started up again. I shall either have to roll up that copy of the *Post* and kill it, Resnick thought, or prize open the window and let it out.

"No, sir," Khan finally said. "Not that I was aware."

"No conclusions here as to why Nicky Snape took his life."

"No, sir."

"And no blame."

"Sir?"

"No culpability attached to any of the staff. No blame."

"No, sir. That's correct."

Is it? Resnick wondered. Maybe it is. At the fourth attempt he levered the lower half of the window far enough upward and used the newspaper to shoo out the fly. "How do you feel about that? Did you feel everyone was being honest, telling the truth? Nothing to cover up?"

Khan's briefs were beginning to stick uncomfortably to his skin; he had to stop himself from easing his body up from the chair and pulling them free. "Inspector, I'm not sure . . ."

"What I'm getting at?"

"No, no. I think I understand that. But . . ."

"But Bill Aston was a senior officer and he has just been tragically killed."

"Yes."

"You don't want to be thought of as disloyal."

"That's correct."

Resnick pushed enough paper aside to make room on the side of his desk and sat looking at the young officer's face; waiting for Khan to look at him.

When he did, Resnick said, "In your own words, what this represents is the basis of a preliminary report. There's nothing here to say that, had he lived, Inspector Aston would not have taken some of this further. He mentioned to me, for instance, he thought supervision on the night of Nicky's death might have been considered slack. Paul Matthews and Elizabeth Peck, I believe that's right."

Khan nodded yes.

"You were present, at their interviews?"

187

"Yes, sir."

"And what was your feeling? Did you think they might have had anything to hide?"

"Matthews, he was nervous. Stuttering all the time, you know. Not stuttering exactly, but stumbling more, over his words."

"And the woman? Peck?"

"Defensive. Yes, that's what I thought. Resentful, as if we shouldn't have been questioning her at all."

"All right." Resnick was back on his feet. "What you do is this. Try and find out when the Social Services Inspectorate are planning to publish their report. Given what happened to Inspector Aston, you might be able to get some idea of which way they're shading, if they think there are any serious causes for concern. Then contact Jardine. Tell him we'll almost certainly need to come back and talk to his people again. Try not to get his back up, get him alarmed. You could always say that there are a few odds and ends need tidying up. In the circumstances, he should buy that. Okay? You can handle all that?"

For the first time Khan felt able to smile. "Yes, sir. Of course."

"Good lad." And, as Khan was opening the door, "There may be no connection, between the attack on Bill and any of this. Ninety-nine percent, there is none. None at all. But we have to be sure."

25

Resnick noticed that Lynn seemed to be wearing more makeup, a dash of color, blue-green, above the eyes. Lipstick, not heavy, not accentuated, but there. A thin roll-neck top under a light check jacket, comfortable skirt. She took off the jacket once she'd opened the car door and draped it along the rear seat. At the passenger side, Resnick clicked his belt tight. He wondered whether she might have started seeing someone again, a man; maybe she was just beginning to feel better about herself. He hoped that was the case. It was no more than she deserved.

A quick adjustment to the mirror and they were pulling out into traffic, heading down toward the city center, the southbound road out toward the bridge.

"His wife," Lynn asked, "Bill Aston's, what's she like?"

Resnick described her: he remembered a shortish woman, not especially lively, but a good listener. Those occasions he had met her socially, police functions, she had kept pretty much in her husband's shadow, but whenever he had been to the house, more relaxed, she had been the one who talked, Bill fading into the background, clearing dishes, making sure the drinks were filled.

"A nice woman," Resnick said. "Straightforward, sensible."

"Kids?"

"Two, I think. No, three. Grown up and left home. One somewhere like Canada, Australia." He seemed to recall that one of them had married, but couldn't remember which. "You know, I didn't really know him that well. The family. We'd not had a lot of contact these past few years."

Lynn made a slight nod with her head, concentrating on the driver in front, who couldn't seem to make up his mind which lane he was supposed to be in. Trent Bridge was only a few hundred yards ahead. You could see the spot where Aston's body had been found, still staked out, cordoned off.

"We haven't come up with any kind of weapon?"

"Not as yet."

There was a lot of water down there, flowing quite fast beneath the bridge.

The young man who came to the door looked enough like his father for Resnick not to wonder who he was. Terry Aston had inherited Bill's facial expression, the color of his eyes, already the same peaking of the hair; he had enough of his mother's genes to be shorter, stockier, set foursquare on the ground. He had traveled up with his wife and eighteen-month-old son from where they lived outside Bedford: Terry, a computer programmer with sidelines in home brewing and ornithology; his wife, Moira, a legal secretary who still temped at ten pounds an hour those mornings when Steven was with the nanny.

Terry Aston shook hands with Resnick, accepting his condolences, nodded a shade awkwardly at Lynn Kellogg, and led the two officers through the house into the living room.

"I'll tell Mum you're here."

Resnick had thought Margaret Aston might have been in bed, resting, somewhere out of the light, alone with her thoughts. But through the French windows, he could see her bending to deadhead one of the early roses, her grandson behind her, running and falling, arms akimbo, onto the graveled path. Stifling his squawl of tears, Margaret scooped him into her arms and held him tight against her, shh-shhhing into his blond hair, until his mother came hurrying and took him from her, hoisting him high into the air and turning tears to laughter. Crushed against Margaret's chest, the white petals of the rose fell aimless to the ground.

"Inspector Resnick?"

The girl who came toward him from the doorway had to be nineteen, possibly twenty, but looked younger, fair hair pulled loosely back, wearing a cream shirt under faded dungarees; the eyes with which she regarded Resnick were alert and half-amused; the hand she offered was smooth and small-boned inside his.

"You don't remember me, do you?"

Resnick looked at her again. "You're Stephanie?"

"Not a bad try. Actually, it's Stella. But I still don't think you really remember."

Resnick shook his head.

"You came here with Dad. I think I was eleven, something like that. Maybe twelve. I remember pestering you about how you got to be a policeman. On and on. It's all I wanted to be at the time, all I could think of, and Dad, well, he wouldn't talk about it. Said it was the last thing in the world I should do. No job for a girl, that's what I remember him saying, it's not a job for a girl." She looked across at Lynn. "Do you think he was right?"

"It depends."

"What on?"

Lynn realized she wasn't certain. If there was an easy

answer, she couldn't call it to mind. "I suppose it depends what kind of a woman you are. But then we all have different ideas, don't we? About what work should be."

"And women," Stella said.

Lynn looked back at her, saying nothing. There was a clear smile at the sides of Stella's mouth, the corners of her eyes.

"But you do like it?" Stella asked. "You enjoy what you do?"

"Most of the time, yes."

"Good. It must be terrible, stuck in some job you can't stand. Boring, nine to five."

"Well"—Lynn smiled—"this certainly isn't that."

"Is it something you're still considering?" Resnick asked. "Coming on the Job?"

Stella laughed. "I think all my dad's propaganda must have worked." Almost apologetically, she looked at Lynn. "He thought it was man's work, I'm afraid. Men of six foot and over." She smiled a little wistfully. "Bit of a traditionalist, Dad, where gender roles are concerned."

Resnick looked into her face for a sign of what she was feeling, talking about her father as she was; she was forcing herself to do so, he thought, making herself talk about him that way in order to keep him alive.

"What are you doing?" Lynn asked.

"I'm at agricultural college."

"You're going to be a farmer?"

Stella shook her head. "Trees. That's what I'd like to do eventually. Get into forestry. Grow trees. Hundreds of them. Thousands."

Lynn was grinning broadly.

"What?" Stella asked. "What's the matter?"

"Nothing. I was just wondering where that came on the list of traditional women's jobs. Not very high, I don't suppose."

"Dad said I'd grow out of it." Stella laughed again. "A

phase I was going through. Bless him, he didn't really understand. Not that or a lot of other things."

She was smiling at Lynn as her mother walked into the room. "All that jollity," Margaret Aston said, "I wondered what on earth was going on."

Stella stepped back, guiltily silent; the smile disappeared. As Resnick moved forward to greet her, Margaret's good intentions evaporated and her brave front collapsed in tears.

"I'm sorry," she said, again and again, as Resnick hovered, uncertain, awkward, offering her a handkerchief, which she refused. "I kept telling myself I wouldn't do this, create a scene."

"Mum," Stella said, "it's okay to cry."

Her mother dabbed at her eyes with a wad of damp tissue, blew her nose, pushed automatically at the ends of her hair. "Time enough for that later. It's not what Charlie's here for, is it, Charlie?" She sniffed. "I'm sure there are questions to be asked, isn't that right? Work to be done."

"Mum . . ." Stella started.

"No. It's what your father would have wanted. Eh, Charlie? It's what Bill would have wanted done."

They had gone out into the garden, the house too cramped for Margaret, too confining, too full of her husband's memory, her grandson's shrill laughter and sudden tears. She had told them all that she could remember, most of what they wanted to know. Bill's early-morning swim, the journeys they had made together to the supermarket and then to the garden center, later in the day. The letter from Nuneaton, inviting Bill to preach on Sunday fortnight; the phone calls from Stella and from their middle child, the son out in Australia, and the call that Bill had taken in the hall, somebody who'd rung him and he'd phoned them back, talked for quite a while, something else to do with his church work, she supposed, Bill hadn't said.

Standing now near the bottom hedge, the three of them, Margaret, Resnick, and Lynn, they were for that moment a silent tableau, while around them, the electric hum of unseen lawn mowers rose up and merged with the dulled roar of a passing plane.

"He was angry, Charlie, you can understand that. These last few years. He felt he'd been passed over; he'd given them everything he had and they didn't want any more, so they hid him away in that wretched place. Offices with closed doors." She smiled. "You knew him, Charlie, better than most. He wanted to be out there, doing things. Real things. Work that mattered. That's what he believed in. He thought that it mattered, what he did. That it made a difference." She half-turned away, shaking her head. "That doesn't mean anything, though, does it? Not anymore. Not now. What you feel. That's old-fashioned. Belief. Values. He was a dinosaur, Bill. That's what he was; he embarrassed them."

"Margaret, no . . ."

"He embarrassed them and that's why they shut him away and waited for him to die."

"Margaret . . ."

"And now this . . ."

"Of course, we . . ."

"All this . . ." She was facing him again, eyes raw not with loss but anger. "All this performance, this great paraphernalia, all of you like headless chickens running around. 'Who did this? Who did this? Isn't it tragic? Terrible?' Of course, it's terrible. He was my husband. But it's what you wanted all along."

"Margaret, you know that's not true."

"Isn't it? Not you, maybe. You personally. But the rest of them, all those smart young men—and women—with their smart young attitudes and sociology degrees. They don't care about him, none of them. Not a one."

"Mrs. Aston," Lynn said, "we'll catch whoever did this, we will."

Margaret Aston looked at her long and hard, this young woman who could almost have been her daughter, so earnest, believing what she said. "And if you do," Margaret said, "what difference will that make? What difference will that make now?"

Resnick waited till they were back in the car. "That call, the one unaccounted for. Have it checked out, the number. Just in case."

26

It turned out that John Anthony Lawrence St. John had walked away from a place on the second year of an undergraduate course in applied mathematics at Bristol University—outside of Oxford and Cambridge, one of the most difficult to get into. His tutor had been convinced that John Anthony Lawrence was on his way to a first; one year for his master's and then the Ph.D. A research fellowship for the asking. Before that, he had left his secondary school in Buckinghamshire—a grammar school, that county being just about the only one in which they still had a right to exist—with four high-grade A levels and ten O's. Glory, glory all the way.

"What buggers me," Divine said, "he's got all that going for him, all those brains, what's he doing, chucking it all away?"

Divine was in the canteen with Graham Millington, tucking into bacon, double egg, and chips and beans, his earlier purloined sausage having sharpened his appetite more than a touch. Opposite him, Millington was slowly forking his way through a meat-and-potato pie that had spent too long in the microwave and whose contents now bore startling affinity to slurry.

"Fancy it yourself, then, do you?" Millington asked. "Groves of academia?"

"Bollocks."

"Well," Millington said, "I suppose that's a point of view."

Divine dashed a large mouthful of egg and beans down with a quick swill of tea. "The way I see it, he's so much sodding cleverer than me, he should be out there using it, making a whole lot more money, right? Sight more'n you or me. Instead of which, here am I, bringing in little enough as it is, all those deductions, national insurance, tax, some of which is going to keep him on the dole 'cause he's too fucking lazy to work."

"His choice," Millington said.

"Live off you and me? Yeah, thanks a lot!"

Millington pushed his plate aside and reached for a cigarette; one of life's little miracles, he was thinking, no matter how much radiation or whatever you zap those pies with in the microwave, there were always those few bits of gristle left intact, like pearls. "Only thing need interest us," he said, "what he told us about finding Aston, it all holds up. Thank him for his help and kick him free."

"Aye." Divine nodded his head. "More's the sodding pity."

The river police had two divers working off their launch, searching the Trent either side of the bridge for a possible weapon or weapons. So far they had come up with two spools of the type frequently used by fishermen, several discarded rods, the rusted frame of a Raleigh bicycle, one picnic hamper, four nasty-looking knives, one of which had several triangular sections chipped out of the blade, a child's tricycle, roller skates, assorted pots and pans, a filing cabinet still containing fifty or so manila files, most likely rolled down the slope from County Hall by a disgruntled clerk, and a sawn-off double-barreled shotgun, which was proving of great interest to the detectives investigating a three-month-old robbery at a bank on Gregory Boulevard. Nothing that might have been used in the attack on Bill Aston.

Forensic had recovered sufficient splintered fragments from the dead man's skull and face to be certain that the weapon involved had been a varnished implement, most likely a baseball bat of some kind. Even in this country where the game was comparatively rarely played, such bats were more and more the preferred weapon.

And blood: quite minute, difficult at first to detect, there were small samples of a second type mixed in with Aston's. As soon as it was properly isolated, it could be checked against the recently established, steadily growing national DNA bank.

The Support Department had gone over the ground with a fine-tooth comb. Dog turds, cigarette ends and discarded cigarette packets, fast-food containers, used condoms and the like notwithstanding, they had come up with only two items of potential interest: a D90 TDK audiocassette tape, unlabeled, which seemed to hold a fairly arbitrary selection of home-taped heavy metal, and a large-sized left-hand leather glove, well-worn, scuffed around the finger ends and smooth in the palm. Both of these items were undergoing further tests.

Scene of Crime had presented Naylor with evidence, mostly partial, of twenty-seven sets of footprints within the immediate vicinity of the attack. A chart showing the positioning of these was still in the later stages of completion, but it already seemed to suggest that of the twenty-seven, nine were strongly present close to where the body had fallen; of that nine, five seemed to have partly circled around it. The impressions of three of these had been made by some kind of running shoe, one by a heavy work boot, the last most likely came from a regular rubber-soled walking shoe.

After being successfully put off by Phyllis Parmenter's secretary for the best part of a day, Khan had installed himself in the outer offices of the local authority inspectorate and settled down with a copy of Vikram Seth's one-thousand-and-five-hundred-odd-page novel, intent upon a long wait.

The WPC walking away from Cossall had an arse on her like a pregnant duck. Cossall's words, though he kept them to himself and supped his pint; all this questioning—publicans and bar staff—it gave a man a thirst. And besides, where women on the force were concerned, nowadays it paid to keep your mouth closed.

He knew a sergeant at one of the outstations, not so much above a month back, who had chanced to make some innocuous remark about a female officer within her hearing and, within an hour of her lodging an official complaint, poor sod had been suspended from duty, pending an investigation. A sure sign of the way it was going, Cossall thought, the writing on the menstrual bloody calendar.

Only that morning he had read in the paper, the first ever woman chief constable had been appointed in Lancashire. A few years shy of fifty and, wouldn't you know it, a graduate from the Open University. And what was her degree in? Psychology. Cossall had read she'd be bringing in over seventy thousand a year salary. Seventy thousand. And a budget of close to a hundred and fifty million to dispose of. How much of that was going to go on setting up crèches, that's what he'd like to know? Counseling sessions? Hiring some poncey interior designer to put in soft furnishings and curtains in the interview rooms, create a more trusting atmosphere.

Still, what had she been quoted as saying? It's never been a man's world, they only think it is. Yes, well, that's where she was wrong: Cossall didn't think, he knew. At least until he chucked it all in, threw in his hand with one of them home security firms, it was his world still.

And if that WPC ever made it to the top, they'd have to buy her a specially reinforced chair. Not that, he reflected, he'd say no to charvering it from behind. Nice tits, too, sort of stretch Dunlopillo, wouldn't mind spreading himself over those. He'd thought that when she first walked in looking for him ten minutes before, Cossall lubricating his tonsils between visiting the pubs along London Road, spaced out between Trent Bridge and the city. Football pubs, most of them; big trade of a Saturday whichever side was at home, Forest or County.

"So what are you telling me, love," Cossall had asked, "the landlord won't talk to you, is that it?"

"He'll talk, right enough. Talk the hind legs off that donkey. It's what he won't say bothers me." No hesitation, coming right back at him, giving as good as she got, Cossall liked her for that. Local, too. That accent. Mansfield, somewhere roundabout. "Take, for instance, there's a couple of windows broken, right? Stuck together with tape, like he's waiting for them to be properly fixed. Well, that's recent, right? And when I had a shufti round back, there's a couple of chairs there, broken, slung out. But when I tried to ask him about them, any of that, he wasn't having any, just wasn't saying. I thought you might get more out of him."

Cossall nodded. "Right, thanks. I'll get right along." And winked. "I'd get you a drink, love, only you're on duty."

She lowered her voice so no one along the bar would hear.

"If I weren't, I'd buy one for myself. But thanks, love, all the same."

Cossall held back his grin until she had turned away and then watched her all the way to the door, an arse on her like a pregnant duck.

He walked off the street into the main bar of the pub; two men in working clothes were sitting off by the back window, Irish, Cossall could tell without knowing them, something about their complexion, broad, high brows, the natural wave at the front of the hair. An Irish pub, is that what this was?

He eased one of the high stools far enough out from the bar to sit down. Through in the side room, he could see a black youth in white T-shirt and dreadlocks, long baggy shorts and high-top trainers, playing himself at pool. No, an equal-opportunity pub, that's what it was.

"What'll you have?" the landlord asked, appearing at the end of the bar and coming slowly toward him. He was a tall man, rangy, with a flattened face that was more like a child's drawing than the real thing.

Cossall told him and watched the man draw a pint, showing him his warrant card when he set the glass before him. With a generous movement of his hand, the landlord waved Cossall's money away.

"I had one of your lot in here earlier," the landlord said.

Cossall nodded. "Tell me about Saturday night." He could see the windows the officer had spoken of, down toward where the two men were sitting, glass cobwebbed over with brown tape.

"I told her."

Cossall tasted the beer, grimaced and shook his head. "If you'd told her, you wouldn't be standing there looking at me. If you don't tell me, tonight you'll be looking at two others like me; and tomorrow there'll be four and so it goes." He set the glass back down. "That's not what you want."

The landlord forced a laugh. "All this over a pane of broken glass and a few lousy chairs?"

Cossall leaned far enough forward for the man to feel his breath on his face. "We had an officer killed, not a few hundred yards from here. Saturday night."

"But that has nothing to do with this."

"Why don't you," Cossall said, "let me be the judge of that?"

The landlord pushed a glass against the optic and gave himself a large Jameson's; sipped at it before, elbow leaning on the bar, he spoke. "These youths come in sometimes, you know, match days. Skinheads, mostly. Lot of noise, swearing and that, but they spend well, so most times I let it go. But this week, one of them gets into an argument with one of the Paddies that use the place all the time. Regulars, like. Well, one thing these lads can't stand, more than the blacks, even, it's the Irish. Just hate them. IRA truce or no truce, it doesn't matter a damn. And this gives them an excuse. One minute these two are squaring up to one another, a bit of pushing and shoving, you know how it goes; next thing, this skinhead's mates start in and before you know it the whole pub's like the last round of a Frank Bruno fight with no holds barred." He drank a little more of the whiskey and wiped the back of his hand across his mouth. "I doubt if it lasted more than ten minutes at most."

"You called it in? Called the police?"

"And risk my license? It's not worth it. That's why I didn't want to say anything before."

"You've been warned, then?"

"Once or twice."

Cossall nodded. "These youths, know them well enough to know any names?"

Slowly, the landlord shook his head.

"D'you notice where they went from here?"

"No. But if I was to guess, I'd say on down toward the Trent."

"And that's all it is, a guess?"

"Afraid so, yes."

Cossall took a final swallow at his pint and pushed the glass away unfinished. "Here." He took a card from his top pocket and set it down on the bar. "If you do hear a name, or if one comes to mind, give us a call." He winked. "It'll count for you, not against. Won't do any harm, someone in your corner, eh?"

The landlord watched Cossall till he was through the door, swallowed down what remained of his whiskey, and allowed himself another. He'd as soon count on a copper like Cossall, he thought, as back himself to win the lottery without buying a ticket.

27

Resnick was on his way back from the superintendent's office when Lynn intercepted him with her analysis of Bill Aston's movements and contacts during the last twenty-four hours of his life.

"It's pretty much all there," she said, businesslike, not quite looking Resnick in the eye. "One or two gaps I still have to fill."

Resnick gave the first sheet a quick glance. "Anything that looks helpful?"

"Afraid not. Trips to the supermarket and the garden center, that's about it. The pool. Walking the dogs."

Resnick nodded, skimming the remainder. A day in the life of a quite ordinary, not especially interesting man. What was interesting about Aston was that he was dead: the manner of his dying.

"Okay, thanks."

"There's one more thing," Lynn said. "You remember you

asked me to track down that call Aston made the day of his death? The one that was unaccounted for."

Resnick looked at her expectantly and she pushed a folded piece of paper into his hand. He opened it, looked thoughtfully at the name, then folded it again before pushing it down into his breast pocket.

"There were two other calls, too. Unanswered, but logged in Aston's office."

"Right. Good." And then, as Lynn turned away, "Are you okay?"

She nodded, still not directly looking at him. "I'd like to take an hour later, personal time?"

"Fine."

They continued their separate ways, Resnick along the corridor toward the CID room, Lynn making for the stairs. Whatever else, Resnick was thinking, she's right about one thing—all this stuff that's troubling her, it doesn't seem to be interfering with her work.

The meeting with Skelton had not been encouraging. One of his best hopes had been that the second blood sample taken from Aston's clothes, the blood that wasn't Aston's own, would prove to have come from someone who was known. But Jane Prescott had checked the records available to Intelligence, made comparisons with all known and processed samples. Nothing. No match. Which left the shoe prints, the cassette, and—most outside of all outside chances—the bat. After that, they were down to information received, unearthing a witness who had seen or heard more than anyone had so far come forward to say. The media appeals had brought in replies, of course, and these were being processed through the computer and the more promising laboriously checked out. But so far . . .

Sheer accident, Bill Aston's murder? An unfortunate victim who happened to be in the wrong place at the wrong time, or was there a more specific motive? Resnick thought again about the name Lynn had given him and was glad he had already arranged to meet Khan and discuss the Snape inquiry. If there was a connection there, he had to tease it out.

Reg Cossall was waiting for him in his office, using an empty coffee mug as an ashtray. With a degree of show, Resnick unfastened the window catch and lifted the lower frame high, before sitting down and gesturing with a hand to indicate Cossall should do the same.

"This could be nothing, Charlie. . . ."

"I doubt that, Reg. If you thought that, you'd not be here."

Cossall smiled his quick, lopsided smile and retold the story of his meeting with the publican on London Road, gracing it with not a few embellishments of the scatological kind. A canny copper, Reg, Resnick was thinking, a man content to wear his prejudices on his sleeve, a glint in his eye like steel as if daring rebuke. Someone like Aston—similar age, equal seniority—they had been able virtually to discard, lost in the shuffle. But Cossall was too valuable, his experience too wide and his arrest rate too high.

"I checked back with the chap on the embankment who'd been moaning on about having his Saturday-night soccer disturbed. He's still not positive, but the youths he saw creating a disturbance, they could be the same ones from the pub. Only could, mind. There's a couple of other reports I'm having checked now, might get confirmation."

Resnick turned it over. A strong possibility, it was true. "This fight in the pub, fracas, whatever. No way we can place any of them with something like a baseball bat?"

Cossall narrowed his eyes and shook his head. " 'Fraid not. But it's got to be a runner, my way of thinking. Specially since we've got Jack-shit else. These blokes, kids, not much more, out on the street, all pumped up from the scene in the pub, tanked up, too. Maybe Bill said something to them, you know how he was. Bit high and mighty, holier than thou, could've told them to keep their mouths down, behave. I can see that, see him doing that, can't you?"

Yes. Yes, Resnick could. He'd been in contact with Bill's Sunday-school manner more than a few times. He'd had more than a tendency toward sermonizing, had Bill. "You want to chase it down, Reg, or what?"

Cossall leaned back, cigarette spooling smoke up from between the fingers of a crooked hand. "Like I said, there are a few things I'm checking into. But keeping on top of all that stuff the computer's spewing out doesn't leave a lot of time."

"I'll have a word with Graham, see if he can help. But this landlord, you think leaning on him some more might loosen his tongue? You think he might know exactly who these youths are?"

"He might. And I'll do what I can." Cossall winked. "Within the rules."

"Divine's got a mate with the Football Intelligence Unit," Resnick said as Cossall walked toward the door. "Might be a contact worth following up. These lads might well be known to them, by the sound of it."

"If they are"—Cossall grinned—"I doubt they'll be County supporters, eh? Need to be drawing your pension, don't you, 'fore they'll as much as let you in the ground?"

With a sly laugh, Cossall was on his way, leaving Resnick standing beside his desk, picturing the group of young supporters at the last match he had attended. They had been lined up at the back of the stand, Union Jack draped from the wall behind them, raised fists clenched toward the opposition, one of them shielding his face inside a balaclava. He could hear their shrill young voices, lofted in anger. "No surrender! No surrender!"

It had looked more like news footage from Northern

Ireland, a Loyalist rally, than an otherwise tame end-of-season encounter near the foot of the Endsleigh League First Division.

Two of the phones in the CID room were in use as Resnick walked through, late for his meeting with Khan, and when the third phone rang it was Lynn, on her way back in, who picked it up.

"Lynn Kellogg, CID." Working on autopilot, not over-friendly today. And then, as she held the receiver toward Resnick, "For you."

He pointed toward his watch and shook his head.

Lynn brought the receiver back toward her and asked who was calling. "Hannah Campbell," she said, mouthpiece covered now with her hand.

Surprised at hearing the name, Resnick felt himself beginning to flush. He started toward the desk but stopped short, changed his mind. "Tell her," he said, "I'll call her later."

"Later this afternoon or . . . ?"

"Probably this evening."

She was looking at him now, interested. "Shall I get a number?"

"No." Resnick over his shoulder, departing. "It's all right. No need."

Lynn asked anyway, a matter of procedure. Resnick was already descending stairs, two at a time, angry with himself for feeling embarrassed, remembering without pleasure what it had felt like to be twenty-three or -four.

For his meeting with Resnick, Khan had worn a blue-black blazer, lightweight wool, tan trousers, highly polished brown shoes. His tie, a deep dull red, almost rust, was one that Jill had given him a month after their second date and the first time they had slept together.

"What's this all about?" he had asked, amused.

"Call it an anniversary, if you like."

"Starting off as we mean to carry on, is it?"

"Something like that."

One month later he had given her a pair of minute white bikini briefs, with tiny bows at the sides, blue, he had said, to match her eyes.

She had punched him, surprisingly hard, on the arm; so hard the bruise didn't fade for days. "My eyes are brown."

Khan laughed. "How should I know? One way or another, they're usually closed."

This time he had caught the fist inside his palm. They were sitting in Jill's living room, TV and stereo both switched off so that they could hear any of her kids if they woke and decided to come downstairs.

Khan was thinking about that now, what had happened next, how it was possible, right down to those last moments, to stay quiet, when he saw Resnick hurrying up the short flight of steps and through the door leading into reception. He had imagined they would talk there, one of the rooms, temporarily spare, at central station, but Resnick insisted that they walk the short distance to the market, Resnick not really wanting to talk until he had downed his first espresso and ordered a second. Khan, not a great drinker of tea or coffee, content to sit and watch, watch and wait, the hubbub of trading all around them.

"Okay," Resnick finally said, "how far've we got?"

Khan told him that Phyllis Parmenter had given him a hundred reasons why she could not conceivably reveal the inspectorate's findings ahead of publication, then hinted quite heavily that in her view there had been no serious lapses in security, nor any reasons other than the balance of his own mind why Nicky Snape had taken his own life.

"And Jardine?"

"Defensive, basically. One minute almost aggressive, the next not able to do enough to help."

"Then he'd no objections to our re-interviewing the two staff on duty that evening?"

"None, but"—Khan smiled—"Paul Matthews is off sick, quite serious, Jardine says, doesn't know how long that might go on, and the woman, Elizabeth, er, Peck, she's on annual leave."

"Since when?"

"This last weekend apparently."

Resnick's second espresso gave hot chase to the first. "Come on," he said, getting to his feet. "I think we should pay Mr. Jardine a call."

"D'you want to ring him first? I could—"

But Resnick was already on his way. "Let's make it a surprise."

Sounds of Blur and Nirvana, identifiable to Khan if not to Resnick, squeezed from beneath a dozen doors. To the accompaniment of swearing and laughter, two youths played pool in one of the larger downstairs rooms, others sitting around watching, waiting their turn. In the television room, on a large-screen monitor, bought from the proceeds of a recent car boot sale and a sponsored run, another few were deep in shabby armchairs with a video recording of the previous season's Forest highlights. Good job it's not County's, Resnick thought, scarcely have time to settle back before you'd be reaching for the remote control, pressing rewind.

Jardine kept them waiting only five minutes and then greeted Resnick with a firm handshake, a surprising show of warmth. "Afraid we might have got off on the wrong foot last time, Inspector. Put it down to the strain of what had happened, shall we? But now, come in, come in. Please, sit down. Inspector, um, Constable, what can I get you? Tea? Coffee? Mineral water?"

Both Resnick and Khan declined. Khan took his notebook from his inside pocket as he sat down, uncapped his pen. The veins crisscrossing Jardine's face were even more pronounced, Resnick thought, than before. He let his eyes slide again along the rows of photographs on the wall, one at least for each year.

"Well, it looks as if, unofficially as yet of course, but it looks as if the report will put us in the clear. The staff here." Jardine treated them to his best PR smile, the one more normally saved for the occasional middle-class parent or visiting minor politicians. "I spoke with Mrs. Parmenter only an hour ago. Fortuitous, really. It seems as if she'll be giving us a clean bill of health." Abruptly, he leaned forward, arms resting on the surface of his desk, serious now, smile set aside. "Of course, it does nothing to minimize the awfulness of that boy's death."

If he expected agreement, a sharing of sympathy, congratulations even, he got nothing; Resnick let his weight ease back in the chair a little more and crossed his legs, deep creases in the trousers of his suit.

Nervous under Resnick's gaze, the director flicked at the dandruff on his shoulder, tugged at the lobe of an ear. He looked from Resnick to Khan and back again. "The, er, officer, DC Khan, explained there would be questions you might wish to put to me. . . ."

"Your staff."

"Sorry?"

"There are questions I need to put to your staff."

"Of course, if . . ."

"Mr. Matthews and Mrs., Miss Peck."

One of Jardine's hands swatted the air in Khan's direction. "As I explained to the young man here, unfortunately neither of them are currently available. . . ."

"Unfortunately?"

"I'm sorry, I . . ."

"You said, unfortunately."

"Yes, I . . ."

"Not fortunately?"

Jardine seemed to be suddenly short of breath. "Inspector, I don't see . . ."

"Miss Peck, she's on holiday?"

"Part of her annual leave, yes."

"Arranged a long time ago?"

Jardine's head swiveled partway toward the chart attached to the wall behind him, annotations and arrows, neat in colored inks. "Usually such things are arranged, you know, at the beginning of the year."

"So there was nothing sudden about Miss Peck's decision to take her leave now?"

"Oh, no."

The green lettering denoting her absence looked, to Resnick, remarkably new; he raised an eyebrow in Khan's direction and the DC made a note in his book.

"You've no idea, I suppose, where she's decided to take this leave? Abroad, maybe? At home, redecorating the bathroom, something like that?"

Jardine shook his head. "My staff, their private lives . . ." He shrugged, as though they could be none of his concern.

"And Mr. Matthews," Resnick said, relaxed still, quite relishing this, Jardine's discomfort, relishing it in a way that was unusual for him and perhaps not exactly understanding why. "I understand he's off sick?"

"I'm afraid so."

"Tummy bug? Flu? Something more serious?"

Jardine was giving his ear a little more attention; when his hand brushed, inadvertently, against his hair, another little fall of dandruff showered down.

"What is wrong with him, Mr. Jardine?"

"I believe the doctor's note mentioned nervous exhaustion."

"Brought on by what happened here to Nicky Snape?"

"The note gave no indication. . . ."

"But that's likely the reason, wouldn't you say?"

"I don't know if it's wise to conjecture. . . ."

"A member of your staff, you would have realized if he was unduly upset. He found the body, didn't he? That morning I spoke to him, he seemed distressed."

"Naturally. Paul is a very caring man. Dedicated." For a moment, Jardine's eyes switched anxiously toward Khan, as if unnerved by the movement of his pen. "Something like that, he would be bound to be affected."

Resnick was nodding agreement. "Then there's nothing else, no other reason that you can think of, no other cause for Mr. Matthews to be suffering from—what was the expression?—nervous exhaustion?"

"No."

"He wasn't apprehensive, for instance, about the results of the inquiry?"

Jardine shook his head. "He had no need to be. He would have known that. And rightly. As I said, Mrs. Parmenter—"

"I meant the police inquiry. DC Khan here. Inspector Aston."

"Certainly not."

"And Miss Peck, as far as you know, she wasn't unduly concerned about Inspector Aston's findings?"

"If she was, she certainly never expressed these concerns to me. Quite the reverse, in fact. After her interview, as I remember, she said that she thought it had been less of an ordeal than she had feared." Jardine was feeling secure enough to try a smile again. "I'm sure in no small way due to your colleague here."

Resnick nodded. "I see. You've no idea, then, why she left messages twice at Inspector Aston's office, or why, when she finally did get to speak to him at his home on the day that he died, they apparently talked for almost three quarters of an hour?"

Jardine's head dipped forward and he closed his eyes. You

crafty old bugger, Khan was thinking, looking across at Resnick, you sat on that one well enough.

"Mr. Jardine?" Resnick said.

A vein at the side of Jardine's head was beginning to throb. "I'm sorry, I know nothing about that at all." He held Resnick's stare for several moments. "I don't even know if it's true."

"I'd be obliged," Resnick said, getting to his feet, "if you would let DC Khan have some addresses and telephone numbers for both Mr. Matthews and Miss Peck. You might as well furnish them for the rest of the staff, while you're about it. I can't be sure how many I might need to speak to and it'll save time later on. Oh, and if you could arrange for a copy of that medical certificate you mentioned?"

Angry but uncertain, Jardine gave it a last try. "I don't see that you have any right, Inspector. . . ."

"Mr. Jardine"—Resnick leaning toward him, over him, his own anger taking over—"not only has a boy died while in your care, a police officer, the one looking into that death, has been murdered. Just how much right do you think I need?"

28

The first few times Lynn had seen Petra Carey it had been at the hospital, the psychiatric wing, a forlorn section toward the back, close to the kitchens. After that it had been in the large Victorian house the therapist shared with several others; group sessions were held in the lower rooms, individual consultations on the upper floors.

The room in which they met was arranged so that Lynn sat facing a high window, too high to see anything more than the top branches of trees across the broad street, snatches of roofs, the sky. There was a lot of sky. Lynn's chair was comfortable, but not too much so, with polished wooden arms and a back that curved away, a decently cushioned seat. Petra Carey sat to one side, a similar chair placed at right angles, a low square table between them which always held flowers; today they were yellow tulips, already beginning to bend and scoop their swanlike necks. Tulips or not, the room, Lynn thought, smelt of roses just the same. Was it Petra Carey's perfume or something that she sprayed into the air?

Sometimes Lynn would turn her head and look at the therapist when either of them spoke, but usually she stared ahead, following the slowly shifting kaleidoscope of clouds.

"So, Lynn, how are we today? How have you been since we last met?"

Always the same opening gambit, and always a pause, which seemed to her unnaturally long, before Lynn could bring herself to answer. So aware of the delicate ground on which she might be beginning to tread. "Fine. I've been fine. At least, I thought so."

"D'you want to tell me what's happened? What's caused you to change your mind?"

Petra Carey was, Lynn guessed, in her early thirties, not so very much older than Lynn herself, although, without perhaps meaning to, she made Lynn feel young, younger. Lynn was sure the room had something to do with it, that feeling of being summoned there; it reminded her of when she had been at school, the situation more than the room itself. Those occasions when she had been found wanting: you know, Lynn Kellogg, we expected better of you than this.

While Lynn framed her answer, the therapist waited patiently, her only jewelry the broad wedding ring on her left hand.

"The case I've recently started working on," Lynn said finally. "The policeman who was just killed. It's that. To do with that."

Petra nodded. "Go on."

Lynn told her about visiting the victim's family with Resnick, and Margaret Aston's reactions—her anger, the way even that had seemed controlled. And the daughter, Stella, telling them how she had wanted to join the police when she'd been younger; follow, Lynn supposed, in her father's footsteps. How it had been Resnick whom she had asked

216

about it. And now she was studying forestry, the daughter, agriculture, pining to go off and do things with trees.

Unusually, Petra Carey smiled.

"What?"

"Nothing, no, go on."

"But what's so funny?"

"Nothing's funny."

"Then why are you laughing?"

"I was smiling."

"What at?"

Touching her ring, forefinger and thumb, Petra Carey turned it around on her hand. "There's so much there, in that story."

"Tell me," Lynn said.

But the therapist shook her head. "That's not the way it goes."

And once Lynn had begun to talk, think it through as she spoke, she thought she could see why Petra Carey had been amused. It was all there, much of it, the things that had been worrying her. Niggling away. Undermining her ever since the time she had been held prisoner by that sick bastard; the first time he had spoken to her directly, after leaving the hospital in which her father was being treated for cancer. Her father, whom she had feared was dying. And here was Bill Aston, near enough her father's age, beaten to a pulp and leaving his wife and family to manage. Wife and daughter. The daughter who wanted to be a policewoman. "Oh, Lynnie!" Lynn remembered her own mother's disapproving cry. "No. No, please no." And, unlike Stella Aston, she had done it anyway, gone ahead and joined. And her father had got sick and now he was in remission. Lynn and her mother waiting, not saying, waiting for the cancer to come back.

"Yes," Petra Carey said once Lynn had finished speaking, "of course, you're right. It's no wonder it troubled you, all those similarities, echoes. Your fears about your father's health; that he might die and leave you. The guilt that persists about going against their wishes and joining the police, as if somehow that has contributed to your father's illness."

They had talked about that before, over and over, around and around—Lynn's sense of guilt. The therapist trying to maneuver her into seeing that her father's cancer was not her doing, there was no cause and effect. His sickness was not in Lynn's gift, not in her control.

"What else is there?" Petra Carey asked. Faint, from outside, electronic sound, drifting and melodic: one of the other therapists, she had explained, liked to use music with his patients, to have them lie on the couch, eyes closed, and think themselves back into the womb.

"What do you mean," Lynn asked, "what else?"

No reply: not quite silently, the clock continued to tick round. Fifty minutes, it wasn't long. At least, for maybe the first half it was; it seemed then as if the hand was hardly moving, as though everything had slowed almost to a halt. And then the final twenty minutes seemed to race. Always. Burdened by the pressure to say something, Lynn sometimes froze.

"What else," Petra Carey said, "do these two stories have in common? This man whose death you're investigating and your own. Is there a common factor we haven't talked about?"

"I suppose you mean *him*, don't you? My boss. That's what you're driving at." Lynn was close to anger now, a pinch of color in her cheeks.

"Inspector Resnick."

Lynn looked away.

"The daughter," Petra Carey said, "Stella, I think you said. What's her relationship to Resnick in this story you've told me?"

"I suppose she looked up to him. I mean, he's the one she

asked about the police, not her father. Even though her father's a policeman."

"And why do you think that might have been?"

Shaking her head, Lynn smiled; just a little, around the eyes. "Because he's her father. She sees him all the time. He's always there. Ordinary."

"And Charlie Resnick?"

"He's different. He's from outside. More, oh, I don't know, glamorous, I suppose you could say. Not so everyday."

"But he and her father, they were roughly the same age?"

"Round about."

"And Stella was how old?"

"Eleven, twelve."

"You think she could have had a crush on him?"

"Oh, now look." Alert, Lynn leaned forward in her chair, looking at the therapist directly.

"Yes?"

"I know what you're trying to get me to say."

"What's that?"

"Listen, I'm not eleven or twelve."

A small shrug of the therapist's shoulders, a disarming smile.

"And I don't have a crush on my boss. That's so stupid. It's not like that. It's not like that at all."

"All right," Petra Carey said, encouragingly. "What is it like?"

"It's not like anything."

The clock showed there were only two minutes to go; it was one of Petra's rules, she never overran.

"I don't see," Lynn was saying, "why it always has to keep coming back to this."

"It was your story." The therapist smiled quietly. "It was what you wanted to talk about today."

She was on her feet now. The session was over. But Lynn continued to look at her, stubbornly, from her chair. "It was

219

because of my dad, because I'm afraid of him dying. That's what made me think about it. That's why."

"I know that. That's clear."

"Well, then?"

The therapist was standing by the door, looking pointedly at the clock. Anger and distress were clear on Lynn's face and in the way she rose reluctantly from the chair and reached for her bag and coat.

"In your story," Petra Carey said, "the daughter, for whatever the reason, might not be able to express her love for her father, all of her love, so she offers it to his friend instead. A man who's like her father, an idealized version of her father. It's part of the normal pattern of growing up. Growing away. Little girls love their fathers. Usually, then, they replace them with other men. Because once you reach a certain age, that love of the father, part of that love, is associated with guilt. Society considers it inappropriate. But if that other man, the man to whom she, the girl, wants to give her love, is too much like her father, she may fall prey to the same taboo. What she ends up feeling is guilt. And guilt is a destructive feeling. It eats away at us from the inside, makes it impossible for us to act."

There were people moving around on the stairs outside. Lynn walked past the therapist toward the open door.

"I'll see you at the same time next week," Petra Carey said. "If you need to get in touch with me beforehand, please ring."

The music, wherever it had been coming from, had stopped. Partway down the carpeted stairs, Lynn swung her head around. The door to the therapist's room was already closed.

220

29

Hannah had devised strategies so as not to think about him, this big, bulky man with the sad eyes. That day, at work, it had not been too hard. The demands of thirty adolescents at a time, so often eager for anything but learning, failed to allow her much space for personal daydreaming. Her attempts to draw Nicky's former classmates into a discussion on gender politics, based around Lady Macbeth's cry of "Unsex me now," had foundered disastrously. But when, discussing with her sixth-form group one of her favorite Jayne Anne Phillips stories, in which a former dancer visits her dying father, she found herself thinking not about the restraint and control in the writing, but the surprising grace with which Resnick could walk across a room, she knew, restraint or not, she was going to call him the first chance she got. And when what she got was Lynn Kellogg's peremptory voice informing her that the inspector was busy and he would try to call her back later, Hannah thought it no more than she deserved.

Whatever had happened to cool?

Back home, she watered the tubs of flowers and the hanging baskets in the backyard, pulled a few weeds away from around the shrubs that were newly planted along one side of her small front garden, and considered cutting the grass; finally she brought out a mug of peppermint tea and the lemon cream biscuits she had bought on the way home, and sat on her front step, sweater round her shoulders, reading Marge Piercy. She found herself feeling so fiercely angry at the efforts the central character was prepared to make to hang on to a husband forever having affairs with younger women, that she forgot to ask herself if anger wasn't precisely what Piercy wanted her to feel.

When the phone called her indoors, a part of her sang with a sweet degree of expectation, but it was only her mother, and when the two women had talked long enough for Hannah to realize she was no longer listening, had not really heard anything her mother had said for at least five minutes, she made an excuse and hung up.

She took a ready-to-heat mushroom bake from the freezer and slid it into the microwave. After pouring herself a glass of wine, she began to make a list of all those fiddling little jobs she would do that evening, another of all the friends she should call.

Considering what it had cost, the wine was surprisingly good. The mushroom bake, as usual, was fine. Wanting some bread to go with it, and regretting that she had forgotten to stop for any on the way home—the biscuits had come from her corner shop, but the bread they stocked was pre-sliced and not worth considering—she found some oatcakes in the back of the cupboard, carefully enough wrapped that they had not lost all their bite.

The first two people she called were seemingly out and

Hannah declined their invitation to speak after the tone; the third was engaged, the fourth had for some reason been disconnected. In the living room she channel-hopped for all of five minutes before switching off. It was either too late or too early to take a bath. She would do some more reading, listen to the stereo. The way she was behaving was extraordinary: all right, she had slept with the man once, but it had not exactly been like Paul on the way to Damascus. No startling revelations, no blinding lights. Just competent, almost comfortable sex. She remembered to switch off the Gregson and Collister CD before it got to "Last Man Alive," but then realized she had listened three times in succession to "Baby, Now That I've Found You"—not the old original version by some pop group she vaguely remembered from when she was a child, but this new one, bluegrass, sung by Alison Krauss. Now that I've found you, dum, de-dum, dum, dum, da-dum, gonna build my life around you. Madness, Hannah was certain, that way comes. Time for a slow, hot bath and an early bed.

She was tipping in the peach and honey cream foam when the phone rang again.

"Oh," Hannah said, flushing, "it's you." And, "Yes, okay." And, "You want to come here?" And, "No, no, half an hour would be fine. Till then, okay, good-bye."

God, Hannah, she thought, checking the temperature of the water before slipping in, are you a cinch or what?

In the event, it was just short of the hour by the time Resnick's cab had dropped him off near the entrance to the recreation ground and he had walked along the shrouded strip of unmade road, once again past the house where Mary Sheppard had died. So many parts of this city from which Resnick now averted his eyes without ever being able to shut the images from his mind.

The front door to Hannah's house was open and his

adrenaline immediately began pumping, sensing an intruder, a burglary, something worse. But no, it was only Hannah, shooing a ginger cat along the narrow hallway, the animal pausing on the front step to look back at her balefully, ears flat to its head.

"Not yours, I take it?"

Hannah made a show of shuddering. "Can't stand them, I'm afraid. That one especially." Taking in Resnick while she was talking, the effort he had made to look informal, pale blue shirt, the top two buttons unfastened, light gray trousers, a dark tweedy jacket that had seen better days. "I woke up one night, not so long ago, that wretched animal must have sneaked in somehow and stayed—anyway, I heard this sound, just light, you know, but like someone else in the room, breathing, and there it was, stretched out on the bed next to me, paws right out, fast asleep."

"Some people," Resnick said, "would consider that an honor." It didn't come out sounding exactly the way it was meant, but like some corny line, the kind he could imagine coming from someone like Divine. "The cat, I mean," Resnick said, trying to retrieve the situation. "It must have felt comfortable, trusted you."

"Yes, well, when it comes to who's sharing my bed," Hannah said, "I like to do the choosing myself."

Resnick bent toward the animal, which was sitting there cleaning itself, unconcerned. Watching him stroke the cat's head, Hannah imagined him wearing one of those loose linen suits, creased and a little baggy, cream-colored, or, no, stone; that was it, stone.

She gave a wry smile. "You obviously don't feel the same way? About cats?"

"There's something easy to like about them. Independence, I think." The ginger one was now purring quite loudly, a little saliva issuing from its jaw. "I mean, they'll take any amount of this fuss, all you can give, but as soon as it's

224

over, that's that. It doesn't seem to matter if you never go near them again."

Not such a bad description, Hannah thought, of men. Some, at least, whom she'd known. "You've got one of your own?"

He did that smiling thing with his eyes. "Four."

"Four cats?"

"It was sort of accidental. I didn't intend it to happen."

Hannah laughed. "Nobody can have four cats by accident."

"Well . . ."

"And how many of them get to share your bed?"

"Oh, one or two."

Then thank God you've come here, she thought. "Why don't you come in?" was what she said.

The wine was already open. They sat in the small front room, made smaller by his presence, and chatted back and forth. Resnick asked her about her day. He asked her if she'd heard about the policeman who'd been found by the Trent, murdered, and when she said yes, she had, a little, told her that was what he was working on.

"Is that what you always do? That kind of thing?"

"Murder, you mean?"

Hannah nodded: maybe it explained the look, vaguely haunted, behind his eyes.

"Not always," Resnick was saying. "Despite what you might read, there aren't so many of them. But yes, I suppose, yes, quite often."

Hannah edged forward on her seat: "But doesn't it get to you? I'm sure it must." Something about Macbeth, so far steeped in blood.

"Sometimes. It depends." What got to Resnick, what really touched him, was the whole thing: everything he saw. The way people could be with one another, the things they could do: the things they could be made to do in extreme situations—guilt, impotence, poverty, love.

"You become used to it, is that what you mean? Become—what's the word?—inured. Hardened to it, I suppose."

Resnick wondered whether this was what he wanted to be doing, talking about this. "To a degree, yes, otherwise you couldn't do the job." He wanted to go across the room and touch her, but, what had happened the last time notwithstanding, he didn't know how. He wondered if he was guilty of staring too obviously at her mouth. He looked instead at the glass in his hand and drank some more wine.

Hannah was moved by it, the shyness of him. "A penny for them, Charlie. That's what my dad used to say."

"Your dad called you Charlie?"

"No." Laughing. "You know what I mean."

Resnick thought that he did. "So did mine," he said. "Except that it was in Polish. But I suspect it was more or less the same."

"So what were you thinking of?"

He didn't answer.

"Not murder?"

"No." He shook his head.

Hannah set down her glass and got to her feet. "Just so long as you don't think that whenever you come here, the first thing we do is tumble into bed."

"No." Looking at her mouth again, openly this time. "That's not what I think."

"Good." She was holding out her hand.

He was aware of her moving beside him, felt a touch of her shoulder, warm and smooth, as she turned. In the almost dark of the room, he looked at his watch and was surprised that it was only a little after two. He felt as if he had been asleep for hours.

Quietly, Hannah slid her legs from beneath the duvet and

sat up. A small gasp as Resnick reached out and touched her back, the knots of spine against the skin. She reached behind and circled her fingers around his wrist.

"Don't stop. That's not to make you stop."

He kissed the back of her hand, the space between her shoulder blades, her neck; she moved her hand from his and ran it along his chest.

"I was going to the bathroom," she said. And then, near the door, "Can I get you anything?"

He looked at her, naked beneath the skylight, unself-conscious now, the dark wedge of hair between her legs that he might cover with his hand. Everything, part of him responded silently, that part to which he usually paid no heed.

"Water, anything?"

"A glass of water would be fine."

They sat together in her kitchen, dunking biscuits into tea, contentedly not talking, at least not a great deal, Resnick dressed save for his jacket, Hannah wrapped in her dressing gown, already the beginnings of what seemed like routine.

"What's happening . . ." Resnick began.

She pressed a finger close across his mouth. "Not now, Charlie. Not now."

His eyes asked her why.

"If anything's going to happen, there'll be time enough."

On cue, there was the sound of a cab approaching the rear of the house.

"Maybe next time you'd like to come round to me? I could make a bit of supper, something like that." He was shrugging on his coat.

Hannah smiled. "All those cats."

"They're not always all four there at once."

"Oh. I suppose that makes it okay."

At the door she went to kiss him on the cheek and deftly

227

he moved his head so that she kissed him on the mouth instead. At the end of the alley, the taxi driver sounded his horn twice.

"Isn't there supposed to be a law against that?" Hannah smiled.

"Kissing?"

"Using your horn after dark."

For a moment, he touched her breast beneath the soft fabric of her gown. "I have to go."

"Yes."

Stooping his head, he kissed her where his hand had been.

She watched him walk away toward the light and already those first familiar feelings of pain were swaying inside her.

30

As far as Kevin Naylor was concerned, this was not a good day. It had started when Debbie walked out of the bathroom that morning, not saying anything, but the expression on her face telling him everything he needed to know. She had got her period. Punctual to the minute.

"Deb . . ."

But she had brushed him away, opening the fridge to stand there, head angled toward it, staring between the flavored yogurts, the leftover lemon pie, the lettuce, and the film-wrapped cheese at what she could no longer see.

"Deb . . ."

"Leave it, will you! Just leave it."

And he had, slurping down the last of his tea, grabbing a piece of toast, which he ate on the way to the car. The traffic was a bastard as usual that time of the morning, and all the while Debbie's unspoken accusation knifing into him, as if it was all his fault.

"Maybe we should go to the doctor," she'd ventured once before when they'd been trying. "See if there's anything, you know, that he can do."

"I'm not going to see any doctor. Fuck the doctor!" Kevin had replied.

"Okay." Debbie grinning. "If you think he'd do a better job."

"Fuck you, too," Kevin had said, but with a smile. And he had, but it hadn't made a difference, then or now.

"Don't worry," she had said last night, taking him in her hand. "You fret too much about it, I reckon that's what it is. I was reading, you know, this article in *Cosmopolitan*, how anxiety, it, you know, it's—what do you call it?— inhibiting."

Sometimes he even wondered if that wasn't right; after all, when making a baby had been just about the last thing on their minds, there wasn't any problem at all. And they'd had their two years of sleepless nights to prove it.

And as if all of that weren't enough, there was this, waiting on his desk for him when he walked in: the analysis of the footmarks around Aston's body. The regular shoe, size eight, had been recently repaired with a rubber, stick-on sole and a quarter heel, the kind that were fitted in over twenty instant shoe-repair shops in this and any other city. Anonymity guaranteed. The work boot was a Caterpillar, size ten, well worn. Eight local outlets, God knows how many hundred sold. And the trainer—a Nike indoor sports shoe, badminton or squash, a kidney-shaped zigzag pattern, deeply cut, below the ball of the foot, another, similar, but shaped like an elongated heart, beneath the heel. Relatively new, or, at least, sparingly used. The kind that had a color flash at the side, a scored section in a contrasting color just above the heel. *Fabrique en Thailande.* U.S. size twelve, U.K. eleven, European size forty-six. One of Nike's more popular lines.

"Jesus wept!" Naylor said, pushing the report to the other side of his desk.

"What's up?" Divine asked, squeezing past on his way to the gents.

"Nothing. Bloody nothing."

"Suit yourself."

Naylor sat down, spun a pencil round and round on top of the envelope the report had arrived in, retrieved and reread it, looking at the patterns more carefully this time, and then reached for the phone and began to dial.

Divine stood close up against the stall, grimacing, trying not to notice the burning sensation as he tried to pee. Trying and failing. Even when he wasn't feeling it, which had not been often in the past thirty-six hours, he couldn't seem to shake it out of his mind.

If that little slut he'd picked out round back of the Orchid had given him a dose, he'd seek her out and give her a good backhander before she went off to get her penicillin.

Jesus! Ow! Christ almighty, that hurt.

Almost, but not quite as much as the time he woke up early morning and stumbled out for his regulation slash and there it was, clear even to his befogged eyes, blood washing around in his piss. That wasn't what had really hurt. It was later, on his back in the clap clinic, this male nurse, chubby little bastard—black, too, that had really been the icing on the sodding cake—telling him, smiling all the while, "The bad news, you're going to feel this. Nothing we can do about that. But the good news, it'll be over so fast, you won't believe it's happened. Okay. Now just try to relax." And before Divine could protest he manipulated him a little, before pushing this umbrella-shaped needle down into the end of his penis, down into the opening, and scooping it back out. "There now, all done." Still grinning, he had patted

Divine on the shoulder and for a moment Divine had thought he was going to give him a sweetie for being good, Divine lying there in that narrow cubicle, unable to believe what had just happened to his dick.

Although, he had thought, trousers back up and putting a brave face on it as he walked down the line of men waiting to go and get theirs, it could be a sight worse. Quick dose of NSU, that's all it was. Not like some of these sorry buggers, take a look at 'em, if it wasn't AIDS this time, then likely it would be next. Still, bollocking shirt-lifters, they got what they deserved. Divine shuddered and cupped his gear into his jockeys before zipping up. Anyone who'd get his jollies sticking it up some bloke's arse . . . the thought of it made him want to puke.

Back in the CID room, Millington broke off in the midst of a delicate rendition of "When I Fall in Love" to remind Divine that they needed to be on their way in the next ten minutes or so, a man to go and see about a pub. Though if Reg Cossall hadn't been able to get names or detailed descriptions out of the landlord, Millington was doubtful they'd have better luck. But it was ground that had to be covered. Good police work, steady and predictable, that's what got results. Well, sometimes . . .

Shane Snape had discharged himself from the hospital and picked up a taxi on the Derby Road, close by the university roundabout. His face still showed signs of bruising and his ribs would have to stay taped up for the next couple of days, but otherwise he was feeling better than perhaps he had a right to, the beating he had taken.

Norma greeted him with a kiss and a hug that made him wince, and Peter grinned and reached up from the settee to shake Shane's hand and say welcome home, as though it was his sodding home to welcome him into.

"How much longer's he staying?" Shane asked Norma out in the kitchen, not bothering to lower his voice.

"Come on, love," Norma said. "Don't be like that."

"I'm not being," Shane said, "like fucking anything."

Less than half an hour later he was off out again, ignoring his mother's questions about where he was going and when he might be back. He caught one bus into the city center and then another out to Ilkeston; it was little more than a ten-minute walk from the bus station to where his mate Gerry Hovenden lived.

Hovenden was one of the blokes Shane hung around with, drank with at weekends: a good mate. When Shane came round the corner, Hovenden was down on his hands and knees by the front path, the exhaust of the motorbike he was repairing laid on an old length of oily blanket near the front door.

"Hey," Shane said, "how's it going?"

"Slowly. How about you?"

Shane grinned. "Slowly, too."

He stood for a while on the threadbare patch of front garden, feigning interest.

"Not a lot of use asking you to pitch in." Hovenden grinned. "Lend a hand."

"Not a lot."

"Go on inside if you want, nobody's in. You know where everything is."

Hovenden lived in the place with his dad, his mum having gone from there to a refuge five years before, before moving to Birmingham, where she was living with a long-distance lorry driver who hated Gerry's guts. Since she'd left, his dad had taken up with a woman who worked in the local garden center and he spent more time at her house than here. Added to which he worked shifts. So mostly now, it was as if Hovenden lived there on his own.

It was a flat-roofed fifties house on a spent-up estate, a few of the places owner-occupied, but mainly not. The council, as usual, was behind on maintenance, paint flaked away from around the window frames, and once enough water had gathered on the roof, it found a way through.

Shane switched on the TV and wandered off without really looking at it. There were four cans of Strongbow in the fridge and he snapped one open and sat down on the folded piece of foam that served as a settee, someone blabbing away on the TV screen, Shane still not bothering to watch. He pulled a bundle of comics toward him and started to leaf through them; finding a Judge Dredd, he read it from cover to cover. Shifting it to the bottom of the pile, he found—what was this?—not a comic, some kind of fanzine. A magazine. *The Order.* The cover showed a large white death's-head on a black background. One of Gerry's old biker things, Shane guessed, back from when his hair was long and his leather stank of engine oil and never being washed for years on end. But inside, above a picture of a crowd of youths standing outside iron gates, he read: *The Holocaust is a load of bollocks. C18 experts examine the myth.*

As he was starting to read it, Hovenden came into the house, wiping his hands on a piece of rag.

"Oh," he said, seeing what was in Shane's hands. "You found that."

"I didn't know you was into politics," Shane said.

"Yes." Gerry Hovenden shrugged. "Now and again."

Standing in the queue at the sandwich counter across the street, Resnick pondered on a largely fruitless day. He had driven out with Khan to the house in Colwick where Paul Matthews lived. At first, the place had been so quiet, they'd thought nobody was at home, but then Matthews's mother had come through the side gate that led from the rear of the house. A birdlike woman in a yellow dress. Paul, she informed them, had been terribly upset by what had happened, that poor, poor boy—Resnick had assumed she was referring to Norma's son and not her own, but wasn't sure. The doctor had signed him off work, nervous exhaustion, yes, that was right, signed him off with medication and told Paul to take a rest. Ordered him. He had gone down to stay with a favorite aunt, in Wales, South Wales, Rhossili Bay. Resnick knew it, perhaps? Resnick did not. Ah! Beautiful, still a little wild, you know. And quiet, this time of the year. So restorative, the sea.

"Color-blind," Khan had said, back in the car.

"Mmm?"

"Color-blind. Every word she said was aimed directly to you. I don't think she knew I was there."

Elizabeth Peck's house, one of those new pseudo-Georgian places off Wilford Lane, was locked up tight. Blinds pulled, curtains drawn, burglar alarm armed, not one but two Banham locks on the front door. The neighbors knew her but not well; knew, at least one of them did, that she had gone away. Holiday. She did not know where. Or when she might return.

Resnick had considered dismissing Khan to the further reaches of the Welsh coast to talk to Matthews, but for now opted to keep that particular powder dry and save on travel expenses to boot. It was Elizabeth Peck whom Bill Aston had spoken to and now Resnick wanted her to speak to him. What he sent Khan off to do was establish whether or not she owned a car; then check with the travel agencies, East Midlands Airport, the railway station, see if he couldn't get a line on where she'd gone, when she might be expected back.

Before Resnick could carry his sandwich into the comparative privacy of his office, Naylor intercepted him, his day looking up at last. "This shoe stuff, sir, inconclusive's putting it mildly. But I had them look again at the markings and one thing's pretty much agreed. Whoever was wearing the boots, you can tell from the movement, variations in pressure and the like, he was the one did most of the damage, really heavy blows that did for Aston, he was the one."

"Good work, lad. Well done."

He was just about to bite into the sandwich, stray mayonnaise already on the cuff of his shirt, when Millington knocked and entered.

"Any luck, Graham?"

"Not a lot, still claiming not to know any names, but he's agreed to go down to Central and look at some photos, may come up with something that way. Did catch a word with one or two regulars who were in there on the Saturday when the fight broke out, though. Confirmed these lads throwing their weight around had been at the match earlier in the day. Regular supporters by the sound of it."

"Right, Graham. Tell Mark to contact that pal of his in the Football Intelligence Unit, set up a meeting."

Millington was scarcely out of the door when Lynn Kellogg came in. Resignedly, Resnick pushed the sandwich back in its paper bag and shut the bag in his desk drawer.

"I've been going over that breakdown I did," Lynn said. "Aston's last twenty-four hours. And there's one period I'm not clear about. He met you in the Partridge on the Friday evening to talk about Nicky Snape and didn't get back to the house until pretty late, between eleven-thirty and midnight Mrs. Aston said."

"And I left him at around half nine, sitting with half an inch of mild."

Lynn nodded. "According to Mrs. Aston, he said he was there talking to you the whole time. Made a point of it."

Resnick shrugged. "She could have been getting confused."

"She might. Or Aston might have lied."

Resnick looked at her seriously. "In which case he'd likely have had good reason."

"I thought," Lynn said, "before taking it any further, I'd pop out there and talk to Mrs. Aston again, see if she's still saying the same. If that's okay with you."

Resnick was already reaching for the phone. "I'll call her first, then ride out with you. We can ask her together."

31

Stella Aston met them at the door, wearing jeans and an over-size sweater; her hair hung slightly damp against her shoulders, washed and imperfectly dried. She smiled a greeting and stood back to let Resnick and Lynn enter, but there was a tiredness behind the smile that she couldn't disguise.

"Mum's been lying down," she said. "Why don't you come through to the kitchen? She's just getting dressed. I don't suppose she'll be very long."

Stella made instant coffee, chatting with just a slight awkwardness to Lynn, Resnick off to one side, staring out at the garden. Although he imagined it had not long since been done, the grass would soon be in need of cutting again.

When Stella carried over Resnick's cup, Lynn watched her without knowing exactly what she was looking for, a change of expression on her face, the way she smiled. *You think she could have had a crush on him:* Petra Carey's words. Well, why not? Others had, Lynn was certain. Fleetingly, Stella's fingers, surely by accident, brushed against the back of Resnick's hand. *Little girls love their fathers. Usually they replace them with other men. But if that other man is too much like her father, what she ends up feeling is guilt.* More of Petra Carey's words.

Petra bloody Carey! What I might do, Lynn thought, is cancel my next appointment, not go back at all.

By the time they had finished their coffee, Margaret Aston had come downstairs and was waiting for them in the living room, the curtains pulled mostly across. No matter how much powder and foundation she had used, she had not been able to hide the extent to which she had, in these last days, yielded herself up to tears.

"Margaret," Resnick said gently, "are you sure you're up to this?"

"Yes, thank you, Charlie. I shall be fine."

Seated on the carpet close by her chair, Stella reached up and patted her mother's hand.

"Mrs. Aston," Lynn began, "you remember there was a phone call your husband made, late on the Saturday afternoon?"

"Yes, of course. Someone rang him and he called them back from the hall."

"Why did he do that?"

Margaret Aston shook her head. "They hadn't finished their conversation, I suppose."

"Yes, but why go out into the hall? Why not ring them back from where he was? The same phone the person had called in on."

Margaret Aston looked bemused; she transferred her gaze from Lynn to Resnick and slowly back again.

"I mean," Lynn persevered, "wouldn't that have been the simplest thing to do?"

"I really haven't given it any thought, but Bill had his reasons, I'm sure."

"What were you doing, Mum, at the time?" Stella asked, looking round.

"Oh, I don't know, dear. Reading, I suppose. Yes, I was, a book from the library, I can't remember . . ."

"There you are, there's your answer," Stella said. "Dad didn't want to disturb Mum's reading, that's what it was. Nothing sinister at all."

Resnick and Lynn exchanged glances.

"I don't suppose you've been able to remember, Mrs. Aston," Lynn said, "who it was your husband spoke to? You couldn't when we talked before."

She shook her head. "As I told you then, Bill never mentioned who it was. But it'll have been someone from the church, I'm sure. For years he's been a lay preacher. Quite famous, isn't he, Charlie, you would know. Famous for it."

Nodding agreement, Resnick leaned forward lightly in his chair. "I wonder, Margaret, does the name Elizabeth Peck mean anything to you?"

She gave it several moments' thought. "No. No, I can't say that it does. But I expect you're about to tell me that's who Bill was speaking to, is that it?"

Resnick nodded. "It was her number that he called."

"So who is she?" Stella asked, the beginnings of agitation in her young voice.

"A social worker. She's employed at the place where Nicky Snape died."

"Well then, of course," Margaret Aston said, seizing on it quickly, "that's why she would have wanted to talk to Bill. The inquiry. And why he would have been careful to have spoken to her in private. Confidentiality. He was very scrupulous about things like that, Bill, even from me. Charlie, you should know that yourself."

"The trouble is, Margaret, that only makes it more difficult to understand why he would agree to a long, private conversation with one of his principal witnesses. Especially when it was so clearly off the record."

"Oh, no, I'm sure he would have made a note at least."

"I'm afraid not. I've been through all of his papers, notebooks, everything. There's nothing about any such conversation having taken place."

Margaret Aston sighed; she seemed to have shrunken even deeper into her chair. "Stella, dear"—touching her daughter's shoulder—"I'm feeling very tired. I wonder, would you help me back up to bed. Charlie, you'll excuse me, I know."

Resnick and Lynn stood as Stella assisted her mother to her feet. Resnick opened the door and as Margaret, leaning on her daughter's arm, passed by him, he asked a further question. "One thing, Margaret. What time was it Bill got back here on the Friday night?"

She stopped. "Almost midnight. A quarter, ten to. You should know, Charlie, it was you he was with. I remember him coming in and coming up to my room—I was in bed by then, of course. Knocking gently on the door to make sure I was still awake. He sat on the bed for a moment and held my hand, told me what a nice evening he'd had. Charlie, he'd enjoyed talking to you. You could see it, see in his face, some of that old life again. 'Long time since I've done that, love,' he said. 'Me and Charlie Resnick, closed the bar together. I shall sleep well tonight,' he said, and kissed me here, on the top of the head, before saying good night."

Unusually, Resnick took the keys and slid behind the wheel. Less than half a mile down the road he signaled right and pulled in outside a small parade of shops. Lynn imagined that he intended to get out, buy a newspaper, or go to the off-license for beer. But, engine idling, he sat there, forearms resting on the wheel.

"You think she's lying?" he said finally. "Holding something back?"

"No."

"Telling the truth, then?"

"Yes. As she sees it. All she knows, yes."

Resnick released a slow breath. "It would be easier perhaps if she was lying, if she knew there was something going on."

"And is there?"

As Resnick turned to face her, a middle-aged man coming out of the newsagent stopped and stared at the car, only slowly starting to walk away, *Post* rolled inside his hand. Resnick saw him and wondered what they looked like, himself and Lynn, another mismatched couple, caught in the middle of an affair, one of them married, most likely him.

He had observed couples often enough himself, had leapt, sometimes inappropriately, to the same conclusions. Most usually, though, he had been right: lovers caught in their own cold, sticky web.

"You think it's the woman? Peck?"

"How d'you mean?" Resnick asked.

"Well, you know . . ."

"That he was having an affair? Bill?"

"That is what you were thinking, isn't it? The path you're going down."

"But with Peck?"

"Why not?"

Resnick shook his head, came close to a smile. "He'd only known her less than a week."

Lynn's turn to smile. "Come on," she said. "How long does it take?"

Instead of answering, Resnick turned toward the windscreen and stared out. What he was thinking of, what he was seeing, was Hannah that first time, walking across the front of the school toward her slightly battered red VW, pausing to speak to those two kids, firm enough, not without under-standing; the way, after they had spoken, she placed her briefcase on the roof of the car and then turned back to face him, that flash of red, visible in the swirl of her hair. Her smile.

How long does it take?

For a brief period—what was it? Four years ago now, slightly more?—he would have thought of Rachel Chaplin at that moment, after that question. For a long while, before and since, it would have been Elaine.

"Even so," he said, "it's doubtful Bill would have had the chance during the inquiry to speak to her alone."

"The interview?"

Resnick shook his head. "Khan was there all the time."

"Then it was to do with the inquiry, maybe something she felt she couldn't say at her interview."

"Because she was afraid?"

"Possibly, yes. Or maybe it was something she didn't know at the time, that she only learned later."

"Then why on earth did Bill break the habit of a lifetime and not note it down?"

They looked at each other along the front seat of the car. Three kids, one not much more than seven or eight, went past on Rollerblades, heads bent forward, arms swinging pro-fessionally out.

"You think it's something personal, don't you?" Lynn said.

"I don't know. I suppose I do, but I still don't see how that could have worked. Time, access . . ."

"Maybe," Lynn said, "it wasn't, you know, an affair. At least, not yet. What if there was just a connection, somehow, between them? Something they were just starting to—I don't know what you'd call it—explore."

"What? In his own house in the middle of the weekend with his wife in another room?"

243

"Wouldn't some people find that exciting? The possibility of being found out."

Resnick gestured with open hands. "I wouldn't know."

"And you'd know Bill Aston? Well enough to be sure?"

He shook his head emphatically. "No."

"Him and his wife, they've got separate rooms, isn't that right?"

"Yes."

"Separate beds."

"Uh-hum."

"Do you know for how long?"

"Quite a while, I think. I'm not exactly sure. But that in itself doesn't mean anything."

Lynn smiled. "Surely it means something."

Resnick knew: there were times after he had found out Elaine was having an affair that he lay in their shared bed, unable to sleep, terrified that by accident or habit they might touch, impossible to erase the images his imagination had conjured up so vividly from his mind.

What had happened, Resnick wondered, in the Astons' lives however many years it was ago?

"It is sex, then, isn't it?" Lynn said. "If it's not to do with the inquiry, it is sex." She smiled ruefully. "One way or another, it usually is." And then, a sudden catch in her voice. "It nearly got me killed."

"That was different. He was some kind of psychopath."

Lynn's head was angled away but he heard her well enough. "Don't forget, at first I wanted him."

He drove then without speaking, back toward the center of town. He would call in at the Partridge, find out if the staff remembered how long Aston had stayed in the bar that night. Lynn sat with her hands clenched, mind churning, overbite of her teeth nervously worrying at the inside of her lip.

244

"You have business back at the station, or should I drop you near home? It's not far out of my way."

For the first time since they had moved off, she dared to look into his face. "Stop here," she said.

"I can't, not here. I'll just go up to—"

"Charlie, stop here!" How long—if ever—since she had called him that?

No mistaking the urgency in her voice; Resnick made a left and a right and came to a halt on one of the narrow cobbled roads that ran through the wholesale flower and vegetable market. One glance and he switched off the engine and waited.

Lynn not quite looking at him again, not yet; she was having a little difficulty breathing evenly. "This isn't—I don't suppose there's ever a right time."

Not knowing, partly knowing, afraid of what was to come, Resnick felt his stomach run cold; for just a moment he closed his eyes.

"You remember," Lynn said, "after the kidnapping, the rescue, all of that, something I said to you one day, we were having coffee, I . . ."

"Yes, I think so, go on." When what he wanted to say was stop.

"I told you I'd been having these—I don't know what you'd call them—nightmares, dreams, fantasies. You, my father, him, the kidnapper. All mixed up together. It was all because of what happened, of course, what might have happened. Would have done if you—"

"It wasn't just me."

"If you hadn't saved me. It sounds melodramatic, I know, but that's what you did."

"Lynn." Leaning a shade closer toward her now, though she was still keeping her body, her face angled away. "It could have been any one of a dozen officers. It just happened to be me."

She laughed, suddenly and loud.

"What?" Leaning back again, taken by surprise.

"That's what I say to my therapist."

"And she says?"

"What might have happened doesn't matter. What does is that it was you."

He looked at her serious face, still somewhat round though she had never put back the weight she had lost; short brown hair, wide brown eyes.

"I'm glad," he said quietly. "Glad that you were safe. Glad that it was me."

"Yes. Yes, I know." Her voice so quiet it was almost lost under the noise of cars passing at either end of the street. "At least, I think I know."

He had an instinct to take her hand and another that prevented him: instead she took his. "Charlie, I've got to get this sorted. I mean it's stupid, I can't go on like this. The way I've been lately, walking round you on, I don't know, eggshells; at least that's the way it seems."

"All right," Resnick nodded. "What do you want to do?"

"Nothing. I don't think you understand. I don't want to *do* anything. There's nothing to do."

"But then . . ."

She squeezed his hand once, then let go. "I just needed to say, tell you what's been going on in my mind, not all of it, the stupid details, but that I have been having these thoughts about you. . . ."

"That doesn't matter. . . ."

"Charlie, I've thought about making love to you, but I know that's not going to happen. Only in my mind."

"Lynn . . ."

"I don't think I even want it to happen. Not really. I know I don't. But I had to say it, had to tell you. Because if I keep it all inside any longer, it's going to explode." Slowly, she lowered her face into her hands. "I'm sorry."

"There's no need."

"Isn't there?" Looking at him now.

"No."

It was hot in the small space of the car, claustrophobic. Resnick could feel the sweat gathering in the palms of his hands and between his legs, dampening the hair at the nape of his neck. A kind of free-floating panic aside, he had no clear idea what he was feeling.

"Well . . ." Lynn laughed abruptly. "My therapist will be pleased."

"Getting it out into the open . . ."

"Yes."

"Making it all go away."

She turned toward him in the seat and he thought she was going to take his hand again and he tensed inside, not knowing how he might respond if she did. But she shifted again and leaned forward, face close to the windscreen, staring out.

"Is that what you want?" Resnick heard himself saying. "To make it all go away?"

She looked round at him, surprised. "Of course. What good would it do?"

A car went by too fast on the opposite side of the road, music spilling from its open windows.

"None," Resnick said.

Lynn thought she might get out of the car and walk, not heading anywhere special, just walk. But she continued to sit there, they both did, waiting until the unevenness of their breathing had subsided, until Resnick could trust himself to set the car in gear and drive back into town. "The Partridge," he said. "We could check it out before I drop you off."

The barman in the Partridge remembered Resnick's friend. He had ordered another half of mild after Resnick had gone, but it remained on the table, scarcely bothered, when he left. Fifteen minutes later, twenty tops.

Back home, Resnick fed the cats automatically, made himself strong coffee and carried it through to the front room, where it stayed till morning, cold and untouched. For what seemed a long time he stared at the rows of albums and CDs and saw nothing he wanted to listen to, nothing he wanted to play.

Silent, save for Lynn's words, insinuating themselves into his thoughts no matter how much he tried to keep them out. *I've thought about making love to you, but I know that's not going to happen. Only in my mind.*

Resnick crossed the room to the telephone and dialed. "I was wondering if I could come over and see you," he said.

"I'm sorry, Charlie." Hannah's voice sounded distant and tired. "Not this evening, okay?"

"Of course. It was just an idea. That's fine."

The Stolichnaya was in the freezer: he wondered how much was in the bottle, how long it would last.

32

The first thing Resnick recognized, warm, soft, and resting close against his ear, was a cat's paw. The second, moments after, close and strangely muted, was the sound of a telephone ringing. And the third, realized with painful accuracy as he lifted Bud cautiously clear and gingerly lowered his own feet toward the floor, was that for the first time in many months, he had a hangover of king-sized proportions. He blinked at the clock: six forty-nine. He should have already been up. Louder now, the telephone continued to ring, and fearing the worst, without knowing exactly what that worst was, he lifted it toward his ear.

"Yes. Hello."

"Charlie, is that you?"

"I think so."

"Did I wake you?"

"Not really, no."

"Are you okay?"

"Um, why?"

"You sound as if you're at the bottom of the sea."

"I slept a little heavily, that's all."

"Look, Charlie, can I see you today? Not for long; lunchtime, maybe. Just for twenty minutes, half an hour. I think we need to talk."

No reply.

"I could meet you somewhere."

Resnick wished his head didn't feel like a sack of gently swaying cement. "Look, let me call you . . . No, I will. This morning. Soon. How long are you around? . . . All right, I'll phone before then. Probably in the next half hour."

In the shower, water streaming across the folds and plains of his body, he kept wondering what had prompted Hannah to phone so early, what it was she needed to talk about so urgently, lathering shampoo into his hair now and wincing as he did so, once more fearing the worst.

He hadn't been the only person tying one on last night. The entrance to the police station was crowded with people in various stages of sobriety, many of them adorned with quite spectacular cuts and bruises, most talking at once. Loudly. A uniform sergeant and two of his minions were patiently trying to sort them out.

Resnick pushed his way through, careful not to slip on the blood. From the corridor to his right came the voice of the custody sergeant, giving one of his overnights a good bollocking for throwing up in his cell. A reedy version of "Little Brown Jug" from the stairs alerted Resnick to the possibility that Millington was embarking on one of his unbearably jolly days; and sure enough there he was, descending the stairs, smile in place around his mustache, happy to share with the world choice moments of that old Glenn Miller magic. As

Divine had announced to the CID room moments before, someone had got his leg over this morning and no chuffin' mistake!

"Boss's been asking for you," Millington said breezily. "That new lad in there with him. Least, I reckon that's who it is. Oh, and I've set up a meeting. Eleven. With that feller from soccer unit, all right?"

Resnick continued on his way upstairs. In the gents he ran the cold tap and sloshed water repeatedly in his face, before heading along the corridor for Skelton's office.

"Charlie, come in, come in." Skelton exuded neatly suited bonhomie from behind his desk. "This is DC Vincent."

Resnick's first impression was of a tallish man in his late twenties, around five-eleven, slim, clean-shaven, his dark hair cut quite short; he was wearing a light-colored suit, creased, but unlike Resnick's, fashionably meant to be that way, an olive-green shirt and black knitted tie.

"This is Detective Inspector Resnick. Day to day, you'll be working for him."

The two men shook hands, Vincent's grip cool and comfortable, not giving it too much.

"Carl Vincent, sir. Good to know you."

Resnick nodded and stepped back, Vincent still looking him clear in the eye.

"As you know, Charlie, Carl here's joining us from Leicester. Up a division, eh, Charlie. In a manner of speaking."

Only if you're a Forest supporter, Resnick thought.

"I've filled him in on the Aston murder, Charlie, basic details. I know you'll want to bring him up to speed."

"Sir."

There was a smile in Vincent's eyes now as he watched him, interested to see how Resnick operated with his superior, sizing him up.

"Anything new there, Charlie? Anything I can pass on to

headquarters? These soccer hooligans in Reg Cossall's report, still the most likely candidates?"

Resnick wondered if he should mention his suspicions surrounding Elizabeth Peck, but opted to wait until he had more evidence, one way or another.

"Seems so, yes. There's a meeting with the Football Intelligence Unit this morning; we'll see if that takes us anywhere closer."

"You'll let me know?"

"First thing."

Vincent fell into step beside Resnick in the corridor. "Found anywhere to stay yet?" Resnick asked.

"Not as yet. Figured I'd travel up from Leicester for a bit, give myself time to look around. Not such a bad journey long as you get the timings right."

"You might want to have a word with our admin officer, she's usually got her ear to the ground."

"Right, thanks. I will."

"Morning briefing any minute. I'll introduce you, find you something to get started."

"Right," Vincent said again and then he smiled. "Never easy, are they? Beginnings. First days. Feeling your way."

"You'll handle it okay."

"I'll do my best."

Outside the CID room Vincent hesitated. "I was wondering, what do I call you? Guv? Sir? Boss?"

"Whatever feels right."

The room fell quiet as they entered.

Divine settled for a bacon cob, brown sauce, toast, tea with two sugars, and a Lion bar for later. Naylor and Lynn Kellogg were already sitting at a table by the window, near the rear of the canteen. The air was thick with tobacco smoke and talk.

"Right," Divine said, decanting cup and plate onto the table, propping the tray against the leg, from where it fell onto the floor. "What's going off? That's what I'd like to know."

"We're talking about last night's *EastEnders*," Naylor said pleasantly. "What d'you want to know?"

"Conspiracy of silence then, is it, or what?"

"How d'you mean?"

"You know what I bloody well mean."

"How's that?"

Divine jerked a hand back round in the direction of the door. "This bloke. Vincent. Why's nobody said a sodding thing about the fact he's black?"

"He is?" Lynn said innocently.

"Never thought you'd notice, Mark," Naylor said, amused. "Reckon that's why."

"Anyway," said Lynn, "he's not really black. More a sort of light chocolaty brown."

Naylor nodded. "Milky Way."

"That's it," Divine said through a mouthful of bacon roll, "make a bloody joke out of it."

"Oh, Mark," Lynn said, "come on."

"Look"—voice getting louder by the minute—"if it were anything else, anything else at all, as marked him out of the ordinary . . ."

"Such as?" Naylor asked.

"I don't know, anything. All right, suppose he wasn't a bloke, he was a woman. . . ."

"Transvestite, you mean?"

"No, you pillock, a proper woman. . . ."

"Well, that would be out of the ordinary, true enough," Lynn said. "Just look around."

"Right. Exactly. Anything from a clubfoot to a man with two heads, we'd talk about it, yeah? But no, not this, this is different. No one's supposed to notice, not a blind thing. So there's the boss, introducing him, welcome to the team. And that's it."

"Well, what d'you expect?" Naylor asked. " 'This is Carl Vincent and in case you haven't noticed, he's black'? "

"Why not?"

"Jesus!"

"Because, Mark," Lynn said, leveling her voice, "it doesn't matter."

"Bollocks!"

"What?"

"You heard, bollocks. Of course it bloody matters."

"Mark," Lynn said, "you're so full of crap sometimes."

"Yeah?" Divine on his feet now, leaning toward her, finger in her face. "Well, listen up. It matters to him, you can bet your life on that. And I'll tell you something else, it fucking matters to me."

There was a sudden hush around them at the scarcely suppressed anger in Divine's voice, and through it Carl Vincent walked blithely, carrying a cup of coffee and two pieces of buttered toast. "Mind if I join you?"

"Please," Lynn said.

"Yes, sure," said Naylor. "Pull up a pew."

Divine had a quick swallow of his tea and grabbed what was left of his bacon roll. Sitting in the vacated chair, Vincent turned his head to watch Divine go.

"There's one in every station," he said with a slow shake of the head.

"Only one?" Lynn smiled. "Things must be looking up."

The Football Intelligence Unit had been at its busiest in the eighties, when self-styled firms of young men could afford to invest considerable time and money in promoting violence in and around major soccer grounds. Often they would eschew the match itself in order to ambush unsuspecting groups of visiting fans at railway stations before or after the game. Officers went underground, spending months establishing solid cover before infiltrating the more dangerous of the firms—the Chelsea Headhunters, Arsenal, Oxford, Portsmouth, Millwall.

When a move to all-seater stadiums thwarted one of the most popular pastimes—a sudden vicious charge to take the home supporters' "end"—and with spiraling admission charges ensuring that lots of youngsters stayed away, hard-core fans intent upon trouble followed the national flag abroad. And the Unit went with them. Information about known troublemakers was passed on to other national police forces, and although the violence was to a degree curtailed, it didn't stop. Wrecked bars and cafés, water cannon and baton charges, testified to that.

"Here," Trevor Ulman said, "take a look at this."

Resnick and his team watched the monitor as, on somewhat bleached-out videotape, a mob of chanting youths, mostly in shirtsleeves, Union Jacks to the fore, erupted from a curbside café and charged across a broad square, despite the attempts of heavily outnumbered uniformed police to stop them. Even mounted officers, swinging their long truncheons, could not deter the English supporters as they raced over cobblestones and tram lines, intent upon catching any local fans with fists or feet or both.

"Now watch this," Ulman said as the camera closed in on a group of five young men as they chased, tripped, and then proceeded to punch and kick—especially kick—the single youth who had been their quarry. Ulman paused the video a few frames before a boot made contact with the victim's head.

"Here," he said, pointing. "The lad with the footwork. Chelsea Headhunter, close links with Combat 18. I'll say a bit more about that in a minute. But look here, this bloke with the belly, over to the left—Leicester Baby Squad. And this one here, leaning over to throw a punch—more local, Forest Executive Crew."

Ulman stubbed out his Silk Cut and lit another, using a slim gold lighter with a dangerously high flame.

"That was two years ago, Rotterdam. But this second clip's more recent. February of this year. Most probably, I don't have to tell you where it's from."

"Dublin," Divine said, with an edge of disgust.

"Correct. One friendly international between the Republic and ourselves abandoned, thanks to scenes like this."

The screen, in color this time, showed a man in the upper tier, his face, save for the eyes, hidden inside a dark balaclava; he stood and turned away from the camera, back toward the crowd, and signaled with his arm. Immediately, the rioting began. Arms were thrust skyward, Union Jacks waved, mouths open with shouts of "No surrender! No surrender to the IRA!" and then pieces of guttering were torn away and hurled down upon the unguarded crowd below.

"Combat 18?" Resnick asked.

"Precisely."

"But you're not saying," Millington asked, "that everyone in that upper stand at Dublin, those yobos you showed us running wild in Holland, that they're all political?"

"Well," Ulman said, "I doubt they're all fully paid-up members of the British National Party. But that's not the way it works." Arching back his head a moment, he released an almost perfect smoke ring toward the ceiling. "Combat 18, no matter how much the BNP might now try to deny it, are enforcers. Write a letter to the *Post* complaining about a Fascist rally, stick an anti–Nazi League poster in your window, and the lads from C18'll be round to pay you a call.

"Now, as far as they're concerned, soccer grounds are

breeding grounds; they use football as a way of spreading propaganda, gaining converts who'll stay interested just long enough to let them pull off some stunt like Dublin, Rotterdam, Oslo. Then C18 have got maximum publicity and they can rattle on in *The Order*—that's their magazine—about getting a good result.

"The difference is, their racism is real: they believe it. To the rest, most of them, it's unthinking. The kind that'll throw bananas at the visiting team's black players, jump up and down and make monkey noises, but not apparently notice they've got—what?—three or four black players of their own. Most likely they don't think of themselves as racist at all. And when you get down to it, they're probably not a whole lot more so than the rest of us. It's ingrained. Difficult to shake."

Millington leaned his chair back onto its hind legs. "This anti-Irish thing, that'd fit in with what the landlord told us, out at this pub we're interested in."

"It would indeed. Though, I have to say, we've no record of that particular pub being a meeting place for the kind of nice young character we're talking about. However, habits change. It's possible. What I can't do, at least until you can provide me with some kind of visual identification, a name, is tell you whether these youths who were creating a disturbance the night Aston was killed are known to us already."

"Details about locals who might fit the profile, though," Resnick began. "We can go at it that way."

"Absolutely. No problem." Ulman took two large envelopes from his case and passed them across to where Resnick was sitting. "The quality of some of these is a little suspect, they've been blown up from video, but the rest, ones we've taken ourselves, they'll be fine. You've got brief descriptions here, too, known associates and addresses, though those do tend to slip out of date pretty fast."

"And will some of these," Resnick asked, "be Combat 18?"

"A few. You want to talk to Special Branch. They'll have this area well sussed."

Resnick nodded and thanked Ulman for all his help. Making contact with the local office of the Branch was already high on his list. But not until after lunch.

33

The day was sharp and clear, the sky an almost unbroken blue. They walked along the upper path through the cemetery, close by the red brick wall that separated it from the road. Stone angels stared back at them, empty-eyed. *Also Flora, aged four months. Agnes Hilda Jane, wife of the above. Suffer the little children. Gone to a better place.* Below them, among a maze of smaller headstones and carefully carved epitaphs, the ground leveled out, before rising again with the trees and shrubs of the Arboretum.

Resnick had brought sandwiches from the deli and slices of rich pecan pie; in her bag Hannah had orange juice, pots of blueberry yogurt, paper napkins, plastic spoons: the arrangement they had made.

"You know the best places to take a girl, Charlie. I'll say that for you."

Resnick checked, but she was smiling, that crease that he

was getting used to, quite pronounced, at the right side of her mouth.

"Do you want to sit down?"

Hannah looked at her watch. "Let's walk a little further. Are you okay for time?"

"Fine."

They went through the gate and across Waverley Street, up between the aviary and the small pond with its low, curved railings, climbing the path that wound toward the bandstand, the borders rich with late-spring flowers, purple and gold.

Hannah expressed her approval at the sandwiches, nothing too idiosyncratic, smoked turkey breast with cranberry, egg mayonnaise with cress. Resnick, panicking at the last moment that she might be a vegetarian, had thought this way, at least, they could have one each. But Hannah bit heartily into her half of the turkey sandwich and Resnick contrived, more through luck than judgment, to trap a sudden squish of egg on the back of his hand before it landed on his shirt. He thought he might allow her to take the second yogurt back for her tea.

"These are good," Hannah said.

Lower down the slope, three Asian men in shirtsleeves had spread a newspaper on the grass and were using it as a surface on which to play cards. Mouth full, Resnick nodded agreement.

"D'you always eat this well?"

"If this is well, yes. I suppose so."

Hannah pushed a straw down into the carton of orange juice. "I suppose I think of policemen as eating chips with everything. Or late-night curries, you know, the kind where, no matter what it is, it always tastes the same."

Recognizing the description, Resnick smiled. "There's a lot of that, too. Sometimes. It depends."

Swiveling on the bench, she looked at him. "One thing you don't do, Charlie, is take rejection very well."

He blinked. "You mean last night?"

"Uh-huh."

"Who does? Who would? I just wanted to see you, that was all."

With a slow shake of the head, Hannah said, "Charlie, you were feeling down. I don't know why. . . ."

"I . . ."

"And it doesn't matter, I don't need to know. But there you were, on your own, feeling low, and you picked up the phone. Let's call Hannah, she'll make me feel better, take me out of myself for a few hours. Wasn't that it? Something like that, at least."

Resnick put the uneaten piece of sandwich back down on the bench, appetite lost in the guilty truth of what she had said. "I didn't think . . . I mean, is that so wrong?"

Lightly, briefly, she touched his hand, the back of his wrist. "I'm not a comfort station, Charlie. That's not what I want to be. Waiting around for you to phone so that I can be pressed into service, relieving the stresses and strains of a difficult day."

"I didn't mean it that way," he said and she thought he believed it.

"The other evening, the last time I saw you, you asked—I think you were going to ask—what was happening. Between us. And I stopped you; it didn't seem the right time. And I said the one thing I didn't want to happen, that we were getting into that pattern where all you have to do is call and whenever you came round we ended up in bed."

"But that's not—"

"What's happening?"

"I don't think so, no."

"Oh, Charlie." Hannah looked away toward the rose garden on the other side of the hill, the blackened cannons dragged back from the Crimea. Part of Resnick telling him, Okay, stop it now, you don't need this, get up and walk away.

"I don't know," Hannah said, turning back to face him, reading the concern in his eyes, "if this is going to come to anything. But I've got baggage, Charlie, the same as you." She smiled, almost a grin. "Maybe not quite as much. But I'm being careful here. I know it may not always seem so, but I am. Cautious, in my way. And one thing I'm not prepared to do is become a tidy little corner of your life. The place where you go to get rid of a little passion, whatever's extra, whatever you can't somehow soak up in the rest of your day." She shook her head. "I don't know if that makes any sense; I don't know if I've made that clear."

He touched her then, high on her shoulder, his littlest finger resting against her neck; the other fingers then, circling softly against the skin. She had smooth skin.

Hannah waited for him to say something, make some response, but he didn't speak. "So what do you want to do, Charlie?" she asked.

"You mean now?"

Grinning, "No, not now."

"Well, I suppose that depends, you know, on you."

"God, Charlie!"

"All right, I want to carry on seeing you. I want . . . I'd like to find a way, something you feel comfortable with. . . ."

"You don't want to hide me away?"

"No."

"Your little bit on the side?"

A shake of the head, emphatic. "No."

"Good. Dinner, then. Friday night."

"All right. Where . . . ?"

But Hannah was already collecting together her things, brushing crumbs from her lap, getting ready to go. "You decide. Call me and tell me where you want to meet. Okay?"

"Yes, yes. Of course, that's fine."

"This yogurt," Hannah said, holding it toward him. "Do you want it or not?"

"Probably not."

With a small gesture of acceptance she dropped it down in her bag. "That sandwich, though, you're not leaving that?"

"I'll eat it on the way back."

"You'll get it all down yourself."

"Look," Resnick said, smiling. "Mothering. That's another habit we could do without. Where I'm concerned, at least."

Khan was waiting in the CID room when Resnick returned, head stuck into a copy of the *Daily Mail*. Naylor was talking into the telephone, close to the far wall. As soon as he saw Resnick, Khan hastily folded the newspaper and set it aside. "Elizabeth Peck, sir. Booked herself a holiday through American Express. One of those late-availability deals. Two-city trip to Spain, Barcelona and Madrid."

"Good. Oughtn't to be too difficult to track her down."

Khan frowned. "That's the problem, I'm afraid. The agency was quite good, put me in touch with the hotel, the place she's meant to be staying in Madrid."

At the "meant to be," Resnick's heart sank.

"She flew out, right enough, checked in. Signed up for a coach trip the first day, some kind of orientation thing, but after that it seems as if she's disappeared."

"And the travel company, they've reported this to the local police or whatever."

Khan shook his head. "Apparently they're not too concerned. She left a note for the tour guide, saying she had no complaints about what was happening, it simply wasn't what she'd had in mind. She was going to go off, spend the rest of the week on her own."

"Checked out of the hotel?"

"That afternoon."

"Which means she could be anywhere."

"Do you think we should contact the Madrid police, sir? Interpol, perhaps?"

Giving himself room to think, Resnick walked slowly over to where the kettle was standing, lifted it to test the weight, make sure there was water enough, then set it to boil. "I think what we'll do is send you down to Rhossili Bay after all." There was a faint ring as, along the room, Naylor set down the phone. "Kevin can go with you. Dig out Paul Matthews, see what he's got to say about Elizabeth Peck, why she might have wanted to talk so urgently to Aston. Leave now, you can be down there by this evening. Okay?"

"Yes, sir." Khan had promised he would go with Jill to the Cookie Club, but he would find a way of making it up to her. Besides, they'd been going together long enough now for her to get used to the fact that with a job like his, plans sometimes had to be changed, last minute.

"Kevin," Resnick said, "how's your Welsh?"

Divine bounded up the stairs like an oversized Rottweiler with his eyes on the back of an intruder's bare and fleshy thigh. So intent was he on finding Resnick that he cannoned into a hazy-looking Millington, doing his level best to remember what it was Madeleine had told him not to come home without buying.

"Hey up, youth!" the sergeant exclaimed, spun half around and rubbing his arm. "What's got up your backside all of a sudden?"

"The boss," Divine gasped. "He still around?"

"Off to see DI Woolmer, Special Branch. Only this minute left. Might catch him in the car park if you're sharp."

Divine didn't need any second urging. Back down the stairs three and four at a time, he was through the front entrance and waving both arms as Resnick indicated right to pull out onto Derby Road.

"Won the lottery, Mark?" Resnick asked, lowering his window.

"It's the cassette, boss. The one as was found on the embankment, near Aston's body."

"Music, isn't it? Heavy metal, isn't that what you said?"

Divine was still fighting to get back his breath. "Aye, well, sent it off to one of our tame boffins just in case. What he's found, recorded over, but none too well, are bits of talking, speech like. This bloke going on about an Englishman's birthright, white power'n crap like that."

"Well," Resnick said, a wry smile on his lips, "I'm glad you think it's all crap, Mark. Here, you'd best jump in."

Chesney Woolmer was the inspector in charge of the local Special Branch team, two sergeants and a dozen officers under him. Affable, if a little offhand, a portly man with receding hair, he listened to the cleaned-up version of the tape, some fifteen minutes of blinkered ranting which culminated in some ragged cheering and an even more motley version of "God Save the Queen."

"Her Majesty," Woolmer suggested, "would be shocked and surprised if she knew the amount of odious bollocks that went on in her name."

Resnick asked him if he recognized the voice.

"Not right off. Besides, the quality leaves a lot to be desired. But if you're happy to leave it with me, I'll get some of my lads to have a listen. Compare it to what we've got."

"And there's no way of telling where it might have been recorded?"

Woolmer shook his head. "Some bloke with his own little tape machine, some BNP rally or other. Could be local, but who's to say? Fairly innocuous by their standards, too."

"We've no way of proving the tape was dropped by the

265

people who attacked Aston, but, all other things being equal, it seems likely. Too much of a coincidence to ignore."

"Well," said Woolmer, reaching several perforated sheets of computer printout from his desk, "what I can let you have is a list of known right-wing activists in the area. Mansfield, Sutton, Ilkeston, Heanor—they'll likely be your best bets. Any who've got an association with C18, that's shown. Check these against the other names that've been thrown up by the inquiry, you might strike lucky. Failing that, there's the soccer connection."

Resnick took the list and passed it across to Divine. "If we decide to move in, knock on a few doors, see what we can turn up that way, you think you might have more than a passing interest in whatever we come across?"

Woolmer smiled. "Always grateful, Charlie, for any little tidbit you care to throw our way."

"Ah, I was thinking of more active participation than that."

"Bodies on the ground?"

"Just for a day or two, any you could spare."

"Give us a bell tomorrow, first thing. If there's anyone I can lose, short of having it checked off as overtime, I'll tell you." Woolmer grinned broadly. "Never like to miss a chance to give some of our white supremacist friends a spin." He walked with Resnick and Divine toward the door. "Last time we did, we turned up bomb-making equipment and a Russian-made rifle that had found its way to Mansfield Woodhouse by way of Iran and the UDF."

Gerry Hovenden throttled down and brought the bike through a slow curve that ended outside the house where Frank Miller lived. Couple of years now, him and Frank would spend Saturdays at the match, away games especially, those were the ones they didn't like to miss. Few pints beforehand, more than a few after the final whistle. Blokes to meet. Once in a while it turned heavy and then it was well good, worth the journey—that Frank, didn't know his own strength.

"This is it." Removing his helmet, Hovenden nodded toward a two-story brick building, its front door square onto the street; a hand-lettered sign in the frosted door glass, telling callers to go round to the back.

Shane, spare helmet Gerry always lent him in one hand, waited while he lifted the bike onto its stand.

"Frank?" Hovenden pushed at the back door and as usual it swung inward, unlocked. What cretin'd be fool enough to burgle Frank Miller?

"Frank? 'S'Gerry."

"Through here." There was music coming from the front of the house, heavily amplified rock.

Hovenden entered, nodding for Shane to follow. The back room was a kitchen, blackened chip pan on the cooker, mugs and plates overflowing the sink. Old newspapers spread across the table, more in piles on the floor. A shelf with books about the SAS and the Falklands, the Second World War.

"Bit of a reader, is he?" Shane asked.

Hovenden didn't reply.

Frank Miller was standing in the middle of the front room, bare to the waist save for tattoos on his back and arms—St. George, a Union Jack. He had pushed back to the wall the one piece of furniture in the room, a leather settee one of his bailiff pals had done him a deal on, and had been doing push-ups with alternate hands. There was a television set on the floor, a VCR, a four-section Marantz stereo with speakers mounted high on the ceiling. Right then it was playing Saxon, *Gods of War*.

Miller turned down the volume, but not much. He grinned at Hovenden, nodded abruptly at Shane. "Beer?" he asked.

"Yeah," Hovenden said. "Thanks."

"Why don't you get a couple of cans, eh, Shane? In the fridge."

The moment he was out of the room, Miller grabbed Hovenden between his legs and began to twist. "What is it with you two, anyway?" Miller hissed. "In and out one another's pockets, the whole fuckin' time, like a couple of fairies."

"Christ, Frank, leggo!" Tears in his eyes already. "It's nothin' like that, honest."

"It better not fuckin' be."

"Be what?" Shane asked, leaning against the doorway, three cans of Special Brew balanced on two hands.

"Never you fucking mind."

Shane stared at him, Miller staring back. You fat bastard, Shane was thinking, you reckon I'm afraid of you like all the rest. And one of these days you're going to have to learn it just ain't true.

"You got a problem," Miller asked, half a pace toward him.

"Maybe, yeah?"

"What's that, then?"

"That," Shane said, nodding toward the speakers, "it's a fuckin' row."

"No," Miller laughed. "That's Saxon. They're the best." But he turned it down some more and Shane tossed him a beer and all three of them drank and started to chat and for now everything was cool.

34

Days into the inquiry, the photographs of Bill Aston's beaten body had been in danger of becoming little more than part of the incident room decor, scarcely deserving a second glance. But now with some concrete information from Special Branch and the Football Intelligence Unit to work on, potential suspects to target, the adrenaline was pumping again, spirits were high, voices boisterous and loud. Aside from the regular squad assigned to the murder inquiry, there were six officers from Special Branch, a further six from the Support Department, a dozen more drafted in from other duties—among these, two out of Vice, one of them Sharon Garnett.

The map showing a thirty-mile radius out from the city had been newly marked with pins in three distinct colors: blue for the Mansfield area to the north, green for Ilkeston to the west, red for addresses within the city boundary itself. Along with Lynn Kellogg, Sharon would be working with Reg Cossall on the green team; Graham Millington was supervising red; Chesney Woolmer, invited in by Resnick to assist with the briefing, would be running blue.

"Some of these people we're going to interview," Woolmer said, "may surprise you. Some will look like nice law-abiding insurance salesmen with a wife who works part-time and the regulation two-point-whatever kids. Likely not what you're expecting at all. That doesn't mean they haven't got regular subscriptions to a magazine with step-by-step instructions on how to construct a letter bomb and ideas of where to send it. Other times, you'll open the door to three bloody great Alsatians and a bloke with a tattooed beer gut hanging over his jeans and you'll think, Okay, stupid fat sod, I know where I am here. Don't be fooled. These are people—some of them—capable of running a network of like-minded souls that takes in not just this country, but most of mainland Europe as well. Don't underestimate them. And don't turn your back on the sodding dogs."

Resnick stepped forward into the ensuing laughter. "Remember we haven't got warrants here, we're not going barging in. What we're doing is asking questions, establishing links—where were they the night of Aston's murder, where did they go drinking, where were their mates?"

"But if you do get inside"—Woolmer again—"if you are invited in, be aware, keep your eyes skinned, anything that might be of potential interest to the Branch, I want to know."

"All right," said Resnick, "any more questions?"

There were none: within three minutes the room had cleared. What questions there were snagged in Resnick's mind: he knew much of the circumstantial evidence pointed to a vicious, random attack—the spiraling pattern of footprints, the nature of the blows—and it seemed certain there had been a gang of probably drunken, possibly violent youths in the vicinity at the appropriate time, and yet . . . And yet . . . he could not let go of the idea that what had happened to Bill Aston had its roots in something more specific, more personal than a random attack in which he was a victim solely by chance and circumstance.

Resnick looked again at the blurred black-and-white images on the wall. Was it only a kind of sentimentality that urged him to see Aston's death as having had reason and purpose, that and nothing more? He looked at his watch: Khan and Naylor should be making contact with Paul Matthews at any time. There were other avenues still open.

Khan and Naylor had spent the night in a B&B in Swansea, close by the old docks, now a smart new marina surrounded by brightly painted rows of flats and a heritage trail. Their landlady had insisted on serving them eggs and bacon accompanied by lava bread. "It's a delicacy, see. Local." Whatever it was, Kevin Naylor thought, it wasn't bread. Black and somewhat slimy, it tasted suspiciously of whelks. As soon as they stepped outside the front door into the bright spring day, they could clearly see both hills and sea. Rhossili Bay was little more than fifteen miles along the Gower Peninsula.

Paul Matthews's aunt didn't disappoint. Her cottage was at the end of a rutted lane outside Llangennith, on the north edge of the Rhossili Downs. Two rusted cars lay on their sides, the new year's nettles growing up around them. A van, unlicensed but apparently still running, sat by the side gate, a black-and-white collie growling at the two detectives through bared teeth.

The aunt walked out into the yard, scattering chickens from around her slippered feet. Face brown and lined beyond her years, hair falling thinly away from a wispy bun, she was wearing an apron with a small floral print and muttering in Welsh.

"It's not lost you are, is it?" she asked, lapsing into English.

When they assured her they were far from lost and explained why they were there, she insisted on sitting them down and making them tea. Paul, she said, had gone off early, down toward the bay most likely; that was what he'd done, most days since he'd come.

"Something wrong with that boy," she told them. "Not right in the head. Oh, I don't mean he's crazy, mind. Not like that. But troubled." She smiled at them hopefully. "Anything you can do now, to ease his mind."

They found him on a high reach of cliff, gulls riding the currents above his head and wheeling down to where they were nesting on the almost sheer face of rock.

For a fearful moment, Naylor thought that he was poised to jump, but he was simply standing, staring out at the dark smudge of a tanker slow-sliding down the horizon, north to south.

"Mr. Matthews," Khan said, speaking quietly, not wishing to startle. "Paul."

He didn't seem surprised to see Khan there, simply nodded toward him and Naylor and went back to looking out to sea. The wind was beginning to whip the tops of the waves into crescents of foam. On the horizon, the ship seemed scarcely to have moved.

"Paul? Paul, this is my colleague, Detective Constable Naylor. We need to talk."

"But we've already . . ."

"We need to talk some more."

"About Nicky?"

"Yes."

Matthews looked out beyond the cliff edge toward the pencil-thin line bisecting sea and sky. "Mr. Jardine, does he know?"

"That we're here?"

Matthews nodded.

"No. Anything you say, it's just between us. You have my word."

"Because he warned me, all of us, we weren't to say anything, anything at all, not without him or a solicitor being there. He—"

"But he's not here, Paul," Khan said, reassuringly. "Look around you. He need never know."

Matthews took them to a place that stood alone with white peeling paint, little more than a hut, an owner who had retired there from southeast London, Camberwell, and now sold cans of drink with names neither Naylor nor Khan had ever heard of, and tea from a large and battered silver pot.

They sat outside on rickety bench seats, sheltering from the freshness of the wind.

"I can't stop thinking about him," Matthews said. "Seeing him everywhere I look."

"Nicky, you mean? Nicky Snape."

"I found him, you see. It was me, I was the one."

"I know." Khan nodded.

"I should've took him down. The towel, I should have loosened it from round his neck. Took him down." His eyes were like the wings of small dark birds, never still. "I was frightened. Afraid. I don't suppose you can understand."

"Yes, Paul," Khan said. "We can."

Matthews looked at him and read the lie. "It doesn't matter, not now."

"Paul," Naylor began, "we wanted to ask you—"

"I held him, you see. I did that. I held him. Against me, like this." He spread his arms from his body and then folded them back carefully through space, enfolding the imaginary boy with tenderness to his chest. "He was still warm."

Naylor glanced across at Khan. "He was still alive?" he asked.

Sobs choked from Matthews's mouth and nose as he shook his head from side to side more and more vigorously, rhythmically, as if dangling from a rope. "I don't know," repeating over and over. "I don't know, I don't know, I don't know."

Embarrassed, Naylor fished out a pocket-sized pack of Kleenex and gave one to Matthews, then another, Khan inside ordering more tea, sweet this time, three sugars.

Ten minutes later they were walking, Khan alongside Matthews, Naylor several paces behind. This is the sort of place I should come with Debbie, Naylor was thinking, get her mum to baby-sit one weekend; somewhere like this, right away from everything, it'd be different here. Relaxed.

"Elizabeth Peck, she was on duty that evening?" Khan was asking. "The two of you together, right?"

"Yes, of course. We went through all of this. You know that."

"And she was the one who called emergency services, I think that's what you said?"

Matthews nodded yes, yes.

They were starting to climb again, the path well-trodden, earth at the field edge almost white.

"You haven't any idea, Paul, have you, why she might have got in touch with Inspector Aston? At home. Privately, you know."

Matthews had stopped walking and Naylor, still partly daydreaming, almost bumped into him from behind.

"Elizabeth, you don't know what she would have wanted to talk to him about?"

Matthews seemed dazed, out of focus. Off to the west a group of gulls was noisily baiting a lone crow. "She did that?"

"Yes. Quite a conversation, apparently. Whatever it was, they found a lot to say. We wondered if you had any idea what she might have talked to him about?"

"I think," Matthews said, "I should go back now. I can't walk too far. I'm not well, you understand, I've not been well. The doctor . . . that's why I'm here. My aunt . . ."

He started to walk back the way they had just come; Naylor standing there, not hurrying to move aside.

"What did she know, Paul? About what happened to Nicky. Something she hadn't told anyone before, that's what it must have been."

Matthews shook his head and made an ineffectual attempt to move past, but sharp to his left there was the cliff edge and the other way was Khan, arms folded, smiling.

"Paul?"

"What? I . . ."

"You can tell us. Whatever Elizabeth would have talked to Inspector Aston about—tell us now, Paul. What would she have said? What did she know?"

Matthews stepped back, back toward the sea. One foot skidding the coarse grass, arm flailing, he was arching over as Naylor caught him, low about the waist and swinging him inland, snatching him, almost, out of the air, the pair of them falling, bodies awkwardly intertwining across the edge of the path, the first stubby growth of the year.

"Good catch," Khan said to Naylor, and then, to Matthews, helping him gingerly to his feet, "You okay? You need to be a bit more careful, narrow paths like these. One foot in the wrong place and then . . ."

There were tears in Matthews's eyes again, clinging there, refusing to fall.

"Come on," Khan said. "What d'you say? Why don't we go back down?"

It was, as Reg Cossall would say later over a pint of Shippos, one of those fine spring days when to describe the stink of stale farts and cheap lager breath that greeted them in every doorway would have beggared even the sodding poet laureate's invention.

Exactly so.

Their questions were answered with deviousness, vulgarity, polite lies, numberless requests for them to fuck off out of it and mind their own bleedin' business, and, on one occasion, by a bucket of what startlingly resembled warm piss descending from an upstairs window in a virulent stream.

At least Chaucer could have dealt with that one.

Or Divine.

Divine, who suffered a long harangue from an out-of-work twenty-one-year-old, living with a seventeen-year-old woman and their two kids in a council house in Kirkby-in-Ashfield. "You," he said, jabbing a finger toward Divine's face, "you ought to be ashamed of yourself, you know that? Goin' round roustin' blokes just 'cause they show a bit of patriotism, right? Not afraid to stick up for their fuckin' country, right? You know what I'm saying? I mean, you look around you, look around you, okay? Every fuckin' business, who owns it? Pakis, right? Pakis and niggers everywhere you fuckin' look. And the Irish . . . honest to Christ, I hate the fuckin' Irish. Treacherous, murderin' bastards. I mean, look, this country, this country used to be great, right? Look at a map, look at a fuckin' map sometime, we used to own half this soddin' world, three quarters of it, and now we're nothing. Less than nothing. And me, blokes like me, we're the only ones standing up, makin' ourselves fuckin' heard. 'Cause we care, right? About this fuckin' country. It's your fuckin' pride, okay? We care and we ain't afraid to let it show and you, you and your mates, as should be standing up with us, side by side, to make this country what it once was, what it could be, without all the nignogs and the Pakis and the Jews, all you do is come round hassling us, right? Ought to be fuckin' ashamed!"

Eyes alight, he hawked up a thick gob of spit and

unleashed it on the ground some yards wide of Divine's feet. Divine listening, thinking, though he wasn't about to say so, that one way or another, the bloke had a point.

Lynn Kellogg and Sharon Garnett had almost given up trying to rouse anyone from this house, the last but one in the road, what remained of the front lawn blackened with engine oil. Sharon was giving Lynn the thumbs-down and turning away when there were footsteps and a muffled voice from the other side of the front door.

It was a runty little man in a singlet and jeans, scratching himself and yawning, blinking at the light.

"Sorry to wake you," Sharon said, identifying Lynn and herself. "We're looking for Gerry Hovenden. That wouldn't be you, by any chance."

Unaware, possibly, that he was now standing there scratching energetically between his legs, the man shook his head. "Not by any chance. That's the boy you're wanting and he's away."

"Away where?"

"Buggered if I know."

But the sound of a motorbike approaching provided all the answer they needed, Hovenden, moments later, swinging his leg over the rear of the machine, Shane already standing there, helmet in hand, thinking, Fucking law, what in fuck's name they after now?

It was soon clear.

"Can you tell us, Gerry," Lynn asked, "where you were last Saturday evening?"

"Home," he replied, without hesitation.

"Last Saturday," his father said dismissively. "I never saw hide nor hair of you all evening."

Colored brightly from his neck, Hovenden shook his head. "Home round Shane's, that's what I mean. Couple of videos and a curry, eh, Shane?"

"That's right," Shane said. "All evening."

"You're sure about that?" Lynn said, moving a touch closer and fixing him with her best stare.

But Shane was not about to be intimidated. "I said, didn't I? Sure." Those hard, brittle eyes, daring Lynn to call him a liar.

"Well, in that case," Lynn said, "we'd best have your name and address, too. You never know when we might want to check."

"Shane Snape," Resnick said, "that's interesting." Lynn and Sharon had reported back to Reg Cossall initially and then to Resnick direct. The three of them were in his office, the sky through the window slowly darkening toward evening.

"Came up on the back of the bike, large as life," Lynn said.

"Yes," Sharon said. "Gave this Gerry Hovenden his alibi."

Resnick looked at the two officers, one to another. "And you didn't believe him?"

Sharon shook her head.

"Not Hovenden, certainly," Lynn said. "Lying to his back teeth, if you ask me. Covering up about something, I'd bet on that."

"And he's on the Branch list? Political?"

Lynn made a face. "Marginal, really. Not a member of any extremist group, as far as is known. Hangs about with them, that's all. Spotted up a couple of times at rallies. Nothing criminal recorded."

"Right, let's follow it up. Once we've got some more information in, check Hovenden's contacts with the rest, see if he fits in with anyone else that looks interesting."

"And Shane Snape?" Lynn asked. "Do you want us to process him as normal, or . . ."

"I might go round myself," Resnick said. "Have a word."

"Right." Lynn hesitated at the door after Sharon Garnett had passed through. "About the other night," she said quietly. "All those things I was saying . . . I know it's difficult, I've probably made it difficult, but it's not going to get in the way . . . I mean, we can work together, it hasn't stopped that?"

"No," Resnick said, "of course not, it's fine."

"You're sure?"

"Sure."

Resnick's phone rang and as he reached toward it, Lynn slipped out through the door and closed it behind her.

35

It was a little after seven in the morning when Resnick realized he was thinking about Hannah, that he had been doing so for several minutes, ever since hoicking a recalcitrant Dizzy from the center of the most comfortable armchair and sitting down with his second cup of coffee of the day. He could see her sitting on that bench in the Arboretum, face angled toward him, fixing him with that serious stare as she delivered her lecture on rejection and how not to take it. The schoolteacher in her, he thought; those earnest, serious eyes. And then the phone rang and it was her. Resnick felt uneasy, as if somehow thinking about Hannah had made it happen.

"Charlie, it's not too early . . . ?"

"No, no, I've been up awhile."

"Good. Only . . . look, dinner on Friday. You haven't already booked somewhere, have you?"

Air sucked cold through Resnick's stomach: she'd changed her mind. "No, not yet," he said cautiously.

"Oh, good, because—"

"Something else has cropped up."

"No. Yes. Well, not exactly."

Resnick fought to keep the disappointment out of his voice. The last thing he wanted was another lecture on rejection. "Not to worry, maybe some other time."

"No," Hannah said, "it's not that, Friday's still fine. It's just . . . well, I feel stupid after making such a fuss about you being the one to decide. . . ."

"That didn't matter, it's okay, I—"

"The thing is, there's this film, at Broadway. . . ."

It would be, Resnick thought.

"It's something I really want to see and Friday's the only chance I've got."

"Look," Resnick said, the soul of reason, "that's all right, you go and see your film. We can meet another evening."

"I was thinking more that you might come with me."

"Ah."

"We could get something to eat afterwards; we could eat there even, the food's not bad." She drew breath, waiting for a response that didn't come. "What do you think?"

"This isn't," Resnick asked warily, "another film from Tunisia about—what was it?—silence?"

Hannah laughed, just a little. "No, you're quite safe. It's in English. Well, American. *Vanya on 42nd Street*."

A memory jostled deep inside Resnick's brain. "That's the Marx Brothers, isn't it?"

Hannah laughed. "Not exactly."

"Oh."

"More Chekov, I think." And before he could say anything else, "If that's okay, why don't we meet there? In the foyer. A quarter past eight."

"All right."

"See you then. And Charlie?"

"Mmm?"

"Next time I will let you choose, I promise."

When he looked back across the room, Dizzy had taken the chance to nip back into the chair and lay there curled, one paw tight across his eyes.

"This carries on, Dizzy, my friend, the way she feels about cats, your days could be numbered."

When Norma got back from her morning stint of cleaning, there was Sheena, feet up in the kitchen, smoking a cigarette while Peter boiled eggs for his breakfast, his or Sheena's, it was difficult to tell. At least father and daughter were in the same room together and, if not exactly talking, not shouting either.

"That place," Norma said, shucking off her coat and dropping it onto the back of a chair, "don't know if the bitter was off last night or what, but the state of that gents this morning, floor were like a bad night in the scuttering abattoir."

"Thanks, Mum." Sheena grimaced, stubbing out her cigarette. "For sharing that with us."

"Yes, thanks, love." Peter grinned. "Just what I need to give me an appetite for these eggs. P'raps I should have them scrambled after all."

Sheena leaned over the side of her chair and mimed being sick.

"What I could do with . . ." Norma began, lighting up herself.

"Is a fag and a nice cup of tea." Peter began it and with Sheena joining in, they finished in unison.

"You two seem perky," Norma said, filling the kettle at the sink.

"Been getting on all right, haven't we, Sheena?"

"Okay, yeah."

"Then I'd best not ask you, young lady, why you're not at work, had I? Spoil this grand mood you're in."

"Leave her be," Peter urged, bending forward and carefully spooning the first of his eggs from the pan.

"Or where," Norma went on, "you got another new jacket from? And don't waste your breath telling me it's borrowed. Or that you bought it from what you've earned, 'cause the number of hours you've been working lately, it's you that'll be owin' them instead of the other way round."

"Norma, love, leave it."

"S'all right for you, you'll be off out of here soon enough. I'm the one whose pocket'll hurt if she gets her cards."

"Yeah, well," said Sheena with a sniff, "shows what you know, 'cause I already did."

"What! You soft cow, what's the matter with you? What d'you want to go and do that for?"

"I didn't do it, did I? It were done to me." Sheena swung her legs round from the seat of the empty chair, revealing a new pair of ankle-length black boots, still bright from their first shine.

"You what? And what about those shoes?"

"What about them?"

"You nicked them, that's what. No two ways about it. You and those fancy new friends of yours. You want to watch out, my girl, else you'll end up inside."

"Yeah? Well, a fucking lot you care."

Norma coming to stand over her now: "I've told you before, don't use that language to me."

"No?" Sheena on her feet, face jutting forward into her mother's. "I'll use what language I sodding like. You don't own me, you know."

"Is that right?" Norma swung her arm wildly, and if she hadn't ducked into it instead of away, Sheena would never have got hit. As it was, the heel of her mother's hand caught her hard alongside her mouth and she stumbled away, bleeding from her lip.

"You bitch!" Sheena yelled. "You bloody bitch!"

Norma let out a sound somewhere between a scream and a howl and weighed into Sheena with both hands, Peter saying, over and over, "Sheena, Norma, cut it out!" and doing his best to drag Norma back; Sheena covering her face with her arms and Norma crying now, Norma and Sheena both crying. "Sheena, Norma, stop it now." Peter carrying on till Norma turned on him and pushed him clear across the kitchen. "Stop wingeing on, you pathetic little shit. You get on my nerves something rotten, you sodding do."

Sheena seized her moment and ran from the room, up the stairs into the bathroom, where she locked the door and sat on the loo seat, arms gripped to her sides, shaking with anger and fear.

She hadn't stolen the boots, Diane had, from Dolcis the other afternoon. And as for the jacket, there they'd been, the whole gang of them, walking down through the city center by Debenham's, when this girl came down the street in the opposite direction and Janie reached out and grabbed her by the hair and told her to take off her leather jacket, she was having it, and the girl, of course, she said, no way, so Janie pulled her hair tighter, then pushed her hard up against the wall, and when she bounced back, smacked her in the face with the heel of her shoe and told her to take off the fucking jacket, which now, no problem, the girl did, Janie bowing and laughing and saying, how kind, thank you so very much, and, now that her shoe was back on, giving the girl a good kick before carrying on across the street, not running or nothing, jacket round her shoulders; top of the street, Janie'd stopped and looked at herself in the mirror, crap, she'd said, I look like fucking crap in this, and she'd tossed it over to Sheena, here, you have it, it'd look all right on you, and pranced on across the street in front of the traffic, expecting it to stop for her, which, of course, it did.

Awesome, Sheena had thought. Fucking awesome!

And she still thought the same now, sitting there on the loo, almost able to feel the bruises coming out on her arms and neck.

Khan and Naylor stood respectfully across from Resnick's desk and told him about their conversation with Paul Matthews; told him and then waited patiently for his response. It was interesting, Resnick had thought as he listened, how the pair of them were seemingly alike in some ways, yet different: with Naylor, you felt the deference was natural, in part a product of a lack of confidence, whereas Khan seemed to be reining himself in, not wanting to seem pushy or overbright.

"He reckons he might've saved Nicky Snape's life if he'd acted quicker; that's at the root of it, then?"

"Yes, sir," said Naylor. "Seems that way."

"You don't think there's anything more?"

Naylor shook his head, but Resnick was looking at Khan.

"I don't honestly think we could have got anything more from him that day; he was in a pretty het-up state. But I'm sure he's not told us everything," Khan said after a moment. "Not yet."

"And you think he will?"

Khan nodded. "I hope so. For his sake as well as ours." He allowed himself a slight smile. "Kevin here's not always going to be around to stop him throwing himself off the edge of the cliff."

"You gave him your number, in case he decides to contact you?"

"Yes, sir."

"All right. Meantime, let's have a closer look at Jardine. Dig around in his background a little. Previous appointments, whatever you can find. Let's see if there are any other reasons for him wanting to keep this all under wraps. Okay?"

As the two men turned to leave the office, Naylor automatically stood aside to let Khan through the door first.

It was almost an hour later that Resnick met Skelton near the head of the stairs, Skelton just back from a meeting with the Assistant Chief. They were discussing the meeting when Carl Vincent walked along the corridor in front of them, heading toward CID.

"How's he settling in, Charlie?" Skelton asked, voice low.

"Early days yet. But okay, far as I know."

"No trouble, then? On account of his color. You know the sort of thing I mean."

Resnick knew well enough what it would have been like in days not so long past: whispering campaigns, closed ranks in the canteen, loud references to spooks and sooties, nignogs and monkeys, spades and coons. Pakis. And the jokes: What do you call a nigger in a three-bedroom semi? A burglar. Bananas and travel brochures advertising holidays in Africa, the West Indies, all the personal details filled in, those and worse left for black recruits to find. Once, hanging down from the locker-room ceiling, a white sheet with eye holes cut in the manner of the Ku Klux Klan. The bad old days.

"I've not heard of anything going off."

Skelton nodded thoughtfully. "And you've talked to Vincent himself?"

"Just about to. Off to see Shane Snape, check an alibi he's given for a mate, I thought Vincent could ride along. I'll have a word on the way."

"What you mean is, Charlie, you thought he could be your driver."

Resnick grinned. "That, too."

There were roadworks south on the Ilkeston Road and an articulated lorry had got itself wedged across the entrance to

Garden Street, so they cut left along Kimboulton Avenue, down Ashburnham, past the brightly painted nursery and the recreation ground, swinging out onto the Boulevard and then over the crossroads, through the lights.

"How's it compare, then?" Resnick asked. "To Leicester?"

Vincent smiled gently, an eloquent shrug of the shoulders.

"Have you been getting any hassle?"

Vincent looked at him, perhaps for longer than he should, considering he was at the wheel. "You mean on account of being black?"

"That's what I mean, yes."

"It's cool."

"You mean there hasn't been any, or there has and you're not bothered, you can handle it?"

"Nobody's spoken out of turn, no—what's the term?— racial epithets." Quickly this time, he glanced across the front seat. "Would you expect me to report it if there were?"

"Yes," Resnick said. "Yes, I would."

Vincent nodded, thinking it over. "Which turning?" he asked. "Must be pretty soon now. On the left, yes?"

It was Peter who answered the door, a slight figure in a singlet and a pair of old cords, absurd almost with his little belly sticking out from below his concave chest. Resnick identified Vincent and himself and by that time Norma was there, filling out the hall. From inside came the sounds of the two-fifteen from Doncaster.

"How's it going, Norma?" Resnick asked, friendly. Norma thinking he had come about Sheena, worried the stupid gillifer had got herself caught in the Broad Marsh Centre, some uptight store detective feeling her collar the minute she set foot outside the shop. But no, not this time.

"Your Shane," Resnick said. "He around?"

He was in his usual place when home, stretched out on the settee in front of the TV, can of Carlsberg within reach. Most days, if he didn't come out ahead at the bookie's, he didn't finish up so far behind.

He looked round at Resnick with flat, cold eyes; took in Vincent and dismissed him with a glance. The signs of the beating he had taken at the hands of the Turvey boys were fading but yet to disappear.

Resnick nodded in the direction of the television and Vincent went round behind the settee and turned the volume down; horse with a white noseband seemed to be winning by seven or eight lengths. "That pal of yours," Resnick said. "Gerry Hovenden."

"Yeah, what about him?" Shane watching the screen, the last runners fading past the post.

"Last Saturday night, you gave him an alibi."

"So?"

"I thought now he wasn't here, you might change your mind. Remember things a different way."

"You're not saying I lied?"

"Loyalty," Resnick said, "it's a funny thing."

"Mum," Shane said, pushing himself up onto one elbow, raising his voice toward the kitchen, "where was I Sat'day last?"

"Here." Norma answering with prompting, walking through. "Here with that pal of yours. Gerry. Brought back those videos, remember? *Elm Street* and that other one. Horrible bloody things!" And then, looking at Resnick, "He was here, Mr. Resnick. They both was." Waiting for him to say otherwise.

What Resnick did was move closer to where Shane was sitting, sit down himself, on the arm of the settee. "You into the same things as him, Shane? Aside from horror movies, I mean. Combat 18 and the like. Extremist stuff. Fascist rallies, racist attacks."

Shane shifted his glance over toward Vincent, standing easily near the back of the room, and then back again.

"'Cause if you were, I'd be surprised. Thought you had more brains than to be taken in by stuff like that."

Shane made a circling motion with his shoulders before looking back toward the screen and the winning jockey, dismounting in the unsaddling enclosure. After a moment, he reached for the remote and switched the sound back up.

"Take it carefully," Resnick said, back on his feet. "Don't get yourself into any trouble you don't need to."

Shame didn't budge, gave no indication that he heard or heeded Resnick's advice.

Norma walked with the two detectives to the door. "The old girl," she said, "the one, you know, my Nicky—"

"Doris. She's getting slowly better, Norma. On the mend. They both are, her and her husband."

Norma nodded. "Good. I'm glad for that at least."

Resnick and Vincent walking away then, back to the car, Vincent unlocking the doors and the pair of them getting in, kids along the street and parents at their windows, watching.

"What in Christ's name," Norma shrilled at Shane the minute she got back in, "have you been up to now?"

"Relax," Shane said. "First horse of the afternoon just come in, twenty-five to one."

36

As luck would have it, Stella Aston answered the phone when Resnick called; yes, of course she'd meet him, how about the Town House? Did he know it? That street off Bridlesmith Gate. Low Pavement, is that what it was called?

It was. Resnick got there early, one of those places he had walked past numberless times in the last three or four years. Slim, pale wooden tables and waitresses who were studying fashion at Trent University; either that or they were sixth-formers from the high school, giving off equal quantities of good breeding and disdain. Inside, casually smart young men whose designer socks and underwear, Resnick guessed, cost more than he spent on clothes in a year lolled back in dark glasses and looked cool. An elegant young mother—or was it the au pair?—fed what looked like purple yogurt to a toddler in a high chair. One elderly woman, gray hair unraveling round her lined face, sat unhappily over the remains of her toasted sandwich, looking as out of place as Resnick felt.

"One, sir?" the waitress asked, friendly enough.

"Er, I'm meeting somebody."

She gave Resnick a look that seemed to signify "as if" and consigned him to a table near the coffee machine, where she promptly forgot about him till Stella walked in. Stella in a bright top, colored tights and clumpy boots, and a skirt so short as to be hardly worthy of the name.

Resnick half-rose to greet her, embarrassed by her youthful attractiveness and conscious of those eyes watching from behind dark glasses, weighing up the nature of their relationship.

"How's your mum holding up?" Resnick asked, once Stella had sat down.

"Oh, you know, pretty well considering. Sometimes I think it still hasn't properly sunk in. Maybe it won't while I'm still around."

"How long's that likely to be?"

"I ought to go back, oh, the end of the week."

Resnick ordered a double espresso and Stella a fizzy mineral water and a piece of chocolate cake that came, small and rich, marooned in the middle of a large white plate.

For ten minutes or so they talked about nothing very much, Resnick relaxed enough now to enjoy Stella's company, the way she would throw back her head and laugh aloud at one of her own anecdotes about college. They think I'm her father, he thought, sneaking an hour off work to spend with his daughter, one of her rare visits home from university.

"I don't know what to call you," Stella said suddenly. "I know my dad always used to call you Charlie."

"Charlie's fine."

But she shook her head. "Not serious enough."

"Is that what I am?"

"Aren't you?" Cake finished, she surprised him by taking a packet of cigarettes from her bag, signaling to the waitress for an ashtray. "You see, you're disapproving."

"Am I?"

"Yes." Drawing the first lungful of smoke down deep. "You think, Nice young girl, into the environment, ought to be taking care of her body in the same way. Something like that, anyway."

Resnick supposed she might be right.

"You're not—what's the word?—frivolous, are you, Charlie? You have to do things for a reason."

Despite himself, almost as if to disprove her, Resnick laughed. "How do you know, I mean, here you are, the first time I've seen you in years. Certainly the first time we've ever . . ."

"Been alone."

"Had a proper conversation . . ."

"And I'm analyzing you."

"Yes."

She smiled. "Charlie, I don't just know about trees. The reason we're here, for instance, it's not casual. You didn't call me on the spur of the moment. Not that there'd be anything wrong in that, but you just wouldn't do it." She grinned. "Even if it occurred to you, you'd hold back. Too many possible complications."

Uncomfortable, Resnick looked round for the waitress. "D'you want anything else? I'm going to have another espresso."

She watched him while he ordered, waited while the waitress cleared their used crockery away. "Well? I'm right, aren't I?"

Resnick leaned forward. "I wanted to ask you . . ."

"Yes?"

"Your parents, they had separate rooms."

"Yes, Dad's insomnia . . ."

"And this first happened when?"

"Oh, I don't know. Two or three years ago, maybe. But why do you want to know?"

"You were still living at home then, when they made this decision?"

"Doing A levels, yes."

"And did they say much, d'you remember, about why they were going to make this change?"

"Yes, like I said, my dad, he couldn't sleep properly, he thought it would be best for my mum, they both thought it would be—" Stella broke off abruptly and reached for another cigarette; there were things she didn't want to see forming behind her eyes. "You think something was going on, don't you? You think he was having an affair? My dad. That's what you were on about the other day, all that fuss about that phone call. God, Charlie! You think he was sleeping around."

Slowly, Resnick shook his head. "I don't know."

Stella shook her head and laughed. "You didn't know him very well after all. He just wasn't like that. I know that's what you'd expect me to say, but it's true. He just wasn't. Apart from anything else, there was all that religion. His preaching. Even if he'd been tempted, he'd never have let himself." She held the smoke inside her mouth, releasing it through her nose. "If it was either of them having an affair, it would have been Mum. Not him."

It was Resnick's turn to be surprised. For some moments, he tried to imagine Margaret, small, dumpy Margaret . . . "Why do you say that?" he asked.

"Because she was the one who had nothing else."

"She had children, you."

Stella laughed again, brittle and raw. "I was seventeen, eighteen, my brothers had long left home. I had this boyfriend, older than me. We were sleeping together. Mum and I, we never talked about it, but she must have known. It's not

293

so difficult to imagine what that's like, your baby girl out there having sex and enjoying it, night after night, and you . . . I doubt if she and Dad had done it for years."

Resnick's mind was on overtime. "What you're saying . . ."

"Do I know it for a fact? No, not at all. I certainly didn't think it at the time. But then I would have been so wrapped up in what was happening to me, I think she could have done it on the kitchen table and I'd hardly have noticed." She giggled, suddenly young again. "Well, I think I might have noticed that."

She stubbed out her half-smoked cigarette. "About Mum, you won't need to say anything, will you? Ask her, I mean? It probably isn't true, none of it. Just my fertile imagination, and besides, even if there was some truth in it, it couldn't have anything to do with what happened to my dad, could it? I mean, how could it?"

Resnick shook his head. "I don't know. But you're right, it's difficult to see."

"Then you won't say anything to her, to my mum?"

"I shouldn't think so."

Stella beamed and ordered a hot chocolate. "You notice a bit of a theme here?" she asked. "Hot chocolate, chocolate cake." And then, "All those times you used to come round to the house with Dad, I used to hang around, follow you from room to room. I always wanted you to notice me, but you never did."

"I'm sorry, I . . ."

"I used to think you were lovely. I had this photograph of you, I'd cut it from the paper. I used to keep it in my room, hidden in case anyone saw it. You never even noticed I was there."

Resnick was blushing. "God, Stella, you were about twelve."

Stella laughed, spilling hot chocolate over the table. "I

can't help it, I was advanced for my age." She was dabbing at the table with her napkin. "Now I've shocked you."

"No."

"Yes, I have. All these steamy revelations about the Aston family women in one afternoon."

The waitress was weighing in with a cloth, murmuring something about coming back to mop the floor. Stella scraped back her chair, smoothing down her skirt onto royal blue thighs. "I think we ought to go, don't you? Before we turn this place into a wreck."

Resnick thanked the waitress and paid the bill.

On the cobbled street outside, for a moment Stella took his arm. "So, Charlie—I like calling you that now—how about you, have you got a girlfriend or what?"

It took him a while to answer. "Yes," he said. "At least, I think so."

"Ooh," Stella laughed, "I should make sure, if I were you. You never know, whoever she is, she might not see it that way at all."

37

He saw her rounding the corner into Broad Street, hurrying a little, but not so much that she didn't pause to check her reflection in the window of an Italian restaurant: a linen jacket over a pale blue top, dark blue, wide-cut linen trousers. She looked, Resnick thought, lovely.

"Charlie, I'm sorry I'm late."

"No, it's me. I was early."

In a slightly proprietorial way, Hannah touched her lips to his cheek. "I phoned ahead," she said, "and reserved two tickets, just in case."

Resnick reached for his wallet, but she stopped him, her fingers circling his wrist. "My treat."

They took their seats just as the film was about to start. A street scene in what Resnick presumed was New York: the Alfreton Road it certainly was not. Too bright, too brash, too fast-moving—all those garish signs and yellow cabs. But then the camera followed a number of the people into the calmer space of an old theater, men and women dressed casually, greeting one another as old friends. Actors, Resnick supposed. Hannah had told him—all she had said by way of warning—it was about actors rehearsing a Russian play. Well, that, he supposed, was what this was.

A fortyish man complaining to an older woman about how hard he has been having to work, so many jobs, different times of the day. When they sat down, she asked him if he would like a drink, and the man shook his head ruefully and told her he was trying to stop drinking vodka in the middle of the day.

Vodka: Resnick's attention perked up. And as they continued to talk, this couple, their language barely changing, he gradually realized that what he was hearing was the beginning of the play. Without announcement or much preamble, the thing itself had begun. *Uncle Vanya.* They were watching it now.

For close to two hours, Resnick fidgeted a little in his seat—legs too long, body weight not distributed quite right—but his attention rarely wavered from the screen, and when it did, it was only to glance across at Hannah, her close profile, the degree to which she was held rapt. Near the end, the way she pulled a tissue from her bag and dabbed away the tears.

"Well, Charlie, what did you think of that?" They were on their way downstairs, people milling round them in a haze of conversation.

What did he think?

That he had recognized them, these people, quarreling endlessly about the estate on which they lived and worked, promises not clearly made and never kept, love which remained undeclared until it was too late. The best hopes of their lives had passed them by because they had been afraid to act. To speak. To say what they felt. These people he knew.

"I mean"—they were down at the ground floor now, others spilling round them on all sides—"did you like it? The film."

Smiling, Resnick surprised her by taking her arm. "Yes, I did. Now"—steering her over toward the CaféBar—"did you say something about eating in here?"

It was busy but they found a table close against the back wall and Resnick ate small pieces of chicken steeped in garlic, while Hannah picked at something spicy with red peppers and aubergine and talked about the film. Resnick content for the most part to listen, sneak occasional glances around the room, chip in the odd word or two, sip his wine.

"Come on," he said, outside, "let's get a cab. I'll see you home."

"It's a nice night," Hannah said. "We could walk."

And they did, through the square and up Derby Road, Hannah asking him about his marriage, what had happened, no need for him to talk about it if he didn't want to or if it made him feel uncomfortable, it wasn't any of her business, but talk he did, mapping the slow shifts of his and Elaine's relationship in a way that moved her, as she had been moved earlier, in the cinema. His slow, careful telling of it affecting her with the pain it still rekindled for him, the sense, still there, of loss; the generosity, finally, with which he spoke about Elaine, despite her leaving him, falling in love with another man.

"Do you ever hear from her, Charlie?"

"Not really, no."

They were crossing at the lights below the Savoy, not so far to go, down past the small hotel and then a left turn onto the path beside the park that led to Hannah's house. Which was where, some fifty yards along, the man stumbled out of the bushes directly in front of them, Hannah jumping back with a stifled scream and Resnick instantly on guard, adrenaline firing in. The man swayed, face a pale blur in the light from the upstairs windows opposite, and then made to hurry past, but when Resnick moved across to block his path, raised a hand to detain him, he cowered back and began to shout.

"It's okay, it's okay," Resnick said, cautiously moving close, the man not shouting now, but mumbling over and over, words draining into one another, "Keepbackkeepback-keepback."

He made a sudden dart, trying to squeeze past between Resnick and the fence, and Resnick caught him by the arm and swung him round and all resistance went out of the man and he cried. There were cuts, Resnick could see now, high on his face, a broad gash above his left eye, a graze all down one cheek.

"It's all right," Resnick said quietly, and then, to the man, taking another careful step toward him, "No one's going to hurt you, it's okay."

"What can we do?" Hannah asked anxiously.

"Nip home. Phone for an ambulance."

The man began to scream.

"Go on," Resnick said, Hannah hesitating. "Do it now."

"Not the hospital," the man was moaning. "Please not."

"Why don't we take him to my place?" Hannah said. "He could sit down a minute, calm down. The hospital's only up the road after all."

Resnick was thinking, thinking about the marks on the man's face, how they might have been caused. "All right," he said. "Maybe that's best."

Hannah moved past him to the man, who flinched when she made as if to touch him, but agreed finally to walk beside her toward the terraced houses at the end, walking slowly as if each step hurt.

He was older than Resnick had first judged, mid-thirties he now would have said, wearing black jeans with patches of dirt down one side and below the knees, a collarless black shirt spotted with blood, white Nike Air trainers with a blue stripe.

"Here." Hannah coming toward him with a dampened cloth to wipe away some of the blood, the man sitting at her kitchen table, blinking in the light.

Resnick stopped her with her name, not loud but firm, and she looked across at him, head tilted in a question. "Gloves," Resnick said. "Kitchen gloves, something like that. Use them. Just in case."

Hannah hesitated on the verge of questioning him, challenging, then did as he said. While she cleaned the man up, Resnick made tea.

"What's your name?" Hannah asked, and when he didn't reply, said, "I'm Hannah. Hannah Campbell. This is my house."

"Declan," he said, so quietly they had to strain to hear. "Declan Farrell."

"Would you like to tell us, Declan," Resnick said, sliding a mug across the table toward him, "just what happened?"

Farrell stirred sugar slowly into his tea, eyes flicking from one to the other, never still in his seat, forever shifting, forward and back, crossing and recrossing his legs, tugging at his jeans, not making any attempt to lift the cup to his mouth.

"You were going to tell us," Resnick said, "how this happened."

Farrell started, stopped, started again. "This man . . . This man . . ." He closed his eyes, began, almost silently, to sob. There was a wedding ring, Resnick noticed, broad and dull, on his hand.

"Go on," Resnick said gently when the crying had ceased. "This man . . ."

Farrell sniffed loudly, wincing, rubbing tenderly at his eyes. "I was in the park," he began, then stopped a second time.

"Isn't it locked up at night?" Hannah asked. "The park."

He nodded, fidgeting again on his seat. "You can get in, it's easy. Over the fence. People do."

Resnick nodded, sitting forward; he knew what people did. "I think you should tell us what happened," he said.

"I was in the park, walking, cutting across like, you know. On my way home from the pub. I was caught short. Needed to use the gents." He paused and looked at the floor. "I was just coming out when this bloke, he . . . he just come at me with this thing, this—I don't know what it was—bat, I suppose."

Resnick thinking, remembering: *mud and grass stains on the dead man's clothes, a smear of earth thick on the fleshy palm of his right hand, a varnished implement, a bat of some kind, baseball seemed the more likely.*

Farrell continuing, saying, "He just started hitting me, here, you can see. I yelled at him, tried to get away, but he wouldn't stop. I couldn't run anymore, all I could do was lie down on the ground and cover my head until . . . until he stopped."

"He just stopped, no reason?"

"One minute he was hitting me, shouting, you know, bastard, things like that. Then he ran off. I heard him going, but I was too frightened to look up. Not for ages. And then, when I did, well, that was when I met you."

"He didn't take your wallet, ask for money, nothing like that?"

Farrell shook his head, not able to look at Resnick for more than moments at a time, squirming on his chair.

Resnick leaned a little toward him and Farrell flinched. "Would you like a cushion?" Resnick said. "You don't seem comfortable at all."

"No, no, no, it's okay. I really ought to—my wife, she'll be worried, you know. . . ." Half out of his seat now, the wooden chair on which he had been sitting patched with blood.

Watching Farrell all the while, Resnick beckoned Hannah to the doorway between the two rooms. "Phone the ambulance," he said. "Then the police. Tell them to bleep Graham Millington, have him call Maureen Madden and then contact me here. Tell them assault and suspected rape."

In the quiet of her house, shock leaped from Hannah's eyes. Resnick touched her hand and held it for a moment, the fingers unnaturally cold. Farrell was sitting with his eyes tight shut, arms clenched across his chest as if it was the only way to hold himself together.

Quietly Hannah rose and went to the telephone and when Declan Farrell started to cry, tears that would never stop, Resnick sat and held him till the ambulance arrived.

38

Maureen Madden was the sergeant who ran the rape suite, an attempt, largely successful, to make rape victims—the ones who came forward—feel more at ease than they would in the functional brusqueness of the normal police station. Comfortable chairs, subdued lighting, carpet, pictures on walls, the facilities for medical examination all present. In the three years or so that Maureen had been working there, she had not had one victim to deal with who was male.

And this had begun differently, at the hospital, no time for anything but the most rudimentary counseling before the doctor on duty carried out his examination. Maureen was uncertain whether Declan Farrell would have been relieved to discover that the doctor was male, or whether by that stage he even cared; she had no clear idea how he would respond to talking to her rather than to a man about what had happened. It crossed her mind to contact one of the members of the Lesbian and Gay Police Association, but then, she had no way of knowing if Farrell himself was gay. A married man, two kids apparently—she wondered if he knew himself. He had pleaded with them, when they informed his wife of where he was, not to give her the details of what had happened.

Now Mrs. Farrell was pacing the waiting area, chewing stick after stick of Dentyne, dropping coins into the vending machine for lukewarm cups of tea, and Declan was unburdening himself little by little as Maureen, patient, trained, won his trust.

Millington had rousted out Naylor and Vincent, but found Divine impossible to track down. No surprise. "Round midnight of a Friday," as Millington had pointed out, "state Mark'll be in, likely neither use nor ornament."

The toilet was in one corner of the recreation ground, close to the gate on the southern edge and in the shadow of the church. They checked the interior, a short stand of unseparated urinals and one cubicle, careful not to disturb anything Forensic might turn to good use later. The small, low building was ripe with the stink of stale urine, its walls festooned with barely decipherable graffiti and gouged here and there with slogans: *MUFC Rule! Colleymore Walks on Water* (from which someone had erased the *l* and substituted an *n*) and *Niggers Out!*

Lights were still showing in a good number of the houses in Church Street and Church Grove, as well as along the Promenade, so they began the slow and diligent business of knocking on doors. Uniformed officers, using emergency lighting, made an initial search of the mainly grassed area between the toilet and where Farrell had climbed the fence onto the path where he was found. At first light, the same process would be gone through more thoroughly, taking in the thick area of shrubs along the church wall.

"Charlie," Hannah had asked, face still pale, "how did you know?"

"I didn't at first." Resnick had shrugged. "Not for definite. Not till I saw the blood."

"Oh, Christ! It's horrible."

"Yes." Holding her now, hair across his mouth, one hand to his chest. "Yes, I know." Except I don't, he thought, not really. I can't. And hope to God I never do.

The doctor was young, Australian, working on a short-term contract he didn't expect to be renewed, though that was due to a lack of funding rather than any fault of his own. The room in which he spoke to Resnick and Maureen Madden was small and white-walled, the overhead lighting so strong it discouraged you from raising your eyes. His voice was occasionally slurred and Resnick might have thought he had been drinking if he were not so obviously tired.

"The cuts to the face were pretty much as you've seen; he took quite a few stitches and he isn't going to be looking in any mirrors for a while, but other than that it's not too serious. There is evidence, though, of quite severe bruising on the neck."

"Finger marks?" Resnick interrupted to ask.

The doctor shook his head. "More like some kind of bar, I don't know, something hard, some sort of stick, you know, like a walking stick. Pulled back against the neck below the Adam's apple."

"Forcing back the head?" Resnick asked.

"Yes, quite possibly. We'll know better once the bruises've come out more. But yes, it could be." He cleared his throat and looked up into the brightness of the light and then at the floor beneath his feet. "Look, I'm sorry, I seem to be avoiding the issue here."

"It's all right," Maureen said, "take your time."

Resnick caught himself wondering, Would he be so reluctant if this were a woman he'd just seen?

"There was penetration," Maureen prompted him.

"Yes. Without any doubt. But not . . ." For an instant, he caught Resnick's eye. "I mean it was sexual, clearly, but I think what was used was some kind of, well, instrument."

"What, you mean a vibrator?" Maureen asked. "A dildo? What?"

He shook his head. "I don't think so. Nothing that appropriate. It probably would have been better for him if it were. No, this was quite large, two to three inches in diameter at the end and solid, probably not tapered toward any kind of a point. Not sharp edged, though, or the damage would have been even worse than it is. But whatever it was had been used with a lot of force. There's quite a bit of tearing of the sphincter muscles and around the orifice itself, and considerable rupturing of blood vessels along the anal canal." He shook his head again. "Poor bastard," he said.

The story Declan Farrell had told Maureen Madden was this: He had needed to use the toilet on his way home from the pub and shinned over the gate. Easy, he'd done it before. The man was there when he went in; inside the cubicle, so Declan didn't see him. But he had followed Declan out, jumped him from behind. Hit him across the face with some kind of club. Almost knocked him out. Forced him to kneel down on the grass, pulled down his trousers and his pants. Told him he was going to give him what he wanted. His words: *This is what you want.* And then . . . and then at that point Declan's voice had choked and Maureen had held his hand and said, "Okay, now. It's all right. Declan, it's okay."

"I'm going to have to talk to him, Maureen," Resnick said. "Tonight?"

"Sooner it's done."

She nodded. "I suppose so. You want me with you?"

"Please."

"Let's take him back to the rape suite, then. Not here."

Resnick agreed.

"And his wife?" Maureen asked.

Resnick looked back at her, unblinking.

"All right," Maureen said, "I'll speak to her before we leave."

Skelton was at the station when they arrived, waistcoat unfastened, no tie; like the reformed nonsmoker he was, cigarette never far from his hand.

"So, Charlie, this little effort, we're not thinking there's any kind of link with the attack on Bill Aston?"

"Bit early yet to know what we're saying."

"But this—nancy boy pickup gone sour, that's what we're dealing with surely?"

Nicely put, Resnick thought. "Sexual, certainly," he said. "Of a kind. Victim's wallet was still on him, nothing stolen. But to what degree there was ever consent . . ."

"I thought we were talking rape?"

"I mean, whether or not there was anything between them beforehand . . ."

"You show me yours, I'll show you mine, that sort of thing? Bit of hanky-panky up and down the stalls."

"Something like that, sir, yes."

"Scarcely matters, does it, one way or another? Bit of flashing in the gents not that much different from walking into the pub with half your tits hanging out—provocation, not an issue anymore where rape's concerned."

Resnick was far from certain that was true, when it came to juries at least. "I'm interviewing him, sir, now. I'll bring you up to speed soon as I can."

"That's it, Charlie." Skelton winked. "Get to the bottom of it, eh?"

◆◆◆

"Bastard asked for it, didn't he," Divine said, finally tracked down after one of those rare Friday nights when he had failed to pull. "No question. Went out looking for a bit of rough and got more than he bargained for. Now he wants us to say 'There, there' and hold his hand. Well, not bloody me, and that's a fact. Kev, while you're over there, be a mate, will you, and fetch us a tea."

Declan Farrell had refused tea or coffee, didn't want anything to drink at all; he sat there, between Resnick and Maureen, unmoving in the hushed quiet of the room. Numb. Except that's what he wasn't, numb: only what he wished to be.

"The man who attacked you," Resnick asked for the third time, "what can you tell us about him?"

Eleven minutes past two.

"His voice, his appearance . . ."

"I didn't see him."

"You heard his voice. He spoke to you at least once, you said."

Nervous, Farrell touching the stitches scissoring above his eye, the worst cut and the deepest, fingers going back to it like a tongue unable to stop itself from probing a bad tooth. Farrell sitting in hastily borrowed clothes, his own carefully labeled, packaged, and shipped off to Forensic.

"Semen?" Resnick had asked the doctor.

"Not really. None around the area of penetration. A trace inside his clothing, probably his own."

His own?

"Why don't you try and concentrate," Resnick said, "on the voice."

As if he could ever forget it, Declan thought. As if there'd ever be a night again when he wouldn't hear it: *This is what you want, you bastard. You fucking cunt!*

"The voice," Resnick asked, "was it young or old?"

"Young," Farrell said, so quietly that both officers had to lean forward to hear him. "At least, I think . . . Oh, God, I don't know, I don't know."

"An accent? Did he have an accent?"

An age before Farrell answered and then, "Yes, maybe."

"Local?"

"'Sort of. I mean, around here, yes, but not strong."

"Is there anything else," Maureen asked, "that you can help us with, about the voice?"

Making him play it back, again and again, six seconds on repeat. "It was rough."

"Rough?"

"Sort of rasping."

"As if he had a cold, that sort of sound?"

Farrell leveled his gaze and stared. "As if he was excited," he said.

Seventeen minutes to three.

"Declan," Resnick said, "no one's judging you here, you know that. Maureen and I, we're not passing judgment on what you do. Whatever you've done. That's not what this is about."

"Then what is it about?" Farrell asked, a sudden unsuspected shout. "Why can't I just go home? That's what I want."

"What this is about," Maureen said, "part of it, is making sure that whoever it was did this to you won't do it again to somebody else."

Farrell was leaking tears again; they came and went so frequently now, he scarcely bothered wiping them away.

"You're sure you didn't know him, Declan? This man?"

"I told you, I told you I never even saw him. How can I know if I've seen him before?"

"But you have been there before," Resnick asked. "Those toilets?"

"Of course I have."

"I mean, to meet someone. For the purposes of sex?"

"No."

"Declan . . ."

"No! I've told you, I'm not queer, I'm not gay, not any of the things you think I am."

"Declan, please . . ."

He was on his feet now and making for the door, Maureen looking quickly across at Resnick, wanting to know should she stop him.

"Declan," Resnick said, "I think you have been there before, after closing, around the same time. I think sometimes you were lucky, met someone you fancied, sometimes you didn't, gave it up and went on home. I think whoever was shut in the cubicle tonight you thought had gone there for the same reason as you. Now, I don't know what you did, whether or not there was some signal between you, whether you showed yourself to him through a hole in the door, hole in the wall. But when you went out onto the Rec, I think you thought he would follow you and he did. And Declan, I don't care about any of that, I honestly don't. But what happened next, that's what I care about. This person, whoever it was, viciously assaulted you, assaulted you in the most terrible way imaginable. And as Sergeant Madden said, we want to ensure he doesn't remain free to do this again. To someone else. And because you know what it's like, Declan, you must want that, too. So I am asking you, please, to help us as much as you can."

After several more moments' hesitation, Declan Farrell opened the door and walked out. Maureen looked across at Resnick and slowly shook her head, closed her eyes.

◆◆◆

When Carl Vincent came into Resnick's office, he was looking a little tired, a man who had been up all night and only snatched a half hour's sleep, slumped across a table in the canteen. There were a couple of marks on the sleeve of his lightweight suit, picked up during the search, and his collar was somewhat awry, but otherwise he didn't look much the worse for wear.

A sight better than Resnick himself. "Carl, what can I do for you?" he asked.

"This business last night, the talk is you're not making any connection with the Aston murder."

"That's pretty much right."

Vincent drew a deep breath. "Look, sir, maybe I should've said before, but I saw him a year ago, Aston, in a gay club in Leicester."

For a second, the pulse beating at the side of Resnick's head seemed to stop. "What are you saying?"

"I'm saying Bill Aston was gay."

39

Not even minutes, Resnick seemed to have been sitting there for a small eternity.

A year ago . . . a club in Leicester . . . gay.

It was not only tiredness, but anxiety in Vincent's eyes.

"This club," Resnick said eventually, "you were there on duty?"

Fleetingly, the eyes closed and when they looked at Resnick again there was no avoidance, no guile. "No, sir."

Resnick breathed through his mouth. He said, "You'd best sit down."

Vincent crossed one leg over the other, uncrossed it, sitting with his hands resting just above his knees.

"And Inspector Aston," Resnick said, "there's no way he was there on duty either?"

Vincent shook his head.

"You're sure? Positive?"

"He left with somebody," Vincent said.

Resnick was seeing Aston's wife, her plumpish little body ill-fitting in black, her voice fierce against the afternoon. *You knew him, Charlie, better than most.*

"And you couldn't have been mistaken? Misinterpreted the situation?"

But Vincent was already shaking his head.

"A year ago," Resnick said.

"The reason I remember, someone pointed him out to me. Someone I knew there, in the Job. He'd seen him at some course, I think. Aston. Knew he was from up here, this force. Said he'd come across him before, you know, in Leicester, once or twice."

"You didn't speak to him?"

For a moment, Vincent smiled. "Not my type."

"But you are gay?"

"It doesn't mean we fancy everyone, you know."

"I know," Resnick said. "But what you're saying is you're gay but you've not gone public about it."

"That's right."

Resnick shook his head. "What's really worrying me is why you didn't tell me about Aston before."

Vincent didn't respond right away. "Because I wasn't sure. I mean, I hadn't known his name. And the photograph . . ." Resnick staring at him, waiting for all of the truth. "No, all right, I thought I recognized him, the connection was made, but then, it seemed to have nothing to do . . . I couldn't see the relevance to what had happened. Gay or not gay, sexuality didn't seem to be an issue."

"Except for yours."

"I'm sorry?"

"Except for yours. Your sexuality."

"Look . . ."

"No, you look." Resnick leaning forward now, head slightly to one side, fingers beginning to point. "The reason you didn't come forward with this information sooner was personal. To do with you. Give up Aston and you're giving up yourself. In keeping silent, you were protecting yourself."

Slightly muffled through the door, the constant, shifting sound of telephones, their call and response. Someone knocked on Resnick's door and, receiving no answer, turned away.

"It was an issue for me, yes," Vincent finally said.

"*The* issue."

"No, sir. If that was the case, I'd never have come forward now. I'd have kept my silence, prayed it didn't matter, or if it did, it'd come out some other way. But as soon as I heard, you know, last night, what happened to the guy in the park, there was no way I could keep quiet then."

"Even though it means exposing yourself like this?"

Vincent shook his head. "I'm a copper, just like you."

Not just like me, Resnick thought. "Carl," Resnick said, "I don't care what you do in bed or who you do it with." Not even sure if that was true. "The only place it affects me is here, when you let it affect you, how you do your job. And what prevented you from acting as you should, it wasn't the fact of your being gay, it was that you've kept that fact a secret. That's what was wrong."

Vincent stifled a laugh. "You think I should come out?"

"That's up to you."

"But that's what you're saying."

A shake of Resnick's head. "What I'm saying, as long as you don't, there'll be other incidents like this, judgment calls you feel you have to make. And they'll be to do with protecting yourself, your secret, and not your job."

"I'm sorry," Vincent said, "I'm finding this a little difficult to take in."

"That I want you to be honest about yourself? Tell the truth."

"That here's my senior officer, telling me I have a duty to come out as being gay."

"I don't think I shall be able to trust you, your judgment, not fully, unless you do."

"And if I did?"

"Your instincts are good, you seem to talk to people well, work hard. You're clearly bright." He shrugged. "No reason you shouldn't make a good detective."

"You'd keep me on your team?"

Resnick thought for longer than probably he should. "Yes, why not?"

Vincent smiled, pleased like a kid who'd been handed a prize, confused; he touched his hands together and rocked back in his chair. "I don't know. . . ." Openly this time, he laughed. "You think it isn't difficult enough, getting on in the Job being black, without having to stand up for being gay as well?"

Skelton had not been having a good twenty-four hours. His daughter had telephoned him in the middle of dinner to tell him she was thinking about dropping out from university to become part of a medical outreach team in Zaire; his wife, whose only recent communication with him had been by means of grunts or notes stuck to the door of the fridge, had launched into a diatribe about setting up a new regime, which seemed to be going to start with Skelton laundering his own underpants; and then there had been the call-out on account of that poof who'd been raped on Lenton Rec.

Now this.

"Jesus, Charlie! They're everywhere."

Resnick offered no comment.

"You can't switch on the television nowadays without there's some clever little bastard smarming on about equal rights for gays. Strikes me, we'll soon be the ones needing extra rights. Blokes on *EastEnders* holding hands and dying from AIDS; lessies all up and down *Brookside*. And the BBC—the BBC, mind, not Channel Four—have started this—what is it? *Gaytime TV*. As though it was all a big laugh. Whatever happened to normal, eh, Charlie? Normal blokes with normal families, that's what I'd like to know."

What happened, Resnick thought, was they turned into Bill and Margaret Aston; or they turned into you.

"And I'd figured him for a decent lad, Vincent," Skelton said.

"So he is," Resnick said, earning himself an old-fashioned look.

Skelton fidgeted with papers on his desk, no longer as meticulously ordered as it used to be. "You really think, Charlie, this radically changes things?"

"I think what it does, maybe, it helps to make more sense of things that up to now have never felt quite right. Aston's murder as a mugging. One thing, however drunk you are, if you're looking for an easy victim, why pick someone strongly built, close on six foot? And then there's the degree of force. Way more than necessary, even assuming Bill was fighting back. Those blows to the face and head, that isn't greed, not even ordinary anger, that's rage."

"Queer bashing, then? That's where we are."

Resnick sighed. "It looks likely, given what we now know. If Bill wasn't above a bit of occasional cottaging, it might have started off that way. You'd have to say, if he was that way inclined, he'd have had opportunity galore. All those times he went out last thing with his dogs; little dogs like that you can leave in the car."

"Come on, Charlie, this is conjecture, nothing more."

"We know he went to Leicester, socializing, picking up men. Maybe other places, too." The expression on Skelton's face, listening, was that of someone who has just bitten into a peach to find the inside rotted and sour. "But closer to home—if he got the urge, where would he go? Not to one of the pubs or clubs here, too great a risk. But somewhere more anonymous, in the dark? He just might. Toilets at Ollerton roundabout, Titchfield Park in Mansfield, Sherwood Library maybe. Where then?"

"Any sodding where nowadays!"

"Closest to where he lives, gents on the embankment. Maybe one of them as attacked him saw him there, inside or just hanging about."

"Even if that were true—and I'm not for one minute agreeing that it is, I don't know what I think about the kite you're flying here—it doesn't prove a link with last night. What happened to Bill, thank Christ, wasn't the same."

"The anger was," Resnick said. "The rage. What happened to them both, it was punitive. Sexuality aside, it was about the same things: power and pain."

Skelton rose to his feet and half-turned toward the window: the same buildings, same vehicles, same people walking the streets, but underneath, the world had turned upside down. "Once the press gets hold of this, Charlie . . ."

"I know."

"His poor wife and family . . ."

"Yes."

"Jesus, Charlie! I went to church once when he was preaching; Billy Aston was up there in the pulpit, rabbiting on about the wages of sin."

And the one about throwing the first stone, Resnick thought, was that one of his favorites as well?

Resnick's briefing was coming to an end. The revelations about Aston had been greeted with shock and loud disbelief; Resnick had let it diminish and moved on. Nothing as good as definite, but some of the boot marks taken from the Rec were at least a partial match with those lifted, more clearly, from the embankment; and the weapon—it was within the realm of possibility that the implement used, both to strike Farrell and to violate him, was the same baseball bat that had killed Aston.

"Lateral thinking, isn't that what they call it?" Divine muttered. "Making the most of both ends."

"So we're going to be double-checking back on our files, all reported homophobic incidents, attacks, complaints made and followed up, anything that can be checked against our nationalist friends. Okay? And now, before you disperse, DC Vincent has something he wants to say."

When Carl Vincent stepped forward, Resnick could see his right hand trembling at his side. But his voice was level and clear. "Especially in view of these cases we're investigating, I think it's important that you all know that I am homosexual." Just for one second, he almost smiled. "I'm gay."

40

They sat in the near silence of the cloistered room, curtains once more pulled tightly together, soft patterns in which brown and gold leaves drifted carefully down. From out along the street, muted, came the intermittent rattle of a road drill as workmen dug trenches to lay cable, bringing in a wider world. Margaret Aston sat small in her favorite Parker Knoll chair, bought when real wood and solid craftsmanship were virtues to be praised and admired. Stella—no smile for him today—had left the moment he arrived, and Resnick had waited for Margaret to negotiate the stairs, the slow passage—refusing his arm—into what she would always call the lounge.

Abruptly the drilling stopped and all he could sense in the room were loss and regret, the broken reed of her breath. In less than two weeks she had aged ten years.

"Margaret . . ."

When she spoke it was not to him, yet she knew he was

there, and whenever he moved, no matter how little, she paused, her fingers plucking at the thread that had come unraveled from the beading on the chair's arm.

"It was after the boys had left home. Stella, she was still here, but"—Margaret sighed the first of many sighs—"she had this boyfriend and she would find reasons for not coming home. Simply excuses, I knew that's what they were; anything so that she could spend the night with him." Another sigh, pluck, and sigh. "She had discovered sex, my daughter, as we all do, and it was all that she could think of. They used to come round here in the afternoons, when Stella should have been in school, upstairs with the door locked and then running off, giggling and smirking the minute I came home. No shame. Even with a father like Bill, my Stella knows nothing of shame." She looked up. "I wonder, Charlie, if that's such a bad thing?"

A pause before she went on. "I would go sometimes then and stand in her room. Instead of throwing open the window, I would lock it closed. Keep in the smell. Do you know how it makes you feel, Charlie? When the children you nursed and carried are old enough to enjoy sex?"

Curtly, Resnick shook his head.

"No, no, of course, Charlie. You wouldn't. Perhaps you never will. So I'll tell you—it makes you feel old, used up. But it does something else, too. It makes part of you, that part of you, come alive again. Pictures of them wrapped there—am I shocking you, Charlie?—those young girl's legs that had once held tight around this pathetic body of mine, they had been wrapped around him, that feckless youth, there on that bed."

Resnick looked at the leaves, still trapped midfall, the long, tapering slice of light.

"I had a body again, Charlie, my daughter had given me back my body and what was I going to do with it now? Bill and I, we had not had relations for years. Scarcely since after

Stella was born. And during all that time I had lain down next to him every night and never once had I minded. But now"—her fingers worked more nervously at the thread—"I did all the things a woman, even a woman like me, old and fat, is supposed to do. I went to the hair salon, the beauty parlor, I was—what's the word?—made over. I bought new clothes, satin nightdresses and silk underthings in which I felt and looked a fraud. I begged him, Charlie, pleaded with him. I had no dignity. I needed him—needed someone—to make love to me." The thread that she was twisting snapped in her hand. "I could see in his eyes the thought of touching me made him feel sick. He told me he was moving across the corridor, into one of the empty rooms. He was having difficulty getting to sleep and he thought if he had his own bed it might be better. For both of us."

She shriveled a little more inside her chair.

"It was then that he started going out. Not so frequently at first, and then more and more. Swimming every night. Or so I thought. Twice, sometimes at weekends. He just needs, I thought, to get out of the house, get away from me, what I've been putting him through." She glanced up at Resnick hastily. "I was feeling guilty, you see, thought I'd been unfair. Making demands." She found a new end of thread and worried it with finger and thumb. "After a while he started going out late at night, too, walking the dogs. I did think, it did cross my mind once or twice that he might be having an affair with one of those fine-minded women from the church. And then when you came here asking questions about that woman who called, I thought, Yes, yes, it's all right, that's it."

She looked at him, dull eyes sharpened by deceit.

"But that wasn't it, was it? That wasn't it."

He thought that she would cry then, but if there were tears there, they were still to come. The drilling had started up again outside. She had said what she had to say and now it was done. Resnick sat across from her, trapped in that closed room, willing himself to be patient, trying not to notice that the undersides of his thighs were growing numb.

POLICE MURDER: GAY SEX LINK? the headline suggested. Startling revelations revealed exclusively to our reporter today . . . There were photographs of Bill Aston in uniform; one, poorly taken, of Margaret's startled face as she turned outward from her front door. A family portrait, paid for or purloined, of Declan Farrell with his wife and child. Detective Superintendent Jack Skelton would today neither confirm nor deny that one of the detective constables under his command . . .

Hannah phoned Resnick at home, but of course he was not there; she left a message for him at the police station that he should ring her that evening if he found time. She would be home.

"What amazes me," Divine said, troughing through pie and double chips in the canteen, "is any of that lot being queer at all. Thought they were all so busy fostering the old myth, our black brothers, that they're all hung like a fuckin' horse, the last thing any of 'em'd do'd be own up to having a limp wrist."

"Reckon that's what it is, then, Mark?" said one of the constables, winding him up. "Big dicks. All a myth?"

"How the bloody hell'd I know?"

"Play your cards right," the PC said, "this could be your big chance to find out."

Sometimes, in Diane's flat, Sheena would sit with the baby, Melvin, for so long she would forget everything else. Times they'd been smoking dope especially. The others, not Sheena, they were popping all those pills, too. Sheena was happy to stick to the spliffs Dee-Dee had taught her to roll— one of the skills Dee-Dee's Pentecostal father had never taught her. The stuff, though, it came from Diane's brother—Jamaican. That was what he said, and who was she to deny it? Umm, wherever it came from, it was good. Sheena leaning against the sofa, sitting back alongside it, head against the wall. Little Melvin with his thumb stuck in the corner of his mouth, slobbering just a little, eyes closed and Sheena rocking him. That music that was playing, a tape Irena had boosted from one of the stores. Mouldy? No, Moby, that was it. Moby with his funny little pixie face, black eyes staring out of the blue. Orange robes on him like he was one of those Krishnas or something. And water: that's what all that blue was around him. Water. Moby in the middle of it, slowly drowning. Sheena wondered what it would be like, lying there. Drowning. Slowly drowning. A girl's voice singing: *When it's cold I'd like to die.*

"Come on! Get a fuckin' move on!" Sheena could hear Janie's voice, shouting from across the room. Janie in black leggings, Doc Martens, black leather jacket, a bottle of Absolut in her hand.

And Lesley, close alongside her, boots and a black miniskirt that stopped halfway up her thighs. Irena squatting in a corner, searching for something in the black and purple rucksack she always carried, taking everything out and spreading it over the carpet, then stuffing it back. Tracey was still pulling up her jeans as she came out of the loo.

"Diane!" Janie shouted over the sound of the ghetto blaster on the table, the music faster now, more like dance music . . . *Every time you touch me it feels like I need more.* Diane listening, lost in it, starting to shimmy, a dip of her hips and she's shaking it, the other girls starting to laugh and Diane playing up to them, pretending.

"Diane, will you stop that shit? I ain't waitin' too much fuckin' longer!"

Diane just wafting her arms now and smiling, her eyes a little out of it; Dee-Dee finally catching hold of her and pressing her wrists down to her sides, telling her to get it together. Diane nodding: Right, girl, right.

Dee-Dee then, going over to where Sheena was sitting, her mouth moving lazily with the music, the girl's reedy voice singing, the joint dead between her fingers. Melvin dribbling onto her skimpy T-shirt, the shadow of her childish breast.

"Sheena, you wake up now. You look after him, right? Melvin. You keep your eye on him. Feed him when he wakes. Girl, you hear what I saying?"

"Yeah, yeah, no problem. Sure."

"Better not be, that's all."

Dee-Dee straightening then, pulling down the hem of her denim skirt. With Diane out of it as much as she was, it was just as well she was there to look out for little Melvin, make sure he was going to be okay.

"She all right?" Janie asked, looking over toward Sheena. The other girls were bundling through the door.

"Her?" Dee-Dee said. "Just asked her, she fine."

Janie laughed. "Looks like warmed-over shit to me." And she slammed the door closed and followed the others down the landing toward the lift that would not be working again.

Norma had picked up a paper on her way home, only glanced at the front page while she fumbled for her keys at the front door.

"Peter? Hey up, Peter, love! Clap your eyes on this."

But Peter wasn't there, not upstairs or down. His mug and the plate he liked to use for his toast, the one with three concentric yellow rings and cracks, faint, across the center, had been rinsed under the tap and left to dry.

"Peter?"

He had brought nothing with him, so it was no use checking to see if his things were gone.

Norma set the kettle to boil, changed her mind and took one of Shane's cans of Tennents from the fridge. Warm, she opened the back door to the whining of the dog. There were turds in neat, whitening piles near the gate. Norma sat down with her newspaper, lager, and a cigarette and began to read.

Suppertime, Peter would be back, she was sure.

What Gerry Hovenden liked to do, work the weights at least an hour each afternoon. Oh, he'd make a change once in a while: rowing machine, one of the bikes, he'd even tried the aerobics once, but felt a fool, jumping around with all those women with their headbands and little water bottles, two-tone leotards disappearing up the cracks in their arse. No, it was the weights, then the steam room, after that a shower, cold and then hot, hot and then cold. Toweling down.

Some days, like this afternoon, he'd persuade Shane to come along. Cost sod as long as you were on the dole. Shane in a torn T-shirt and a borrowed pair of shorts, sweat pouring off him, stinging his eyes. Shane, he always overdid it, didn't know when to stop.

"Here," Gerry said, still moving, press and lift. "You hear about that bloke as got raped on Lenton Rec?"

"Looking for it, wasn't he?" Shane said.

"Prob'ly."

"Well, then, cunt got what he deserved."

"Yeah," Hovenden agreed. "Most likely." Watching the way the sweat ran down across the flat of Shane's belly, making the skin glisten, the downward curve of tiny hairs shine gold.

The assistant manager of the audio department assured his would-be customer that there was no problem at all: once in a while the machines backed up and it wasn't possible to get immediate clearance from the card company, and she could see why, with an amount that size, close to six hundred pounds for a state-of-the-art, wide-screen television receiver, twenty-six-inch screen, well, company policy dictated and so on and so on.

Sally Purdy stood there in an old air force jacket that smelled of port wine and a dress that swept the floor when she walked, hiding old tennis shoes on her feet. Sally, certain that if she could just get a decent TV into the place she was squatting, that'd make all the difference. Fuck all this time spent sitting out with a lot of old alkies on benches, she was going to get to grips with herself, start a new life.

Only without a poll tax form or something similar to verify her address, hire purchase was out of the question; she knew enough people out there on the street who would get her a set cheap, but it wasn't going to be one like this.

Sally saw herself sitting round all summer, watching Wimbledon and Ascot in all their glory, those hats they got themselves up in at Ascot, Ladies' Day, something to dream about. And musicals, she loved musicals—the old ones, not rubbish like *Grease*, but really old: *Gentlemen Prefer Blondes, It's Always Fair Weather*. She was sure she'd got the signature right, times she'd practiced it, over and bloody over.

"Yes, madam." Bloke returning now, suit and striped shirt, staff tie, all smiles. "Please accept my apologies for the delay." Smarmy bastard, Sally thought. "Now, if I can explain how to get to our dispatch department in the basement, by the time you've collected your car and driven round there, your set will be packed up and ready for you to take."

Car? What fucking car was this? "I thought," Sally said, "you'd deliver it, right?"

"Certainly, madam. That would be Tuesday or Thursday of next week."

No way, José! "How about this," she said, "a cab. I'll get a cab, take it home in that. Easy, right?"

"Absolutely." Smiling his unctuous smile, he gave her the directions to Dispatch.

The extra time it took Sally Purdy to walk to the nearest rank meant that by the time she drove up to the door marked DISPATCH, the two uniformed officers were waiting for her inside.

"Sorry, mate," one of them said to the cabdriver, while his oppo was hauling a reluctant Sally to the marked car, "want to collect on your fare, you'll need to nip over to the station, fill in a voucher."

When they were booking her, Sally Purdy cursed them all from there to perdition, the custody sergeant downward.

It was the sergeant, going through Sally's possessions, in particular the small pile of credit cards she'd been carrying in a purse Velcroed to the inside of her dress, who had spotted the name and signature of William Aston on one of them.

Lynn Kellogg picked up the call. Inside fifteen minutes she and Kevin Naylor had Sally sitting across from them in an interview room, tapes identified and rolling, stolen credit cards spread out before them like a hand of solitaire.

"This one, Sally," Lynn said. "Aston. Tell us where you got that, we might go easy on you for the rest."

"How easy?"

"Easier," Naylor said, "than you deserve."

She didn't have to think about it for too long. "Shane. I got it off of Shane."

"Shane Snape?" Lynn asked, almost unable to believe her luck.

"No. Alan fucking Ladd, who d'you think?"

41

"This interview," Resnick stated, "timed at five twenty-seven."

They had picked up Shane a couple of streets from his home, winnings that he'd collected from the bookies stuffing out his back pocket. "One lucky lad, Shane, and no mistake," the man behind the counter had said, smiling grimly as he counted out the notes. "One lucky bastard."

Divine and Naylor had been in the lead car, Millington with Carl Vincent fifty yards behind. Two squad cars were waiting at the house, a couple of uniformed officers in the alley out back. Norma Snape on the front step, cursing them out to the world.

Shane had slammed his bag into Naylor's chest, Naylor staggering back winded against a garden wall, while Divine moved in close, hands outstretched. "Come on, then, pal. You want to try it? Come on." Fingers beckoning him, let's go for it. Divine so clearly wanting it: the pair of them about equal height, Divine maybe an inch taller, certainly heavier; Shane probably the fitter, despite another season for Divine in and out of the first fifteen.

"Don't be daft, lad." Millington from the edge of the curb. "Look about you. You'll not get anywhere but hurt." A third squad car was arriving fast from the opposite end of the street, siren wailing.

And Shane had stood there, not ever really taking his eyes from Divine, thinking about it, wanting it, too, but feeling that first rush of adrenaline start to drain out of him, knowing that he could have taken him, cocky bastard, that someday he would, he'd have him right enough, he was certain of that, but knowing that moment wasn't now.

The instant Shane had lowered his hands toward his sides, Divine had been in on him, fast, spinning him round, cuffs at the ready, propelling him hard toward the side of the nearest car.

"Together, behind your back! Hands together!"

"Fuck you!"

"Now! Do it now!" Divine bending him forward over the car roof while Naylor, recovered and standing alongside, read Shane his rights.

The metal of the cuffs was biting into Shane's wrists, yet somehow he managed to twist the upper half of his body until his face was inches from Divine's, eyes brittle as ice glaring into his face. "One of these days, I'll fuckin' kill you!" Spittle lacing Divine's mouth and cheek.

"Mark!" Millington in fast, seizing Divine's shoulder seconds before Divine would have head-butted Shane in the face.

"Mark, leave it. Let it be."

And Divine, with a final stare, had stepped away. Millington had pushed Shane into the back of the car between Naylor and himself and ordered Vincent to drive off sharpish. Divine could follow on his own.

"I hear," the solicitor's clerk on call said wearily, "my client was subject to physical intimidation in the course of his arrest."

"Your client," Millington told him, face close enough for the clerk to smell peppermint fresh on the sergeant's breath, "came within a virgin's tit of being charged with assaulting a police officer in the course of his duty. Maybe you should suck on that."

Resnick and Millington would handle the questioning, interview room A. The same scratched table scored with cigarette burns, the same stale smoke lingering in corners, the stickiness of the floor that tugged at the soles of your shoes, the faint crackle of thin cellophane as it slipped reluctantly from around the pair of audiocassettes: the words, the same or similar. "This interview . . ."

Just over an hour in, the solicitor's clerk leaned forward and asked for a break. "My client—"

"Not now."

"My client—"

"Not yet." Resnick's voice raised to the edge of irritable, weary of Shane's persistent stonewalling.

"Where did you get the card?"

"I don't know what you're on about. Which card?"

"Inspector Aston's credit card. Sally Purdy says she bought it from you in the back room of a pub on the Boulevard."

"Well, she's mistaken. Either that or she's lying."

"Why would she do that?"

"Slag. It's what she does."

"What?"

"Look at her, the state of her. Pissed out of her brain. Wouldn't know the truth if it crawled out of her arse."

"Not like you, then, Shane, eh?" Millington taking over from Resnick, lighting another Lambert and Butler and leaning toward Shane, almost smiling, a definite twinkle in his eye. "Expert on the truth."

Shane looking back at him, defiant. Where were we going now?

"Two Saturdays ago, for instance, you and your pal Gerry. All cozy at home with your old lady and her fancy man, watching videos and kicking the family cat."

"What about it?"

"Pack of lies."

Sneering, Shane turned his face away.

"Lies, Shane, beginning to end." Millington grinned. "Pork Farm pies."

"Bollocks."

"Exactly." Millington triumphant.

"Where you were, Shane," Resnick said forcefully, "that Saturday, was out drinking with Gerry Hovenden and some of his dubious friends. Doing the pubs between London Road and the bridge, already a bit of excitement on the way, few fists flying, and then on the embankment, pissed the lot of you, that's where you came across Inspector Aston, out walking his dogs, and you went for him. The pack of you. Stole his wallet, cash, credit cards, *this* credit card, and left him for dead. That's where you were on that Saturday night."

Unblinking, Shane stared Resnick square in the eye. "Bollocks," he said quietly.

"For someone who's not exactly an idiot," Millington said, "your conversation tends toward the boring."

"Then why not stop all this crap and let me go? I don't know nothing about any credit card, nothing about no bloke beaten up on the embankment, nothing about any of it, right?"

"My client—"

"All right." Resnick quickly to his feet. "Twenty minutes. No more."

"Surely he's entitled to a meal?"

"Half an hour."

"This interview," Millington said, "suspended at six thirty-nine."

"You think he's lying, Charlie?" Skelton was pacing the length of his office between door and desk, conscious of being harassed from above, harassed from below, the local media, national press.

"Sure of it," Resnick said. "But I'm not sure about what."

"Christ, Charlie, don't play games. What the hell's that supposed to mean?"

Resnick was standing also, conscious he had already been sitting too long and likely would be again. "I put it to him straight, the whole business, Aston, everything. He never as much as blinked. I know he's cool; one of those as can hold it all in tight until something goes and he explodes. But a dead copper, he must know we're not going to mess around. But Shane, he could've been holding a razor blade to his own throat and there'd not have been as much as a nick."

"Then why's he lying?"

"I don't know."

"This credit card business, we've enough to charge him?"

Resnick looked doubtful.

"We could stand the woman up in court, sworn statement, her word against his."

"With Purdy's record they'd not believe the day of the week, even if it was staring at them off the calendar. And Shane knows it."

"He'll bluff it out, then."

"He'll try. But I'd like to hang on to him a while longer. If he wasn't there when Aston was killed, likely he knows somebody who was."

"So he's covering for somebody else?" Skelton was round

behind his desk, swiveling his chair so he could lean against the back, hands gripping its sides.

"Could be."

"This pal of his, then . . . Hovenden?"

Resnick nodded.

"Let's have him in. If we can't budge the one, let's try the other."

But Resnick was already shaking his head. "What I'd sooner do, as long as you're agreed, is make sure Hovenden knows we're holding Shane. Let him stew awhile. More reason then for him to wonder exactly what his mate Shane has said. If we finesse it right, maybe we can persuade him it's more than it is."

"No chance of him doing a runner?"

"I doubt it. Must know that'd draw attention to himself quicker than anything else. But we can always keep an eye."

Skelton levered himself away from the chair. "Play it your way, then, Charlie. But only for now. Twenty-four hours tops."

Resnick nodded and moved toward the door. Now that he had some food inside him, Shane might be feeling more amicable: he'd give it another shot.

"She's got something against you, Shane, has she, Sally Purdy? Something personal?"

Shane glanced at Resnick and shook his head.

"Your family, then? Her and Norma, maybe? Argument of some kind, goes back a long while?"

"My mum wouldn't pass wind on her, never mind the time of day."

"What is it, then? Some kind of death wish?"

"How d'you mean?"

Resnick straightened his back, hands flat near the table's edge. "I mean, why you? When she gets picked up and she's got to give a name and it's not going to be the truth, wouldn't she have to be stupid pointing at you? I mean, of all the names she could choose. What did she think you were going to do? Next time you see her, slip a fiver into her hand? 'Thanks for thinking of me when you were talking to the law.' " Resnick shook his head in disbelief. "No, Shane, the only way she'd give you up is if it was true."

A smile now, wavering about the corners of Shane's eyes, beginning to think, They've got nothing, really nothing, what I can do, relax and enjoy this a bit.

"Mr. Resnick," he said, polite as could be.

"Yes?"

"Prove it."

They tried. Questions about how Shane put money in his pockets (the horses); where he got the cash from to make his bets (stand in line at the post office and cash me giro check like everyone else); about his relationship with Gerry Hovenden (mates, we work out together, down the gym); about Gerry's right-wing connections (politics, no, we never talk about it, what's the point, Labour, Tory, they're all the same); what they were doing the night Bill Aston was killed (round my place watching some videos, how many more times).

Not many.

When the solicitor's clerk asked for another meal break for his client and the chance of a rest, Resnick readily agreed. Lynn Kellogg had phoned in by then: she and Kevin Naylor had spoken to Hovenden and told him the police were holding Shane; it looked as if Hovenden, nervous, was about to make some kind of move. All right, Resnick had said, stick close, observe. Anything urgent, you can reach me at home.

◆◆◆

When finally they kicked Shane free with a warning they'd be speaking to him again, chance brought Shane and Divine onto the stairs at the same time. Shane walking down with Millington as escort, Divine on his way up to CID.

"Remember," Shane said softly as they passed, "me and you, sometime soon."

"Yes," Divine said. "In your dreams."

42

It was late enough for the streetlights to be showing clear against the purpling dark of city sky. Khan and Naylor were in the CID room chatting about the relative merits of the city's Indian restaurants when Resnick strode in, nodded in their direction, and went on through into his office.

"The Shand," Khan said, reaching for the folder on his desk. "For my money, that's got to be the one."

Instinctively, he straightened his tie and pushed a hand through his hair before knocking on the inspector's door.

"Jardine, sir. You said to make a check."

"And?"

"It wasn't easy, getting hold of some of this. I'm afraid it's only sketchy in places. And there are still one or two items I need to double-check. I—"

"Khan."

"Yes, sir?"

"Just get on with it." All of that waltzing around with Shane Snape had done little to improve Resnick's patience.

"Well . . ." Khan flipped open his folder. "Before being appointed to his authority, Jardine worked in Staffordshire and Leicestershire. Regular social work to begin with, but pretty soon he moved into residential care."

"Staffordshire," Resnick said, "that's where there was all that furor about kids being tied to their beds, held in isolation?"

"Yes, sir. Excessive physical restraint. Pindown, that's what it was called. One of the homes Jardine worked in was involved right enough. I've got a copy here of the inquiry report. But compared to some of the other staff, Jardine comes out of it pretty well. The worst that was said about him was that he must have known these practices were being carried out and he did nothing to try and prevent them or to inform his superiors. But there's no suggestion of any direct involvement.

"Not so long after that he moved across to Leicestershire. Promotion. And this might be more interesting. It seems that while he was in acting charge of one of their residential homes for difficult children, there were complaints of sexual abuse—"

"By Jardine?"

"No, sir. One of the members of the staff."

"These complaints, were they proved?"

Khan sighed and shook his head. "Again, it's not really clear. The man concerned claimed that a small group of the boys had a grudge against him and made up the whole story to get at him. The medical evidence is, well, hazy at best. There was some talk of prosecution, but by then the man had resigned and in the end no charges were brought."

Resnick sat forward. "What did Jardine have to say about all of this?"

Khan smiled. "Pretty much what you'd expect: the alleged incidents, which in any case were unsubstantiated, would have taken place before he was appointed; since he'd been in charge, there was a more open regime, staff and boys were encouraged to air their grievances in public." Khan paused to read from his notes. " 'I give my word that no child under my care need ever have anything to fear.' Interview with the Leicester *Mercury*, 1989."

Resnick rubbed his eyes with the bases of his palms. "Maybe he should've tried telling that to Nicky Snape."

Khan closed the folder, reversed it, and set it on the desk.

"All right, let's have another go at Matthews. See if he's any more willing to talk. Chances are he's still down in Wales, but best check."

"Sir, I wonder . . ."

"Yes? What is it?"

"Well, it's just . . . I think if I went back to him too soon, pushed him again, all would happen, he'd clam up even more. It might even be enough to drive him over the edge."

"What are you saying, then? That we should leave well enough alone?"

"No. Just give him some more time. Even if it's only a day or two. If we let him stew in it a little, he might even come to us."

"To you."

"Yes."

Resnick sighed. Not so many hours earlier he had been making a similar request to Skelton, asking a superior officer to trust his judgment.

"Okay, forty-eight hours. Meantime plug the holes in this report. Let's make sure if we need to use it, it's watertight."

Gerry Hovenden had found out that Shane had been taken in for questioning, but not that he had been released. After several hours of sitting around worrying himself half-sick, he had decided to seek out Frankie Miller and get some advice. Frank Miller, the kind of man whom some people turned to when they were in a fix.

Miller worked security in the clubs, pubs; squeezed himself into a cheap dinner jacket or a shiny fake-satin jumpsuit with a matt-black headset crammed down onto his head like a crown of thorns and he was in business. Smiling face, raised hand—not now, sunshine, looking like that, no way, try the place down the street, patience, let's have a little patience and an orderly line. Quite often they'd look at Frank—not so tall, more than a little overweight, out of condition, had to be pushing thirty—and think, You fat bastard, you're not going to tell me what to do, where I can go, no way. Frank loved that. Kids giving him some mouth, showing off for the scrawny tarts they'd have up against some back wall later, a quick shag before a late-night curry and the long walk home. He loved the look on their sweaty faces when they finally gave him a push, threw a punch, and he didn't give ground. Frank smiling before he started punching back.

Once in a while, he had to admit, things would get a little out of hand; when they did, whoever was in charge—no hard feelings, Frankie, eh?—they'd have to let him go. No sweat. There was always another pub, another door, another Saturday night. And if not . . . well, there were other things. Mate of a mate needing a bit of muscle, friend of a friend. He had this arrangement with a bloke who lent out money, you know, when the talking bank wasn't talking no more, council suing for rent arrears and the bailiffs on their way in. Of course, the interest was high, what did they think this was? Social fucking security or what? Frank had a way of making sure the debt was paid or, if not, ensuring folks saw the error of their ways.

Frank Miller? Bit rough, but underneath it all, decent enough. Tell you what, any trouble, he's the one I'd want alongside. Frankie. Good bloke, really, good bloke.

Frank was in his local pub in Heanor, not hurrying his last pint, when Gerry Hovenden came in wearing leathers, helmet in his hand.

"What the fuck's the matter with you?" Miller asked. "Look like the rats've had your balls for breakfast and now they're startin' on the rest."

"It's Shane," Hovenden said, short of breath, near to knocking an empty glass from the table as he sat down.

"What about him?"

"The law, they've got him. Picked him up this afternoon."

"What the fuck for?"

"I don't know. I don't know. I haven't had a chance to talk to him, have I?"

"Then calm down. May not be anything at all. You know what coppers are like. Shane, he's done time, right? They'll have him in for nothing at all."

"I know, but—"

Frank Miller's hand clamped itself round Hovenden's thigh, squeezing at the muscle behind the knee. "He won't talk, your mate Shane. And if he does, without dumping himself in the shit, what can he say?"

Hovenden blinked, catching his breath, trying not to notice the pain in his leg, Miller's thumb weeviling away against the bone.

"Trust him, don't you?"

"Yeah, yes, yeah, of course."

Miller released his grip and tapped Hovenden on the arm a couple of times playfully with his fist. "Nothing to worry about, eh, then?" He lifted his pint. "I'd get you one in, only they called last orders a while back. 'Sides, drinkin' and driving. Don't want you coming off that bike of yours. Loss to the human race, Gerry, you taking a

340

tumble round Cotmanhey and fetching up in the Erewash Canal."

Resnick hadn't forgotten Hannah's message: he thought he'd make himself a sandwich first and then give her a call. Lollo rosso, cucumber, watercress; goat's cheese; a tin of anchovies which he opened, pouring off some of the oil and then mashing the contents into a thick paste with black pepper and some dried basil; the last few pieces of sun-dried tomato fished from the jar and cut into strips. Johnny Hartman drifting through from the other room, Howard McGhee on trumpet. His friend Ben Riley had sent it out of the blue from New York. *Charlie, down here on a visit. Got myself conned into seeing the new Eastwood movie and actually liked it. Well, almost. Anyway, this guy sings all over the soundtrack and I thought you might like him. Always assuming your technology is up to it. Your friend, Ben.* Ben, sounding more acclimatized with every postcard, every year. And now, Resnick's technology was fine.

He cut bread, covered it with lettuce and the other salad things, spread over that the anchovy mixture and sun-dried tomato, finishing up with thin circles of cheese.

While he was waiting for the grill to warm, he went back to the phone: engaged. At the last minute he dribbled thick, green olive oil across both slices of bread and, licking his fingers clean, opened a bottle of Old Speckled Hen out of the fridge.

Johnny Hartman, deep-voiced: "They Didn't Believe Me."

This time when he tried the phone it rang and rang and rang.

Why couldn't he see Shane Snape joining in with a bunch of yobs for whom queer bashing was a legitimate sport? Trying not to get too much of his supper over the front of his shirt, he broke off a corner of crust, scraped it through the anchovy paste, and offered it to a mewing Bud. One of those coincidences: as the track ended, the telephone rang. Hannah, Resnick thought, reaching round for the receiver; Hannah calling him. Or else it could be Lynn.

It was neither. "Sir?" Carl Vincent's voice, as recognizable to him already as the regular members of the team. "Sir, I think you'd best come in."

The man sitting in Resnick's office was forty-two or -three; his hair was medium brown, quite thick, slightly long at the back and in need of a trim, perhaps, where it was beginning to curl around his ears. He had a neat beard, tight to the jawline; spectacles without rims. He was wearing what seemed to be a good suit, navy blue, one narrow stripe of a darker blue alongside one of gray. The knot of his tie was precise and unfashionably small.

"This is Mr. Cheshire," Vincent said, standing between Resnick and the door.

Resnick nodded and when Cheshire offered his hand, Resnick shook it, observing the slight tremor, the patchiness of sweat.

Resnick moved behind his desk and sat down, motioning for Vincent to close the door and do the same.

"Why don't you tell the inspector," Vincent said, "just what you told me?" And then, "Don't worry, it'll be fine."

Cheshire's accent was regulation, well educated; whatever local variation might once have been present was now almost totally submerged. "Ever since I read the story in the newspaper," Cheshire said, "the man who was attacked in the recreation ground, I've been considering coming to see you. You see, I couldn't be certain, positive that it was the correct thing to do."

"If you've got information for us, Mr. Cheshire, anything that might help us with what happened . . ."

"No. No, you see . . ." A nervous glance round toward

Vincent, who nodded encouragingly. "It isn't about that, at least not directly."

"Go on."

"Several months ago, six, six to be exact, six months and seven days, I was attacked by a man on the Promenade alongside the park, the same park." Cheshire removed his glasses from his face and rested his head forward at an angle into the palm of his hand. "I was . . . I was struck to the ground and almost throttled from behind. I was threatened with what would happen to me if I screamed . . . and then I was forcibly . . . I was raped, Inspector, that's what happened. Six months, a little more than six months ago."

It was quiet in the room, just the breathing of three men above the barely audible electric hum.

"This incident," Resnick said, "you didn't report it at the time?"

Cheshire shook his head.

"Not your doctor, hospital . . . ?"

"No."

"Did you tell anyone about this at all?"

"No, I did not."

"It's okay," Vincent said reassuringly.

"I feel as if I'm being accused here."

"No," Vincent said, glancing across at Resnick.

"No, Mr. Cheshire," Resnick said. "I assure you, that's not the case at all."

"Because if I hadn't thought this important, I would never have come forward at all."

Resnick nodded. "We understand that." And then, "And the reason you've come forward now, you think there might be a connection between the two attacks . . . ?"

"Well, yes."

"A possibility they might have been carried out by the same man?"

"Yes, of course. I mean, it has to be likely, doesn't it, after all?"

"There's something I have to ask you, Mr. Cheshire," said Resnick, leaning slightly forward, hands loosely joined. "When you were in the recreation ground that evening, had you gone there with the possibility in mind that you might meet someone, for the purposes of sex?"

"Look, I'm sorry . . ." Cheshire was on his feet and turned toward the door, Vincent half out of his chair to intercept him.

"Mr. Cheshire," Resnick said. "Mr. Cheshire, please sit down."

Cheshire took a handkerchief from his suit jacket pocket and wiped at his face, cleared his nose, turned back to face Resnick. "I'm sorry." He resumed his seat. "And yes, your assumption, as to my reasons for being there that night, it is correct."

"And this wasn't the first or only time you had been there in similar circumstances?"

A slow shake of the head.

"Are you married, Mr. Cheshire?"

He glanced toward the third finger of his left hand, the indentation gone now but the skin where the ring had fitted still a touch paler than the rest. "Not anymore."

"Your job?"

"I work for an investment company, pensions and loans."

"And this side of your life, no one else knows?"

Avoiding Resnick's eyes, "That's correct."

"The person who attacked you," Resnick asked, "can you describe him?"

Cheshire shook his head.

"Not in any way at all?"

The silence was long. "He was strong," Cheshire finally said. "Very strong. I thought—of course, there is no way to be sure—but I thought he might have been under the influence of drugs."

"Because?"

"His strength seemed so unnatural, and his anger. I think—I thought—he wanted to kill me. That was what he really wanted to do. And instead he . . . he . . . he tried to cause me all the pain he could."

Cheshire's glasses fell from his hand and he cried. Fingers meshed across his face, he cried. After some moments, Vincent went over and stood close beside him, resting a hand across his shoulders. Only when Cheshire had begun to recover himself did Vincent move away to his own chair and sit back down. Resnick fetched a glass of water and Cheshire sipped at it, then gulped, choked a little, thanked him, wiped at his glasses with his damp handkerchief, set them back on, took them off again.

"There's one more thing," Vincent said quietly, "I wonder if I could ask you, about what happened."

Cheshire nodded. "Go ahead."

"Penetration, when it took place . . ."

"A bottle," Cheshire said, eyes clenched shut, remembering. "He used a bottle and then smashed it on the railings when he was through."

43

If Hannah had woken earlier than usual that morning, and looked out from her upstairs window, she would have seen several men in overalls down on their hands and knees among the bushes that grew along the railings separating the recreation ground from the Promenade. She would have wondered exactly what, with their reinforced gloves and careful manner, they were looking for.

Up early himself, scarcely able to sleep, Resnick had driven out there and stood, hands in pockets, while the officers were making their search. He was present when one of the men, triumphantly, uncovered one section of bottle, a piece broken away from near its mouth and now wedged full of something dark, excrement or earth or both. Inside a curved oval of glass, there were dried streaks of what was almost certainly blood.

Just to contemplate what had happened, how these things could have come to pass, was enough to make Resnick drive the ends of his fingers hard into the palms of his hands. *He used a bottle and then smashed it on the railings when he was through.* Who, Resnick wondered, did the person who could perform such an act hate most, his victim or himself? Who was suffering the most pain?

He walked down toward the small row of terraced houses nearest to the church. No lights showed on the ground floor of Hannah's house; one only, burning high toward the roof. He thought of knocking, but knew he would be waking her for nothing; there was precious little time for anything approaching conversation and there was nothing he might say at that moment that he could imagine her wanting to hear.

Resnick got back in his car and drove the short distance along Derby Road to the station. Millington and Carl Vincent were sitting at one side of the CID room, Lynn Kellogg standing close behind them. The latest list Jane Prescott had supplied from Intelligence was on the computer: names of those cautioned for violent behavior during recent gay-rights rallies in the city center. Four charged with various breaches of the peace, 1993, charges dropped before coming to court; six officially warned, three charged, 1994, charges dropped; four warned, two charged, 1995, charges dropped.

"Really got behind these in a big way, didn't we?" Vincent said, sarcasm soft but clear in his voice.

"Evidence," Millington said, "not prejudice. Look at the figures for looney lefties trying to break up right-wing meetings and I'll bet it's just the same."

Vincent gave the sergeant a wry smile, unconvinced.

"Notice anything interesting here," Lynn said, pointing at the screen, then scrolling it round. "Miller, Frank. Three years out of three, a perfect score."

Resnick had come over to stand with them. "Miller, that's who Hovenden went to see."

"Last night," Lynn said, "right."

The door to the office opened and a sleepy-looking Kevin Naylor walked in, followed by Divine, who from somewhere had unearthed a slice of cold pizza and was eating it with gusto.

"Okay," Resnick said, "all the names on this list, they'll be matched with the ones we've already had from Special Branch, checked out today. The assumption we've got to go on is that what happened to Farrell and to Cheshire likely weren't isolated cases. It took six months for Cheshire to come forward; there'll be others who never will."

"And we're still thinking," Millington said, "these incidents and Aston's murder, they're linked?"

"Other than the fact," Lynn said, "that all the victims are gay?"

Resnick nodded. "That's what I feel. So what we're going to do is move in fast, follow up on those we know. Snape, Hovenden, Miller—that's the chain, and Hovenden, he might be the weak link. Lynn, you and Carl come with me, we'll catch him on the hop if we can. Graham, take Kevin and Mark, see what this Miller's got to say for himself; we still don't have a satisfactory alibi for him at the time Aston was killed." He looked round the room. "Questions, comments?"

"Only," Vincent said, "in case it was someone in here, I'd like to thank whoever put the condoms and Vaseline in my locker. One small point of sex education, though—small but important—Vaseline with condoms isn't really safe, it has a bad effect on the rubber. K-Y jelly"—and he winked at Divine—"now, that's the thing."

Kevin Naylor laughed uncertainly; Lynn shook her head in dismay.

"This isn't the time," Resnick said, "but any repetition of

incidents like that and I'll make it my business to find out who was responsible and have them out of here too fast for their feet to touch the ground."

Expressionless, Divine dumped what was left of his pizza into the nearest bin.

Resnick was in the back, Lynn driving; fast, northwest out of the city. Vincent was sitting alongside Lynn, half-turned toward the rear of the car.

"Local gay organizations," Resnick said, "they'll be informed as a matter of course. Encouraged to ask members to come forward."

"Problem there is," Vincent said, swinging further round, "most of the men likely to have been involved won't be on that scene anyway. And even if they were . . ." He shook his head. "There's still a lot of distrust."

"Well," Resnick said, "we can step up patrols around toilets and open spaces. . . ."

Vincent laughed. "That should fetch a few of the gay community out on the streets, protesting a violation of their civil rights."

"What right's that?" Lynn asked sharply. "The right to go out and put yourself at risk?"

"Hey!" Vincent smiled, backing along the seat. "Don't get at me. I didn't say that was my point of view."

Lynn swung wide to overtake a milk truck, smoothly changing gears. "What is your point of view, then, Carl?"

"About cottaging, you mean?"

"Um-hmm."

He shrugged. "It's not what I would want to do, not for myself. Not doing the job that I do. But I can understand why people feel the need."

"But not you?"

"Not me, no. Least, not anymore."

None of them spoke again until Lynn signaled left and slowed the car to a halt. "That's the house, over there."

Millington glanced down at his watch: it was still shy of seven o'clock. It was quiet in the street. Here and there among the lines of dilapidated houses, the odd one had been spruced up with a lick of bright paint, louvered shutters fitted across the upstairs windows, new doors with brass knockers that shone. Not here. He read the notice inviting callers to go round to the back.

"Let's keep it quiet now. No sense waking him till we have to."

There was a sour-sweet smell seeping across the backyard like blocked drains. Divine, ever hopeful, eased his hand against the rear door and to his surprise it slid open. Eyebrow raised, silently he questioned Millington and the sergeant nodded. Divine pushed the door all the way back and took a step inside. A tap was dripping against the clutter of pots that threatened to overflow the sink. They could hear clearly now, the sound of snoring, harsh and arrhythmic, from the adjoining room.

With the curtains pulled to, Miller had fallen asleep on the settee where he lay, a flotilla of empty cans adrift on the stained carpet, stale tobacco flat and thick in the air. Miller's T-shirt had worked loose from his jeans and was wrinkled up across the hump of his belly, jeans belt unfastened, zip partway down. He was on his back, one foot touching the floor, one arm thrown back, face to one side close against the cushion, mouth open.

Satisfied that they had not disturbed him, Millington pointed to the stairs, back out into the garden to the lean-to shed that was more falling than leaning. After all, the door had been open and Miller hadn't voiced any objections to their looking round.

◆◆◆

Late for the early shift, Gerry Hovenden's father had been leaving the house as Resnick and the others approached. "Inside," he said brusquely, scarcely slowing to examine Resnick's ID, "out the bathroom by now, if you're lucky."

"What the bloody hell's this?" Hovenden emerged into the postage stamp of a hallway, hair wet, an old Forest away shirt hanging over his sagging boxer shorts, bare feet.

"Inspector Resnick, CID. DC Vincent. I believe you know DC Kellogg already."

Lynn gave him a quick smile, not her best.

"I don't know what you think you're doing," Hovenden blustered, "but you can sod off out."

"Why not pop upstairs," Vincent said politely, "put a few more clothes on. Time you're back down, I expect we'll have figured out where the kettle is. Coffee or tea?"

Millington had been standing in the kitchen, idly leafing through Miller's well-thumbed copy of *Above All, Courage*, and wondering what exactly possessed someone to go off and join the SAS, when Naylor beckoned him outside. There in the corner of the shed, soles thick with mud, stood a pair of Caterpillar work boots, size ten.

"Been doing a spot of gardening," Millington observed.

"Looks like," Naylor said.

Divine appeared in the doorway behind them. "Seems as if he might be coming round."

Millington grinned. "Let's give him a hand."

The Saxon CD was still in the machine. Divine turned the volume up to full and pressed play. Miller, startled, tried to push himself up, overbalanced and rolled off the settee to the floor.

"Morning, Frank," Millington mouthed, waving his warrant card in front of Miller's incredulous face. "This is your wake-up call."

Hovenden had pulled on a pair of jeans and wore old trainers, unlaced, on his feet. Carl Vincent had made tea in mugs that Lynn had first carefully rinsed under the hot tap.

"Must have a bit of trouble," Resnick said innocently, nodding toward Hovenden's feet, "always finding shoes to fit."

Hovenden sat awkwardly and said nothing.

"Elevens, are they?" Resnick asked.

"What?"

"Size? I said elevens, twelves?"

"What sodding difference?"

"Just making conversation."

"Elevens, for fuck's sake! They're elevens, satisfied?"

Resnick smiled.

"You know," Lynn said, "we've been talking to your friend Shane."

"What of it?"

"He had some interesting things to tell us, that's all."

"Oh, yeah? About me, I suppose?"

Lynn looked at him, her head angled to one side. "Now, what d'you think he could have had to tell us about you?"

"Sod all!"

Lynn nodded. "Just about that credit card."

"What credit card's that?"

"Oh, the one he sold to Sally Purdy."

"Who?"

"Sally Purdy," Resnick said. "She was the one who told us she bought it from Shane."

"What bloody credit card you on about?"

"Inspector Aston's," Resnick said.

"You know," said Lynn. "The police officer who was killed."

"The night," Resnick said, "you seem to be confused about where you were."

Hovenden pushed himself clumsily back in his chair. "Which night's this?"

Lynn said, half-smiling, "You see what we mean?"

"No, look. Look." Hovenden not looking, not at any of them, not at the table, not at the floor. "That night, I told you, right? Before. I was home."

"Is this a different story, Hovenden?" Resnick asked. "Because if it is . . ."

"Shane's, I was round Shane's. That's what I meant."

"By home?"

"Yes."

"Not here?"

Hovenden stared around. "This shithole?"

"Shane, then," Vincent asked, leaning close over him, "he's what? Like your brother?"

"Yes. I s'pose, yeah."

"Not being very brotherly, then, Shane," Vincent said. "Some of the things I hear he was saying yesterday."

"You're lying."

"Not exactly brotherly love, dropping you in it the way he did."

"You're lying!" Hovenden's face was almost white with strain.

"What would you say," asked Lynn, "if I told you he claimed he got Inspector Aston's credit card from you?"

Hovenden scrambled to his feet, knocking back his chair, face thrust forward. "I'd say you were a lying cunt!"

Vincent clicked his tongue against the roof of his mouth twice. "That's no way to speak to a lady."

"Fuck you!"

Resnick was standing now, time to move on. "Had all you want of this tea, Gerry? Or d'you want to finish it before we leave for the station?"

"Turn off," Frank Miller shouted, "that fucking noise!"

"Worried about the neighbors, Frank?" Millington said. "That's nice. World could do with a few more like you."

"Saxon, though," Divine said, flicking open the drawer and removing the CD, "always did like them. DeMontfort Hall, ooh, must be six or seven years back now. Go down and see them, did you? My ears were ringing for days."

Miller turned to stare at him: what the fuck was all this about?

"But then that's the way you like 'em, isn't it? In the ears? Fact, I think we might've found a tape of yours a while back. That had quite a bit of Saxon on it. Good, too."

"I don't suppose," Miller said, zipping up his jeans, "there's any way you lot of comedians'd crawl back out the way you crawled in?"

"Course, Frankie," Millington agreed, "just as soon as you're ready."

Miller snorted and scratched his left armpit energetically. "Oh, yeah? What is it now?"

"Someone's been putting themselves about amongst our friends in the gay community," Millington said. "Looking at your record, you've done a bit of that in your time."

"Poofs? Yeah, why not? It's what they fuckin' deserve."

"You don't need a coat," Millington said, leading the way, "but if I were you, I'd lock this back door. Never know who might come waltzing in."

354

44

Khan had woken that morning with Jill's leg hooked over one of his own, her hip pressed against his. It had been light enough in the room to see the inward curve of her spine, the swell of her buttocks when he slipped back the sheet. Fifteen minutes before he had to be getting ready for work, twenty at a push. Experimentally, he tensed himself against her body and felt pressure in return. He knew there were two things he could do and one of them was to bend forward and kiss her lightly between the shoulder blades, slide his leg free, and swing out of the bed. He looked at the way she was stretching, legs parted, and knew how warm she would feel if he were to move his hand a little higher along her thigh. She gave a sleepy, satisfied moan when he did this and that was that. Twenty minutes, he thought, would be fine.

In fact, it was closer to fifteen. Khan stood buttoning his pale blue shirt, fading a shade now, the one his last girlfriend had bought him at Next.

"I swear," Jill said, sitting up higher in the bed, "you only wear that to annoy me."

Reaching for his tie, silver with a blue stripe, Khan laughed. "Have to get some kind of reaction, don't I?"

She threw a pillow and he ducked low, reaching for the end of the duvet.

"No!" Jill shouted. "Don't you dare!"

Which was when the phone rang and Khan, chuckling, went to answer it. Paul Matthews's voice was nervous yet unmistakable, a smile broadening across Khan's face as he listened. "All right," he said finally, "give me twenty minutes and I'll be there."

Back in the bedroom, he kissed Jill languorously on the mouth: five minutes, he was thinking, more than I gave you.

Given the seriousness of the crimes concerned, the weight of evidence, circumstantial at best, had been enough to argue the necessary search warrants. They had twenty-four hours, plus a possible extra twelve, within which either to charge Miller and Hovenden or let them go. Under new regulations, they were allowed to take samples from all suspects in order to establish their DNA; these samples would then be checked against the new national database in Birmingham. Comparisons with the DNA from the blood found on Aston's body would be crucial. But it would not be quick.

"This can't be right," Frank Miller had said to his solicitor. "There's no way they can make me agree to this."

The solicitor was sorry, but under the new law indeed they could.

"And if I won't stand for it?"

"We'll have to find ways"—Divine had grinned hopefully—"of taking your legs from under you. Nothing to stand on."

Miller had shaken his head. "Know what this means, don't you? This DNA business, it's like a fingerprint, right? Once you're in their books, they're gonna come chasin' after you every chance they get."

"It doesn't work that way," Naylor said. "The only times we hang on to the samples is if you're actually convicted, or officially cautioned for a recordable offense. Otherwise, they're destroyed."

Miller threw back his head and laughed. "Believe that, you believe the moon's made of fuckin' green cheese!"

"Don't tell me," Divine said, disappointed, "that it's not?"

The first thing the search team did at Miller's house was to bag and label the boots in the shed. There was a car ready and waiting to whisk them off for analysis. The house itself, though, proved a disappointment. True, there were back issues of *The Order* and a few other bits of right-wing paraphernalia, but nothing to get Special Branch worked up into a sweat. In a tatty address book, they found a few phone numbers that would ring bells with Trevor Ulman and the Football Intelligence Unit, but again, there were no major surprises. The collection of top-shelf porn devoted to women with abnormally large breasts was well-thumbed, but compared to some of the stuff that was routinely confiscated, this was very small beer indeed. And they turned up no likely weapons; nothing resembling a baseball bat.

Once you got beyond the main downstairs rooms, the house Gerry Hovenden shared with his father was indeed a shitheap of the first degree. Hovenden senior was a classic hoarder and the only prerequisite for being an object saved seemed to be that whatever it was, it was covered in dirt. There was a layer of grease along the banister rail, on all the shelves and surfaces, over everything they touched. Engine parts, old clothes, yellowing newspapers, fuse wire, cycle blocks, quarter heels for sticking on shoes, bottles of oil gone rancid, copies of paperback Westerns with the pages bent back, rusty tools. And, in the midst of all of this, the glove—the one that Gerry had hurled there, back among the recesses of that upstairs back room, thrown there among the cobwebs and the musty boxes, the rat droppings and the silverfish— the leather motorcycle glove that matched the one found on the embankment near Bill Aston's body. Its identical opposite. Its partner. Its twin.

Paul Matthews's mother sat at her kitchen table, picking crumbs from around a piece of seed cake and lifting them absentmindedly to her mouth. "Be gentle with him, won't you? He's never meant any harm."

Matthews was upstairs in a bedroom that had scarcely changed in the last fifteen years. Scouting certificates hung on the wall beside a color photograph of the Forest team from 1981 and a map of South Wales; framed on the window ledge was a picture of a smiling Paul, newborn lamb in his arms, in the lane alongside his aunt's house.

"How was the rest of the visit?" Khan asked. "Are you feeling any better?"

Tears at the edges of his eyes, Matthews turned away.

"I'm glad you phoned," Khan said gently. "I think it was the right thing." A pause, then: "You'll feel better, after you've talked. Got it off your chest."

"I can't."

"Yes, it's all right. You can."

"I can't tell you everything. I don't know . . . Oh, God!"

"It's all right." Khan put his hand on the base of Matthews's neck and let it rest there. "Just tell me what you can."

After some moments, Matthews reached into his pocket for a tissue and Khan moved his hand, sat back, and waited. He thought Matthews might break down again and cry, but instead he simply sat there on the side of his bed, telling his story, the one he had told so many times inside his head out walking the cliffs, watching the waves break back upon the shore.

He described how this particular group of youths, the older ones, half a dozen of them, had got up from the television room earlier on the night that Nicky died, and swaggered toward the door. How the biggest of them, at least as big as Matthews himself, if not bigger, had sauntered back over to Paul and fixed him with a grin and told him to stay where he was, carry on watching whatever he was watching—unless he wanted to go up and watch them.

And then they had gone up to Nicky's room, all six of them, and locked the door from the inside. And he hadn't known what to do. He'd been frightened, scared of them, the way they would swagger about the place and smoke and swear and sometimes there were these drugs they got from somewhere, and they would mock him, call him names, make threats, and he knew it was too late to stand up to them, far too late, and when the screams from Nicky's room were so loud they could be heard, even downstairs, all he had done was go over to the TV and turn up the sound.

"You didn't tell anyone?" Khan said after a moment.

"No, not at first. Not then."

"But later?"

Matthews's eyes were closed. "I told Mr. Jardine."

Something akin to pleasure lurched deep in Khan's throat. "You told him what you've just told me?"

Matthews nodded.

"Paul?"

"Yes, yes."

"And what did Mr. Jardine say?"

Matthews opened his eyes. "He said there was no need to mention it to anyone else, especially at the inquiry. He said it would only muddy the waters. He said anyway it wasn't relevant at all."

"What about the other staff member on duty? Elizabeth Peck? You didn't say anything to her?"

Matthews pressed the tips of his fingers against his temples so hard that when he finally withdrew them, there were pale ovals clear against the skin. "She wasn't there. Not all evening. Not until I phoned her and told her she'd best come in."

"She was ill, sick, what?"

Matthews shook his head. "She was working at another job."

Khan got to his feet and went across to the window. On the roof opposite a workman was sitting, a brightly colored scarf tied round his head, drinking from a thermos and reading a newspaper.

"These youths," he said, uncapping his pen. "What are their names?" And Matthews told him, each name like a nail.

Resnick and Millington had decided to take Hovenden first. The glove they had found in his house? The one matching that discovered at the murder scene? Yes, Hovenden had agreed, it was his, but so what? He'd chucked it out months ago, before Christmas probably, after he lost the other on a ride up through the Peak District. Late November, that would have been. Snow on the tops, he remembered that. Whatever they'd found down by the Trent, no connection, nothing to do with him.

Resnick didn't tell him that Forensic was even now checking out the body fibers from inside the glove found near Aston's body, microscopic particles of skin, matching their DNA against Hovenden's own. That could wait till confirmation came through; enough for now to leave him rattled.

"All right, Gerry," he said, "play it that way if you like. We'll go and have a chat with your pal Frank Miller, see if he can't throw a little more light on things."

Hovenden nervously laughed. "Frank'd not as much as cock his leg on one of your lot if you were on fire."

"Okay, Gerry," Resnick said pleasantly, getting to his feet. "Have it your way. For now."

"Cocky bastard!" Millington said, once they were out in the corridor.

"Bravado," Resnick said. "Nothing more. Behind it all, he's one unhappy boy."

"Thinks his mate Frankie's about to dump him in it, you reckon?"

Outside the second interview room, Resnick grinned. "Let's see if he isn't right."

Frank Miller claimed only vague memories of a Saturday night's drinking. Yeah, yeah, this pub and that; a pint with this bloke here, a few more with these pals there. Dinner on the way home, curry maybe, fish and chips. Come to think of it, wasn't that the night he never got back at all? Fetched up at his brother-in-law's place in the Meadows, sharing the floor with the pair of Rottweilers his sister was hoping to breed from. Long as they didn't do it, you know, while he was kipping there. Why didn't Resnick send someone round, find out for himself?

Resnick less than well pleased, another alibi depending upon close family more likely to commit any amount of perjury before seeing their nearest and dearest end up in the nick.

"Meantime," Millington said, "why don't you try telling us about these?" And with something approaching a flourish, he produced the Caterpillar boots.

"What about 'em?"

"Well, do you recognize them, for a start?"

Miller shrugged. "Hundreds of pairs like that, must be. Thousands."

"Are you saying they're not yours?"

"What I'm saying"—a cocky strut to Miller's voice—"is that I don't know. They could be mine, and then again, they could not."

"Maybe you'd like to try one on?" Millington suggested.

"What is this? Fuckin' Cinderella? 'Cause if it is, we got the Ugly Sisters well cast, I can tell you that."

"These boots were found," Resnick said, "in your garden shed. This morning."

"Really? Amazing, in'it, searched for them bastards everywhere."

"Lost," Millington mused, "and then were found."

Resnick sneaked him a quick sideways look. For a man whose only confessed religious experience seemed to have been Petula Clark singing one of the songs from *Jesus Christ, Superstar*, biblical references were unexpected, to say the least.

But Millington was not through. "Interesting what was found on them, too. That style of boot, you see. All those deep cracks and crevices in the sole, you'd be amazed what gets stuck in them." He paused, Miller watching him carefully now. "Or maybe not."

Miller slouched back in his chair, head round for a moment toward his brief, one eyebrow raised. "So tell me," he said.

Millington flipped the cover of his notebook back. "Mud, for a start . . ."

"Yeah? Surprise, fuckin' surprise," said Miller, but his heart wasn't in it.

"Earth," Millington went on, "consistent with that found on the section of the embankment where Inspector Aston was murdered. Not only that, we found blood, small traces of blood across the tongue of the left boot, the same blood type as Aston."

Blood was now in short supply in Miller's face.

"Something else we found," Resnick said, leaning in, "a

cassette tape with a lot of music by a band called Saxon, a favorite of yours I believe? And that's not all—it seems whoever's tape it was had used it before, recording made at a BNP rally, autumn of last year. Shouldn't be impossible to check if you were there."

Miller sat there for several moments, arms resting on his knees, staring at the ground. Then he looked up and pursed his mouth into a perfect O. "Got a cigarette?" he asked. "I need a fag."

His solicitor tapped him on the arm. "You're under no obligation to talk about this now, not without discussing it with me first."

"What you can do," Miller said politely, politely for Miller, "fuck right off. And poke me in the arm again and I'll break every finger in your fuckin' hand. Understood? I know my rights better'n you."

It was understood.

A knock on the door fetched Resnick out of the room and the expression on Naylor's face told him the news faster than words.

"Fuck!" Resnick said, not a word he often used, or lightly. It seemed certain that the surplus blood found on Aston's body had come from neither Hovenden nor Miller.

He was on his way back into the interview room when Khan appeared at the end of the corridor, smiling: not all news was bad. After listening he sent Kevin Naylor in to sit with Millington—he wanted to confront Jardine himself.

45

The suit was different, double-breasted with wide lapels, dark with a narrow pinstripe running through, but the amount of dandruff that had fallen from Jardine's graying hair was the same. The veins etched into his nose stood out more prominently; the corners of his eyes were watery, clouded yellow.

He began by offering Resnick his hand, and when it was refused, sat back behind his desk and folded his arms across his chest.

"DC Khan and myself have just come from the police station," Resnick said, each word spoken with special care, "where one of your staff, Paul Matthews, has made a statement about the events leading up to the death of Nicky Snape on these premises."

Jardine flinched and covered his mouth with the opened fingers of one hand.

Resnick nodded toward Khan, who took an envelope containing several sheets of paper from his inside pocket. "I would like you to read that statement now."

Jardine hesitated before reaching out and taking the statement from Khan's hand; he still avoided looking either officer in the eye.

"Read it," Resnick said, "all of it, carefully, before making any response."

Jardine's eyes stalled at the end of the first paragraph and then started again. At the end of the second paragraph he glanced sideways toward the wall, the photographs where his career was smeared. By the time he had reached the end and had pushed the sheets away across his desk, there were tears in his eyes but not enough.

"What Matthews says is basically correct?"

Jardine nodded: yes.

"He told you those youths had been in Nicky Snape's room the evening he died?"

"Yes."

"That in his opinion they had been bullying him, at the very least?"

"Yes."

"And that in his belief, that bullying had been of a sexual nature?"

"There is no proof—"

"But that was what he said?"

"Yes."

"The staff member in charge?"

"Yes."

"And you did nothing."

Jardine glanced from Khan to Resnick and shook his head.

"You told Matthews to do nothing, say nothing?"

"Yes."

"Would you mind telling me why that was?"

After a pause, Jardine said, "It would only disturb the smooth running of the home. I didn't see what good would be served."

"And why was that?"

Jardine looked at him directly for the first time. "Nicky Snape was already dead."

On his feet, Resnick retrieved the statement from the desk. "Copies of this statement have been sent to Director of Social Services, to Phyllis Parmenter, the member of the Social Services Inspectorate who chaired the original inquiry, and to the Crown Prosecution Service. Detective Constable Khan will question the youths named in the report as soon as you have arranged for a parent or legal representative to be present. Is that understood?"

Jardine nodded, head once more bowed, and Resnick, after a quick glance toward Khan, left the pair of them in the room. Now that it was done, he couldn't wait to shed himself of the sad, corrupt smell of that room, that man, that institution.

One night on the thin mattress of the police cell had been enough to bring Frank Miller to his senses. Talking his way out of the blood on his boots, the voices on the tape, he knew would be difficult—and why? To save the hides of a pair of queers—he was sure they were, no matter how much they denied it—who just weren't worth saving. Commit perjury for the likes of them! Bugger that for a game of soldiers!

So Miller began banging on the inside of his cell door a little after seven and by nine he was sitting back in the inquiry room with Millington and Naylor and a tape machine. The story he told was this: his brother-in-law, Ian Orston, had had words with some of the Irish who used this pub on London Road and had asked Frank and a few other mates to come and help sort them out. Teach them to pay some respect. Frank had tipped the wink to Gerry

Hovenden, who, in turn, had enlisted Shane. But Shane never showed, not then. And it was Ian who brought along the baseball bat, a Christmas present to his kids.

They'd done the business in the pub.

Frank couldn't remember whose idea it was to walk on down to the river, maybe look in at the TBI, but that's what they'd done. After closing, they all headed back across the bridge, pretty pissed by now and noisy, pushing one another around for the fun of it, because there wasn't anyone else to push. Ian and himself had wandered off in front, aiming for Ian's place in the Meadows and going to take the path across the playing fields, back of the Memorial Gardens. It was somewhere around then, on the other side of the Trent, that the others must've met up with Shane, who was already in an argument with this bloke. The one who turned out to be the copper. Poor bastard!

Anyway, there was so much shouting Frank hadn't been able to hear everything, except he remembered that Shane had accused the bloke of being queer—which was a bit rich, Frank thought, coming from him—and of trying to grab hold of Shane's balls in the gents. Next thing you knew, they were all over him, shouting "Fucking poof!" and the like, kicking the shit out of him.

Frank and Ian had stood back on the path, watching. Frank fancying a bit of it himself, he didn't mind admitting, but the way they were swarming round the bloke there was sod all room.

And then Shane had broken away and came at a run for Ian's bat; gone back in there and smashed the bloke about the face like he wanted to take his head clean off. In the end, Gerry had pulled him away. Tried to give Ian back his baseball bat, but Ian said no way.

"I went over and looked at him," Frank said. "Total bloody mess." He shrugged. "That must've been when I got his blood on me boots."

"And at no time while this was going on," Millington asked, "did you raise a fist in anger or deliver a blow?"

"Me?" Frank Miller said. "Not one. You got my solemn word." And he grinned.

Hovenden denied all of it: every word. The results of the tests on the fibers from the glove had still not been returned. "Let him chew on it awhile," Millington said.

"This Ian Orston," Naylor called from over by the computer, "he's got some previous. D'you want me to pull him in, see if his account tallies?"

"Yes, get on it now. Take Carl here with you, okay? And stay sharp, the pair of you."

They were leaving when Resnick returned, sullen and sad-eyed. Millington waited while the kettle boiled and the tea had mashed before filling him in on all the details.

"Right, Graham," Resnick said, fortified. "Let's get over to the Snape place, you and me, see if we can't lay our hands on Shane. Mark, Lynn, you'd best be along for the ride."

When Norma opened the door to Resnick, midafternoon, she was still wearing what she had slept in, an old dressing gown pulled loosely round her. One look at Resnick and she turned back into the house. The curtains in the front room were closed and the television was on. Norma had one cigarette in her hand, another, forgotten, smoldering alongside cold toast.

"Norma," Resnick said, "what's happened? Are you all right?"

She looked at him as if she hadn't properly heard what he had said.

"Norma, it's Shane. Is he here?"

A slow shake of the head.

"We've got a warrant to search the house."

"What do I care?"

Resnick nodded at Millington and Divine and they moved quickly toward the stairs. He waited until Norma had flopped down into the settee and then he switched down the sound on the TV; outside, in the backyard, the dog was barking frantically to be fed.

"Should I let him in?" Resnick asked.

Norma didn't care about that either.

He motioned for Lynn to stay with Norma while he tipped dog biscuits into a bowl and unlocked the rear door, careful to keep well to one side when the dog tore in. He could hear Millington and Divine moving around, heavy-footed, upstairs. Back in the front room, he sat across from Norma, waiting for her to focus on him.

"It's serious, Norma, this time. That alibi you gave him, him and his pal, it doesn't stand up." Her eyes flickered as if still only half understanding what he was saying. "Where is he, Norma? Shane. Where is he now?"

Footsteps on the stairs were followed by a slow shake of Millington's head, its expression telling Resnick they'd found nothing, neither Shane nor any weapon: burned it or hidden it, Resnick thought. He imagined the baseball bat floating off down the Trent, hurled there after Aston's murder and never found—except for what had happened to Declan Farrell, the particular agonies he'd been put through. *A varnished implement, solid, hard.* They had searched along a half-mile stretch of railway line, between overgrown gravestones, in among bushes and across fields. Every dustbin, backyard, and cranny.

He smashed this bloke about the face like he wanted to take his head clean off.

Resnick pictured Shane standing there, sweat on his lip, breathing hard, hatred and anger bright on his face.

Why?

"Your Shane," Resnick said, "when he's not hanging round with this Gerry, are there any other friends he sees? Special, I mean?"

Norma didn't answer.

"Girlfriends?"

"Sara Johnson," Norma said scornfully. "Slag."

"You know where she lives?"

Norma didn't have a clue, couldn't have cared less, but she thought she worked in the Viccy center, in the food court, somewhere like that.

"Make sure the house is watched," Resnick told Millington when they were back outside. "Front and back. And keep in touch with the station. Lynn, let's you and me see if we can't find this Sara Johnson."

At the curb, he turned back. "Look sharp, all of you; be on your guard. Think on what he's maybe done. He's young and he's strong, likely he'll not come easy."

"Just give me the chance," Divine said, once Resnick had gone. "Shane Snape, one on one, see how easy he comes then."

Once in the food court, steering his way between the shopping trolleys and the prams, Resnick realized he had seen Sara Johnson before; she had served Hannah and him with coffee and now she did so for him and Lynn, strong, small espressos in waxed paper cups. They identified themselves and asked Sara if she wouldn't mind answering a few questions; carried the coffees to one of the nearby tables and sat down, Sara, pretty in her pink uniform, a fine sculptured face and lazy eyes, seventeen.

Self-conscious, she lit a cigarette and wafted the smoke away from her face with her hand.

"I don't know," she said in answer to Resnick's question. "I haven't seen Shane for a week or more now."

"Sara, you do understand this is important?"

The tip of her tongue pressed for a moment against the underside of her upper lip. "I'm not a liar, you know."

"I'm sure."

"I've not seen him. Besides, he wouldn't come round to me, if that's what you're thinking."

Near them, a man in a shabby overcoat, once someone's best, but a long time ago, was coughing repeatedly into the back of his hand, rough-edged and raw. It was enough to make Resnick's throat sore. "Why d'you say that?"

"He just wouldn't, that's why." There was irritation, mixed with amusement, in her eyes. "For one thing, on account my old man can't stand him, won't have him inside the house, right? For another, I finished with him. Two weekends ago now."

Resnick reminded himself not to ignore his espresso.

"Why did you chuck him, Sara?" Lynn asked.

Sara tilted back her head and released a thin plume of smoke. Her nails were painted, Resnick noticed, with some kind of varnish that glittered, like the hundreds and thousands kids liked sprinkled over ice cream. "We went out, right. The Sat'day. Going to the pictures, that's what I thought, but no, he didn't fancy that, so we went up the Malt House for a drink. After that, I don't know where. The Dog and Bear? Anyway, after that we come back down the Square and Shane, he calls a cab, so I think, Oh, right, his mum must be out, back to his place, usual thing, as if that's all he's got on his mind. Blokes, you know. Though in Shane's case, you had to sometimes wonder why he bothered. Anyway, I get in the cab and he tells me he's not coming, promised to meet one of his mates. Give the driver a fiver and tells him to take me home. Well, I wasn't having that. I told him if that was how he felt, maybe he should spend all his time with his precious mates and stop wasting it on me." She looked at Resnick and gave a little shrug. "That was that."

371

"How did he react?" Lynn said. "When you told him that?"

Sara glanced back over toward the counter where she worked. Watching her, Resnick caught himself wondering if she knew just how pretty she was. "He didn't care," she said. "I don't think he ever did."

The coughing had been joined by a small child's shrill wailing and Resnick waited for the ensuing shout and slap. Through hidden speakers, a tinkly organ with percussion accompaniment was following "The Skye Boat Song" with "How Are Things in Glocomorra?"

"Look," Lynn said, lowering her voice, "I don't want to pry, but you said, well, you implied, sex with Shane, it wasn't all it might have been."

Sara grabbed at her packet of Silk Cuts and fidgeted back in her chair. "What d'you want to ask about that for?"

"Sara, I'm sorry, I know it's personal, but believe me, we're not asking for no good reason."

She took a long drag on her cigarette and momentarily closed her eyes. "It was like, you know, he always wanted it, just never . . . well, not never, but . . . Everything was always okay when we, when he . . . Look, I can't believe I'm sitting here telling you this, it's like being on that, what d'you call it, Ricki Lake show. But sometimes, well, let's put it this way, what he was in such a hurry to start, he couldn't always finish. How's that for you?" She stubbed out her cigarette and hurried to her feet, glancing back again at the unattended coffee machine. "Now I've got to go, I shall get my cards. All right?"

"Yes, of course," Lynn said, leaning back. "And Sara, thanks."

Resnick watched her go, the tight swish of her legs inside her pink uniform. Why was it, since Hannah, he had begun again to notice these things?

"Good," Resnick said. "You made a sight better job of that than I would."

Lynn gave him a quick smile and drained her cup. They found a phone near the Mansfield Road exit and Resnick called the station; so far, there had been no sign of Shane. But twenty minutes previously, the fibers found inside the leather glove had been successfully identified as coming from Gerry Hovenden. Nothing now to stop them from charging him with the murder of William Aston.

"Right," Resnick said, passing on the news to Lynn as they headed for the lift. "Let's get back sharpish."

"What you mean is"—Lynn grinned—"you want me to drive. Again."

46

Naylor and Vincent relieved Millington and Divine ten minutes short of six o'clock; not that Millington himself was in any hurry—his wife, he knew, was all set for one of her evening classes, and leftover mushroom lasagna, neatly wrapped in environmentally friendly cling film, would be all there was to go home to.

"The daughter," Millington said, "Sheena, is it? She came in about an hour ago, left ten, fifteen minutes back. Aside from that, about as quiet as the proverbial."

Divine and Vincent contrived to change places without exchanging either a look or a glance.

"Nearly forgot," Millington said, leaning back in through the car window nearest to Naylor. "How'd it go with Frankie Miller's mate, Orston?"

"Clammed up at first," Naylor said, "much as you'd expect. Once he started talking, though, everything he said pretty much agreed with Miller's version of events. Right down to standing there while them others beat Aston senseless. I asked him if he hadn't been tempted to step in, try and put a stop, but he said, no, it weren't none of my affair. Only thing he was sorry about, callous bastard, was that Shane had used his baseball bat to lay into him with."

"Makes you wonder, doesn't it?" Millington said. "What it's all coming to, blokes like that."

"Good bloody thumping," Divine said, "that's what he needs. Only thing his sort bloody understand."

While Naylor and Vincent were on duty outside the Snape house and Millington was watching *The Bill* and washing his microwaved lasagna down with a can of Carlsberg, Divine was mooching around his flat, unable to get interested in either of the videos he'd rented from Blockbuster, *The Specialist* and *Highlander III*; the pizza he'd phoned out for sat cold in its cardboard box.

By ten-thirty he was so edgy that he dialed the number of the staff nurse from the Queen's who'd spent nine months getting him to change his ways and then, when he almost had, had dumped him just the same. At the sound of Divine's voice she set down the phone.

Once in the car, he was on his way along the Radford Boulevard before he was wholly conscious of where he was heading or why.

Naylor was sitting in the unmarked Sierra, seventy yards back along the road, with an unimpeded view of the Snape house.

"Must want something to do," Naylor remarked, as Divine got into the seat alongside him.

"Reckon so," Divine said. "Anything up?"

Naylor shook his head. "Mrs. Snape left. Norma. Some woman friend of hers came round and they went off. Had this small bag with her. Suitcase, like. Asked her where she was going and she said round to this friend's for the night. Made a note of the address just in case."

"You don't think she could have been sneaking out some clean clothes to her Sonny Jim?"

Naylor laughed. "Not unless he's into dresses and frilly bras."

"Never can tell nowadays. Speaking of which, where's our Carl?"

Naylor pointed toward the house. "Watching the back entry."

"Who better?" Divine said.

Naylor gave him a look but left it at that. He knew better than to get into an argument with Divine about what was politically correct.

After forty minutes of sporadic conversation, Divine lit another cigarette and said, "Why don't you get off home, Kev? Keep Debbie company. No point us both sitting here."

"No, you're okay."

But when Divine asked him again, twenty minutes later, he agreed. He was getting out of the car when Vincent appeared, out of the alley entrance and walking toward them across the road.

"Seen anything?" Naylor asked, hopefully.

Vincent shook his head. "Only the back of the house with all the lights out. Upstairs curtains drawn. Only sound's from that dog of theirs, carrying on every once in a while to get let out."

"Mark," Naylor said, "if you're serious about hanging on, why don't you go round the back for a spell? Then Carl can take my place here for a change. I'll get off home for a bit. All right?"

Divine didn't like the idea of doing Carl Vincent any kind of a favor, but he agreed all the same. At least round the back he could pace up and down if he'd a mind, better than getting a numb bum in the Ford. And that's what he did: walk, lean, light a cigarette; lean some more, walk.

He was just approaching the house from the further end of the entry when he saw something move in the yard. A shadow, low against the wall.

Divine waited till his breathing had steadied and then moved on slowly, careful to lift his feet, not to kick a stray stone or stumble. By the time he had got to the gate, he realized it was the dog.

All right. The breath punched out of him with a sigh. Only the sodding dog. And then, instantaneously, his palms began to sweat. The dog: the dog was inside, Carl had said so. Whining inside the house, wanting to be let out. And for him now to be out, someone must have gone in.

He lifted the latch on the gate and eased it open. Half a dozen paces and he was at the back door. Listening, he heard no sound. He thought the door would have been locked again from the inside, but it wasn't. At the doorway leading off from the kitchen he paused and listened again, nothing but the pump of his own heart. Sweat was in his hair now, running the length of his neck. Holding his breath, he stepped quickly into the front room and waited to let his eyes become more accustomed to the light. Nothing beyond the usual.

Divine turned toward the stairs.

Only once, when he hesitated midway up the stairs, did he ask himself the question he would ask himself a thousand times later: Why hadn't he called Vincent for backup before going in?

Three of the four doors were open, partly at least. Divine's mouth was dry and he ran his tongue across his lips; started counting to three inside his head, and on two, turned the handle and pushed the fourth door back as fast as he could. Flicked on the light.

A girl's room, posters of Take That and Keanu Reeves on the walls. Cuddly toys on the bed. The small wardrobe was crammed with clothes, some on hangers, many not.

Maybe, Divine thought, Vincent had been wrong; what he had heard was the dog in the backyard, yammering to get in.

He could see the shape of a double bed through the doorway to the next room, covers all in a ruck. Norma Snape's room, he supposed. Shoes scattered across the floor, haphazard piles of clothes, pairs of tights hanging from the dressing table mirror—Jesus! What a mess! He stepped over a discarded pair of jeans and a high-heeled shoe and that was enough; some sense alerted him, so that he swung his head toward a sound felt rather than heard and turned smack into the full curve of a baseball bat, swung with all the force of a young man, fit and in his prime, striving to strike the ball clear out of the park. The crack as Divine's cheekbone fractured was sharp and clear, and as he catapulted back across the room, before he lost all hearing in that ear, he heard Shane say, smiling, "This what you're looking for?"

Divine bounced forward off the wall and Shane swung the bat again, down onto the top of his shoulder, breaking his collarbone.

"Didn't I tell you it'd be me and you?"

Without Shane having to do anything more, one of Divine's legs buckled under him and he went sprawling to the floor, crying out as his injured arm fell against the base of the bed.

Shane grabbed him by his other arm, the collar of his coat and shirt, and lifted him up, throwing him down again upon the mess of sheets.

Divine wanted to shout, but somehow he couldn't think how. Shane on one knee on the bed beside him, reaching underneath him, feeling for his belt. Oh, Christ!

"Didn't I say I'd have you?"

A wrench and Divine's legs kicked upward as his trousers

were yanked down about his knees, his boxer shorts next, Divine struggling to fight back, use his elbows, arms, the back of his head, anything, but when he did the pain that seared through him was enough to make him cry out and that was before Shane slid one arm around Divine's neck and began to squeeze it back, his other hand feeling between Divine's legs, fingers beginning to push against the clenched sphincter, all the time repeating words Divine could barely hear.

"Slut. Whore. Cunt. This is it, this is what you want, you know it is."

Shane pulling at the front of his own jeans, freeing himself and then kneeling above Divine, one arm still so tight about his neck that Divine was close to fainting, wishing he could faint, praying for it, rocking his body backward, trying to throw him off, trying . . . Oh, God! The pain was sudden like a knife and sharp and then Shane was pushing into him and shouting louder and louder that litany of words again.

"Whore! Cunt! This is what you want, you bastard! You fucking cunt!" Shane throwing himself across Divine as he came, sinking his teeth into the flesh at the back of his shoulder and puncturing the skin.

The sound of the door slamming downstairs must have registered seconds after it happened. Shane pulling away and clutching at the top of his jeans, trying and failing to cover himself and at the same time reach for the baseball bat that had become jammed between the mattress and the foot of the bed before Carl Vincent burst through the door.

Vincent, diving at Shane headlong, the top of his skull striking Shane's breastbone as the bat flew from Shane's hand and he fell backward against the wall beneath the window. Vincent punching him once, twice, then slamming the point of his elbow hard into the center of Shane's face, before seizing his arm and turning him, one knee driving down into the small of his back, Vincent's cuffs in his hand now, one of them fastening about Shane's wrist and the other half locked around the pipe from the radiator.

"You do not have to say anything," Vincent beginning. "You do not have to say anything . . ." but stopping, wanting Shane, please, to turn his head and look at him, look at him so that Vincent could hit him again, so that he would have a reason.

Vincent getting up and leaving him cuffed to the radiator, going to where Divine lay sobbing on the bed, sobbing in his embarrassment and pain, and covering him carefully with one of the sheets, as carefully as he had ever done anything in his life.

47

"How is he?" Hannah asked.

They were in her small front garden, overlooking the park. It was two days later. Through the trees, the light angling low across the grass was beginning to fade. A few elderly men stood chatting, pausing on the curve of path as they walked their dogs. The last cries of children rose and fell from the playground at the further side. Some of the cars heading into the city along Derby Road had switched on their lights.

Hannah had been sitting in her doorway when Resnick arrived, cushions piled beneath her, leaning back against the frame. A pile of folders beside her, pen in hand. A wineglass by her side. When she heard the gate and saw him approaching along the path, she smiled. "Just let me finish this . . ." but he gestured for her to stay where she was and stepped around her, moving on inside the house. The opened bottle of wine, a Semillon Chardonnay, was in the door of the fridge and he removed it, letting the door swing closed, and turned to reach a glass down from the shelf.

There was a postcard, propped against a stack of blue and yellow bowls, a reproduction, he supposed, of a painting: a town house in reddish stone, steps that climbed quite high to the front door and a couple standing there, he in a waistcoat, white shirt, and tie, the woman wearing a blue dress and leaning back against the curve of railing beside the steps. Beyond the house, to the right of the picture, half in shadow, there is a spread of almost impossibly smooth grass and beyond that, rising suddenly, a wall—is it a wall?—and a rich cluster of green trees, the tallest of which is catching the last of the sun. The dull orange glow on the stone, Resnick realized, that was caused by the setting sun. Evening, and this couple, they are both looking out toward the light.

Resnick turned over the card to see who the painting was by and before he could do that or put it back he read instead, in purplish ink and lettering that was fussy and none too clear, *Nice to see you again*, and *missing you*, and the name. Jim. The postmark was unreadable, smudged against the stamp.

"Charlie! Have you got lost or what?"

He picked up the bottle and the glass and carried them out.

"Divine," Hannah said, after she had sipped her wine. "How is he?"

"He's a strong lad. Bones'll mend."

Hannah looked at him, the weariness in his eyes. "And the rest of him?"

Resnick shook his head. So far Divine had refused to talk about what had happened, not to the doctor who had examined him, not to Maureen Madden, to Resnick, anyone. Shane's statements had so far been only patchily coherent, but what seemed certain was that he had encountered Bill Aston in the public toilets on the embankment late on the

Friday evening, the day before the murder, and that something had happened between them, something sexual, but exactly what and how mutually consensual, it was difficult to tell. But when Aston bumped into Shane again, presumably by accident, back on the embankment the following night and approached him, Shane reacted with anger, called over his mates and encouraged them to set upon him, bloody poof, beat him to a pulp. A bit of fun.

Along with Gerry Hovenden, Shane had been charged with the murder of Bill Aston, and on his own account had been charged with two cases of indecent assault and one of causing grievous bodily harm; they were holding back on the charge of rape.

Listening, Hannah reached up and squeezed Resnick's hand.

During the time that Resnick and the team were preoccupied with Shane, Khan had continued to be busy. The youths who had terrorized Nicky Snape had given conflicting accounts of what had happened leading up to Nicky's death. It was uncertain how far their threatening sexual byplay had gone on that occasion, but what was clear almost beyond dispute was that if they had not forced Nicky to take part in oral or anal sex there and then, they had made it clear that the next time he wouldn't be given any choice. Khan also established that, while in care, at least two of the boys had gone out at night for the purposes of engaging in prostitution.

And when he had checked again with Elizabeth Peck's neighbors, several claimed to have seen her leaving the house in uniform, usually in the evenings, nurse's uniform, and arriving home early, between six and seven. Not regular, but quite a few times just the same. Khan checked with the hospitals, the nursing agencies in town. He was waiting for her when her car arrived back from East Midlands Airport, parked across the street with a copy of Nancy Friday he'd borrowed from Jill's bedside. *Women on Top.* He'd given up on Vikram Seth.

When Elizabeth Peck swung into the drive of the neo-Georgian house, on which she was still three mortgage payments in arrears, he walked across and offered to help her with her bags.

At first, she was dismissive, haughty, insistent on standing by rights she didn't have; later, in the living room with its stone fireplace and fake leaded windows, she was penitent, sniffing back the tears. Khan gave her several clean tissues and waited for the sniveling to stop. Weighed down by debt, unable to sell the house, even had she wanted to, its current market price so far below what she had paid for it, she had been working as an agency nurse at the City Hospital, most often nights, when the pay was better and there was the greatest need. If her shifts at the local authority accommodation clashed, Paul Matthews covered for her, signed her in and out. On the night that Nicky Snape hanged himself, she had been doing her second job out at the hospital and Matthews had been there alone.

"I don't feel," she told Khan, "any real guilt. I mean, whatever he did, he would have done whether I'd been there or not. Well, he would, wouldn't he?"

At the station, Resnick went out of his way to compliment Khan on the way he had handled his side of the inquiry and assured him he would pass that on to Jack Skelton. Khan tried to disguise his pleasure, without ever quite succeeding.

By then the story of what had happened to Divine, rumor and counterrumor, had ricocheted around the station and Resnick and Millington had been chipping away at Shane's belligerent stonewalling the best part of fourteen hours.

Off duty, Carl Vincent had driven out to visit Divine in his side ward at the Queen's and Divine had turned his back and closed his eyes and stayed like that even after Vincent left.

Then, on the second morning, when Resnick entered the interview room, Shane, as the result of a long discussion with his solicitor, began to tell them about what had happened to him when he was taken into care as a boy. About the deputy head of the first children's home he'd been in, who had given Shane cigarettes if he let him slip his hand up inside Shane's short trousers, and a crisp new five-pound note if he would let him pull the trousers down.

"It wasn't the same man?" Hannah asked.

"The same . . ."

"In charge. Of the place where Shane was abused. The same as the place where Nicky died?"

Resnick shook his head. "I'm afraid that would be too neat," he said, and gave her a wry smile. "That sort of thing only happens in books. Not real life."

What happened in real life was that those who had power all too frequently abused those who did not; and that those who were abused, abused others in turn. What happened was that many of those grew up, for whatever reason, confused about their sexuality, and often succeeded in damaging themselves and others, trying to live up to what they thought of as the norm. What happened in real life, Resnick thought, was all too often a helpless, bloody mess.

They were facing each other in Hannah's bed, features just visible in the opaque light from the ceiling window. "Just so long as you stay till morning," Hannah had said. "Six, at least."

Now she said, "How do you deal with it? All of this awfulness."

He sighed. "I went to see Norma Snape this afternoon, before I came round here. She had a friend with her and she'd been drinking, both of which were probably just as well. What else can she do?" He touched Hannah's shoulder lightly with the back of his hand. "Seems Nicky's dad—the one who came back out of the blue—he's gone off again without a by-your-leave. She doesn't know what's hit her. Likely never will." He kissed Hannah's fingers when she brought them close against his face. "First Nicky and then Shane. How can she ever hope to understand?"

"All my pretty ones," Hannah said.

"Mmm?"

"Nothing. A line from a play." And then, "Do you? Do you understand?"

"Only that there's nothing people won't do to one another, if the circumstances are right. No dreadful thing."

"Or wrong," Hannah said. "Surely, if the circumstances are wrong?"

"Yes." He reached his arm behind her, hand open across the curve of her back, and she eased herself toward him, face close to his face. "Yes, I suppose that's what I mean."

After a while she said, "If they're right, if things are right, do you think, what we do to one another, it can be good?"

"Yes," Resnick said, kissing her. "I do think that. I want to." Hannah brushed her lips again against his mouth. "It's what," he said, "I want to believe."

Before Peter had left he had written a letter to Sheena and put it on the pillow in her room; there had been nothing, not a message, a blind word for Norma herself. Tears so strong she had not been able to see clearly, Norma had ripped the letter again and again until all that was left were little pieces, unreadable save for the odd word. *Love* and *home*. Norma had scooped the fragments up into her hands and carried them to the sink and burned them. Ashes by now.

Sheena had come home when she'd heard about Shane, but she hadn't stayed. Her mum bawling and scraighting and wanting to grab hold of her all the time, she couldn't cope with it. It was too much. And besides, Rosa was there for her mum and she was her best friend, after all. She'd look after her, make sure it was all right.

Back at Diane's, Dee-Dee had got some acid, ten quid for a small strip, and Sheena was just in time for her share; the others were well away, with the baby crawling between them, nappy filled, and nobody paying attention until he started to cry and then Diane pushed him at Sheena and told her to get him into the bathroom and sort him out and Sheena had giggled and done as she was told.

"And get a fuckin' move on," Dee-Dee had called. "We're already late as it is."

They were meeting Janie in town, near the bowling alley. Janie on speed or something when they got there, had to be, she was really manic the way she was carrying on and screaming. Sheena watched as she pushed her way past this bloke, not much older than her but wearing some uniform like he worked there, wasting his breath telling Janie she had to leave. But Janie had laughed in his face and then felt between his legs, just for the hell of it, to see what he'd do.

The bloke saying how if they didn't leave he'd call the police and Janie grabbing hold of him and pointing at Sheena, saying, See her, her brother he just killed a fucking copper, so just you fucking watch out. And then leaving anyway, 'cause he'd run off into the office, probably pissed his pants.

Diane shouting from the burger bar, "Wait! Hang on a fuckin' minute, I in't got my chips yet."

But Janie didn't care and they pushed their way outside and went off down the street, arms linked, blocking the pavement, singing this stupid song at the top of their voices.

Then there was this guy, just this old guy, Sheena saw him first, weaving across the road toward them, drunk, right up to Janie, big smile all over his face, singing along even though his was a completely different bloody song. "Come on, sweetheart! You and me, eh? You and me."

And this drunken old bastard, must have been forty or fifty years old, pulls up his shirt and starts rubbing his chest all up against Janie. "Come on, sweetheart, you an' me." Which is when Janie pulls out this screwdriver she's got inside her jacket, just a screwdriver, broken off halfway down the blade and sharpened to a sort of point, and she sticks it in this drunk's disgusting fat belly, right above the buckle of his belt, and he falls there, down on his knees, this thing sticking out of him, almost to the hilt, and Janie, she's laughing, pointing, and the rest of the girls, most of them, are running.

Diane is standing there outside the bowling alley, chips falling between her fingers, watching Dee-Dee trying to pull Sheena away. "Come on, for Christ sake, girl! You mad? Let's get out of here."

Sheena staring at the blood beginning to swell up around the man's white belly, fascinated, and Janie, out of her head beside him, laughing.

"Come on, girl! Move it!"

Running then, leaving Janie to face the music, the first sounds of a police car approaching at speed along Canal Street and Sheena, as she allowed herself to be dragged away, turning now and stumbling, looking back and thinking, awesome, truly awesome. I mean, absolutely fucking brilliant! Brilliant, right?

one another, if the circumstances are right,' Resnick concludes. And yet, the hope lingers that sometimes what people do to one another can be good. 'It's what I want to believe,' Resnick says; in the passion of his wanting lies the power of Harvey's fiction."—Bill Ott, *Booklist* (boxed and starred)

"Absolutely brilliant."—Andrew Vachss

"What makes Harvey's grim world bearable is his compassion: Even Nicky's hapless mother is wretchedly human."—*Publishers Weekly* (starred)

"The novels combine the stark urban realism and testy departmental conflicts of 'Prime Suspect' with the rip and raunch of Elmore Leonard's mysteries and the arcing personal histories of Ross Macdonald's classics."—*Chicago Sun-Times*

"Crimes and Pulps can no longer be hived off as poor cousins to what writers such as Martin Amis or Patrick McGrath, with their manifestly literary pretensions, are up to. And, of course, if genre fiction's day has come, or come back, John Harvey is its eminence."—Valentine Cunningham, *The Times Literary Supplement*

"Pick of the Week. Operating somewhere between the police procedurals of P. D. James and the psychological thrillers of Ruth Rendell, fellow Briton Harvey claims a compelling turf: the nightmare streets of an England on the dole. Detective Charlie Resnick pinches small victories from the urban slaughterhouse. *Easy Meat* is a tale that will stay with readers for a long time to come."—J. D. Read, *People* magazine

"With each of his crime novels, John Harvey goes deeper into the heart of urban despair. . . . Nora Snape and her children [are] a family so blighted that only the clarity of Harvey's writing can make them bearable to approach. He gives them faces, and they are not easy to forget, impossible to simplify."—Kate Regan, *San Francisco Chronicle*

"Harvey's terse style is just about perfect."—Linnea Lannon, *Detroit Free Press*

"Without question, *Easy Meat* is John Harvey's best."—Jim Harrison

"Harvey's 24-karat British procedurals have always led the field, but in *Easy Meat* he's surpassed himself."—*Kirkus Reviews* (starred)

"What makes a Resnick investigation ring so true is not just the impeccable detail, the crisp dialogue, or the multilayered interplay between cops; it's also the crushing sense of futility that surrounds Resnick and his colleagues like an evil fog: finding the truth about Nicky Snape only confirms its inevitability. . . . Without romanticizing or oversimplifying, Harvey forces us to see Nicky Snape whole, and we fear him every bit as much as we empathize with his plight. 'There's nothing people won't do to